In the Shadow of an Obsession

Book 5

A Fareview
Fairytale

By Maci Aurora

Maci Aurora Books

In the Shadow of a Wish, book 1
In the Shadow of a Hoax, book 2
In the Shadow of a Dream, book 3
In the Shadow of the Truth, the Novellas, Book 4
In the Shadow of an Obsession, Book 5

The Accidental Seraph, Carran Hollow book 1

The Secrets of Roan Island written with Thea Masen

Coming Soon

Book 2 in the Carran Hollow Series

Book 2 In Roan Island Series written with Thea Masen

CL Walters Books

Swimming Sideways
The Ugly Truth
The Bones of Who We Are
The Messy Truth About Love
The Stories Stars Tell
In the Echo of this Ghost Town
When the Echo Answers
The Letters She Left Behind
The Ring Academy: The Trials of Imogene Sol

Coming Soon

The Ring Academy: The Cipher of Tolo

In the Shadow of an Obsession

A Fareview Fairytale

Book 5

By Maci Aurora

Mixed Plate Press
Honolulu, Hawaii

In the Shadow of an Obsession
Fareview Fairytale Book 5
©2025 Maci Aurora w/ Mixed Plate Press
Honolulu, Hawaii

cover art: Sara Oliver Designs

ISBN: 979-8-9924456-0-2 (paperback)
ISBN: 979-8-9924456-1-9 (eBook)

About this book: *In the Shadow of an Obsession* was inspired by a mash up of Grimm's Fairytales, "The Glass Coffin," "Rumplestiltskin," "Snow White and Rose Red," and "The Six Swans." It contains explicit sexual situations and is intended for mature audiences (18+).

DEDICATED TO

My readers...

You are the perfect ingredients.
Jessamine embodies your resilience.
Johesha, your persistence.
This story is for you.

Author's Note

In the Shadow of an Obsession is a reimagined fairy tale filled with potions, magic, and true love, but even fairy tales traverse dark roads and face scary monsters. While Jessamine's story is a romance that focuses on that happily-ever-after, it doesn't preclude her (and others in her story), and thereby the reader, from facing some very real and possibly disturbing obstacles. It is important to share what could possibly be triggering for those who wish forewarning. **If you don't want to know, please stop reading here, turn the page, and begin the story.**

Scarlett, the Fareview's mother, has been lying to her family. While her lies have been told with good intentions, they have resulted in a loss of power and choice for each of her grown children, unaware of her duplicity.

One unintended consequence is the abduction of Jessamine Fareview by a man claiming to be her father. Using magic to keep her captive, he forces magic on her person and others without their consent. He uses mental and emotional manipulation that result in mental trauma as well as physical torture against an imprisoned non-human being. His methods include gaslighting, trickery, emotional manipulation, and physical control. While none of it is glorified or explicitly described, this story touches upon loss of agency, entrapment, abduction and torture. Please note, that given the fantasy elements, there are some dark creatures with frightening intentions depicting violence.

Though this inclusion of what is harmful isn't intended to be glorified, there are other kinds of gratuitous situations in this story including strong language, graphic sex (consensual), poisoning to intend death, and even death. Please rest assured that I have done my utmost to care for the various characters (and my readers) in the narrative scope of these situations. My hope is that all scenes are presented with that in mind, and we journey to the happily-ever-after.

Thank you so much for being willing to take a chance on *In the Shadow of an Obsession*. I hope you love Jessamine's and Johesha's story as much as I enjoyed writing it, and that this heroine and hero are exactly what you hoped for when you picked up this story to escape into another world.

The Fareview Fairytales Cast

(In alphabetical order)

Aurielle (Auri) Fairview: The fourth daughter of Scarlett and Tomas Fareview. She found an enchanted key in the Whitling Woods that trapped her in the spelled labyrinth of Nixus Uraiahs, where she was given three wishes.

Brendsen: A guard in Prince Lachlan's forces tasked with looking for Johesha.

Brinna Fareview: The third daughter of Scarlett and Tomas Fareview. She is inherently good-natured and the nurturer of the family. A romantic dreamer, sometimes her dreams have seemed to come true.

Credence Crendell: Owner of the Copper Pot Inn and supporter of Tarley Fareview.

Crue: (aka the Wizard) the dark sorcerer who is looking for Azleah (Scarlett). He abducted Jessamine. The wizard controls the darkling. No one knows his true name.

Henro: A boy living in the manor Crue owns.

Horance Forte: Brother to Credence, he helps her run the Copper Pot Inn.

Jessamine Fareview: The oldest daughter of Scarlett and Tomas Fareview. She is dependable and responsible. As her mother's right hand, she become a gifted healer in Sevens but rarely leaves Scarlett's sight.

Johesha Malinor: The captain of the guard for the Crown Prince of Jast, Lachlan Nikolas. He is loyal, brave, and heroic. He was instrumental in saving Tarley Fareview from marauding assassins.

Jude: New captain of the guard to Lachlan Nikolas.

Lexa Uraiahs: Oldest goddess sister of the god twins

Lucian and Nixus. She is the goddess of death and ruler of the underworld.

Lachlan Nikolas: The crown prince of Jast, he recently married Tarley Fareview. She saved him from certain death.

Lucian (Luc) Uraiahs: Elder twin brother of Nixus Uraiahs. He is the god of light and day. Due to his meddling in his twin's life, he inadvertently trapped Nix in a spell (where Nix met Auri). He's recently been promoted to take over as God of the Vasmost. He and Brinna Fareview saved the family from a sleeping spell.

Mary: A maid working for Crue at the manor.

Mattias Fareview: The youngest child and only son of Scarlett and Tomas Fareview. Now, twenty-one, he's getting a handle on his power to move through time and has taken his mother back in time to search for Crue's true name.

Mrs. Gerrick: The cook at Crue's manor and mother to Henro.

Nixus Uraiahs: The younger twin brother of Lucian Uraiahs, he is the god of dark and night. He fell in love with Auri Fareview when she saved him from a spell where he'd been trapped. Her sacrifice saved him and inadvertently changed the world.

Ruhnna Graham: Mattias's new friend he saved from a forced marriage in Echo.

Scarlett Fareview: Mother of the five Fareview children and wife to Tomas, she is a healer and extremely protective of her family. She was keeping secrets from her family but has finally told them the truth of her past.

Tarley Fareview: The second daughter of Scarlett and Tomas Fareview is fiercely independent. Considered the rebellious daughter, she is often at odds with her mother. She saved Lachlan, was asked to marry him by Queen

Keyanna for the treaty with Jast but fell in love with him.

Tomas Fareview: Father of the five Fareview children and husband to Scarlett, he is the voice of reason with his wife, but also unfailingly keeps her trust by maintaining her secrets.
The Darkling: a magical creature with the ability to shapeshift, it lives on blood and will imprint on its victims, choosing either to kill immediately or satiate (turn them). A darkling can see magic spells, even those that have been designed to be concealed.
Trevis: The stable boy at the Copper Pot Inn.

Dear Reader,

In case you feel like you need a refresher . . .

Once upon a time there was a family called the Fareviews. Tomas and Scarlett had five grown children: Jessamine, Tarley, Brinna, Aurielle, and Mattias. They called the land of Kaloma home, residing in a cottage located in the Whitling Woods near the village of Sevens. Though peasants, the Fareviews were content to remain hidden from the oppressive world in which they lived.

Scarlett, you see, had dark secrets from which she'd run. And to protect her family, she'd obscured them all under two protection spells the witch of the woods helped her cast. One spell was a magical hedge wrapped around the cottage veiling their home from beings able to use magic. The second spell was in the form of a ribbon tied around her children's wrists, but it came with a warning: *falling into true love would break the spell.*

For twenty-seven years, the Fareviews lived behind the

hedge in their cottage in relative peace. But as with most things, the truth of Scarlett's past closed in. The land's oppressive marriage laws caught up with the family, forcing Tarley, Brinna, and Aurielle to present themselves at the marriage market, a horrible prospect for a poor family in the backcountry of Kaloma.

One day, while out in the woods imagining ways she could save her family, Aurielle uncovered a golden key *(In the Shadow of a Wish)*. Unbeknownst to her, the key had a powerful enchantment, and the moment she touched it, she was captured by the spell and trapped with an embittered god—Nixus Uraiahs—who had also been a captive for over a century. The only way to escape the enchantment and get back to her family was to make three wishes and face three consequences for making them. Then she would be faced with a final choice: escape the enchantment or save Nixus, the spell's villain.

With a special wisdom, Aurielle began to make her wishes, growing to enjoy the broody god the more she learned about him. Working together, they discovered they were fated-mates—a godyolk. She saved Nixus from the spell and escaped the clutches of the enchantment. When she returned to her family, her ribbon was gone—she'd fallen in love with Nixus Uraiahs—and the Marriage Law in Kaloma was changed into the Law of Means.

Aurielle's strange temporary disappearance that claimed her ribbon made things more complicated with Scarlett attempting to control them all because of it. With the Law of Means keeping women from controlling their livelihood, Tarley Fareview tried her best to make her way in the world *(In the Shadow of a Hoax)*. While working at The Copper Pot Inn, Tarley got into an altercation with a man that forced her to flee into the Whitling Woods.

While there she came across a dying man washed up on the shore of the River Grimz. Afraid of the danger men presented for women, Tarley pondered leaving him to nature, but couldn't stop thinking about her own brother and relented. Using the healing arts Scarlett taught all her children, Tarley nursed him back to health. Little did she know, however, she'd saved the heir to the throne of the neighboring kingdom of Jast, Prince Lachlan Nikolas, who was the victim of an assassination attempt.

When they eventually returned to Sevens, they discovered that the Queen of Kaloma was there under Scarlett's care, having survived an assassination attempt as well. His disguise now ruined, Lachlan and the Queen forge a treaty, part of which made Tarley Lachlan's reluctant bride. Over time and with Lachlan's efforts, Tarley realized that being with Lachlan was something she wanted, that she loved him.

But the assassins caught up with them, and Tarley was abducted. Simultaneously, the sorcerer after Scarlett, discovered her whereabouts and sent a terrible monster called the Darkling after the family. The monster became infatuated with Tarley and pursued her into the woods. In the middle of a meadow in the Whitling Woods with Lachlan intent on rescuing his future bride, Tarley, Tomas, Jessamine and Mattias, the King and Prince of Jast and their army, along with the god of night and dark, Nixus as witnesses, the Sorcerer revealed himself. Though the wizard saved them from the Darkling, he demanded that Scarlett return what was his.

Confronted by her family, Scarlett agreed to tell the truth, but only after Tarley and Lachlan's wedding. After the wedding, with the family assembled around the table inside their cottage to hear Scarlett's story, she covertly slipped them a sleeping potion *(In the Shadow of a Dream)* and chanted a new spell that changed the hedge around their home into an impenetrable entity, wanting to protect them from the wizard. Her actions, however had dire consequences by splitting up fated-mates, Aurielle and Nixus.

With the power to dreamshare, Brinna learned she could dream with Lucian Uraiahs, Nixus's twin brother, the god of day and light. Though they were reluctant allies, they knew they had more to gain by working together to solve the mystery behind the reason Scarlett cast the spells. With Brinna dreaming and Lucian awake, they worked to uncover the clues, meeting with one another as Lucian slept.

While Lucian pretended his aversion to Brinna, the truth was he'd fallen for her long before Aurielle and Nixus even met. The more time they spent together, Brinna found she loved Lucian, losing her ribbon. But they were racing against the clock. Nixus and Aurielle were dying, the separation tearing at the god-yoke. Lucian was left with a terrible choice to separate Nixus from his memories to save him. Then, hoping that when Nixus saw Aurielle again, his memory would return.

Lucian led Nixus and Lachlan through the hedge to

wake up their true loves with true love's kiss. While he succeeded in waking Brinna and Lachlan, Tarley, Nixus couldn't remember loving Auri. Brinna was able to wake her sister with her true love. Once the whole family was awake, they discovered Jessamine was missing.

Now, with Scarlett's duplicity and lies revealed, she finally told the family the truth *(In the Shadow of the Truth)*. Left reeling in the horror of Scarlett's secrets while also trying to find Jessamine, the family separated. Tomas and Scarlett faced what came after Scarlett's lies *(In the Shadow of a Vow)*. Brinna and Lucian tried to find a happily-ever-after amid the pain of grief *(In the Shadow of a Kiss)*, and Aurielle had to rebuild a relationship with the love of her life who didn't remember her *(In the Shadow of a Memory)*. Finally, Mattias was coming-of-age with newfound powers and the means to help find the true name of the monster that had abducted Jessamine *(In the Shadow of Time)*.

And that is where we begin Jessamine's story . . .

PART 1

"Awake, dear heart, awake.
Thou hast slept well. Awake."
– William Shakespeare, *The
Tempest*

The Spell

A drop of this potion— two, three, or four—
will call to the Deep Sleep and close the door,

to slip into Dreamland locked up nice and tight,
with a magical beastie guarding with might.

One whose heart is bound and pure
Can face the beastie and endure.

A true heart to be veiled from sight
to reach the dreamer bound to endless Night.

Upon True Love's kiss, the spell will break,
and into True Love's arms, the dreamer will awake.

Crue

Crue—though not his true name because his true name was hidden where no one save him would ever find it—stood in the musty, warm comfort of his sanctum. Housed in the bowels of the manor he'd cheated from some down-on-his-luck lord in the land of Kaloma, surrounded by the dark, dank stone of the under house, he felt… secure there among the items of his workshop. Among the plethora of herbs, powders, animal parts, and other ingredients that helped him brew his spells, the origin of his genius, he was untouchable. Though spells weren't the entirety of his magic. He'd gained access to so much more power over his lifetime. But his usual contentment, or perhaps purpose, seemed to melt away, offering him instead a bereft existence of loss.

He sighed and added a pinch of shaved bear claw to the bubbling mixture.

He should be happy. He had what he wanted, mostly. And yet, nothing he wanted. The line he walked was a tightrope strung between twin peaks of promise, and he was only halfway across the abyss below. Behind him, one peak was his unprecedented ability, but he was facing the next peak—unparalleled power. The most complicated obstacle remained in his path, even if he had everything he wanted within his grasp. Azleah—or Scarlett, as she was now called—was at his mercy once more, their daughter was in his clutches, and all he had to do was find a way to break the tether to the darkling to achieve his greatest magic yet.

He grinned smugly, pondering the taunting letters he'd sent Scarlett, crowing his impending victory. Scrying as the crow who'd carried both missives allowed him to watch the unfolding drama. Her hope, then her rage, followed by her fear and sadness. Watching her cry had brought him a bittersweet sense of satisfaction. He had loved her once, but the warmth at the thought gave way to darkness as he considered who she'd chosen over him. Him!

That feeble giant Tomas.

The moment he'd realized he'd been passed over for that formerly minuscule sprite still grated on him. He could picture Azleah swollen with Crue's child. Two god hearts! And Tom, no bigger than her thumb, riding her shoulder like some bug needing to be squished. No power. No abilities. Nothing to offer her. That's who she'd chosen. It rankled.

Crue would get even. She would get her comeuppance.

He scoffed and focused on the steam drifting from the cauldron, his gaze unseeing, as his mind swirled with the problems at hand. His progeny was still trapped in the sleeping spell Scarlett had cast with that awful witch in the woods. That and the tether.

He glanced at the woman—his daughter—still asleep in the protective glass case he'd created with his magic. A beautiful box of artistry made from wood, ice, and obsession. Frosted with etched inlay of the forest around her, trees, vines, leaves, berries, branches, and woodland creatures but for the clear space that framed her lovely face. A face so much like his own. Her dark hair spread about like a dark halo.

Despite his centuries of experience with spells, potions, and incantations, he hadn't been able to wake her, even as he was at work on another potion to try. He knew why. The glow of the spell on her, a gentle, golden light threaded with amethyst, swathed her form like a magical sarcophagus. He needed another thread from the sorcerer who'd created the damned spell. He'd hoped to make a trade, having used his only thread to get through the hedge, and despite trying to find that witch, he couldn't seem to summon the bitch.

He sprinkled some clipped phoenix feather into his palm and lit it on fire to sprinkle the ash into the mixture.

From its cell tucked into a vestibule in the room, the

monster chittered in its cage. It used to screech at the sight of fire, but in the year since Crue had imprisoned it, being around a controlled blaze had become something to which the creature had grown more accustomed.

"This isn't for you," Crue said without looking at the cell, "but it could be."

"I burn. You burn," it said. It had changed its form. He knew because its usually monstrous voice, like shards of glass cutting up the inside of a throat, now sounded even and masculine. It was probably wearing the doctor's face.

Crue didn't check. "Which is why you have nothing to fear from this fire."

It snorted its irritation. Crue could feel its gaze on him, as if studying, buying time. "The magic won't let you through," it said.

Crue knew it was talking about his sleeping daughter; about the magic it could see. It was why they were tethered, after all. "Has it changed?"

"No."

He knew that, but not for want of trying, and added the ash to the potion. Circumstances as they were, he didn't really need to wake his daughter for what he intended to do. He only needed her beating heart, but that wouldn't get him what he truly wanted. This sleeping beauty was his only leverage over Scarlett, who still had his other gifts. He wanted them back in his possession. Needed them. Or—

No. He wouldn't ponder failure. It wasn't an option.

He'd never failed—except with Azleah. And that miscalculation would be remedied soon. Scarlett's heart was as good as his, now with their daughter in his control.

He could achieve the same ends to his greatest achievement, and Scarlett would pay. She would experience his wrath and vengeance. Because she'd ruined everything!

With a shout, he plucked up a spoon and threw it. His impotence—in more ways than one now—had never been more apparent. He followed the spoon with a heave of his pestle and mortar. It created a divot in the wall then fell to the floor with a thud, cracking the stone beneath it. His rage heaved inside him, his withered heart lurching under the stress. He pressed a hand against his chest.

The darkling hissed.

"Shut it," Crue snapped, pulling the bone flask from the inner pocket of his vest, uncapping it, and taking a swig of the potion inside. Warmth crept down his throat, heating all the spaces inside him, attaching itself and weaving magic around each of his cells, sluicing through the connections to his soul. He tilted his head back and closed his eyes as the heat slithered over his bones, his muscles, and hugged his organs.

His dick hardened.

With a smile and the desire to find a maid, he adjusted himself and looked to the door, knowing the effect wouldn't last for long.

"You are weak," the darkling said.

"And so are you," Crue replied.

"Let me hunt," it said. "Strength will return."

"I said to shut it!" Crue slammed his hands down on the countertop and leaned against it. He hated that the sound of the darkling instantly curbed his rigid cock, making it flaccid once more. Incantation! He hated the cursed thing. Curse the day he'd ever thought it was a good idea to tether himself to the magic seer. Granted, the monster had helped him find the thieving Scarlett, but now that he had what he wanted, undoing his own genius was proving more difficult, and the darkling was at the root of it. He might need to summon one of the demons for the answer, he just hadn't wanted to. Demons were a dangerous business regardless of the protections in place.

Starving the creature had become an experiment to see if it would weaken the connection between them, but the darkling was right. Crue could feel the weakness right along with the it.

"Tell me how to break the tether, and I'll feed you," Crue said.

From within its cage the darkling clicked and snuffed. "I didn't create it, Wizard." It grew quiet.

Crue hated that the creature was right. Crue had been the one to create the tether. He'd traveled into the deep death of an island of ice and winter where the last darklings lived, and with will and magic had trapped and tricked the creature. Creating the tether had been easy. Destruction was proving more difficult.

Finally turning toward the prison, Crue could picture the creature's red eyes pulsing as if bleeding, though no blood oozed, and stepped closer, his ear toward the solid door of the prison.

With a startling thud and a screech, the darkling threw itself at the door, bending a divot out toward him.

Crue jumped back with a shout. "You devil!"

"Let me out!"

"Quit your incessant complaining." Crue bent forward, the deep pain of the darkling's hunger gnawing at his own insides. He would have to feed it, soon. Torturing, withholding food, forcing it into other forms. Nothing worked, but then again, knowing he had such a power over the creature was satisfying. He would eat, and while he would feel satisfied, it would add to the creature's hunger.

Crue smiled at the prospect and retrieved the pestle and mortar from the floor, replacing them on the wooden countertop.

The darkling moaned again within the confines of its cell, and discomfort slid through the tether. "I groan for my freedom."

Crue pinched his brow and sighed. "You know the price."

Its growl deepened. "Perhaps I will just end you instead."

A chill rushed down Crue's spine as a threat slid along the tether, as if the darkling had increased in size.

It couldn't be so. It was weak. But Crue could feel the tether stretching and pulling, tugging on his innards. "It isn't," he said. "And I'm trying to find the answer to our dilemma," he added to pacify the creature.

"Not soon enough," the darkling growled, its spiky claws curling around the bars of its cage.

"Are you questioning me, darkling?" Crue chanted a spell, opening his palm, and a blue flame flared to life.

The darkling shrank back from the door, from Crue and the other worldly flame, screeching. Crue could feel the faint echo of terror slide through the tether, this hint of a sensation rather than the raw pain of hunger. Physical sensations were more visceral than the emotional ones. It wasn't as if they could read one another's minds. Thankfully. Crue didn't want the darkling to understand his intentions any more than he wanted to know how the beast ate.

Crue fisted the flame, sending it back down the tether to the Netherrealm from where he'd called the magic, for the first time worried about being linked to the monster. Even though Crue wasn't sure how to break their connection to release the creature, he knew letting it go wasn't even possible anymore.

"You promised to let me return home," the darkling hissed, referring to their bargain.

Crue had made promises. But he knew releasing the creature was too dangerous to himself. Even if he could break it without ending himself, he couldn't guarantee the stupid beast wouldn't turn on him. The tether between them was the only thing keeping Crue safe. Their lives connected. The darkling understood this as much as he did, but he told the creature what it wanted to hear. "As soon as I have what Scarlett stole in my possession, I will release you."

The darkling hovered in the viewport of the door a moment more, assessing the truth behind the Wizard's words, and Crue was grateful it couldn't sniff out lies like it could magic. Then without another sound, it receded from the door of its prison and disappeared from Crue's view.

The steam from the cauldron sputtered, and Crue frowned. He glanced at the sleeping woman's glass case, to the magical sarcophagus glowing around her. He needed to figure out how to wake her, and soon. The last year had been too long, and he wasn't sure how much longer he could keep her alive, keep the darkling contained, keep himself... well. He'd figure it all out. If the sleeping woman died, he'd be left with nothing. No heart. No means for vengeance. Then this godsdamned tether would have been for naught.

With a sigh, he realized he was hungry.

First, he'd eat.

He rubbed his forehead. That would make things clearer in his mind and would make the darkling feel the pain of what it was missing. Then Crue would return to the safety of his sanctum and feed magical potions to his daughter, if not to wake her, then to keep her alive. A little while longer, at least.

Jessamine Fareview, first daughter of Scarlett and Tomas Fareview, was in between, trapped like a specter inside her own body. But for all intents and purposes, she could sense everyone believed her to be asleep. Except her mind was actively awake, locked within the silent space of her form. She could hear, and smell, and think, and feel despite being as blind to the world as the world had been to her.

Before.

Growing up in Sevens, she'd known something was different about her, about them all. To put it mildly, her mother Scarlett wasn't just overprotective, she was overbearing. Strangely so, and more so with her than the rest of her siblings though Jessamine couldn't quite identify why, couldn't match words with her thoughts as if there were a lock on her tongue.

Her sweet words were often at odds with her dark thoughts. Sweet Jessamine, or so everyone said. Such a perfect child. But things didn't add up, as if an elixir contained too much cruel weed, poisoning the whole batch. Rarely out of her mother's sight, Jessamine had learned the healing arts and remedies as her mother's apprentice. And she had a knack for it which had given her a sense of pride. The question was: was Jessamine the cruel weed, or was it her mother?

The way others had interacted with her when Jessamine had accompanied her mother on a call had always been strange. Adding to her unease was the way they would look at her, then look away. Their eyes skimmed past as if they understood she was there but then would immediately forget. Even Jessamine, herself, struggled to identify what made her unique, made her… well, her.

She existed. She felt and loved. She interacted with her family, her sisters, with others, only nothing remained to fill her and flesh her out into a wholly unique being. It was as though she were a living, breathing vessel, no more filled than that of an empty vase waiting for flowers. But once offered the flowers, they would die, wilt, and leave her empty once more.

Except for those dark thoughts coursing through her unable to latch onto her voice.

She suspected it had something to do with the ribbons. Her siblings wore red ribbons at their wrists, as did she, but her crimson ribbon was twisted up with a second, a deep shimmering opalescent pink, like that of a pearl, entwined with violet threads. Beautiful, yes, but different. Just like her.

When Auri returned from the *Great Nap Escapade* without her ribbon, then Tarley less than a year later, both with new loves, Jessamine had suspected. When her mother had refused to answer questions, she'd wondered if magic was at work. But her suspicions felt locked inside her throat, and even if she'd wanted to voice them, she couldn't, as though even if she'd been awake, she'd been asleep. A living, breathing doll, no more or less than the assignments she'd been given by her Master—her mother.

But something had changed.

Because now she was locked in her body. And sometimes she dreamed of Brinna.

Brinna standing at the edge of the forest, waving Jessamine to come to her.

Brinna standing on the other side of a ravine calling to her. The sound and echo of her cry lost to the raging river flowing below.

Brinna trapped on the other side of a mirror, her palms hitting the glass until it cracked.

Brinna crying in the dark, and Jessamine with a single candle nearly burned through to illuminate her. She wondered what would happen if the candle went out?

Then—because Jessamine did have periods of sleep— when she cycled back to awareness, there were the voices of men. One was a stranger. The other was on the edge of one.

Each day—she assumed, because time was strange in this in-between where she existed moving like both the rush of a river's current, but also the slow meander of a viscous, muddy mixture—both men would visit. The first, the stranger, would speak, the sound of his voice sat forward in his head, a thin sound like wind in the reeds along the River Grimz. Fragile somehow but laced with condescension and rage. His touch was the skittering of spiders over her skin. She didn't like him; he made her unnerved and uneasy. He told her of his workshop, of his needs, of what he wanted from her which was to wake up.

The men had the same goal, but she couldn't make it happen even as much as she wished for it.

The second voice, the one that felt familiar, brought comfort. He would open the box where she lay and take her hand.

She couldn't see the box, but she'd come to believe that to be the case. The men's voices were muted, as if she held her hands up to cover her ears, and when either man visited, she could hear the creak and groan of something being opened. She'd experience the sensations of new temperature rushing across her skin. Only during the second man's visit did she also experience the gentle warmth of his calloused hand on hers, the rest of her sensations waking as well.

"I'm here, Jessamine," he would whisper each time.

His voice was deep, rich, but rough and layered with an edge of something feral, as if he were a wolf hidden in the darkness watching her from the shadows. Only she didn't feel fear, she felt protected.

Her heart bloomed at his attention.

When she was small, before Mattias had been born, their parents had taken her and her sisters for a picnic. Jessamine had been around eight at the time and remembered the vibrant green of the trees and explosion of color in the wildflowers as they'd walked through the forest toward the River Grimz. It wasn't very often that the whole family left the confines of the hedge.

"We'll have an adventure." Her father had smiled and swung Auri up onto his shoulders. Her youngest sister had squealed with delight.

Their mother's annoyance at her father's insistence had been a storm following them for some time, but eventually, even Scarlett had relented, pointing out herbs and ingredients to healing elixirs along the way, her hand held protectively over her belly, an unborn Mattias growing inside her.

With Tarley's hand in Jessamine's on one side and Brinna's in the other, she'd led her sisters through the Whitling Woods following their parents. They'd stopped in a meadow and set up their picnic. Hoping to please her mother, Jessamine had ventured into the woods to go back for a special flower Scarlett had mentioned was a rare find. Only the next time she looked up, she didn't recognize where she'd wandered. The voices of her family had gone silent in the shadowed darkness of the forest.

She'd screamed, cried out for them until her voice had grown hoarse.

There'd been a small light, glowing like a lightning bug. She'd followed it, crying. Like a hero from one of her mother's stories, her father appeared from the shadows of the trees, crushing Jessamine against his giant chest where she'd felt utterly safe and secure in his arms.

That was how this stranger's voice made her feel. His touch brought a surge of warmth and light to what otherwise was cold and dark.

"I'm here, Jessamine."

She craved these moments with him.

Today, his thumb ran back and forth across the back of her hand. "I'll be hunting today. I'm going to see how far I can go," he said, then muttered something about *the cursed spell*. "But I will return for you, Jessamine. I will always return to you."

In the beginning—when he'd first began speaking to her—he'd told her they were in the manor of a sorcerer without a name, known as Master. He provided her with facts and details about her circumstances. She didn't believe he was one for many words. The words he shared were stark and honest, pointed and focused. He told her of the sleeping spell, the witch, the broken hedge. He told her she'd been taken by the Master from her parent's cottage. "I followed," he'd said, matter-of-factly, as if there hadn't been another choice. "I promise to get you home." The comforting voice reminded her of her family, speaking their names. Reminding her. Keeping her connected to life when it might feel so easy to let go.

"I'm going to get us out of here." His hand squeezed hers.

She strained toward his voice, longing to open her eyes. As he spoke, she thought of horses and the forest. Of the sensation of strong arms encircling her. Of a sturdy chest. Of her heart's pitter patter and the movement of a horse beneath her. Of a soft exhale against her neck. Of dancing, dark eyes curled slightly at the corners. She could smell leather and pine, the crispness of an outdoor chill.

But time passed and the scent of him changed to a springtime forest layered with petrichor, to the summer woods and wildflowers, to the fall forest and the depth of earthen pine, until the crispness of winter cool was on him once more.

Time was passing, and she remained locked in. The voice she longed to hear, whose touch she longed to feel, never wavered. But she could hear the weariness in his sigh.

"Every time I leave, I forget. I don't know how to get past the spell." His thumb moved back and forth over her wrist. "Gods, I hate magic."

Heat bloomed under skin each time he touched her, intensifying her desire to hear him, to open her eyes and see him. If only she could.

"I'm failing," he said. "I'm letting everyone down."

She wished she could comfort him. Wished she could lift her arm, place her hand on his, feel him with her own fingertips. Wished she could thank him for being with her. And if she could, she would assure him they'd figure it out together.

Except she couldn't. She was useless. Locked in the prison of her own body and a spell.

Nothing new had happened to change this.

"I'm afraid I might be losing my mind," he said, his voice heavy and strained. His thumb stopped moving for a moment, then resumed its tender journey back and forth over her skin.

She wanted to touch him.

Wanted to reciprocate the comfort he brought her with each visit, with his words and his gentle touch.

But as much as she fought against her prison of silence, there was no escape. She thrashed and cried, screamed and yelled inside her own mind.

It didn't change anything. She was locked in just as she always had been.

Today, after sharing his words, he sat with her silently, his thumb moved back and forth across her wrist.

Jessamine concentrated on that comfort and connection. On his callused thumb, on the warmth spreading through her as she pondered more than just this simple, innocent touch. The way his rougher skin felt against the smooth, sensitive flesh of her inner wrist.

Then suddenly, it hit her. Her ribbon was gone.

Johesha

Johesha Malinor held the bow string taut with one hand, his fingers tucked around the arrow notched and ready to fly. The smooth, arched wood limb of the bow held securely with his other hand; he waited for his prey. The woods were winter quiet as a light snow dusted the forest, muting sound but for the buck foraging late fall grass, snuffing cold, white powder as it went. Johesha's heartbeat was calm and steady, his muscles taut, but ready. This—hunting for the benevolent Master—was what he knew best, and he was very good at it.

Johesha was fortunate to have his position with such a

great estate. Working for the Master for a little over a year, his gratitude pulsed through him like golden light, warming him inside and out.

The buck he was hunting walked out from behind the thicket of trees and looked up at a noise.

Johesha released the arrow.

The buck started, sensing danger. But it was too late, and the beast fell, victim to Johesha's true aim.

He didn't miss.

After dressing out the buck and the other small game acquired on his hunt, he hiked back through the woods toward the estate, hauling his catch over his shoulders. He climbed a hill, skirted an outcropping of rocks, followed the stream before it narrowed to the place he could cross it. Once on the other side, he retraced his steps back to the game trail.

The sound of footsteps in snow and the hush of voices carried on the breeze stopped him.

He ducked with his load behind a thicket of trees as two men appeared. Soldiers. They were dressed finely, their supple leathers quietly creaking as they moved, well taken care of. One bent to examine a track, pushing one side of his cloak over his shoulder. He looked closer at a footprint Johesha had left on his way into the woods.

"Do you think we'll find him?" the younger of the two soldiers asked. His freckles were stark against his alabaster skin, bright pink in the cold. "It would be nice to give the prince more than just 'we found tracks.'"

The second soldier sighed as he stood, the dark cloak falling back into place. "The captain will be found only when he wants to be. But…" He paused and looked about, his cornflower blue eyes searching the surrounding area. The second was older than the first. In charge. There was something about this one that spoke a common language to Johesha, as if to say, 'I know you.' But that seemed strange. The soldier continued speaking.

"I can't figure out why he hasn't sent word."

"How do we even know these are his?" the younger one asked.

"The tread. That's a Jast soldier's boot," the older soldier answered. "Come on. Maybe we can catch up to him."

Johesha waited until the men disappeared, then looked down at his boots. Soldier's boots. He lifted his foot awkwardly to look at the tread, confused. He had the vague awareness of having been a soldier once, a lifetime ago, but the memory was hazy. Were they looking for him? His heart raced, as if perhaps he was in hiding, and that was how he'd ended up with the benevolent Master. He couldn't remember just then. With a sense of urgency, he moved back toward the manor—to safety.

He followed the path, cutting through a meadow usually filled with wildflowers in the spring and summer, but now dormant and bare, asleep under winter's spell. There, he slowed, as he always did, a pervasive feeling of being watched piercing him between the shoulder blades. He turned in place, checking his surroundings: no soldiers, no strangers. Even still, he unhooked two hares from his kill line and laid them at an opening in the forest—a sort of walkway marked by two black rocks stark against the snow that appeared to have faces. Without a clear reason and though he wasn't a superstitious man, leaving the game felt right, so each time he hunted, he got more than required and left it as an offering of sorts. To whom was a mystery. Maybe the forest itself. But it was always gone when he walked back through.

After, he kept on through the forest until he came to the final stretch of the tree line that abutted the Master's fields. When he reached the edge of the woods, Johesha stopped to survey his surroundings. The manor house stood in the distance, a dark wood and stone edifice in the valley, with steeply pitched roofs and tall, glass windows, glowing now with warmth. Smoke rose from the many chimneys. While in spring and summer, the fields, trees, landscape around the manor effervesced with verdant life, just then, snow dusted everything. The evergreens, situated like guards around the house, were coated white. From Johesha's vantage at the edge of the woods, the roadway to Rockwell Village appeared to be a stone's throw, but he knew it was quite a distance from the manor.

The snow-covered Jast Mountains rose dark and steep like sleeping giants in the distance. Johesha's eyes always reached for the mountains as if they were a beacon. He was curious about what lay beyond, but unsure why. He couldn't recall ever having been to the other side, and looked down at his boots, stomping the idea away into the fresh snow. Why would he long to leave the Master's manor where he was taken care of by such a benevolent lord?

"Captain?"

Johesha spun at the word, at the voice cutting through the forest. The soldiers from earlier had tracked him. He'd been stupid to let his guard down. Now that they were closer, he could see the finery of their uniforms, impeccably dressed in dark leathers and dyed green linen. Their leather cuirass was stamped with what appeared to be a tree, though it was covered by the buckles and straps that led to their weapons on their backs. Dark green cloaks were draped around them, hoods deep to cover most of their faces now, though clearly disposable should they need access to their weapons. Dressed in their head to toe black-dyed leather, they were imposing and outfitted finely, with boots just like his.

"Do I know you?" he asked.

"Johesha Malinor?" The younger of the men took a step toward him.

They knew his name?

Johesha took a step back, wary, one hand tightening on the buck draped across his shoulders. He didn't want to dump the game, but he would. He had to return to the manor. He had to! The other hand shifted around the hilt of his dagger. "Do I know you?" he repeated.

The second soldier—the one in charge—held up an arm, stopping the first, his eyes dropping to Johesha's dagger. He pulled his hood back to reveal his face. "We've been looking for you, sir."

Sir? Confusion crackled inside him, and he felt sick with it. "I don't know what you're talking about."

The men exchanged glances. "The Prince has been looking for you," the older of the two said.

Johesha looked around them for said prince, then returned his attention to the soldiers. "Prince? Prince of what? What for?" he asked, suddenly worried that perhaps he'd committed a crime and that was how he'd gotten his boots. "I think maybe you have the wrong man. I'm just a huntsman."

The soldiers looked at one another again, their brows bent with their own confusion. "I'm Brendsen." The one in charge pressed a hand against his chest plate. The young man tilted his head toward the other. "This soldier is Kobb."

"You're our captain, sir," Kobb said. "On my honor. We've been looking for you for over a year."

On my honor.

A year.

Johesha's throat constricted as if his body had gone to war with itself, fighting for dominance and tearing his mind apart in the process.

He'd been working for the benevolent Master for a year. What came before was… hazy.

"Did you desert?" the one named Kobb asked.

Desert? What? He shook his head and squeezed his eyes closed, his thoughts a jumble, then snapped them open. Wary.

"Magic," Brendsen whispered, the back of his hand against the other's chest. "I'd bet my life on it."

"But we found him. Should we take him?" Kobb asked.

Johesha's eyes narrowed, and he pulled his dagger. Over his dead body.

Brendsen held both his hands up, one to Johesha and the other gripping the younger soldier. "No. Sir," he said directly to Johesha. "Kobb, stand behind me. The captain will end you, son. We aren't here to fight, sir," he told Johesha, his eyes shaped with appeal and his hands conspicuously free of weapons. "We just want to find a way to bring you home. You and Jessamine Fareview."

Jessamine.

Jessamine.

The name was so familiar, but Johesha couldn't put the puzzle pieces together. Frustration began to fill in the cracks that the confusion had ripped open. He brandished the dagger. "You have mistaken me for someone else," he said through gritted teeth and a tight jaw.

"Okay. Okay," Brendsen said. "We're sorry."

"But–" Kobb started, but the older soldier silenced him.

"We're sorry for the mistake."

Johesha watched them back up, then fade into the forest. He didn't think for a second that they were gone, so he backed away, keeping watch. When he was far enough, he turned and raced for the manor just as huge snowflakes began to fall to cover his tracks.

But he knew full well it would never cover his trail in time. He was leading them straight to the manor.

Johesha

When he finally reached the entryway to the house's kitchen, he stomped his feet to clear them of the snow, then pushed into the vestibule, the heavy wooden door groaning as he did. He glanced back over his shoulder once more, thinking about those soldiers as he stepped into the house.

The moment he crossed the threshold, the heavy weight of memory dumped on him, as if he were held down underwater. He gasped, rocking forward, grabbing the chopping block at the center of the room to keep himself standing as everything he knew about himself and why he was in the manor rushed back into his mind. The heavy buck slipped from his shoulder and fell to the wood floor with a thump.

I am Johesha Malinor.

I am the captain of the guard for Prince Lachlan Nikolas of Jast.

I am here for Jessamine.

Johesha straightened and took a deep breath, reorienting himself to the truth of his circumstances. He'd followed a man who'd abducted Jessamine. He'd left his post, and the guilt of that slid through him, even though he knew the prince would have insisted he go after his wife's sister. Disguised as an ordinary huntsman, Johesha had sought employment, unaware that the moment he'd crossed the threshold of the manor house, some kind of magic took hold. Without fail, his desire to leave, his awareness of his circumstances, the bulk of his memory would flee as soon as he crossed to the outside world, only to return when he stepped back inside. A cruel trick. And it was the same for everyone who worked for the man who called himself The Master—an arrogant nod to his prowess as a wizard.

Johesha spun back toward the open door. Brendsen. He'd seen Brendsen!

He studied the tree line, sure the soldier had followed him, sure that even now, the guard Johesha had trained himself was obscured in the shadows of the trees watching the manor. Certain that Brendsen now knew where Johesha and Jessamine were. The snow fell harder, covering any traces of where he'd been, but he was positive that wouldn't be the last he'd seen of Brendsen. The catch was if Johesha would remember it.

"Close it! Hurry now," Mrs. Gerrick called. "You're letting out all the warmth." She appeared in the kitchen doorway, a tall, thin, pale woman, her skin now pink with the kitchen's heat, wiping her hands on towels tucked through her apron strings. Her brown hair, threaded with traces of silver, was escaping her functional bun. "What did you bring me?"

"A buck and some winter hares." He shut the door and picked up the buck once more, resituating the massive deer across his shoulders with a grunt. "Is *he* here?"

She hummed, stepping out into the dark anteroom and stalking around him looking at his offerings, but she didn't comment on his question. "Leave the hares. I'll have Henro skin them. Will you prep the buck for me? A bit big for the boy."

"I'll take it down to the curing room in the basement. Send Henro when he's done, and I'll teach him."

She tapped his forearm, then tilted her head, and with a whisper said, "*He's* down there again." Her distaste was clear from her tone, leaving no question who she was referencing. She harrumphed a noise and disappeared into the kitchen as she talked, normal volume now. "Size of that buck, we'll be eating good for the next few days, at least. Good thing too, with this storm coming in."

His gaze jumped to the door that led down to the under house. The wizard was at it again in the basement, which was where he spent most of his time in the manor house. Day in and out tinkering with… it was hard to ascertain in Johesha's mind what it was he was doing. But the man crowded the room, brewing, stirring, ranting, reading, muttering to himself as he mixed concoctions. Johesha's gut clenched with worry for Jessamine. Though the wizard hadn't hurt her, the man's frustration at his own inability to break the spell that kept her locked away did concern him. The sorcerer's patience was the edge of a knife.

"Make it last," Johesha called to Mrs. Gerrick and dropped all but the two unbutchered rabbits onto the block. "Looks like it'll be a blizzard."

Mrs. Gerrick snorted loudly.

He carried the heavy load down into the depths of the cavernous space of the manor house. There were several entry points to the basement, one of which was in the vestibule near the kitchen. The stone under house ran the length of the large home, following the pattern of the upper house, but whereas the upper house was fit for living, the basement was dark and damp. Most of the floors were stone, but some stone had worn away to reveal the dirt beneath. Roughhewn beams hung low enough that Johesha had to duck down. Lamps ran the length of the narrow halls and into various rooms, but they weren't often lit, as the creature locked up in the Master's workshop screeched inconsolably at the sight of fire. Only a few were now lit and wafting thin threads of smoke, and none in view of the wizard's workshop.

Johesha heard the Master before he saw him and could only imagine what was happening in the strange little workshop where the man did his magic. That was where

Jessamine was preserved in an etched glass box. It was also the room where the monster was jailed in the attached dungeon.

The Master yelled, and the echo rebounded through the hallway like an eerie slap, painful in its frustration and leaving a mark on Johesha's ears. It was followed by a deep thud that stopped him in his tracks. He waited, listening, the thump of his heart picking up speed and climbing up his throat, anxious for Jessamine. But he was nothing if not controlled, even in the face of fear.

The wizard needs her, Johesha reminded himself. Though he wasn't sure if that was true or if it was a lie he told himself to feel better.

There was a squelch of something thrown against a wall. "Curses!" the Master yelled again, his voice now muted and dim as it passed through the stone hallways, grating dull scratches along the walls. Johesha shuddered.

"Blood," the dark creature hissed.

"Well, if you'd reveal your secrets, I could let you go!" the wizard snapped.

The monster screeched. "I have no secrets!"

Johesha wished he could cover his ears at the sound of the creature's strange voice, the gravel of it scraped over glass, reverberating like sharp shards in his ears and making him feel nauseous.

Hoping to make it past the open door unseen, he took a deep breath and slipped through the hallway toward the room where he stayed.

"Hunstman!" the Master yelled. "Huntsman? Is that you?"

With a sigh for fortitude, Johesha turned and retraced his steps back to the doorway of the workshop, the buck still draped over his shoulders.

The monster groaned.

Inside, the Master stood between a closed door where the monster was imprisoned and the glass box where Jessamine lay asleep. Behind him was a counter strewn with herbs, steaming pots, bubbling potions. The wall was a collection of different ingredients. Johesha had made the mistake of looking a little too closely on one occasion and discovered hair, dried mouse eyeballs, rat tongues and tails, and other sorts of strange materials the man used in his concoctions.

"Master?" Johesha bowed his head and shifted the heavy buck on his shoulders.

"A buck?"

"As you see, sir."

"Anything else?"

"A few rabbits."

"Cottontails or hares?"

"Hares."

"Oh!" The wizard moved quickly past him, a clear dismissal. "I need some eyes and nails and tails."

Johesha adjusted in the doorway so the shorter man could pass, then watched him race for the kitchen, the haze of the smoke swallowing him in the narrow hall. The dismissal was exactly what he needed to get Jessamine out of there, except he needed to figure out a way past the magic. He knew the moment he left with her, all he'd want to do was find his way back. He also needed Jessamine awake. It was one of the reasons he'd waited this long. If this master wizard couldn't do it, how was he supposed to?

"Hungry," the creature hissed, pulling Johesha from his worried thoughts. The monster made an inexplicable sound, unnerving and frightening, as the cell door rattled. There wasn't much of a space to see the creature through the locked door, nothing but darkness and shadow, but its dark, thin fingers with long, sharp claws worked their way through the opening.

Johesha hated listening to the pathetic creature. "I've already drained the deer," he said, knowing that the monster needed fresh blood. He'd regrettably seen the Master feed it.

Ignoring the creature's strange sounds, Johesha continued down the hallway to another room where he had a large table to butcher the kills. There were knives, hooks, and all manner of implements organized by kind, used to prepare the meat for the kitchen and tan the leather. Everything hung in its proper place along the walls. Once the buck was on the table, Johesha removed his outer hunting clothes, hung them neatly, and unhooked the remaining hares from his line.

Then he returned to the workshop.

"I brought you some meat," he said, holding up the undrained animals.

The creature made an unnatural noise. Pitiful. "Hungry," the creature repeated.

While Johesha didn't like the creature, he felt sorry for it. It was trapped. Alone in this room at the whims of the Master, just like them all. So rather than watch the Master starve the creature, Johesha had begun offering it small kills.

He dropped the hares where the monster could reach them.

The monster hissed, snatching at the fur and dragging them one at a time between the bars; the small creatures' bones crunched as it did. A grotesque sound.

With a glance at the doorway, Johesha took a few steps across the room to Jessamine's glass case. He flicked the closure open, the creaking competing with the crunching of bones behind him.

Jessamine looked beautiful.

Of course, he'd always thought she did—though the origin was hazy. He could remember her more clearly now, see her face in his mind's eye, but when he thought back, the impression of her lingered in small points of light disconnected from the rest. That impression existed in the back of his chest. In sleep, her beauty was something to behold. Her long, dark hair was sleek and shiny black. Her skin, a warm hue, was soft. He only ever touched her hand, as he was just then, the velvet of her a contrast to the roughness of his own touch. Her eyes were closed, long dark lashes framing the ridge of her cheeks, but he knew her eyes were a deep brown, dark and layered. Her nose was straight and led to full lips. Kissable lips, not that Johesha allowed himself to ponder that.

That was too dangerous.

"I'm here," he told her.

It wasn't useful or prudent to wonder then or now. Considering who he was then, his role as the captain of the prince's guard, or now, because if he was caught with her, it might just be the death of him. But admiring Jessamine, imagining a life with her even if it was futile, had been a way to pass the torturous time. It wasn't that he was in love with her, but he'd spent the better part of a year watching over her. Protecting her. Her vulnerability brought out his protective instincts.

That was all. He was certain. It wasn't the way he was attracted to her, which felt strange to consider given they'd hardly talked. It wasn't the dance they'd shared, or the kiss she'd pressed upon him after. No. Those moments he felt added up to curiosity and were best forgotten. Nothing more. He might be married to his position as captain of the guard, but the idea wasn't abhorrent even if he couldn't—wouldn't—allow himself the luxury of wanting a normal life with a wife who loved him, with a home, with children.

He took Jessamine's hand in his anyway, feeling deep down that even if she was asleep, perhaps if she heard him enough, it would help rouse her. "I got a buck," he said, running his thumb across the back of her hand. He frowned, thinking she probably didn't want to know that, but he hadn't spent much time talking to a woman. "Large."

It didn't matter, he figured.

"Henro is going to come and help me cut and cure it."

He paused, waiting, his thumb moving back and forth across her skin. The pad of his finger warmed. "It's snowing. Looks like we might get our first blizzard of the season." He thought about the guards and wanted to tell her, but then, he didn't know who was listening in.

The creature screeched.

Johesha jumped and glanced over his shoulder.

"Blood," it whispered.

"Not yours," Johesha answered.

"Yours?" it asked.

He'd never had a conversation with the creature before, and though it was unnerving, he decided he needed to set it straight so it didn't get ideas about Jessamine should it escape its enclosure.

"Yes," he lied. "Mine." And he hated that his heart tugged on his gut, wanting it to be true even if it never could be.

Johesha

The snow prevailed throughout the next day and the next, locking in the house's inhabitants. Winter white coaxed the world into quiet, creating the picture of serenity. Except the wizard's manor was anything but as Johesha cracked open the door to his work room in the basement to listen to the man's mumbling. His unhinged ranting about needing his vengeance was a constant theme, mixed with the screeches and hisses of the monster's replies.

Desiring to go unnoticed, Johesha retreated to the little space where he worked to maintain his proximity to

Jessamine. Though it had several small windows in a row along the top of the wall, they were now packed with snow, so Johesha lit the oil lantern. A small alcove housed a cot where he slept and stored his things. Down the hall was a room where he cut the meat of the big game before he delivered it back to Mrs. Gerrick, and where he tanned the hides. Though the Master didn't care for the leather, Johesha had been raised not to waste things, so he did the work. It was useful and kept him busy. Like cleaning his hunting weapons and tools, as he was doing now: knives, bows, arrows, and arrowheads, all laid out on the worktable in the middle of what he'd come to think of as 'his' room.

As the oldest and only son of three children to Jomiah and Rozzi Malinor on a farm in the Jastian province of Ussan, Johesha had been raised to know how to do all these things. It was the way of subsistence and survival. His father had believed strongly in self-reliance and imparted those lessons to Johesha and his two sisters, both younger. It had been the expectation that Johesha would eventually take over the farm, but he'd left home at fifteen to join the Jast guard—an honor—even if it had broken his father's heart. Johesha hadn't wanted to be a farmer, not then when he'd been young, brash, and seeking adventure.

His father had taught him to trust what he could do with his two hands. His mother had offered him the sustenance of her love and the nurturing of his spirit. She was a dreamer and perhaps was why he'd wanted to follow a dream, a dream that began with her stories of brave warriors and romantic notions of heroism. But these things had nothing to do with magic, not beyond the beauty of the rhythm of life and the adherence of dreams. He'd taken his lessons to the palace in Opalant City and trained, using his father's work ethic and tough love, and clinging to memories of his mother's love until he was the best, until he'd moved up the ranks in the guard to captain of Prince Lachlan's detail. At twenty-six, the youngest captain ever granted the position, he'd been given that assignment, and he'd done it well for the last ten years.

Until recently.

He'd left his post.

He picked up an arrow and the tool to sharpen it.

Now that he was older, wiser, he could recognize a sort of wisdom in that life, the farmer's life. Despite the heavy toil, there was the beauty of cycles. The predictability of seasons. The simplicity of work and rest. Perhaps if he were ever able to find a way out of this mess with Jessamine, he'd return to his homeland and honor his father's wish. It might be all that remained to him having left his post.

But what could he do against the wizard? The answer was nothing, should the confrontation turn to magic. With his hands, with his weapons, Johesha knew he would be a difficult man to best. He'd been trained to be the best. But he had no knowledge of magic. Hard to, when he hadn't known it existed.

"Huntsman."

Johesha straightened, startled by the Master in the doorway of his room, but he shut down any surprise he might feel as he waited for the wizard to speak.

It was clear the other man was frustrated, his usually

neat dark hair threaded with silver in disarray on his head, as if he'd been yanking on the strands. His usually warm skin was brightened even more with his ire. He frowned, clearly displeased, and his dark eyes appeared darker. "I need some things from the market."

"Is the market open, sir?" Johesha wasn't usually the one to go. That duty fell to one of Mrs. Gerrick's underlings. Though not in this weather.

The Master snorted. "Yes. But it will have moved indoors." He stepped into the room, then back out again, wrinkling his nose. Johesha knew the room smelled gamey, like the copper tang of blood, wet fur, dirt, and the musk of dank dampness of the basement despite his best efforts at cleanliness. He didn't mind, since it kept the lord of the manor away.

"Come next door," the wizard ordered, then disappeared from the doorway.

Johesha followed and stopped short at the framed opening. Jessamine's glass case was open. She lay still, her hands folded serenely over her middle, still dressed in her barely pink frock—such a strange contrast to the dim room glowing with ethereal glowing orbs of light, strange luminescent worms in bottles and a single flickering candle on the workbench. She also glowed with a soft golden light threaded with lavender tendrils wrapped around her, still asleep.

But the Master—Johesha's eyes jumped to the man— what had he been doing?

Johesha's heartbeat kicked up with concern like it always did when it came to Jessamine. It was maddening.

He prided himself on his ability to remain calm, to stay tempered and even under pressure, but somehow reason and clarity flew when he was worried for her.

He swallowed.

His thoughts trailed back to the night before the hedge had appeared. It had been the night of the prince's wedding. Johesha had watched Jessamine dance, his eyes chasing her, losing the view of her despite knowing she was there, as if her form was too much for any one person to consume. His heart had beat then with a different beat, as if each time his gaze reconnected with her, he was seeing her for the first time. Except his mind surged with knowing, like he'd forgotten from one second to the next, and then, when saw her, relief would careen through him like standing under an ice-cold waterfall.

Then he'd look away. And forget. And the cycle would begin anew. He'd experience the loss of the feeling, find her, and his heart would surge with awareness. *There she is,* it would say between thumps.

Since the hedge, however, in the aftermath of her being taken, he could see her clearly, and she never dissolved in his mind's eyes like she once had. He saw her as clearly in his memory as he did now, looking at her, and worrying. He told himself the pounding of his heart had nothing to do with attraction. That everything pulsing through him now was nothing more than protectiveness due to her vulnerability. He had a job to do, and it required his focus.

"I haven't found the means to wake her," the wizard admitted.

Johesha's eyes jumped up to meet the Master's, hoping

his anxiety for Jessamine's safety wasn't written on his features. He thought it strange the wizard was even admitting it but watched the man run a delicate finger across an etching in the glass, gazing down at her. Johesha couldn't name the look. It wasn't reverent, but nearly so, and didn't seem to align with what he'd come to learn about the wizard.

"Yet," the wizard added with just enough arrogance that his usual confidence overtook anything else that might have been inside him. He straightened, then turned to face Johesha. "Which is why I need you to go to the market for me."

"But Mrs. Gerrick's staff–"

"You all do as I say." The wizard huffed an annoyed sound, and a spray of sparks drifted from the workshop counter. The monster in the cage screeched. "And I can't send them in this weather. You're used to it."

That didn't mean Johesha liked it, but he didn't say anything.

"I need this done with some delicacy, as well. I'd usually do it myself. But you…" He paused, his gaze taking Johesha's measure. Then he said, "You're quiet, Huntsman, and I like that."

Johesha hated that this man liked anything about him, but playing the part was necessary. For Jessamine. He dipped his head in acknowledgement.

"There will be a man selling red-clay pottery at the market. Tell him that Crue sent you, and that I need some particular ingredients."

Crue. The Master's name was Crue.

Crue held out a small scrap of parchment inked with a list but didn't move, forcing Johesha to enter the room. "Repeat it, Huntsman."

Johesha did, taking the list on the scrap.

"Hungry," the monster said, the sound like a rattling of chains.

"Shut up," Crue shouted without looking at the creature.

"Should I bring it something—"

"No!" Crue's dark eyes jumped from staring at Jessamine to meet Johesha's eyes.

Johesha's gaze darted to the door, where the creature's long fingers disappeared from the opening as it slunk back into the cell. He knew the creature didn't deserve his pity, but he felt it just the same.

"Does the potter have a name?"

"A name?" Crue snapped, his impatience clear and bright, his tone like a bell ringing on a crisp, clear, morning.

"The potter?"

"Insignificant and unnecessary. He'll be the only red-clay potter. Now go," Crue said, turning his back to Johesha.

He had the fleeting thought he could snap or slice the sorcerer's neck just then, kill him, take Jessamine and flee. It would be easy. But it also meant he would have to find a way to wake her. He also didn't know what magic was involved, what kind of protections were in place. Just like he knew the moment he crossed the threshold, he'd forget. What would happen if he tried to escape with a sleeping Jessamine and all he wanted to do was return? He'd lose access to her, perhaps his life. What would the spell do if the wizard died? Kill them too? Trap them forever?

No. It would be more prudent to wait until Jessamine was awake or he could find a way around the stupid spell on the manor. One battlefront at a time.

Once he was ready, though there were several ways in and out of the basement, he climbed the stairs to the doorway he always chose, the one closest to the kitchen. The warmth of the room hit him when he opened the door. He added the outer layer of his cloak before taking the slides from the wall. Then he stopped at the wooden door knowing that the moment he crossed he'd forget but hopeful he'd see Brendsen again.

With his hand on the wooden door, he closed his eyes. "Remember," he whispered to himself. Though he'd done it before. He'd always made plans to venture farther, to get as far as he could to Sevens to get a message out. But every time he stepped beyond the threshold, the spell would take control. He'd tried leaving himself notes stashed in his pockets, but upon finding them he'd discard them as nonsense. He'd tried marking his skin. Nothing he'd tried had worked. He needed a way to stay cognizant, but he hadn't yet discovered how.

"You're going out there?"

Johesha looked over his shoulder at Mrs. Gerrick standing in the doorway, Henro, her eleven-year-old son, just in front of her. The boy's skinny arms were crossed tightly over his narrow chest, his dark brow furrowed, bent and tense like the rest of him.

"It's stopped snowing. Master ordered me to the

market. Need anything?"

"What if there's another blizzard?" Henro asked, his concern clear.

"I'll be careful," Johesha answered the boy. "And we've talked about how to survive if you're stuck, right?"

Henro nodded, but his tense features hadn't eased, and Johesha was struck by how much the boy cared. Then again, Henro hadn't had any men in his life, not since his father's death when he was just a small boy. Over the last year, Henro had been like Johesha's shadow.

"Do you think that ever matters to the Master?" Mrs. Gerrick asked in a hushed voice. Then she cleared her throat, wiping her hands on her apron. "I could use some sugar. A pound should do it. If it fits."

Johesha nodded and affixed his mask and his gloves before drawing up his hood. Then he pulled open the door.

"Johesha," Mrs. Gerrick called before he crossed over.

He glanced back.

"Be safe and come back, yes?"

As if there was ever a choice. Jessamine notwithstanding, the magic insisted on it.

He gave her a reassuring nod anyway, then stepped out into the bright, white of the day.

A warm sensation slipped through, and as he glanced around, he felt sublimely happy and content. The world was wonderful, and working for his benevolent lord was perfect. Even on a frigid day! That he was trusted and tasked to get to go to the market for the Master. An honor.

Johesha attached the slides to his boots and set out toward Rockwell using his guiding hand poles to navigate the terrain. The forest was quiet but for the hushed swish of his skis through the fresh snow, the evergreens weighted with their white coats, the air still. The sun burst across the terrain, and Johesha adjusted his hood to better shade his eyes before setting out again.

By the time he reached the marketplace, he'd worked up a sweat. After removing his sliders and attaching them to his pack, he stomped into the wood building where the goods' exchange was held in the winter. Tables and roughly constructed booths lined the room, leaving a wide walkway. Laughter and chatter bounced around the room, busier than he'd expected, but then, it was the first day the snowing had eased. With enough space to maneuver through the crowd, Johesha went in search of the potter.

Starting down one side of the longhouse, he passed the booth of a farmer and his wife selling canned roots. Another selling jars of honey. There was a booth offering different kinds of milled wheat, barley, and other varieties of dried and canned food. Another, praising the invention of his hothouse, sold fresh vegetables. Johesha passed colorful bolts of fabric for making clothing, soft pink ribbons that made him think of… someone, and it seemed strange he couldn't remember who. He searched his mind for a face, a name, anything, but the concrete details slipped away like a caught fish wriggling from hands back into the water. The more he tried to grab hold of it, the more it slid from his grasp.

Someone yelled, drawing him back into the moment. A man selling ointment promising to cure rashes. Others were selling furs, a tanner, a blacksmith with new arrowheads where Johesha lingered for a moment, an herbalist, all bartering with patrons and some with one another. When Johesha reached the end of the first row, he'd purchased the cook's sugar and a treat for the boy, stashing them in his pack, but he hadn't found the potter.

He started up the other side. A few booths in, he found the man he was looking for. Sitting behind a table stacked with red-clay earthenware, the man spoke with a patron. He was small, his head covered with wiry, gray curls that seemed to need a good brushing. A pair of spectacles sat at the end of his nose. His leather coat was tattered and patched, though weather-proofed with oil and wax. He said something to the old woman, speaking with his hands covered in fingerless gloves, his fingertips cracked and calloused, and shook his head at her with a frown. Johesha hung back until it was his turn, wondering if perhaps they were married and having a row. There was something vaguely familiar about her, which didn't make any sense. She was small, her silver hair wild about her head and hanging down her back in an unbound style that most women didn't favor.

Suddenly, the old man's blue eyes turned to him.

As did the old woman's.

"May I help you?" the man asked.

"I didn't wish to intrude," Johesha replied.

"Well?"

"Crue sent me, and he needs some peculiar ingredients." Johesha held out the list.

The man took it. "Crue, you say?" His eyes drifted to the old woman, still there.

"Yes."

The old woman turned her bright gaze to Johesha. Her eyes seemed both simultaneously colorless and brilliant with it, so much so, it was almost difficult to look at her old face, which suddenly seemed equally young.

Johesha glanced away to get his bearings, and when he looked back, she was just an old woman in a heavy coat, patched with different colored swatches of fabric. Her gaze—gray—jumped over his shoulder, but before he could turn to see what she was looking at, she turned and disappeared into the crowd.

"That woman is a nuisance," the man said. "Always haggling."

"For pots?"

The old man seemed taken aback by Johesha's question, then came back to himself as he looked at his wares. "Right. Yes… Pots."

The potter opened Johesha's parchment and scanned the list. "I have a few of these things, but Crue will need to return for the third item."

"The third item," Johesha repeated.

"Wait here," the potter said before walking away from his booth.

Johesha did try to stay out of the way of people walking past but was bumped and jostled, nonetheless.

"Captain? Johesha?"

Johesha whirled.

The two guards that had found him in the forest days ago stood before him. They looked as they had then, if a bit more haggard, like they'd ridden hard and had yet to rest. Except now they were also joined by two other men. One was tall—like Johesha—with an arrogant carriage, no concern for his safety. He was under dressed for winter. Everything about him was dark, from his curly hair to his black eyes to his dark day-old beard and his strange black clothes and overcoat.

The other—a touch shorter, but no less regal than the dark man—had less of an arrogant condescension and more of a confident entitlement. His brown hair was a touch long, dipping toward his brow, but his hood shielded most of his face. The man reached up and pulled the hood back a touch to reveal himself, and tilted his head expectantly, waiting. He was young, perhaps in his later twenties, his jaw shaped and broad like that of a man rather than a boy. His hazel eyes heavily favored green and were shaped with hope, slightly wide with expectation. A smile touched his lips. "Johesha?"

Important men. And... the haze of his subconscious pressed hard against his memory, but he couldn't grab hold of the thought. Another slippery fish.

"Do I know you?" Johesha asked, taking a step away from them as warmth pressed in against his chest with a desperate tension.

I have to return, he thought.

"It's me, Johesha. Lachlan," the young man said, nodding his head slightly, as if Johesha should know him and completely confident that he would.

There was a brief moment when a light curled inside of Johesha, a sensation of familiarity, but it dimmed as quickly. "Should that mean something to me?"

The young man's smile faded, though his initial affability did not. "You're my captain," he said. "Of my guard."

Remember. The word lanced through Johesha's gut like the stab of a cutlass, and his eyes danced toward the dark one—then back to the man who'd called himself Lachlan. Did he know them? He stepped forward, struggling against an impulse, wanting to say something but what did he want to say? The words slid away, choking him, and the sensation waned until it was just him standing with strangers.

The dark one tilted his head, black eyes narrowing. Unlike Lachlan, he didn't bother concealing his face with a hood, unconcerned with who might see him, and Johesha thought it probably wouldn't matter either way. The man emanated power. It wasn't something Johesha could see, just something skittering over his skin like chills when listening to a spooky story.

The dark man's eyes slid from Johesha's head down to his feet and back up again. "Definitely a spell," he said. "Explains a lot. Maybe Ozland would know." He looked at Lachlan. "We should have brought the girls. They might have been able to see."

"Or they'd do something rash that could endanger Jessamine," Lachlan said.

Jessamine? Johesha's heart skipped at the name, though it meant nothing to him.

The dark one smirked.

"Would you like to come with us?" Lachlan asked Johesha.

Johesha took another step away from him and grabbed hold of the dagger handle at his waist.

Lachlan's eyes tracked Johesha's movement.

"I need to return to my benevolent Master."

The dark one laughed though it contained no mirth. "Is that what he's calling himself now? What's the monster? The all-powerful, blood-sucking henchman?"

Lachlan held up his hands. "No need to feel threatened, Captain."

"I'm not a *Captain*," Johesha seethed, hissing the words through his tight jaw. "I'm a huntsman."

"Everything okay, sirs?" the potter interrupted, though Johesha didn't look away from the threat before him. A threat to his life with the benevolent Master.

"Everything is fine," Lachlan said. "Just fine." He took a step back. "We're done here," he said, his eyes flashing to Johesha's with... concern. Then the men melted into the crowd, disappearing from his view.

Johesha slid the wrapped-up packages from the table into his bag and plopped the lin to pay for it in its place.

"The third item—" the potter started.

"Will be ready next time," Johesha intoned, watching the crowd for the strangers, suddenly worried about getting back to the manor without being waylaid by a confrontation.

"Yes."

Johesha didn't wait for the potter to offer anything else before hurrying for the front door. He attached his sliders and was off, careful to determine if he was being followed, but he didn't notice the men, or any others on his tail.

Twenty minutes from the manor, without sight of the men, Johesha took a breath with tentative relief.

But then he crossed the threshold, and reality washed over him. He almost buckled under the weight of the truth.

Lachlan.

His prince had come for him. Johesha turned in the doorway. Lachlan and the dark god, Nixus. They knew where he was.

He waited, hopeful they'd somehow followed him, but the cold wind whistled through the open doorway and Mrs. Gerrick scolded him to shut it. So he did, feeling like he was closing the door on hope. They knew where he was, but how was he ever going to find a way to break the spells to free Jessamine?

Jessamine

Her body hurt, though it wasn't as if she could explain the pain. Perhaps it was boredom, a need to move. Perhaps it was because she was stuck, and knew she was wasting away. Whatever magic had her locked in the in between had sustained her, but she didn't know how much more time she could exist in this waking death. She wanted to scream, to cry, to beg for an ending. But she couldn't move.

The stranger bent over her.

She couldn't see him, only sense him. He smelled like earth and metal, with a hint of leaves as they decay in late fall after a rain. He was slick, somehow, though she couldn't see him, and cold like a reptile slithering across rocks to soak up the sun. Her innards shivered.

"It's time you wake up," he said and pinched her cheeks together.

Cool liquid poured into her mouth. She wanted to thrash, to cough, to spit but couldn't. She could only acquiesce. He lifted her by the shoulders to ease the liquid, a benign sluice of citrus and something wild, down her throat. Like him, she waited for this latest experiment to yield fruitless results. This wasn't the first time this man had forced a concoction into her. It occurred daily. Now, she only had to wait for his anger at its futility. At least his concoctions offered her body nutrients, she supposed, though locked in this magical stasis, she probably didn't need anything.

But why did her body hurt? Was she dying?

"I think the potion is close, child," he spoke as if to ease his impatience. "Then I'll proceed with the plan."

What plan? she wondered.

"It might just be missing an ingredient now." He was silent for a moment. "But I've sent the Huntsman for new ingredients. This . . ." His voice drifted away.

Jessamine felt nothing.

"Your mother–" But he stopped there, processing whatever was in his mind as he eased her down. Then she heard a slam, a loud and profane shout mixed with an inhuman screech, followed by a crash. "It has to work!"

Only, like all his other attempts, it hadn't.

Jessamine was still locked inside herself.

She heard the stranger close the box, muffling the world once more. But she wasn't alone. She was never truly alone. There was the scritch and movement of something else in the room with her. Though she couldn't smell it with the box closed, she had scented it before. Blood. It smelled of blood, though, of late, it had begun to smell like decay. Whatever it was, was it dying too?

Eventually she succumbed to the rhythm of sleep, drifting into that darkness where her mind didn't stretch with a madness that sought to grab hold. She fought it with the memory of the other man's voice, the one who brought comfort—the way he tethered her to some version of reality outside of her body.

That and that alone was keeping her sane. And sleep, because in her sleep, she could dream.

She stood in the summer forest, the trees dripping green leaves around her.

"Jessamine?" a voice whispered.

She knew that voice and whirled toward it. "Brinna?" she called. "Are you here?"

But Brinna wasn't anywhere Jessamine could see, even if she wanted to.

She walked through the forest, her feet sinking into mud, until the thick squelch and suck of it captured her.

"Help!" she screamed.

"Hush, child," a gentle voice said, a female.

Unable to move anything but her head, Jessamine looked around, but the swampy forest was empty. "Who's there?"

"Old Baba," the voice replied.

Jessamine turned her and saw a woman obscured in the trees. "Brinna?" she called because though she knew it wasn't Brinna, she could see her sister in this woman too, as if the entity were more than one woman.

The woman chuckled, a warm sound that filled Jessamine with ease even if she was stuck in the mud. "Is it your sister you want to see?"

"Yes," Jessamine replied. "She would help me out of the mud. You're not."

"I can't. None of us can. But–" The woman stepped from the forest, no longer a woman.

She'd morphed into a man, tall and shaped with muscle. His skin was a smooth, rich brown, his eyes darker and fathomless. His face was sculpted by the hands of gods, the sharp angles of his jaw, the fullness of his mouth, the strength of his nose. He was beautiful. And she knew him.

"Captain?" she asked.

Like being sucked from the muck, out of the water, she returned to the consciousness of her body.

The gentle swipe of another's skin against her hand drew her focus.

"Jessamine?" he asked, and she suddenly knew who was there with her. It was the captain! He'd been with her the whole time. He was the one bringing her relief from this prison. The one who kept her tethered to what was real and true. He was the one whose voice she longed to hear and whose touch she craved. The one who told her of his day, of his plans, reminded her who she was, and told her of her family.

"I saw them. Lachlan… Tarley's husband," he whispered as if to remind her, his lips near her ear. She could feel the sensation of his warm breath, of his skin against hers. He smelled like the forest today, like the cold of winter and the bite of pine. It was lovely, and she wished she could turn her face into his neck and breathe deeply. "And the god, Nixus. Your other sister's… Well, I don't know what they are. Betrothed?"

Jessamine's heart burst, overflowing with old and new feelings. She wished she could open her eyes, wished she could gaze upon his face. He'd been here! The whole time he'd been here. And now they'd been found? Her throat ached with a desperate need to cry.

"They know where we are," he said. "I just need to figure out how to wake you."

Yes! She wanted to wake up.

"Before Lachlan went into the hedge with the others to wake Tarley, the witch had said it was the kiss of true love." He stopped speaking, and his warmth retreated. "Do you have a true love, Jessamine?" he asked, quietly.

She wanted to scream and shout. True love? Who would ever love her, the invisible girl?

But then she thought of the captain, and she'd fantasized enough about him, even if true love was an impossibility. Lust wasn't. She thought of the night of Tarley's wedding and recalled kissing him. She remembered it like it was only the day before and supposed in her waking life it had been one of her last days awake and free.

That night, the courtyard at The Copper Pot had been

beautiful for Tarley and Lachlan's wedding, a fairyland glowing with soft light filled with the sparkle of dresses and the glitter of smiles. Drinks had flowed and there'd been music and dancing. She'd danced, for the first time not in the arms of one of her sisters, but with men, one of whom had been Captain Johesha.

She listened to his voice now, remembering.

She'd gone to him, recalling now that she'd longed for him to ask her, but he'd lingered at the edge of the courtyard just watching as if that was all he would let himself do.

But his eyes had met hers, time and again, giving her courage.

"Why do you stand here like a statue, sir?" she'd asked and smiled. They weren't strangers, so she'd felt comfortable enough to tease him. "Do you not wish to dance?"

His gaze had met hers, briefly dipped to her mouth then back up to her eyes. "I don't dance," he'd replied as stoic and stern as he always was, gazing out at the dancers once more. The deep timbre of his voice vibrated through her body.

"Why is that?" she'd asked.

"I'm the Prince's guard." He'd turned his head toward her, offering his undivided attention, a rarity for him.

"What does that have to do with it?"

A deep dimple hinted close to a corner of his mouth, but he hadn't smiled, as if he'd been fighting it. He'd dipped his head, looking down for a moment and shifting slightly on his feet. "I've never learned."

"A tragedy!" She remembered watching him fight that smile. "Allow me to teach you? I don't claim to be the best dancer, but I'm passable."

"More than that, I'd say." His gaze had locked with hers once more, and the sizzling awareness of attraction had raced up her spine, her skin heating.

"I'm afraid I would just embarrass myself, and that won't do in front of my men." He'd offered her a smile then, and the dimple appeared. "How could they ever follow a man without the ability to dance with a beautiful woman?"

She'd smiled, then hummed. "It seems to me, though, that dancing is as important as say... fighting." She'd bravely laid a hand along his bracer. "That being a good dancer is probably paramount to being a good fighter. A good—" But she'd stopped speaking then, realizing she'd been about to say lover, embarrassed by it.

And she'd seen in his eyes that he'd known what she'd been about to say.

Instead of backing away, however, she'd led him into the woods, and he'd followed, just far enough from the courtyard that they were obscured by the foliage, though the light, the music, and the laughter were still clear.

"As you wish, Miss Fareview," he'd said. "I'm all yours."

Her gaze had jumped from the tree stamped into the armor on his chest to meet his eyes sparkling in the darkness. He was so tall, it had made her feel small, but not weak.

"Well, you'll have to put your hands here." She'd

directed his hands into hers. "Like this." She remembered wishing she'd taken off her gloves to feel his skin.

She felt his calloused touch now, carving trails across the back of her hand, and heard his whispered voice, still offering her comfort.

That night, his hand had squeezed hers. "And?"

"Then we dance."

They'd both stepped, but in the awkwardness of not knowing which way to go, had crashed into one another. His strong arms had banded around her, crushing her body against his. Rather than stepping away like a prudent woman might have, Jessamine hadn't. Instead, she'd grabbed hold of his supple cuirass and pulled herself up toward him. He'd dipped down toward her and she'd risen onto her tiptoes, and without thinking about it too much, had pressed her mouth to his.

He'd froze.

Embarrassed, she'd pulled away. "I'm sorry. I didn't mean to over–"

But he'd grunted, cutting her off as he'd jerked her up higher against his body, his hands squeezing the backs of her thighs. He'd groaned, his shining eyes measuring her reaction, and when she hadn't protested, his mouth had crashed against hers, taking, taking, giving, taking.

She'd moaned into his mouth and wrapped her arms around his thick neck and strong shoulders, wanting to be closer to him, to crawl into his skin.

As soon as the kiss had begun, it ended.

Johesha had set her down gently and stepped away, breathing heavily and wild. "I can't," he'd bit out.

Unable to form a coherent thought, she'd just stood there, unsure how to respond.

"I'm a Jastian Guard. I took a vow," he'd explained, then shook his head. "I mean…"

Her heart had raced in her chest, constricting with disappointment. "It's all right, Captain. You don't need to explain. I kissed you. I apologize for my forwardness." She'd curtsied and walked away, since it was all she could do to salvage her pride.

He hadn't followed her then.

But he was here now, with her. Somehow. Some way.

Though she knew he didn't love her, and maybe she had only fledgling feelings for him, a light of hope started in her chest that maybe they would find a way.

Johesha

Hunting in the woods, Johesha felt like the best version of himself. While the killing wasn't his first choice, there was something formative in his person about his ability to do it. The weapons, his knowledge of them, the preparation, his skill in using them. The sense of normalcy that overcame him was almost as if he'd been born with his abilities rather than taught. Like tracking the elk herd, finding their trail, and stalking them like the predator he knew he was in his bones.

As he moved quietly through the woods, he wondered how he'd learned. He couldn't remember it. Upon reflection, he couldn't remember much of anything beyond his time with the benevolent Master. He thought of the men from the marketplace, sure they knew him. He thought about the way his body had come alive, a rush of energy moving through his muscles when he thought he'd have to fight. His curiosity about the event captured his mind, and he spiraled over it and around the thoughts again and again, hooking on to the fact that those men had known his name. The beseeching way the one who'd called himself Lachlan had tried to will Johesha toward…something.

With a sigh, he climbed into his stand to wait for the herd.

Several hours later with a fresh kill dressed out, he checked his rabbit traps and collecting several. Grateful, he started back to the manor.

When he got to the meadow, Johesha stopped short.

An old woman stood between the two rocks with faces, clearly waiting for him. Her dark gaze bore into him. She couldn't have stood any taller than his elbow, and her round form was wrapped in clothes and boots that had seen better days, a woolen coat buttoned around a full middle. Her silver hair was long and braided, the thick tail draped over her shoulder. She tapped her cane against the earth. "Hunter."

There was something familiar about her, but he couldn't remember having ever met her. Couldn't recall ever having seen her, either.

"You've been leaving the kills? Between the two faces?"

"Yes, ma'am," he said.

She nodded, then turned to walk up the path. "Come on, then." She didn't wait for him to follow.

He didn't question the wisdom of following her, though he could admit he was probably a more frightening creature than the old woman. Except he was also wise enough to recognize that dangerous things weren't always contained in dangerous packages. He followed anyway and didn't have too far to travel, her cottage just a hefty stone's throw (or two) from where he'd left the meat.

But he'd never noticed it before.

A miniature reflection of the manor house in the valley, the cottage was pushed deeply into the forest among the trees. The foundation was made of stone, and the walls of wood. A thatched roof littered with snow and wispy tendrils of smoke rose from the stone chimney. Warm, golden light shone from the diamond-grilled mullioned windows. It looked inviting.

"Leave the buck in the shed. Should keep away the scavengers for the time being," the woman said from the porch.

Johesha followed her lead, stashed his kills, and after removing some meat for the old woman, closed the shed and carried his offering in through the front door of the cottage. The single room was warm and cozy with a square table with two chairs, a rocking chair near the fire, and a small bed covered with a multi-colored patchwork quilt, a curtain hanging at one end for privacy. A fire burned in the hearth, with a steaming black cauldron hanging from a cast iron spit-jack. He saw a cabinet, a chopping block, and a small sink with a pump for convenience.

"For your trouble." He lifted the meat.

"Oh." She offered him a smile. "It's I who owe you a debt, hunter."

"Johesha," he said and set the cut of meat where she indicated on the chopping block. "You have no husband?"

"Why would I want one of those?" She cackled. "More trouble than they're worth."

Johesha had to smile but dipped his head to hide it.

"Lost the first and only one many years ago, so long ago I can only think of him fondly, now. Sit."

Johesha did as he was told. "You didn't think of him fondly then?"

She hummed a note as she shuffled across the wood floor to the cabinet. After pushing aside a curtain of violet fabric, she removed two bowls and carried them to the table. "If I recall, I think I wanted to kill him at least once a day." She cackled again.

"Did you?"

Her gaze met his. Her shining eyes were a bright gray lit up like a snow-filled sky and appeared far younger than her years.

"No, but perhaps I fantasized once or twice. He died of an illness." She started back to the fireplace.

Johesha, seeing her plan, jumped up. "Let me," he said, and swung the jack from hearth, then carted the heavy container back to the table.

"Thank you. Had my husband been so accommodating, I might have taken another." She offered him a bright smile, her eyes gleaming with mischief.

Disarming.

"This smells delicious."

The old woman ladled them each a helping of the hot stew. The fragrance of rosemary and pepper hit his senses and made him think of something homey. A man and a woman with brown skin like his, dark eyes like his, sisters laughing across a table much like this one. But the memory was fleeting, the image of the manor and the benevolent Master taking its place.

"My pleasure," the woman said. "Thanks for all the meals you've gifted me."

"Truthfully, I didn't know I was leaving them for you." He took a bite of the stew and moaned at how good it tasted; how warm it made his insides.

She offered him a hunk of bread with some soft cheese, then took a seat across from him. "Well then, it is even more important for me to offer you my appreciation. To leave food based on a feeling is a blessing offered with nothing expected in return."

It was true, he realized. The more he considered the superstition of it, the more it felt out of character. Unlike the hunting, which was as natural as breathing, heeding something he couldn't see wasn't.

After they'd eaten for several minutes, she asked, "You work at the manor just through the valley?"

"Yes. For the most benevolent of masters," Johesha said, then frowned, as the words sounded strange in his ears. He meant them, only the pitch of the tone was just a touch off.

"The Master?"

"Yes."

She hummed again as she took another spoonful. "What makes him so generous?"

"Benevolent," Johesha said and took another bite. "This is delicious," he told her.

"Benevolent."

Johesha nodded. "He takes excellent care of everyone in his employ. Offering us food and lodging. He even takes care of those who don't work. There's a young woman there…" His throat closed around the words, words he knew but couldn't seem to say. He pictured the woman, the glass box, but couldn't seem to get the information through to his voice.

The woman placed a hand on his forearm. Heat from her touch seeped through his shirt. "A young woman?"

"—asleep in a glass box," he gasped, then coughed.

"Oh! Water. I'll get you some water," she said and jumped up. "A glass box, you say?"

Johesha coughed, the spasm in his throat lingering. "What?" he asked, unclear what he'd said.

The woman set a cup of water in front of him and sat back down, picking up her spoon once more. She tilted her head, and Johesha had the impression she was carefully selecting her words. "Have you ever seen a sleeping woman in a glass box?"

He nodded.

She hummed as she took in that information much like she took another bite of the stew. "Does she need help?"

Johesha nodded, taking another bite of stew.

"Magic?"

Johesha shrugged, his tongue unable to form the words.

The old woman shook her head. "Interesting." She paused. "Take another bite and try again. Magic?"

"I think so," he struggled out, but the words came easier, freer.

They finished their bowls, the old woman asking him questions about the manor, and Johesha answering. He told her about the rest of the servants, Mrs. Gerrick and her son, Henro, the housekeeper and the butler, naming each of those in Master Crue's employ and how all of them were so happy to work at the manor. Eventually, after a second helping, Johesha pushed away from the table.

"I really should get back."

"Yes. Yes. But I have some gifts for you," she said. "Just a moment."

She disappeared around the curtain at the far side of the kitchen, and he listened as she muttered and clanked. There was a whoosh of noise, a void of silence as if all the sound had been sucked from the room, followed by a chill that raced along his spine. When he blinked again, the old woman was there, holding out two things toward him.

"First," she said, "this is a small token of my appreciation."

It was a strip of leather around which was twisted dark green and violet filaments that looked like shiny jewels.

"Oh, I couldn't."

She held out her hand. "I insist. Your wrist."

Johesha obeyed, raising his hand.

The old woman tied on the small bit of leather. It was

thin, no wider than the quill of an eagle's tail feather. "My husband was a tanner," she said as she fastened it. "He would work the leather over and over until it became so soft it felt like soft butter. This is a bit of it. I don't have enough for a second one, though I'd hoped for it. Just know that whoever wears it is protected."

"I shouldn't."

"You should. Allow an old woman her pride."

Johesha bit his tongue, understanding that sentiment. "Thank you." He watched the filaments flash then disappear as if melting into the leather around his wrist. "What—"

"What is it?"

"I thought…" But he didn't know how to explain it, so he didn't and just accepted the warmth sliding through him.

The old woman didn't press and instead presented a bright red apple. "This," she said, "is a treat for you."

"An apple? At this time of year?"

She grinned. "I have my ways," she replied, her gray eyes sparkling. "Don't share it with anyone else, as it is for you and you alone. But save it for when you are in the place with the one whose eyes you wish to gaze into. Do you understand?"

He didn't, not exactly, even if a sensation of understanding knocked between his shoulder blades. So he nodded, taking the fruit. "Thank you."

Once he'd helped her return the pot to the fire and carted the dishes to the sink, she shooed him out of the cottage. "It's getting dark. You must get your kills back."

"Thank you," he said once more.

"Yes. Yes. Now remember. Keep the apple safe. And should you need help, just return here, between the stone faces."

He nodded and turned away, but as he started down the steps, he turned back. "I forgot to ask your name."

But the cottage stood dark and empty, and the woman was gone.

Johesha

With the apple tucked in his bag, Johesha set out toward the manor with the buck draped over his shoulders, pondering what had happened to the cottage with the woman. A glance at his wrist revealed it had been real, the thin wrap of leather still fastened there. But the more he thought about the encounter, the more he struggled to make sense of it. His steps faltered as he considered turning back to demand answers, only his thoughts turned toward Jessamine.

…for when you are in the place with the one whose eyes you wish to gaze into…

Johesha stopped.

Jessamine.

He couldn't remember the last time he'd been outside the manor and thought her name.

"Jessamine," he whispered. The silence around him was suddenly oppressively loud, making her name clear and concise from his lips. Easy. "Jessamine," he said again, louder this time and spun back around toward the cabin, the crunch of the snow under his shoes an accusation.

But the clearing was empty. Not even the cottage remained.

Magic.

"Why can't you magicians ever be straight forward?" he muttered. "Why all the riddles and manipulation?"

There wasn't an answer, not that he expected one. Irritated, he stomped toward the manor. The frown deepened on his face, and when he made it to the edge of the forest, he glanced at the Jast mountains and wished for a moment he was home instead of trying to get Jessamine out of the clutches of the sinister wizard who had her. The realization that perhaps the witch couldn't have said anything plainly because he wouldn't have remembered it being under the spell on the manor hit him like a punch to the gut.

He stopped short, his lungs tightening.

He remembered!

He was Johesha Malinor, son of Jomiah and Rozzi Malinor. Captain of Prince Lachlan's guard. He was on a mission to retrieve Jessamine Fareview from the man who'd abducted her. He just needed her awake to do it.

And he was outside the manor!

He could leave! He could go for help.

He twisted around to look at the forest once more.

How had that old woman from the woods known? He wasn't sure, but that wily old woman had done something to him. The food? He glanced at his wrist. As much as he hated magic, at the moment, he was awash with gratitude. She'd done something to keep his mind clear, even if it didn't solve the problem of Jessamine's sleep.

But the apple. The apple, and however it worked, might. He wasn't exactly sure how, but if it worked, it seemed it could somehow get Jessamine to open her eyes.

And Brendsen! And Lachlan! They knew where he was, where Jessamine was. It was time to make a concrete plan, especially if the apple worked. With more vigor and less vexation in his steps, he hurried across the terrain for the manor, ready to make a plan for the next time he went out hunting. He was certain he could make the trek to Sevens and back in three days without rest if he needed to.

This time when he crossed the threshold of the manor, there wasn't the deluge of memory to drown him. "Where is he?" he asked Mrs. Gerrick.

The cook looked up from the dough she was kneading. She didn't have to clarify who *he* meant. "Haven't seen him today. Mrs. Pennig told us to keep it down. Said he's slept most of the afternoon. Said he was up all night, working." She shrugged and went back to kneading. "He was angry when he came up and appeared ill."

Johesha tapped the door frame with a closed fist, considering this. "I'll take the buck down then."

The cook nodded, and Johesha left with his kills down into the basement. He dumped the deer on the block, stripped out of his hunting clothes, grabbed the hares, and the apple, and entered the magician's empty workshop.

The monster clicked a sound at him, a kind of chirp. This was new.

Without hesitating, Johesha dropped the two rabbits in front of the opening and ignored the crunching of bones as the creature pulled them through. Instead, he walked to the glass case, undid the clasp, and opened the lid. He pulled the apple from his pocket, unsure how he could get her to eat it, then thought back over what the old woman had told him: *This is a treat for you. Don't share it with anyone else, as it is for you and you alone. Save it for when you are in the place with the one whose eyes you wish to gaze into.*

He was the one who was supposed to eat it.

He covered one of her hands with his. "Jessamine." He waited a moment, then said, "I met an old woman today." Talking to her calmed the trepidation he had at eating the apple. It if was spelled, how was he to know it might do something adverse to him instead? Except, the old woman had seemed kind, cooked a delicious stew, and offered him gifts.

But the only magician he knew—the Master—was a manipulative liar.

Save it for when you are in the place with the one whose eyes you wish to gaze into.

He leaned closer to Jessamine, fitted his lips near her ear, and whispered, "She gave me an apple. I think it might be spelled." Then he leaned back and looked at her.

She didn't move.

It would have been a lie to say he felt safe putting his faith in magic. Johesha was a man of action. He put his faith in his fists, in the training he did to make sure he could keep the prince safe, in the men he trusted to back him up. Putting his faith in an unknown woman who suggested a spelled apple could somehow solve his magic problem felt wrong. Magic for magic. He hated it, but he was out of options.

He didn't have much to lose.

Their lives, he figured, but then again, was this really living?

"I think I have to eat it," he said. He looked at it more closely. It seemed rather ordinary. So Johesha—on faith—took a bite.

Nothing happened.

The creature contentedly crunched on the bones behind him as Johesha crunched on the perfectly sweet apple.

"It tastes good," he told Jessamine and sat down on a stool next to her. The workshop remained what it was, for the moment a chaotic mess of a chaotic man's mind.

His bite hadn't changed him. Everything seemed just as ordinary as before. Jessamine lay asleep in the glass case, though it was open.

He took another bite of the apple and worked though his memory, staring at Jessamine's sleeping form, recalling the Fareviews had been locked in a sleeping spell. That's why Lachlan had disappeared into the hedge to go after his wife.

He ate another bite.

Jessamine really was lovely, he thought, twisting his head to get a better look at her as he took another bite. But he'd always thought so from the moment he'd met her. She'd insisted on riding into danger with her brother and Lachlan to find her sister. Johesha had required she'd ride with him, then had instantly regretted it when he'd climbed up onto the horse, her small backside nestled between his thighs, his legs framing her hips, his arms wrapped around her and his body wanting to speak with hers. He'd shut it down. There'd been a job to do.

He took another bite, warmth spreading through him. Contentment.

He considered their one kiss, and his heart pushed its pace inside his chest as he let himself recall it. He hadn't allowed himself to remember the feel of her lips, of her flesh in his palms. Refused to think about how much he'd wanted more than that night. Even trying to forget it, he'd thought about her many nights after knowing she was stuck behind the hedge. Forced himself to forget, only it had been a lie. He hadn't. He'd abandoned his post to go after her.

He ate more of the apple, swiping a bit of juice that dribbled down his chin.

He wished he could look into her eyes once more, recalling the last time they'd danced, at Lachlan's wedding to Tarley. It was hazy, but he vividly remembered her eyes, remembered her hand in his, his palm pressed against her back.

He finished the apple, that warmth inside him settling

into a sensation of resolute urgency.

The night of Lachan's wedding, she'd danced with several of his men, her smile contagious. Johesha hated the jealous feeling that had bloomed inside him watching her, wanting her for himself when he refused to do anything about it. He'd taken a vow.

But she'd acted on the attraction, bravely communicated what she'd wanted. She'd kissed him.

Now, as heat and light warmed his chest, he thought he could let himself do something about it, find the bravery, allow himself to hope and to wish for just this once. That he could kiss her. Just once more.

"I'd like to kiss you, Jessamine," he whispered, reaching out and touching her cheek, his fingers tracing the curves.

And maybe the witch's magic could get this right since what he wanted most to see was Jessamine's deep brown eyes fluttering open.

He'd spent a year with Jessamine, talking to her, holding her hand, working to reassure her she wasn't alone. Did she know? He'd spent a year trying to find a way to get both of them out of this mess, waiting for an opportunity. Now that Lachlan and the others knew where they were, they could do it.

He threaded his fingers into her dark hair. It was silky. He'd wondered.

His heart slammed against the inside of his chest.

When was the last time he'd kissed a woman? It seemed a lifetime ago. And he'd never felt for another woman what he felt for Jessamine. He loved her.

Oh gods! He loved her. He was sure of it. Surer of that than anything else he'd ever known in his life.

He was absolutely in true love with Jessamine Fareview.

Without pondering that thought overmuch, Johesha leaned down, and because his life absolutely could not continue without seeing her eyes, he pressed his lips to hers.

PART 2

"I would not wish any companion in the
world but you, nor can imagination form
a shape, besides yourself, to like of."
— William Shakespeare, *The Tempest*

"Jessamine?" Brinna called from inside a deep yawning darkness of the cavern.

"Brinna?" Jessamine answered from the edge of its entrance.

"You're here?" Brinna voice was cut off as if sliced by a knife.

Jessamine whirled and warmth bloomed across her skin with light. Captain Johesha stepped from the thicket of trees surrounding the cave.

"I'd like to kiss you Jessamine," he said, except the sound didn't match the movement of his mouth.

She was dreaming again.

Heat slid along her body, then invisible hands yanked her from the darkness. Waking up was warm sunshine filling up every part of her body, bright and burning. There was a sensation akin to joy, but also an insistence of fear. A *knowing* that something wasn't quite right. Consciousness pulled her from the haze where she'd existed for far too long, dragging her toward awareness. She blinked her eyes open, and a face she recognized hovered above her.

"You're here," she croaked.

His dark eyes darted around her face, then widened when his gaze connected with hers. "It worked," he whispered, as though surprised.

"It's you," she said and had the impulse to throw her arms around his neck but couldn't move.

She glanced at his lush mouth, the perfect, supple shape of his full lips, and she recalled the way she'd kissed him. Ringlets of wild black hair framed his strong features. He had a beard. She didn't like the way it hid his beautiful, brown face. She sank into the comforting darkness of his dark eyes just then, and reached up, laying a palm against his cheek. His beard was softer than she'd anticipated. "You kissed me?"

He sucked in a breath. Blinked. Shook his head. Then straightened, disconnecting from her touch, and nodded. "I'm sorry. I shouldn't have–" But then he stopped, bit down on the words, his jaw protruding under his skin, and he sighed. "I did." He held out a hand and helped her sit up.

Her body ached with the movement. "I'm really

awake." She was dizzy, weak, her stomach wrenching inside her, angry at being ignored for so long.

"You are."

"I feel terrible." She glanced around at her unfamiliar surroundings. A dim room with no windows but hissing with lights behind opaque glass orbs to hide what undulated inside. A chill made her shiver, and she squeezed the captain's warm hand. The room smelled musty. Of dried herbs, heavy with the scent of wet earth tinged with copper and iron. Amid her unconscious awareness, she might have had a feeling it was like this, but now, being awake, that awareness was like the burn of a limb that had been asleep as blood rushed back inside the tissue. "Where are we? Where is my family?"

He helped her climb out of the box.

Her knees buckled. "Oh!" She grabbed hold of him.

Johesha scooped her up before she could fall. "Your muscles are weak. You've been asleep a long time."

Now, in his arms, her own holding onto his strong, broad shoulders, she searched his face again. "I heard you." He smelled of snow and pine, and a hint of something bright and peppery.

"Heard me? What do you mean?"

The rumble of his deep voice moved through her, hitting all those vital organs with the vibration, sending a shiver through her.

"You talked to me."

He nodded.

Something screeched, and the captain twirled.

"Yours?" the thing behind a door said, a strange, airy,

garbled sound as if it were speaking around pebbles.

"What's that?" she whispered. "It isn't–" But she pictured it on the field that day trying to take her sister and could hear that otherworldly voice. She shuddered and pressed closer into Johesha's strong embrace.

"Yes," Johesha said, and his eyes dipped to hers.

She could tell he looked ashamed for saying it, but she tightened her hold around his neck anyway, as if to assure him it was all right.

"Master," the creature hissed.

"What are you doing here?" A new voice.

The captain whirled again to face the door, Jessamine in his arms.

A stranger stood in the doorway. A man. He was tall and lean, older. Silver threaded his short, dark hair, styled around his face in neat waves. His features were lean like the rest of him aside from his large, deep-set eyes and heavy brow. Handsome and frightening. He looked angry, but when his dark, bottomless eyes landed on her, he faltered. "She's awake!" His gaze jumped to the captain.

"Yes."

"It worked?" He started forward.

Jessamine pressed closer to Johesha once more and looked from the stranger back to the captain. "Do I know him?"

"I have heard her voice!" The stranger clapped his hands together and a delighted smile grew wider on his face. "How I've longed for this. I did it!"

His exuberance failed to alleviate the strangeness of him. She wanted to say Johesha had done it, but the gentle squeeze of the captain's strong arms kept the words locked inside her.

The stranger stopped an arm's length from them. "What are you doing holding her that way? Why are you here?" he asked Johesha, his tone accusatory. "Get your filthy hands off her, hunter." The stranger pulled Jessamine from Johesha's arms, and she lost her footing, her muscles unable to support her. She hated that she had to grab hold of the stranger's wiry frame but was assured by Johesha's hands still on her waist, keeping her upright.

"He helped me get out of the glass box," Jessamine said.

"Unhand her. I've got her," the stranger said.

"Who are you?" She leaned back against Johesha's strength, away from the stranger. "I don't know you."

"Do you know him?" The stranger's head tilted, and his dark gaze slid away from her to the captain behind her, his look menacing.

"Yours," the creature-behind-the-door trilled.

Her instincts told her this stranger was dangerous, so she lied. "Why would I know him?" she asked. "I don't even know you."

Johesha released her waist, but her back pressed against his broad chest, supporting her. And though she was barely standing on her own, she had every faith he would catch her if her legs gave out, which, she was certain, was only a matter of time.

"Leave us," the stranger told Johesha, but he remained where he was.

"Who are you?" Jessamine demanded. "Where is my

family?"

"I am your family now," the stranger said. "Huntsman, you aren't needed anymore."

Jessamine shook her head and stepped back into Johesha's immovable form, his breadth a fortress. Tears filled her eyes at her weakness, her confusion, her circumstances. "You aren't my family. Where is my mother, my sisters, my brother?" She started yelling their names. "Father!" she cried.

"Stop," the stranger shouted.

The thing behind the door screeched loud and full of pain.

"Master," Johesha explained. "She's afraid."

"Fine." The stranger whirled and shouted an order over his shoulder. "Bring her upstairs to her rooms."

Thankfully, it was Johesha who picked her up. Jessamine turned her face into his neck, breathing deeply to find a place of balance as tears leaked from her eyes. His wonderful scent, sharp like a winter day in the forest, offered her some sense of familiarity and comfort. "What's happened?" she whispered against his skin. "Where is my family?"

He didn't answer but his arms tightened around her.

She refused to close her eyes, afraid that if she did, she might go to sleep once more, and she worked through what she knew, trying to recall the last time she was with her family. It was difficult to remember. They'd been in the cottage around the table, but that was all that came to her mind just then. "How long have I been asleep?" she asked, even though asleep wasn't truly accurate, watching the opening to the ground floor grow smaller as Johesha climbed the stairs.

"Over a year," he whispered.

But she'd known it, hadn't she. Thought about the shifting scent of him. Knew that time had passed.

"Where are they?"

"Searching for you, I'd guess."

She pulled back to look at him.

His eyes dipped to her face as he carried her through a doorway, down a dark hallway lit with sconces, then up another set of steps, turning through opulent hallways filled with art, glowing with chandeliers, walls covered with dark fabric.

She didn't ask him any further questions, the implication clear enough.

He took yet another set of stairs and eventually turned into another room. This one—unlike the dank darkness of the one she'd awoken in—was beautiful. The walls were a dark green accented with lush purple and lavender, ivory and gold. It was gilt, gleaming brightly. The large hearth, alive with a fire undulating in its belly, was ornately decorated with a large frame of a woman holding a bunch of lavender sprigs in her hands, her ivory gown twisted around her hips as if someone had called to her as she walked through the meadow. It too was framed with golden pillars that reached to the ivory coffered ceiling above. The seating was upholstered variations of ivory, green, and purple. Plush rugs woven with the same colors overlaid over a parquet floor.

Across the room, beautiful windows and a door framed

with heavy drapery that opened to a balcony. It was snowing outside, the white world awash with the blue of twilight.

"I made this up for you," the stranger said, waving a hand about, then yanked on a cord near the hearth. "Put her in a chair, near the fire, huntsman. Then you may leave us."

Johesha followed the man's order and set her down in one of the chairs near the fireplace. When he straightened, she knew he'd go, and her heart grew anxious at the thought. She grabbed his forearm to keep him, her eyes meeting his. The shape of his eyes softened at her unspoken request.

"Don't you have something else to do?" the other man snapped. "There's a carcass downstairs, yes?"

Johesha's eyes slid from hers to the stranger, then back to the floor. He nodded, but still he hesitated, and she could see the conflict on his face. So she squeezed his arm and let him go, folding her hands into her lap.

"See to it then."

Johesha studied her face one more time, his eyes lingering before he turned and left.

She was alone with a man she didn't know in a strange house, a far cry from the cottage where she'd grown up in Sevens. The disorientation hit her in the center of her chest, an acute ache filled with a terrified beat. "Please," she said and hated that she sounded like she was begging. "Where is my family?"

"Enough sniveling," the dark stranger said. "My daughter doesn't beg."

Daughter?

Jessamine was doused with cold shock and hated that she knew it was on her face. "That's a lie," she said, stronger than she felt.

The stranger smiled and took a seat across from her. He crossed his legs and leaned on an elbow to study her. "That's more like it," he said. "And I'm not lying, but I appreciate the fight."

"My father is Tomas Fareview."

The man chuckled. "That worm."

Rage rose up in Jessamine, but she bit her tongue.

"Tomas Fareview is the man who has lied to you your whole life, pretending to be your father. Your mother… She's spent her life lying to you as well and keeping you from me. She and I," he paused, "well, I don't have to spell it out. You're aware of how children come about, yes?"

A servant entered the room and waited.

"Bring my daughter some food, please. Something bland," the stranger said, his tone barely containing patience.

"Yes, milord," the servant said and disappeared.

"So my mother didn't tell me about you because…" Jessamine asked, enraged by the man.

"Because she's a thief. I assume she didn't want to have to tell you what she'd done." He paused, his eyes assessing, alight with an emotion Jessamine couldn't decipher, and perhaps didn't want to. It almost seemed hungry. Greedy. "And I have found you again."

She shivered. "And so you are–"

"Your father. Yes."

"As you said. And?"

He grinned. "Crue."

"Just Crue?"

"For now." He sat forward in his chair. "A name holds power. It's not wise to go around giving anyone your true name."

"Crue isn't your true name?"

"Of course not." He picked a bit of lint from his trousers.

"And I'm just supposed to take you at your word?"

He shrugged. "That's all you've got."

"I awoke in a glass box in a dungeon surrounded by strangers in your home, and you think I should just trust your words."

He leaned back, still smiling as if proud. "I see your point. Let me clear up some matters. I didn't put you to sleep. I assume you can thank your mother for that."

Jessamine pictured a teacup in her mind. Looked at the contents, the swirling leaves, then looked up at Scarlett sitting next to her. *'Mother, you didn't,''* she'd said, just before everything went dark.

"You remember it?"

She ignored his question. "And how did I get here, then?"

"I am a very resourceful sorcerer. I was able to find a crack in your mother's spell and come to collect you."

Jessamine was a touch short of breath and didn't know how to respond to this. Instinctively, she reached for her ribbon, wrapping her hand around her wrist, but it was gone. And the stranger claiming to be her father watched her with shrewd eyes, missing nothing. "You abducted me?"

"Your mother *stole* you *from me*. Hid you," he said. "Now, I've found you."

She swallowed and watched the servant return, setting a tray on the small table next to her, a steaming cup with a bright blue tureen with white flowers.

"Some broth, miss."

Jessamine looked up, and her gaze connected with the servant's, a young man with blue eyes. "Thank you."

"Don't talk to him," Crue snapped. "Get out."

The servant scurried out of the room.

"And you woke me?" she asked, knowing he hadn't. That had been Johesha.

Crue accepted the credit with a nod of his head. "As I said, I'm very adept."

"You said you were resourceful."

He chuckled. "I like you."

"I don't know you."

"A matter we will rectify." He slid a hand over the black fabric of his trousers.

"I want to go home."

"You are home, Jessamine."

She shook her head. "My home is with my mother *and my father* in Sevens."

He jumped up, startling her. "You want to see them?"

"Yes."

"Fine." His steps ate the distance across the rug.

She pressed back into the chair. When he reached her, he gently touched the top of her head. His touch surprised her.

"Let's make a deal. When you are stronger, when you can walk unaided, you will write your mother a letter, and I will have it delivered to her. You can write, yes?"

"Of course I can write." Anger at his assumption colored each of her words.

He grinned once more as if pleased by her ire. "I'll send a maid to help you. Be sure to drink your broth. You'll need your strength."

Then he was gone, and Jessamine was left alone in that beautiful room feeling as if she'd woken from one nightmare into another.

Johesha

J ohesha stood at the top of the stairs hating himself for leaving her, feeling sluggish with something that didn't feel quite natural. It was as if there were a film over his eyes, painting the world with a rose-colored hue. And at the center of everything was Jessamine. With the fingers of one hand pressed to his eyes and the other flat against the wall, he tried to rub the haze away.

He saw her eyes opening over and over, and the way his body responded to it.

Then the way her mouth looked when she spoke.

He loved her, or that's what his mind told him over

and over, even though another quiet part of him reminded him it wasn't real. That he shouldn't believe it.

Magic.

It's magic.

Magic! his brain screamed.

Still, he stood on the top step that led down into the under house, torn between returning to Jessamine and doing as he was told to keep up appearances. He clenched his hands into fists, needing to turn back around. Needing to grab her and run away.

He took a deep breath and shook his head, trying to shake away the strange feeling muddling his mind, befuddling his senses.

He couldn't take her. Not yet. She could barely stand. She needed her strength, and he needed to figure out how to fight what the spell on the manor would do to her. They'd need to test how she responded to it to make a plan. If she fought him to return, there had to be a way to get her all the way to Sevens. Then again, he could restrain her. But what happened when they got to where they were going? Would she just fight to return?

He thought of the old woman. *If you need anything, find me here between the two faces.* Maybe that was where he needed to get Jessamine.

He descended into the depths of the basement and retreated to the curing room to finish butchering the buck, thinking about how to get a message to her family and failing to clear his mind. A note. He needed to do that again, now that he remembered. So when his grisly chore was completed, he snuck a bit of parchment from Crue's workshop.

"Where is she?" the monster asked, startling Johesha.

"What do you care?"

The creature didn't answer.

Johesha stalked out of the workshop back to his own room and penned a note to Jessamine's family. He wrote about the spell, about the manor and where it was. He shared that Jessamine was awake and healthy. He offered details about Crue and the manor's defenses, including a crude map. Even writing, he wasn't sure how he would get it to her family, but in the event he could, like seeing the prince at the market, this would ensure he had it ready. Then he wrote that he was working on a plan to get her home. When he was finished, he folded up the note and slid it into his pocket, hopeful.

Unable to contain his antsy thoughts, the feeling that he might crawl from his skin waiting to act, he climbed the back steps into the vestibule outside the kitchen and peeked inside to see if anyone was awake. He needed to burn some energy, or he'd march back up into the room and ruin all the work he'd put in to have the run of the place.

Henro looked up from the table. He was bent over an open book. "Heard the girl's awake. Mr. Wright said she ate a little while ago."

Johesha—grateful suddenly for the servants' gossip—nodded at the youngster, sad because he was as much trapped in this house as everyone else. "Yes."

"Henro," his mother said, "go get more wood for the fire. And bring enough for the morning."

"I can do it," Johesha said, pushing away from the doorframe. "I need some air."

"All the same to me," Mrs. Gerrick said. "No matter who does it as long as it gets done."

Johesha opened the door and stepped out into the cold night. The sun had descended some time ago, and all that was left was the shine of the moon on the snowy ground. His memory remained, and with a sigh of relief, he trekked across the trail made between the back of the house and the woodshed. As he stacked another piece into the wheelbarrow, the crunching of snow grabbed his attention. He turned to see Henro walking toward him.

"What are you doing out here?" he asked.

Henro held out a jacket. "Mother didn't like that you came out here without your coat."

Johesha took the offering. "Thank you."

"What's she like?" he asked.

"Who?"

"The girl?"

"Well, first off, she's a woman. And second, like any other, I suppose." Though even as Johesha said it, he knew that wasn't so. No other woman had ever lit him like he was ablaze.

The magic. It was the magic, and he shook his head, reminding himself of it.

"What color are her eyes?"

"Brown."

"Light like Grisom the dog or dark like the benevolent Master's?"

Johesha looked at the boy recognizing the phrasing and

hearing the enchantment. "So many questions. Take this wood to your ma, then bring the barrow back and you can help me with another load." He ruffled the boy's brown hair. "I'm going to chop more."

"Yes, sir." Henro pushed the wheelbarrow down the path.

Johesha grabbed the ax, set up a round, and with a heft swing, split the wood clean through. He did it again and again, working through the convoluted mess of feelings and thoughts moving through him. As he brought the ax down again, he heard something that made him stop, pulling the ax in closer in case he needed it as a weapon.

"Show yourself," he said.

Within the next breath, a faceless voice said, "Don't swing," and a face he recognized appeared just on the other side of the woodpile.

"Brendsen?"

The soldier stood up. "Sir. For all that's holy, you know me?"

Johesha hurried around the pile and ducked down behind it with the guard. "Stars, it's good to see you." And though he wouldn't have ever done something so familiar prior, he tugged Brendsen into a hug.

"But–" Kobb started; his face scrunched with confusion.

"Magic." Johesha pulled away and patted Brendsen's back. "The minute you leave the house you forget everything except this place."

"But how do you know us?" Kobb asked. "Now?"

"More magic." Mostly because he wasn't sure how the

old woman had done it. "How long have you been waiting?"

"Prince Lachlan sent us to wait after the market."

"Oh," Johesha said. "The prince is here?" He frowned. "Who's guarding him?"

Brendsen chuckled softly. "Always working. He was with the god, the dark one. And now Jude."

Johesha nodded, remembering giving Jude his pin, and patted his pockets, looking for the note he'd just written, a bit shocked but grateful he'd done it for a circumstance just like this. Magic again? He pressed the parchment into Brendsen's hand. "This explains everything. I need you to get it to her family. I'm going to get her out, but it might take a bit more time. That spell is going to complicate the escape. But at the next opportunity, I'll get her out."

Johesha glanced at a noise on the walkway. Henro was making his way back. "Get the note to them."

"It's good to see you, Captain." Brendsen smiled and clapped a hand on Johesha's shoulder.

"Mr. Joe?" Henro called.

"Go," he whispered. "Here, Henro." He re-emerged from the woodpile. "All done?"

"It was easy," the youth said.

Johesha glanced up and watched Brendsen and Kobb disappear between the bushes, realizing that this wasn't just about him and Jessamine anymore. Looking back at Henro, he knew figuring out how to leave was about everyone stuck in this house.

Crue

Crue stood at the window of his study watching the huntsman walk from the forest toward the house, a dark speck against the snow. He had yet another dead creature draped grotesquely over his shoulders. The big oaf was unconcerned by the filth coating his outer clothes. Disgusting. Crue couldn't help but sneer, and while he needed the man to provide food now that the darkling was too weak, and well... locked up, he wasn't sure he could trust the man.

A doubt had crept into his mind since his daughter's revival, when he'd walked in to find her huddled against that mortal filth.

Turning away, he carried his drink across the room and sat in a chair to watch the blazing fireplace. He needed to reevaluate his plan. It had been two days, and Jessamine wasn't cooperating. Not as he'd hoped. He'd thought mistakenly that when she'd discovered the duplicity of her mother and her lover that Jessamine could be turned to his side. He wanted her on his side, since he was certain that would hurt Scarlett most deeply. Except Jessamine was proving irritatingly loyal.

And she kept asking for the ridiculous huntsman, which he found bothersome. Some kind of imprinting trick, he wondered.

"Why?" he'd asked her during their breakfast that morning.

"He was there when I awoke. I just want to thank him."

"He's a servant. You don't need to thank anyone." He'd left it at that, but his mind hadn't stopped turning it over, and left him wondering about the huntsman, who had come to the manor a few days after he'd returned with Jessamine.

Crue frowned.

Did they know each other?

He looked through his memories, uncertain. There was nothing in the way the huntsman behaved toward her, even if the man was a closed book. There was nothing out of the ordinary about Jessamine's fixation on the man. He was a handsome specimen. Tall. Broad. Strong. Mysterious.

Perhaps that was all it was.

But something clawed at his insides, so he resolved he needed to keep an eye on them.

Someone knocked at the door, pulling him from his musings.

Crue bade whoever it was enter, and a pretty maid bobbed in. She wore the gray and white livery like all the rest, but he could see her dark auburn hair curling from under her cap. She had smooth alabaster skin, and her eyes lowered in subservience. She reminded him of Azleah.

"My Lord?"

He crossed his legs, wishing to feel the spark of desire in his groin. "Speak."

"Will you be needing anything further this evening?"

He considered her. Given that he was so keyed up with his rage against the huntsman and Jessamine's stubbornness, he considered ordering her to suck his cock but wasn't sure he could get it hard—a horrible side effect of that traitorous bitch, Scarlett. Of her choosing a fucking… imp! One more reason to hate what she'd done to him. The thought of the maid kneeling between his thighs with her mouth around his flaccid flesh filled him with more indignant fury.

"Sir?" the maid asked, reminding him she was still standing in the doorway, awaiting his order.

"No," he bit out. "That will be all."

"Yes, milord." The maid bobbed a curtsy, never once raising her eyes to his face, and hurried away.

The fire snapped.

He took a sip of his personal elixir, enjoying the way the liquid warmed his insides, the way the magic did what it was supposed to, even if it was temporary. His body heated, his joints moved with ease, his skin smoothed, his eyes grew keener. If only it would help with his flagging cock. Temporary effects didn't help. He growled, frustrated, but it was a small inconvenience to achieve his goal. He wouldn't have to worry about impotence ever again when he succeeded. So, with a quiet calm, he watched the fire and waited, content for now because soon, everything he'd been searching for would be within his grasp. Finally.

He smiled and took another sip as his heart grew strong again, and even the waning darkling didn't impact the way he felt. The tethers were bolstered with power once more. For now. But there were things he needed.

He stood, certain the huntsman would be back and have shed the gore by now.

He needed to get him out of the manor, away from Jessamine, and he had just the errand to do it.

It would keep Jessamine from asking for the giant clod again.

Crue found the huntsman in the butchery beginning his chore of hacking at the meat for the cook. He looked gruesome covered in blood and gore; the leather apron he wore to protect his clothes slick with it. The man's dark blue tunic sleeves were rolled to his elbows, giving Crue the view of his massive forearms. The fabric stretched around the muscle of his arms and shoulders.

He was a massive man and had Crue not been superior

with his magical might, he might have felt intimidated.

Though the stench was overpowering, he refused to retreat. He refused to be cowed by such a brute.

"Huntsman?"

The man stopped hacking at a joint, straightening, his dark eyes trained on Crue like... well, like a predator. He didn't say anything, just waited.

Crue could feel the measure in the man's waiting, as if he were assessing Crue, keeping an accounting and filing the bits of information away. Had this appraisal always been there, or had it only appeared since Jessamine woke? He wasn't sure, which bothered him. It wasn't like him to be so distracted not to notice.

Well, not anymore.

She was *his* daughter.

"I have an errand for you."

The man just dipped his chin and set down the butcher's knife.

Crue watched the methodical movement and noted the grace. "Before I tell you, however, I did want a word about my daughter."

The other man's features remained impassive, and Crue found himself wishing for the predictability of anyone else. He couldn't seem to get a read on this man, where others were so much easier. This fact alone was beginning to grate at Crue's patience, to worry him when it hadn't before, though he couldn't identify why that was so.

"She seemed very taken with you." Crue swiped some nonexistent dirt from his jacket.

The man grunted. "I happened to be there, and she was frightened."

Crue expected him to hack again at the carcass, to fill in the silence with something else to divert attention, but he didn't. He just stood there, waiting. "It was fortuitous you were there."

The large man tilted his head, his dark eyes giving nothing away. "I am always here when I am not hunting."

The obvious.

Crue scoffed and nodded. "Yes. That is true. And you have been the best of hunters." He waved at hand at the fresh kill.

"Which will turn if I don't get it cut and hung."

"Yes. Well, I need you to go to the Spine and hunt for a red rupricap. Their horns are especially valuable and an ingredient I need. But bring me the whole animal. There are other things I can harvest for my mixtures."

The huntsman offered a singular nod and picked up the butcher's knife once more.

"Leave as soon as you're done with that." Crue turned to leave but then stopped. "It goes without saying, yes?"

The huntsman looked up from the meat in one hand, the knife ready to make another cut with the other.

"My daughter is off limits."

Then he walked from the room with a self-satisfied smile on his face and in his heart. He felt so full of himself he nearly felt hard.

With the huntsman out of the way for a few days at least, he could work on keeping his daughter's focus. That and he could make more of the temporary potion he needed. It wasn't a full measure fix, but a stop-gap patch.

Then he could begin working in earnest on his plan for Scarlett. He needed the gifts, and he shuddered considering what could happen if he didn't get them.

That wasn't an option.

Jessamine

essamine ran, glancing over her shoulder into the darkness behind her, trying to keep on her feet though terror threatened to topple her. The grunts and growls of the beast chasing her had a scream in her throat. Thorns clawed at her hands, pricking her skin and leaving it bloody. She slammed into a dead-end, leaves raining around her from the hedge that was too thorny to climb. She'd tried and cut up her exposed skin. She whirled around, facing the darkness, back against the hedge, tears streaming from her eyes.

"Go away," she tried to scream, but the words lodged in her throat.

A growl from whatever was chasing her cleaved the darkness.

Suddenly, a brilliant light shone through the spaces between branches, thorns, and leaves to her left chased away the shadows. The hedge shifted. Standing in the opening was the outline of a woman holding out her hand. "Jessamine? Hurry!"

"Brinna!" She darted for the opening, slamming into her younger sister.

A vicious snarl and the brute force of a heavy body hit the hedge just as the natural doorway closed.

Jessamine scrambled to her feet and looked at Brinna, who was no longer on the ground either. Her beautiful sister, the third born, straightened out her pretty blue dress. Of all her sisters, Jessamine was closest to Brinna. Whereas Tarley's spit and vinegar was tempered by the outdoors and Aurielle was boosted by books and conversation, she and Brinna felt at home in the tasks they enjoyed together, namely sewing for their family.

Brinna straightened, and though her light copper hair was askew and tangled with bramble, she waved a hand over it, and it fixed itself as if by magic. "I've been looking for you! Where are you?"

Without hesitation, Jessamine closed the distance, pulling Brinna into her arms. Tears pierced her eyes. "Oh gods, Brin. I was stuck."

"Where are you stuck?"

Jessamine drew back and looked at her sister, soaking

in her beautiful face that seemed to glow with vibrant light. She pressed a palm to either side of Brinna's cheeks. "You are beautiful. I am so relieved to see you."

"I'm relieved to see you, Jess. And I need you to help me. Where are you?"

Jessamine swiveled away from her sister to look at the hedge maze they'd escaped from, only it was gone. Instead, she was standing in an opulent room decorated in greens, lavenders, and golds. Lavender plants began growing between them, and now they were in a field filled with the vibrant purple plants that stretched as far she could see. "Here," she answered, holding out her hands and spinning. "It's so beautiful now. How is it so beautiful?"

Brinna smiled sweetly, patiently. "Where is here?"

"In this field."

Brinna sighed and walked toward Jessamine, the lavender blooms tugging on the blue skirt of her dress. When she reached Jessamine, she grabbed her hand and stood at her side. They faced the snow-capped mountains.

"It *is* beautiful," Brinna said, then looked at Jessamine. "I'm so happy to see you again. To know that you're all right."

Awareness cut through the field, blasting it apart with light.

"Brinna!" She was suddenly afraid to lose her sister after all this time.

"I'll be back. I promise," Brinna said, then broke apart into a million lavender petals before Jessamine's eyes and blew away on a breeze.

Brilliant, harsh light slammed up against her as she

came back to consciousness. She blinked. Squinting while her eyes adjusted, she groaned and sat up in a massive bed, the green and purple comforter making it difficult to move.

She remembered. She was in the mansion of a stranger claiming to be her father. She'd been asleep for over a year. She was suffering the effects of it now. And she'd dreamed of Brinna—the first time she could remember a dream in so long—though the remnants drifting through her mind made her sad. She missed her family and wished she could wake up from this nightmare.

But she wasn't sleeping anymore. It was time to take matters into her own hands.

"Good morning milady," a pert woman said from the windows where she fussed with the heavy drapes until they lay in perfect folds. She was dressed in a starched gray dress with a crisp white apron, her brilliant gold hair glossy and pulled away from her cute face into what must have been a tight bun under the white cap. Her cheeks were rosy, her pink lips curved with a friendly smile.

"It's Mary, right?"

"Yes, milady." She beamed a smile nearly as brilliant as the light outside. "You remembered."

"It's just Jessamine."

"Oh." Mary paused, glancing over her shoulder as she finished with the final curtain. "I couldn't."

"I'm not a lady."

"You're the Master's daughter. He told us."

Jessamine gritted her teeth, angry at the audacious stranger and his ludicrous claim. "I grew up in Sevens in a cottage about the size of this room. I'm not of noble birth,

Mary."

The maid continued to flutter about the room, moving toward a wardrobe where she pulled out a new dusty rose-colored frock, the fabric heavy and layered for the chill in the manor. "I'll help you dress, then I'm supposed to help you take a turn down to the lady's morning room."

When Jessamine didn't reply, Mary looked at her. "Miss Jessamine, then?"

Jessamine smiled and nodded. "Where is my other dress?"

"The laundress has it. Master had these made while you were... ill."

Ill?

There were several hanging in the closet. "How?"

"The seamstress in Bandy Cove, the next township over, is very talented."

Bandy Cove? She'd never heard of it.

Mary brought the dress she'd selected as Jessamine swung her legs over the side of her bed. She didn't want to know how he'd gotten her measurements. When she tried to stand, her legs shook, unable to hold her weight, and she collapsed back onto the mattress.

"Oh Miss! Not yet. You need to regain your strength. That's what I'm here for," Mary said and reached around for Jessamine's night clothes, pulling them up and over her head.

Jessamine used her arms to shield her bare breasts. "I don't–"

"You were ill," Mary said. "It's to be expected."

There it was again. "Ill?" That wasn't true.

"The Master—he told us all. You were very ill, and he was able to use his healing arts to bring you back. Lift." She touched Jessamine's arm, and Jessamine raised her arms up as Mary applied a wrap to bind her breasts. "There's no reason to feel bad that you aren't up to scratch yet, Miss Jessamine."

"And what else did he say?"

"Oh. We know all about the tragedy. I'm so sorry for your loss. I didn't think you'd want a corset, as you're healing right?" the maid asked.

"No corset. What loss?"

Mary hesitated, either confused or wary she'd overstepped, then busied herself with the dress, unbuttoning the pretty pearl buttons that ran down the bodice of the underdress. She lifted it and slipped it over Jessamine's head.

"Please. It seems my... illness has affected my memory." If she had to lie to play along, she would. She needed to find her way out of this place.

"Oh." Mary's eyes drooped with sympathy. "I don't want to overstep, ma'am, and I'm sure that his lordship will help with that. He's very excited you are here. Proud to have his daughter home, you know." The maid helped Jessamine finish dressing until she was in layers of a pink and ivory confection of a dress more exquisite than anything she'd ever worn in her life.

Jessamine had the impression that Mary's vibrant personality wasn't exactly real. There was something that rang false about it. Too much. As if she were playing Jessamine. But there was also something genuine about her, and Jessamine couldn't understand the dichotomy.

After helping her dress, Mary helped Jessamine with her hair, all the while chatting about the manor. Jessamine learned a great deal just listening to Mary talk. She learned about the cook, who, because of a hunting tragedy, had lost her husband. The cook's son also lived at the manor. There was the head housekeeper, Mrs. Pennig, and the butler, Mr. Oto. There were several other servants, Mr. Rathsome, Mr. Wright, Helene and Cora among the names Jessamine couldn't keep hold of just yet.

"Oh, goodness me. You don't want to hear me prattle about."

"And the captain?"

Mary's eyes met Jessamine's in the mirror of the vanity. "The captain?"

Curses. That wasn't what Crue had called him. "The, um…"

"Huntsman?"

"Yes."

Mary blushed. "He's a sight, isn't he?" She grinned and pinned another of Jessamine's dark locks into place. "Johesha has been here about a year."

Jessamine smiled. "Where is he now?" Her smile faded.

A year. He'd been stuck here a year. With her. He'd said it the night she woke, but the information hadn't registered. She'd been without her family for a year. Locked in her body for a year. What had happened in all that time? Were they looking for her? Were they all right? Were they still locked in the sleeping spell? She thought of her dream, of Brinna grateful to have seen her, even if it had just been a dream.

"He's not here."

Her chest tightened. "What do you mean?"

Mary looked at her in the mirror, her brows changing shape over her eyes with confusion. "The Master sent him out hunting."

The panicked tightness eased. "Oh. Right. Because he's a hunter."

Mary smiled. "You know who has a crush on him?" she started, then stopped as if realizing she shouldn't be gossiping.

Jessamine wanted to ask, but was certain everyone, male and female, had a crush on the man. So she ignored the intrigue and asked, "If I wanted to send a letter to my family, could I?" She knew Crue had said they would, but maybe she could get something to them before. Something truthful.

Mary's smile faded. "Oh. Miss Jessamine." The maid patted her shoulder as if with sympathy. "Of course." But the way she said it made Jessamine's skin prickle. "Shall we walk to the drawing room now?"

By the time Jessamine made it to the room, the warm morning sun lighting the lovely white and yellow the interior, she couldn't admire it. She was breathing heavily and struggling to just put one foot in front of the other without leaning on Mary and the cane she was using. When she was finally deposited in a chair at a small round table near a window, both were spent.

"I'll get you some tea and pastries. You must eat to regain your strength."

Mary disappeared, but Jessamine wasn't alone for long. "Finally!"

She closed her eyes and gritted her teeth. "Good morning."

She heard him yank on a cord and opened her eyes as Cruc slid into the seat across from her. He looked different than the night before, though she couldn't put her finger on why. His hair was dark and laced with silver, gleaming in the sunlight. His dark eyes were bright and his smile... perfect. He wore a waistcoat—charcoal gray with darker stripes—with a row of silver buttons over a starched white shirt accessorized with a black tie. He leaned back in the chair and crossed his legs. She noted the black trousers and black boots.

"What did you tell the staff? They seem to think I was ill."

"You were ill, were you not?" He grinned, sliding a hand over the buttons of his waistcoat. A slim golden ring was on his pointer finger inscribed with the initials AR. She wondered what they represented.

"I was trapped in a magic spell. There seems to be a difference."

"Do you think I should tell them that? Shall we see how that goes over when one of them arrives with your brunch?"

She supposed he was right. "What did you tell them happened to me?"

He lurched forward with a quick intake of breath and leaned his elbows on the top of the table. "That is a great story." He smiled. "I really have a knack for it."

She didn't return the smile, waiting.

"Your mother stole you away from me when you were small. And I have been looking for you all these years. The truth."

His truth, she figured. "And the lie?" Though she was sure all of it was a lie to some degree.

"When word came that a ship went down in the Dauntiss Sea—one of my ships claiming to have my daughter and her new family aboard—I rushed to find you. You, my dear, were the lone survivor."

"And who was I supposed to have lost?"

He leaned back. "Your husband and child. All very tragic," he said with a pout.

That was why Mary placated her earlier. She didn't think Jessamine remembered the fake tragedy. "So how exactly did you meet my mother," she asked, "since I don't know that story."

His dark eyes flicked to the doorway as a servant entered, Mary on his heels. "Here's your food, Miss–" The maid's voice died. Jessamine glanced at Mary, who had blanched, but recovered, smiling brilliantly. "Milord! I didn't bring anything for you. Let me rectify that."

Interesting, she thought. Not all was roses as she was being led to believe.

"I have eaten," he said, waving a hand. "I've only come to keep my daughter company."

The male servant stood tableside as Mary unburdened the tray he carried, placing an array of food in front of her. A boiled egg still in its shell, buttered bread and some slices of cheese. Fruit and porridge sprinkled with cinnamon and sugar, a lump of butter melting in the center, finished off with a cup of steaming tea and a glass of fresh juice.

"This is too much," Jessamine said.

"Eat what you will," Crue replied. "You must regain your strength so we can do what we agreed upon last night."

The healing, then the letter.

"How was the walk?" he asked, looking at Mary rather than Jessamine.

"She'll be right as rain before we know it. Right, Miss?" Mary bobbed a curtsy and backed away in a hurry to retreat.

"If I had access to herbs, I could make myself a remedy for strength," Jessamine said.

He leaned back in his chair and grinned. "A healer. Yes."

Jessamine cracked the shell of the egg, pulling off the top. "Learned everything from my mother."

"And the godblood you carry."

It was Jessamine's turn to lean back. "Excuse me?"

"Oh." He pressed a hand to his chest, feigning surprise. "Right. One of those tidbits of information your mother failed to disclose. Her mother was a goddess. And her godblood gift: healing."

Jessamine swallowed, staring at the crack in the egg and wondering if it was somehow prophetic of her own circumstances. The imbalance felt tenuous. She knew she couldn't trust this man, but how could she trust her mother? The woman had drugged her into a sleeping spell.

But she was her mother's daughter, so she shored her defenses and continued forward, breaking the egg to eat what was inside. She knew the only way she would get the answers she needed to escape this prison was to get better and stronger. And she was the only one who could do that.

Johesha

The snow was relentless, a wash of white that made it nearly impossible to see. At least the wind wasn't as intense in the canyon where he'd found shelter for the time being. This high in the mountains, there was little else but rocks, larger rocks and, if he was lucky, a cave. He was so miserable; he wanted to yell himself into an avalanche. The godsdamned malevolent Master had decided he suddenly needed the curved horn of a mountain goat, and Johesha had been on the hunt for one for three days. If luck had been on his side, the hunt would have taken him closer to Sevens, but it had taken him in the opposite direction.

Then there was the threat.

He wondered if Crue had figured things out. That he and Jessamine had a prior relationship. Standing in the basement with Crue two mornings after Jessamine had woken, the shrewd gaze of the sorcerer had unnerved him. That and his questions. Then the threat: *my daughter is off limits*. If Johesha was another man, he probably would have challenged it just because he could.

But he wasn't. He'd already determined for himself that Jessamine was off limits. Besides, Jessamine wasn't a tool to use in a pissing contest between men. And Johesha didn't much like pissing contests.

That made him think of his father and the way he'd turned his back as Johesha had rode away from the farm. When Johesha had stopped to look back, his father hadn't been there. As if that final act would have made Johesha stay. One last pissing contest to see who was in charge. But that was his father. Stubborn to a fault. The memory made his heart both hurt with sadness and harden with pride.

He pulled the blanket tighter around him inside his leather shelter. The wind howled beyond the tarpaulin, grasping on with its fingers and tugging the walls, but at least it wasn't tearing into him. He just had to wait out the worst and restart his hunt for the horned goat when it was over.

In the meantime, he hadn't stopped thinking about Jessamine. While he'd been able to blame his one-track mind on the residual effects of the love potion, now, he knew, the potion was long gone. He couldn't blame anything but his own attraction to her. And the truth was, he *was* attracted to her.

It was her beauty, of course. Her eyes. He kept picturing those dark, fathomless depths that hinted at her wisdom. Then that mouth. That perfect bow shape, plump and luscious that tempted and tamed. Lips he'd now tasted twice. The rich darkness of her hair, like curly shadows, and the feel of her in his arms, her small, slight frame needing him. The spark of her touch on his shoulder, his neck. He'd replay each moment through the last he had, then replay them all over again.

But there was more than just her beauty, as all the interactions he'd shared with her surfaced and collected in the current of his thoughts. From first seeing her in Sevens to the feel of her between his thighs on his horse as they'd searched for her sister Tarley, from seeing her at the cottage, sewing sitting on her lap, and her dark eyes finding him, then slipping away with a blush staining her cheeks.

He remembered the warmth of a waning summer day, of the birds singing in the trees, of Lachlan and his bride-to-be walking ahead of them, and the guilt he felt at wanting to focus on Jessamine beside him instead of the prince ahead. Heat had raced up his arm to claw at his spine each time her arm brushed his. She'd chattered to him about her life, her family, her work.

"What made you decide to be a royal guard?" she'd asked.

He'd looked away from the prince for a moment. "My mother told me stories of heroes."

She'd smiled then, and that brightness lit up her whole

face. "You wanted to be a hero. I love that."

Heat rose on his face, but he'd nodded, admitting it. "Is that why you're a healer?"

She took her time answering him. "At first it was because my mother forced me, but then I noticed how she was a hero." She'd turned to look at him, life dancing in her eyes. He remembered admiring that spirit in her. "We both want to be heroes, I guess."

She'd laughed, her head tipping back and the sight had tugged on his chest.

He recalled observing her laughing with his men, the joy on her face. Then his mind slid to their first kiss in the forest the night she'd tried to teach him to dance. Every moment in her company he'd enjoyed. All of it added up to infatuation—a soul-searing crush.

The thought unnerved him.

It wasn't as though he hadn't ever had a crush before. He remembered being a lad puffed up with youth. He'd been fresh in the ranks of apprenticed guards, boys still, daring one another on a day off for the attention of the maids in the city square. He'd thought himself in love with one such girl—Eleri—the daughter of a rich merchant. They'd taken to sneaking out to meet one another, to test the boundaries of physical attraction. She'd been his first, and he thought his only. They'd spoken of love and made plans to forsake their dreams for one another. He would leave the guard before he took the vow, and she would leave her father's house. They would return to his family's farm. When her father discovered their tryst, he'd put an end to it with very little fight from Eleri, or Johesha for that matter.

Eleri had moved on with another young man, a lordling, and Johesha had suffered his first heartbreak. Eleri had married that man and he'd seen her again and again in court. Seeing her produced nothing but nostalgia and fondness.

That had been child's play.

This was something much, much different.

Johesha could feel the difference. His feelings were more refined, sharper, and steeped in the wisdom of years and experience. It wasn't the fantasy of the physical that had him obsessively focused, though it would be a lie to say he hadn't imagined it, but rather the worry that she was safe, the fear that the wizard might be hurting her, of the anxiety she could slip back into the spell and away from him.

And even knowing all of that, acknowledging it, he knew he couldn't pursue it.

He was the Prince's Captain of the Guard. He may have abandoned his post to save Jessamine, but it didn't strip him of the vow he'd made. A promise to forgo any other entanglements that would remove his heart and mind from service to the crown. He'd promised not to take a wife, at least not while in service to the kingdom. Not that he imagined Jessamine would be his wife. He barely knew her, really, but he could imagine developing the kind of depth of tenderness for her if he allowed these already planted seeds to bloom. He was promised to the Kingdom of Jast and committed to his job which was at the moment getting Jessamine home safe and sound.

He couldn't forget that. Ever.

Eventually the thrum of the wind made him sleepy. He allowed it, needing the distance from his thoughts, and slipped into slumber.

"Johesha."

The sharp crack of his name woke him, and he wasn't alone. A strange woman was in the tent with him. She was beautiful. Her hair was dark, laced with brilliant copper strands, and her eyes were filled with filaments of a multitude of colors. Otherworldly, somehow. She was wrapped in a dark, gauzy shawl that was clearly not enough covering in this weather, but nonetheless, she was hale and healthy, her cheeks, though gaunt, were bright with color. When she moved, it was as if she floated, a part of a world different from this one.

She tilted her head and regarded him, the silence unnerving.

He didn't move, didn't go for a weapon, just watched her watching him. Waiting.

But she seemed content to hover there.

"Who are you?" he whispered. She was familiar somehow, but he couldn't place her.

She tilted her head the other way and offered a short smile, a familiar smile, and his mind turned over people and faces, but the sluggishness claiming him couldn't move his thoughts quickly enough.

"How did you get in here?" he asked, knowing that his hovering on the side of the mountain of the Spine didn't make for an easy trek to his shelter. She should have been shivering, soaked through with snow and cut to the bone by the cold wind.

"Are you a ghost?" Because that seemed the only thing to make sense even if it didn't.

Still, she didn't speak, just watched him.

"Do I know you?"

Her smile widened, and she shook her head, then she coughed, her hand covering her mouth. Then she took the same hand and held it out to him with a closed fist.

Johesha went for a weapon, initially startled by her movement, but the knife wasn't there, which seemed strange. He was never without his dagger.

She flipped her hand over and opened it. In her palm was a bead of golden light.

He wasn't sure what he was supposed to do and just stared at it.

The woman lifted her palm, indicating she wanted him to take it. With a soft touch, he pinched the light with his thumb and first finger, careful not to harm it. Like a seed kernel, only it glowed between his fingers.

"I don't understand," he said, staring at it, then placing it back into her palm.

"For life," she said, then slammed the hand holding the golden seed against his chest, stealing his breath.

Johesha's eyes flew open. He coughed and clutched at his chest as warmth slithered outward from the center of his heart. The tent was empty.

Jessamine

On the fifth day after waking up from the spell, bolstered by an herbal remedy she'd suggested to the cook on one of her walks with Mary—she didn't trust Crue with her remedies—and her forced walks with him down to the basement and back up, Jessamine was stronger. Strong enough to not need to lean on Mary, and nearly strong enough—another few days perhaps— she'd be able to forgo the cane altogether. It was too quick, she knew. Magic at play rather than the physics of real life, but she wasn't complaining. At the first chance she got, she had every intention of leaving, but she hadn't seen Johesha in days and wouldn't leave without him. Mary had said he was still on that hunt and hadn't yet returned.

She hated that this worried her.

Maybe he'd left without her.

Except he'd remained with her for a year, and she thought it strange he wouldn't return considering that fact. Strategically, however, she considered it intelligent not to come back, and hated her selfish hope he would return. She didn't wish this place on him, but she was afraid to be alone here. At least with Johesha here, she didn't feel so exposed and vulnerable. But now that he was free of his obligation—though maybe that was the wrong word to describe why he'd stayed—why would he need to return? He could fly to his old life, share where the mansion was located, and bolster reinforcements. At least one of them could be free of this horrible place and its awful owner.

The disappointment at thinking he wouldn't return, however, was visceral. She couldn't help but think of him and waking up from the spell in his arms. The feel of his broad shoulders under her palms and the safety of his strong arms around her. Or even farther back to their first meeting when she'd been in those same arms. Under duress at needing to find Tarley who had disappeared into the woods, they'd spent hours moving through the forest together on horseback. There hadn't been enough horses to accommodate her, but she'd gone as the group's healer. Rather than ride with her brother in the lead on an unfamiliar animal, Jessamine had been asked to ride with Johesha.

Jessamine had tried to concentrate on the view rather

than being settled between the firm legs of a stranger. It had been the height of summer, the deciduous trees bright with green growth, the evergreens stoic and solid. The birds were quiet as their party of horses rode through. As much as she'd tried to concentrate on the task, the scenery, anything but the stranger behind her, the warmth of his thighs pressed solidly against hers had served a lovely distraction from the fear over Tarley.

She might have filled the awkwardness with conversation, but he didn't seem very talkative until he'd surprised her by asking, "You're a healer?" The deep rumble of his voice had reverberated through her body.

"I am."

Then he'd returned to silence, where he seemed so comfortable.

"Do you have something that needs healing, Captain?" She'd looked over her shoulder and tilted her head up to meet his dark gaze.

He'd looked down at her, and sparks had kindled at the base of her spine, then raced up to her neck with heat. "Sort of comes with my line of work," he'd replied. His mouth had quirked at the corner as he'd stared straight ahead and dropped into silence once more.

She'd enjoyed observing him in action. His efficiency, his focus. Remembered the trepidation as he'd walked all alone into the camp where Tarley had been held captive to collect her, then the relief and awe as he'd walked out with her sister, both unscathed. A seed of attraction for Johesha had been planted in her heart that day, and every interaction they'd had since only nurtured it.

She recalled the depth of his dark eyes when he looked at her, and his rare, unguarded smile on the night of Tarley's wedding to Lachlan. Of their kiss, which made her touch her lips with her fingertips at the memory. She wasn't sure if he would return, but even as she thought it, she knew that was just a lie she was telling herself.

He would come back. She knew it as plainly as the sun rises each morning. That was who he was. A hero. So, she resolved to get stronger while she waited.

That morning, Mary had helped her dress in another of the many dresses Crue had had made for her. This one was a lovely shade of butter yellow whipped to nearly white with matching slippers. Mary had done her hair up with a wide yellow ribbon with curly tendrils hanging down her back. It was the most finery Jessamine had ever experienced in her life, and it was tainted. She was a dress-up doll playing in a macabre play orchestrated by the man claiming to be her father.

She and Mary were just walking through the grand entrance of the manor when the same devil intercepted them.

"You are looking well," he said, grinning. He lingered in the doorway to the main parlor as she and Mary took a turn around the room.

"Time is all she needed, milord," Mary said with that bright tone Jessamine had come to understand was a disguise. But Jessamine hadn't truly gotten to know the woman any better. She was sure it was because of Crue. The help couldn't afford to be friendly with the woman connected to the tyrant who provided their livelihood.

It made her feel even more isolated and was just one more reason she wished Johesha back.

Crue's boots snapped against the parquet floor as he approached. He held out his arm. "Allow me to escort you around the house this morning. It is excellent to see you so much stronger, my dear."

Jessamine swallowed a retort and nodded rather than say anything.

Mary curtsied and fled the room.

They started through the entrance down a hallway that led into the dining room. It was a nice room, though she was certain Crue had no hand in how it appeared. A soft green paper lined the walls to an ivory wainscot rail that lined the perimeter of the room. A healthy dose of light, bright because of the sun's illumination against the fresh snow, steamed through the tall windows, each topped by a valance and draped with thick gold drapes. An oil painting of a horse hung over the hearth, which was cold and empty at the moment, the long table that comfortably seated a dozen bare but for the big floral arrangement filled with greenery and brilliant flowers in its center.

"I take it you don't host many dinner parties," she said as they walked through the room.

"I've never taken to them," he said. "I prefer the cozy dinner for two."

"Is there a reason for that?" she asked.

He led her through a pocket door out into the hallway. It was dark there since the doors were closed, candlelit sconces flickering and smoking. There were oil paintings lining the walls, portraits of long dead people, none of whom, she decided, were related to this man.

"I like to provide my undivided attention."

She didn't reply to that but followed him through another pocket door into the conservatory. It was bright and airy with the many windows in the room. The floor like the parquet in the entrance was covered with a thick blue area rug. The design showcased ivy leaves and yellow daisies. There were several areas to sit for conversation and bookshelves against the entrance wall, and another wall that looked as though it could be moved. The open double doors at the far edge of the room led to a greenhouse, and that is where Crue led her.

"How did you and my mother meet?" she asked.

"I worked for her father." He led her through the doors into the artificial warmth of the greenhouse and refrained from offering any more information. Despite the heat, it was a beautiful room made completely of glass. Row after row was layered with so many different colors of green, with herbs and fruits and vegetables. This was where so much of the food was coming from, she realized. And the ingredients necessary for the elixir she was using to strengthen her body.

"This is lovely," she said and meant it.

"How did you meet the huntsman?"

She turned and looked at him, suspecting a trap. "The day I woke up," she answered without a beat. "That's a strange question."

"You just seemed… familiar."

Jessamine let go of his arm and started down the row to a lovely parcel of ashperghandis, a tiny white flower with a dew-drop shaped yellow center. "Oh! How did you find this? I've only ever seen it sold in Fulstrom." Of course, she didn't say that was as far as she'd ever been in Kaloma.

"I'm able to come by many things. Just tell me what kinds of ingredients you need, and I can get them."

She was certain that was true and moved on to the next herb, then the next, feeling suddenly at home amongst the plants. She didn't like that it was in the company of this man, however, and tried to temper her excitement.

"So... familiar?"

"What's familiar?" She straightened from smelling a wild rose.

"With the huntsman."

"That was the first time I'd seen him, and I haven't seen him since."

"And yet you ask about him."

"He *was* the first person I saw," she said, but that was all she could think to say, so added, "Perhaps that makes me feel slightly more at ease. Is he all right?"

"Still hunting. I sent him on a dangerous task."

When she made it to the end of the row, she paused, leaned over to smell another flower, a white bloom of jasmine as she tried to rein in her thudding heart. She feared for the captain, concerned that perhaps he hadn't returned because he was hurt somewhere. A door at the end of the row with a clear trek through the field to the forest beyond caught her attention.

Crue stopped beside her.

"I love jasmine. The scent is divine. Did you know you can brew it in a tea to reduce inflammation?" She was babbling, but she had a feeling he would appreciate this line of diversion.

"I'm curious to learn all you know about the healing arts," he admitted as he stopped at the door. He turned the knob and opened it.

A heavy rush of cold air burst in.

"Oh, the plants!"

Crue turned to look at her. "You're worried about the plants?"

She nodded and watched him close the door. He led her from the greenhouse, showed her the music room that held a grand piano and the shadowed, closed-up ballroom filled with canvas coverings and shaded windows she was certain had never held a party in all the time Crue had been there. Then he took her to the library, which made her think of Auri and how much her sister would have loved the room and the books that stretched from the floor to the ceiling. Eventually, they ended back in the entrance.

"The house is yours." He bowed. "Enjoy free access to it. Now, I must see to some work."

Then he was gone, disappearing through the side door back to his study. She took a deep breath of relief, tired of worrying about what she might say. With her cane to help, she hurried back through the servants' hallway down a set of stairs until she was in the kitchen with Mrs. Gerrick, Henro, her son, and the scullery maid, Cora.

"Miss Jessamine!" Mrs. Gerrick smiled. "Come for your tonic?"

"Yes. And some company," she added. "Is that all right?"

"Of course. You sit here." Mrs. Gerrick indicated a bare spot on the large island in the middle of the room where there were piles of vegetables to be prepared.

The kitchen was a rectangle room, big in its aspect with a giant stove at one end, sputtering steam from pots that she assumed were for lunch. Bright, clean, and airy at the opposite end were shelves that held empty pots and pans and food items that didn't need special storage. There was an icebox and racks on which herbs dried, arranged from oldest to newest in their cycle. Though it was a massive room, it still reminded her of home.

Mrs. Gerrick set a white teacup and saucer in front of her along with a small pastry. She was a tall, thin woman with an efficient look about her.

Jessamine thanked her as the cook poured the tonic, the spice of the ginger root prominent and the vibrant orange tang of the turmeric taking precedence among all the ingredients. "I appreciate your help, Mrs. Gerrick."

"Well, you're walking in here on your own after your ordeal. It says something, now, doesn't it?"

Jessamine liked the cook immensely, and wished she could speak freely but didn't dare. It wasn't for herself so much as to make sure she was protecting the other woman. So instead of commenting or saying something that might make the woman uncomfortable, she just nodded and took a sip. "May I help chop these?" she asked. "To be useful."

"Oh no. Cora and I have it."

The door to an outer vestibule opened from the outside, startling them.

Henro jumped up. "Mr. Joe?" he called, darting from

the room, leaving behind a mess of whatever he'd been doing.

Jessamine's insides burst with nervous energy.

"Son!" Mrs. Gerrick called after him then muttered under her breath about something related to boys and making-more-work ways as she straightened the mess he'd left.

Jessamine stood and walked around to the end of the workstation, unable to keep still, hoping it was him. Afraid it was him. Afraid it wasn't.

When she heard his rumbling voice before she saw him, relief crashed over her, and tears filled her eyes. She didn't want that to be the case, but she couldn't contain the involuntary reaction. She was relieved as safety wrapped its arms around her once more.

He appeared in the doorway, bringing Henro back into Mrs. Gerrick's fold, and his eyes found hers. They widened with surprise as he froze. Their brown depths dipped, taking in her dress, jumped back up to her face, her hair, back to her face.

Her chin quivered with emotion and her throat hurt, but she smiled. "You're back."

"No worse for the wear?" Mrs. Gerrick asked.

Johesha nodded, swallowed, and tore his gaze away from her, looking back at Henro. "Got stuck in a storm." He looked at her again, as if his words were meant for her rather than the boy.

"Did you use the emergency tent?" Henro asked, all but hanging on Johesha. The boy was too old to do something like that, and yet he clearly couldn't contain his happiness and excitement.

"I did. Set it up on a four-foot overhang in the Spine."

Henro's face was the sun offering worship to his god. "I wish I'd been there."

"No. You don't. It was cold."

"Finish your chore, son," Mrs. Gerrick said.

"I should clean up." Johesha's eyes returned to her as he backed out of the room. He stalled, as if there was something he longed to say or do, but then he committed to leaving and disappeared through the door.

It wasn't until he was gone that Jessamine found she could catch her breath. But her heart continued to race.

Jessamine

Two days! Johesha had been back for two days, and she still hadn't seen him. Jessamine turned away from the mullioned window and moved without assistance to the chair in front of the fireplace in the room she'd come to think of her own space—no fears about Crue interrupting her here. It was a lavish prison, however. She didn't forget that. The room, the house. She sat in a gold jacquard-covered wingback chair facing the fireplace to brood about her situation.

Why hadn't he come to see her?

Maybe he was trying to keep his distance, so Crue

didn't suspect anything.

She wondered if her family had received the message yet, her lock of hair. Crue had made her write it the same night Johesha had returned. Would they believe that it was her? It was difficult to remain patient considering the situation, but there was little to be done about it at present, wondering how she could get away, get to them.

She was stronger now. Could walk unaided. It was time to go.

Which made her thoughts shift to Johesha. She needed to talk to him, but that meant finding a way to see him. Seeing him return two days ago, her heart and mind had erupted with relief, but her body had sizzled with desire.

He'd looked different. Wild. In Sevens, he'd been clean-shaven, a soldier. She could picture his rigid stance, his frowning mouth, his hand on the hilt of his sword as he stood observing activities, his gaze swinging with focus on the periphery of his prince. Now, his edges were as soft as the beard that covered his face. His black hair had grown out, silky with soft curls he tied back at his crown. His clothing was less restrictive than his soldier's gear.

Some things were still the same. The tightness in the shape of his eyes had given way to exhaustion, and his mouth still frowned. He was an imposing man.

There was a faint knock on the large wooden door, and it creaked open.

"Miss?" Mary popped her head in.

"Hello, Mary." Jessamine stood, her hands clasped in front of her.

The young woman slipped through and shut the door,

then turned and bobbed a curtsy. "I've come to let you know we're preparing you a bath before dinner. I've come to take down your tub," she said and disappeared through a curtained alcove on the other side of the room. It hid a small space where Jessamine had discovered the chamber pot and a cabinet. The floor was black and white tilework of alternating natural stones, the bathtub set into a small storage space when not in use.

Jessamine could hear Mary retrieve the metal container, setting it down on the marble, the tenor of the metal against stone thin and brittle. "Dinner with–" She started across the room to Mary.

"The Master. Yes. Mrs. Pennig is bringing you a new dress to wear, something more extravagant. Several came in today. Quite lovely."

Jessamine huffed. "I don't need another dress. There are plenty already." She looked down at the blue one she was wearing, one of the many in various shades of blue, green, and pink. There were more dresses than she could wear in her lifetime.

The maid's head poked out between the curtains, smiling, but at the look on Jessamine's face, her smile faded. "Most ladies would be so grateful. The Master wanted you to have the best from a seamstress in Fulstrom." She disappeared into the bathing nook once more.

Her head snapped to look at where Mary had disappeared. "Fulstrom?" She knew Fulstrom!

"Aye." Mary reappeared and started back toward the door. "Mr. Silas, Mr. Abner, and Henro will be bringing up some hot water soon. I'll be back to help."

Jessamine played dumb. "Is it a big town, Fulstrom? Far away?" She watched Mary cross to the door.

"Not as big as the capital New Taras." Mary stopped and turned back toward Jessamine. She seemed to want to say something and closed her mouth, then opened it, smiling with that false vibrance. "It's about a four-day horse ride directly west."

Jessamine tried not to smile, stifling her excitement and holding it in her chest. West! Directly west! That meant home was north.

Mary bobbed another curtsy and turned, reaching for the door.

"Mary!" Jessamine called before the maid could disappear.

Mary stopped and looked over her shoulder.

"Would you get a message to Johesha, I mean, the huntsman for me?"

The maid frowned, turning her head to glance at the door before looking Jessamine's way once more. "Why?" She'd lowered her voice. "The Master wouldn't–"

Jessamine shook her head. "A secret message?"

Mary's fair complexion paled further, but her cheeks belied her fear with a darkening, pink hue. "I don't know. If I get caught…"

"My–" Jessamine's throat caught on the word, but she forced it out– "father won't know. I just need to–" –she searched her thoughts for a plausible reason to see him– "thank Johesha for his chivalry the other day when I woke up. I haven't had a chance."

Mary's hand came up to her neck as she nodded, then smiled, a blush heating her cheeks. "Oh. Well, in that case," she giggled with a nod. "I'll tell him you wish to see him." Then she was gone, leaving Jessamine hopeful.

By the time she was submerged in her bath, it was going on two hours later and she had yet to see him. Mary had helped her wash her hair, but that was as much as Jessamine needed help with, despite the maid's insistence.

"Did you get the huntsman a message?"

"I did."

"And?"

"He didn't say anything, just nodded after I told him where to find you."

"Thank you, Mary," Jessamine said. "It will be our secret. I can finish up here."

"Shall I return to help you fix your hair for dinner?"

"No."

"But–"

"I don't need to do anything extravagant for dinner with my father," she said, the word cutting against her throat. "Besides, I'm used to doing my own hair."

Her features tight with disappointment, Mary bobbed and disappeared through the curtains.

Jessamine slid down as deep as she could into the copper tub, grateful for the silence. The water sloshed as she scrubbed. The verbena soap smelled clean, and though she was tense about the circumstances of being there, that scent offered her a touch of vigor. She worked the suds down one leg, thinking about Johesha and him being away. Of him standing at the threshold looking so... feral.

She shivered and wondered if he was allowed the luxury of bathing like this. She doubted it, though he hadn't smelled terrible despite his work, which meant he must have found a way to be clean. It made her think about his kiss and the disappointment that wove through her at not being able to remember it, of only coming to that awareness after it had already occurred.

She paused, imagining what he must have smelled like the night he'd returned. That wildness in him, his eyes. Like a man, she decided. Strong and natural.

She washed her other leg, her arms, her chest as she thought about his dark eyes, the depths of which caught her in a trance and pulled her in deeper. She imagined him stalking across the kitchen toward her and pulling her against him. That deep voice rumbling, "I missed you." Of him kissing her again.

Wishing it was so, she brought her fingertips to her mouth. She recalled their first kiss, his hands spanning the backs of her thighs, and replaced that feeling with the fantasy she was weaving in her mind of him lifting her and carrying her to the island in the kitchen. She slid her other hand across her belly as she thought about touching him, about what his touch might feel like, until her fingers were pressed against her sex, rubbing softly. She sighed, needing something, imagining it was Johesha with her.

The water wasn't warm anymore, but the sluice of the water felt good against her skin. Her fingers allowed her a moment of reprieve to release the tension she held inside her. She tested the soft skin, working her fingertip gently between the furrow of her gender until she pressed against that sensitive place of her clit, imagining Johesha's calloused touch.

She sucked in a breath at the sensations in conjunction with her imagination. Of Johesha bent over her, his hands making her come alive. "Johesha," she whispered, and leaned further back against the tub, opening her legs wider. She closed her eyes, sighed, and dropped into the pleasure of touching herself while imagining it was him. She moaned at the sensations, the fantasy overtaking her.

He would whisper in her ear with his velvet voice, "I love touching you, Jessamine." She realized her imagination wasn't very adept at this line of thinking, considering she didn't have any experience with a man—any man—but it wasn't as if she hadn't imagined him before.

She gently rubbed her clit, circling it with her finger. Her toes curled at the heat pulsing from between her legs, rushing to her toes, up her legs, and with a gasp, she grabbed her breast with her other hand. Heat unfurled like a wave inside her, driving pleasure into her belly. She bit her lips to quiet the moan as she came, bright bursts of heat careening down her legs as she jerked against her own touch, both satisfied and so lonely all at once.

Johesha

His cock was hard as a rock, and even though he knew he should back out of the room to give Jessamine her privacy, he couldn't. Her quiet moan, the slight splashes of the water, her gasp made it impossible.

Then he heard his name.

Fuck.

He suppressed a groan.

Closing his eyes, he fisted his hands, imagining her. Her naked body submerged in the water, her hand between her thighs, her head tipped back, her mouth open and eyes closed with torturous pleasure. The guilt he felt at eavesdropping wasn't enough to override his own desire to split the curtain to watch her pleasure herself.

But he didn't because his honor was.

He pressed the heel of his hand against his straining erection, silencing another groan.

It was just a physical need, he lied to himself. Except he'd never thought of another woman like he did Jessamine. He'd been around women over the last year and hadn't once thought of them like this.

He recalled Jessamine standing in the kitchen when he'd returned. The shock and happiness, the relief, and then the desire of seeing her there, waiting, a myriad of emotions had slammed through him. She hadn't been waiting for him, he knew, but he'd imagined she could have been, and something hungry had woken inside him.

What he was feeling right now, listening to Jessamine as she made herself come, was instinctual.

The strain of his cock. The thumping of his heart in his chest. The strain of his lungs. The fear he'd be caught juxtaposed with the desire to reveal himself. He wanted to slide between those curtains, slip his hand into the water of that bathtub. He wanted to touch her, feel the tender give of her female flesh. He wanted to watch her squirm and come apart because of his hands. He wanted to fill her with his fingers and feel how tightly her cunt squeezed him when she came. He wanted to taste her.

But instead of stepping through the curtain, he took a step back, then another. Considering even crossing that boundary with Jessamine was foolish, dangerous, and forbidden.

"Mistress?" a voice called from the door as it opened. "I know you said you didn't need help, but..."

Johesha, never one to panic—there wasn't time for it—stepped back and slipped behind a heavy drapery near the window to conceal himself.

Mary shut the door, and her steps passed his hiding place.

Johesha thought of Mary sneaking down into the basement a couple of hours ago, the fear a living creature in her face. Her wide eyes, her lips thin, her skin paler than it already was.

"Huntsman?" she'd whispered.

He'd stopped scraping the goat hide, surprised she'd dared enter the basement, then glanced in the direction of Crue's workshop.

The maid had shaken her head and walked deeper into the room. "I came from the other end of the house." Obviously having used the entrance that kept her from having to cross in front of Crue's workshop, avoiding it altogether. "My mistress seeks your time."

He'd stalled, focusing on the maid as worry consumed his insides. "Is she all right?"

Mary had held up a hand. "She wants to thank you."

The monster had shrieked as Crue had yelled, still at his experiments, for what was a mystery now that Jessamine was awake. Mary had jumped and a hand had flown to cover her mouth, a pitiful sound escaping between her fingers.

"I'll see to it," Johesha had whispered to get her gone.

He'd stolen up to Jessamine's room the moment he could.

Now, the water sloshed, and Johesha pictured Jessamine climbing from the bath. He wondered about her form.

"Did Johesha say when he'd come?" Jessamine asked.

His heart jumped at the sound of her voice, and he frowned, hating these involuntary responses. Control was important. It was imperative if he was going to get them out of there and back to her family so he could resume his post. That was, if his prince still wanted him after his desertion. Perhaps he would be punished, imprisoned. He could hope for mercy.

"He didn't," Mary replied, her steps returning to the room where he hid. "Mrs. Pennig was busy with something for the Master, so I laid out the new frock for you."

"It is lovely," Jessamine said, her voice now near him.

The pad of steps passed, and he was certain it was Jessamine. He willed himself still but couldn't contain the need to see her. With a steady hand, he peeked out from behind the curtain. Her dark hair was wet, the skin not covered by her robe, shiny with water, her feet bare. He released the curtain, cursing himself for looking, thinking about her bare skin under the robe. Of touching those legs, of spreading them, seeing the promise of what lay between.

He drew in a soft, steady breath, hoping to clear his imagination of her, closing his eyes but then snapping them open because all he saw was her.

He needed his wits about him.

"Beautiful, but wholly impractical."

Mary giggled. "I don't think the Master does things for

practicality."

Jessamine made a noise of discontent, then sighed. "Fine."

Johesha smiled and maintained his position, listening as the women talked. Well, Mary talked. Jessamine listened. There was the sound and slip of fabric, the tug and rub of ties, a rustle of skirts and a hitch of breath, until Mary said, "I'll do your hair."

"I was just going to braid it," Jessamine replied.

"But now you have me to do it for you," Mary nearly whined.

Mary's excited response indicated Jessamine had agreed.

The maid spoke about the Master—all favorable, which Johesha assumed was because Mary didn't know if she could trust Jessamine. She talked about mundane happenings at the manor, about the other workers, about the village and the pie her mother had made for her brother's birthday ceremony the week before. She spoke about polishing the silver, of finding a stray button, and Johesha wished he had a way to shut her up.

Finally, she said, "The Master said he would come to collect you for dinner."

Her steps retreated, then the door clicked shut.

It was silent.

Johesha sighed with relief, then counted to ten before stepping out from behind the curtain. "I didn't think she would ever leave."

With a gasp, Jessamine whirled.

His breath stopped.

She was stunning, dressed in a frock the color of a pearl that shimmered in the low light of the fire and setting sun, not quite ivory but sparkling with pink. Her nearly black hair was pulled up onto her head in an intricate bun of sorts, leaving the bronze smoothness of her neck and shoulders bare. When she released her hand from her throat, her breasts strained over her bodice with each startled breath.

Gods, she was breathtaking.

"You frightened me!"

"I'm sorry."

"How long have you been there?" she asked, her cheeks darkening.

For some reason, he wanted to see how she'd react if he insinuated he'd heard her pleasure herself, but his honor kept him from it. "Long enough to hear Mary talk you into a stupor."

"How?" She glanced around. "I didn't see–"

"I'm only seen if I want to be."

She crossed the room toward him, unaided by the cane, which was excellent progress and great news. "Where have you been?" Her face was filled with imperious indignation.

It made him want to smile, but he didn't.

"Would you like to sit?" She waved a hand at the chairs.

"This isn't a social visit."

She held her hands tightly in front of her. "You're right, of course. He's coming to collect me for dinner." She frowned. "And I'm Jessamine. You can use my name."

He paused. It wasn't as if he hadn't ever said her name. Except for some reason, the sounds felt different just then, saying them to her so she would hear them. But he nodded his head and forced the sounds through his throat. "Jessamine."

She perched on the side of the bed and studied him. "I was worried about you."

He didn't respond, just waited, unsure where this was going.

"Afraid."

"Afraid?"

"That you wouldn't return here."

"I'll always come back." Then worried it revealed too much, he added, "until you're safe with your family."

"According to him, he's my family."

"What?" He felt the surprise on his face, a foreign feeling.

She nodded and stood once more, pacing. "My father."

He could see it. The coloring, the eyes. "But–"

She stopped moving and turned to him. "Johesha."

He swallowed and waited.

"He isn't my family. He's a stranger that's stolen me from them, and we have to leave."

He swallowed and nodded.

She took a step toward him. "Why did you come after me?"

He opened his mouth, then closed it. The truth was, he didn't know. He'd been over and around and through the decision. He'd made an impulsive choice, and there weren't many of those in his life to account for. "It seemed the right thing to do." It was true enough.

"Why did you stay?"

"I wouldn't have left you."

"Honorable. But you didn't have to stay. Do you have a plan? You seem like a man who always has a plan."

"If there wasn't a spell on the house, we would be riding away from here at the very moment."

"What do you mean, a spell?"

"The moment you cross the threshold you'll lose your memories of anything beyond your absolute devotion to this place and the Master. You cease to be."

"And how do you know that?"

"Because the moment you return, you remember."

"That's inconvenient." Jessamine stood, her hand going to her mouth as she walked around the room. "So you couldn't leave," she said, as if it all made sense now. That he hadn't stayed because of her. She glanced at the nail she'd been biting, fisted her hand, and dropped it back to her side.

"I can leave," he said, hoping she understood that even if he'd been able to leave, he wouldn't have left her here.

Her eyes flashed to his, and desire buzzed at the base of his spine. He thought about how easy it would be to close the distance between them, to kiss those lips.

"How?"

"An old woman in the woods. Magic, I suppose. I've been able to leave and return unchanged—since you awoke."

"Why haven't we left?"

"Besides the obvious–"

She bit at the corner of her thumb. "Right. He sent you away."

He stepped closer and took her hand, removing her thumb from her teeth. "I don't know what the spell will do to you. Imagine me trying to haul you across the countryside as you fight to get back here."

She looked up at him, then down at his hand touching hers.

All he had to do was tug her a step closer.

The tension bloomed.

Johesha held his breath, wishing, for just a moment, he was someone else. That he hadn't taken that vow as a guardsman. That he could follow this impulse.

But he didn't. He released her and gave her some space. Himself some space.

Her dark eyes narrowed. He could see the Master's gaze in her eyes just then. "We should go find her."

"That's what I've been thinking as well, even though I hate the idea of more magic."

"Meet me in the greenhouse? Later? We'll test it."

A knock at the door startled them both.

“Daughter?”

Jessamine whirled back to Johesha with a whisper, “Hide!” But he was already gone, as if he’d been a ghost.

She ignored the flare of disappointment and walked to the wide wooden door. When she opened it, Crue stood on the other side, freshly bathed, his hair damp. He was dressed impeccably in a dark green suit with a bright white shirt open at the collar. An informal and strange manner of dress to disarm her, she decided. Like the beautiful dress she wore, a bit of artistry so fine against her skin, that for some reason contributed to the ruse for some purpose only apparent to him.

Crue grinned as he openly admired her from head to toe, then back up again. While he claimed to be her father, his look wasn't fatherly. It wasn't sexual, either but the predatory nature of his gaze warned her she wasn't safe.

"My daughter." He grinned. "Beautiful." He presented his arm. "Allow me to escort you to dinner."

She was a thing to him and ignored his offered arm, stepping from the room as she pulled the door shut behind her.

Crue chuckled. "A lot like your mother, I see." He started down the hallway.

She didn't deign to reply. The hallway was dark, the interior lit with flickering candles in glass orbs set at various intervals into the wall. There was a faint scent of smoke and something else she couldn't identify, along with a cool draft that made her shiver. It made her wonder how much of this place was dripping with magic, not that she had much experience to identify it.

She thought of her mother, missing her. Pictured her in the cottage with her father, bent together at the table holding hands.

"Have you heard from her?" Jessamine finally asked, breaking the silence.

"It's only been two days. I expect at least a few more."

"She will come for me."

He chuckled, but it wasn't a sound that offered joy, rather a sharp sound full of arrogance and derision. "I'm counting on that, daughter."

Perhaps he was the man who had helped to give her life, but he would never be her father. She wanted to tell him to stop calling her that but pressed her teeth together instead, unwilling to push things yet.

Jessamine knew she wasn't familiar with this world. Her lack of experience left gaps in her understanding and her awareness of what to discern about her place and the people around her.

But Scarlett Farview had been her conscience for as long as Jessamine could recall. Even now, her thoughts were in her mother's voice. She could hear her mother's wisdom in her head: *Wait until you understand the whole of a situation. Assess it. After you have all the information, then decide how to respond.* Scarlett had been advising Jessamine about matters related to a patient's health, but this situation seemed in line with that wisdom.

There was much to discover, and she needed Crue to trust her, so she had all the information she needed to decide what to do. It was better to feign acquiescence than to poke this bear with a stick. The worldliness her mother had understood Jessamine now carried with her into the den of her abductor.

Crue stopped at the door to a dining room, waiting for her to pass. These little manners, offering her his arm, walking her through the hallway, pausing to follow her into a room felt like a practiced performance. Ice sluiced over her skin, and she wondered why he'd go to such trouble.

To make you comfortable. So you'll let down your guard.

"And what is it you want from her?" she asked.

"What's mine."

"Which is?"

He pulled out a chair and waited for her to sit before pushing it in under her and taking his own seat. "It's a long story."

"We have the time, don't we?" she asked, removing the napkin from the table and placing it in her lap.

He smiled, then took a sip of the wine after the footman poured it into the crystal goblet. After he'd swallowed, he said, "We do."

Then it was silent, and the footmen placed the first course in front of them. Jessamine studied the bowl filled with a steaming concoction of something orange. It smelled delicious, herbs and spices creating a heady concoction that made her stomach twitch with eagerness, but she worried suddenly that perhaps there was a trick in it, as if she might take a bite and be changed.

She reached for her water as she thought about the last time she'd been at a table with her family, the tea and food tainted with a spell that had put her to sleep. She pictured the herbs in the bottom of the cup shaped like lines pointed away from the handle just before she'd succumbed to the potion.

A journey, she thought, and looked up at Crue sitting across from her.

"Eat," Crue said, and she wondered if he noticed her hesitation.

"How do I know you haven't poisoned it with something?"

He grinned again, took a spoonful of his own, and clearly savored the flavor. "It is good to wonder." When he was done with his bite, he set his spoon down with a clink. "But I need you whole for the time being."

For the time being.

Jessamine didn't want to ponder what would happen when he didn't, but she needed nourishment to strengthen her body, so she picked up her spoon and scooped up a dainty taste. The flavor burst on her tongue, sweet and savory, somehow, a tangy, earthy flavor of a root followed up with sweet, pleasant notes. She took another spoonful. "The story?"

"I met your mother when she was still a princess instead of the pauper she's become."

Jessamine stalled, looking closer at him. "A what?"

"Oh. You didn't know?" Crue laughed, then pressed a napkin to his lips. When the fabric was once again in his lap he leaned forward, his elbows against the table's edge. "So many secrets she's kept from you all these years."

"You said you worked for her father."

She could see he was delighted at the prospect of revealing all, as if it would somehow color Jessamine's perception of her family and add cracks to let him worm his way through her defenses. The idea that Scarlett had been lying to her, to them all, was worrisome, but Jessamine had also spent a lifetime with her mother, learning, practicing, hearing, observing. She knew her mother was secretive, but always purposeful.

"I did."

"And you will delight in telling me all her secrets, I suppose," she said before taking another bite.

Crue just smiled, straightened, and took another bite. When he was finished, he leaned back and watched her. "Her father—King Zollah Cumbria of Echo Landing—secured my magical services after his wife died. Your grandmother."

"I've never heard of Echo Landing."

He took a sip of the red wine in his goblet before saying, "No. You wouldn't have unless your mother explicitly told you. It's very, very far away."

She could hear the weight of the statement, feeling there were words unsaid she couldn't discern. "What kind of magical services?"

The footman appeared to remove the empty bowls, then replaced them with a salad. It was beautiful. Purple endive woken together with bright roots, pungent cheese, and berries. All from the greenhouse. She glanced at Crue before glancing at the window glowing with a bluish light of a winter landscape washed in early moonlight. "So? Magical services?"

"Yes. Right." He took another sip of his wine. "The King was deep in his grief at the death of his wife and wanted to speak with her one more time. That is why I was summoned."

Over the course of dinner, Jessamine ate and listened as

Crue spun a tale of a king lost to his grief who had misguidedly succumbed to the call of necromancy in order to reunite with his dead wife. According to Crue, he'd used his wits to protect Scarlett from the mad king, whose broken mind believed her to be his dead wife returned to him.

"We fell in love," he said simply as he sliced through the meat on his plate. "Amidst the chaos of her father's insanity, we stole away secret moments when we could and to protect her, I gave her my powers. It was when she discovered she was pregnant with you, we made a plan for her escape."

Though entertained, Jessamine reminded herself that this was his side of the story. His version of events, and as much as there was probably a touch of truth, it wasn't the full truth. Her mother had run away, after all, had hidden them in Sevens with magical ribbons. "And if my mother told me the story, would it be the same?" she asked, leaning back against her chair and taking a sip of her wine.

Crue's dark eyes twinkled as if delighted by her question. He smiled and took a sip of his wine but didn't answer her.

"I take your silence as a 'no', then."

"Take it as you will, daughter, but I am excited by your mind." His eyes jumped to hers and held. This wasn't a lie.

"Why is that?"

"You are mine. I see that."

Her smile slipped, and to hide her discomfort she leaned forward, setting her goblet on the table. "As you say."

"That bothers you? Why?"

"I have a father," she said simply. "The man who raised me. You are a stranger."

"A point to be rectified now that we have this time. Which reminds me," he said, tapping his plate and tracking the footman with his gaze as the man retrieved the plate. "I would like to see your talents in action."

"My talents."

"With healing."

"Is there someone that needs healing?"

"I could make someone need it."

She looked at him, unnerved by that statement. "Healing shouldn't be a test, but rather a response. I wouldn't harm anyone just to show off."

He shrugged and sat forward, looking closer at the dessert the footman placed in front of them: a berry cobbler dripping dark red juice on the plate. "As you wish," he said without looking at her, his focus on the berries. He took a bite.

Jessamine looked away unnerved by the red juice that lingered on his lips.

Suddenly, the footman collapsed, his body shivering and shaking on the floor at the end of the room.

Jessamine jumped up and raced across the room. The man's body convulsed. On her knees, she rolled him to his side, foam beginning to collect on his lips. "What have you done?" she snapped, unbuttoning the tight collar at the servant's throat to give him air.

"Like I said," Crue said from her side, "I wanted to see you in action. You haven't disappointed."

She reached for a cushion on the chair and froze, her hands glowing with warm light. She flipped them back and forth, then refocused, yanking the pillow and adjusting it under the man's head, his convulsion abating. "So you poison the man?"

"How did you know it was poison?" Crue asked, bent over at the waist near her shoulder. "He could just as easily have a condition?"

"The color and the scent. Now fix him," she said, looking up at Crue.

"Seems you already have."

She looked back at the footman, whose eyes fluttered open, disoriented.

"It's all right." She helped him sit up.

Crue chuckled. "Impressive. He shouldn't be alive."

Jessamine made sure the footman was safely seated before standing and whirling on Crue. "What?"

Crue sipped of his wine, set down the goblet, then patted his mouth with a napkin. "The poison. Whatever you did counteracted it." He nodded toward the servant. "He should be dead. Your talents are… exceptional, I'd say. Might I even say… magical."

Jessamine

The house looked different at night. The shadows were darker and filled with an inky blackness that seemed to exhale as she passed. Finally strong enough to forgo the cane, she snuck through the manor to their planned meeting place, ready to test the spell. Though they hadn't had time to solidify a plan, she hoped Johesha would be there.

The greenhouse, she'd realized, was the furthest entrance from Crue's room.

With a small candle flickering in the holder in her hand, Jessamine worked her way down the hallway and stairs through the drawing room and into the conservatory. She'd been there in the light of day. At night it was like a tomb filled with the threat of ghosts. After what had happened with the footman that night, she didn't doubt Crue had amassed victims. She shuddered.

The entrance to the greenhouse was closed, so she turned the doorknob and pushed open the door quietly. She closed it behind her, then turned to get her bearings.

Johesha was already there, waiting. He turned upon hearing her, but didn't move.

Her candle didn't quite reach him, leaving him in the blue shadows of the glass room. The night sky, the snow, the darkness of the forest—had it been any other time, it might have been beautiful and romantic, but Jessamine was focused. She wanted out of this house.

"It's just a test?" she said. "If we can get away, let's just go."

"You're going to put up a fight." He held out a coat. "Put this on."

"But I want to leave." She slipped into the jacket he handed her. It was much too big.

Johesha grabbed her arm gently and turned her to face him. "I need to understand how much fight you'll give me if I lead you away."

She swallowed, nervous. "Even if I want to leave?"

He offered her a clipped 'yes'. "The spell doesn't care what you want."

She turned back to the door, then turned the knob. Cold plunged into the room like a deluge of water enveloping her. She pulled Johesha's coat tighter and realized she wore nothing but her slippers. "I'm going to have to get my hands on some boots."

Johesha made a noise. "I'll find you some."

She hesitated and looked at him, suddenly worried about crossing, about losing herself, about losing him.

"It doesn't hurt," he said.

She glanced at him, took a deep breath, and stepped through the doorway.

Contentment filled her chest. She was happy, even in the cold, and took several steps from the threshold. It was so beautiful outside in the moonlit dark, the blue light shining off the snow, and though it was cold, the stars above were brilliant. She felt like twirling and glanced over her shoulder to see a man in the door.

The stranger followed her out into the snow.

Her heart faltered in her chest. "Do I know you?"

"Yes."

"I don't–" She paused, her heart racing with trepidation, at the handsome stranger so close. Foolish to have ventured from the house. "I need to go back to the benevolent Master. He takes care of me," she said, and moved to step around the stranger.

Only he grabbed hold of her waist. "Not yet."

"Don't," she said as his large hand closed around her wrist. "Wait. No." She pulled against him as he tried to lead her away from the door. She tried to jerk from his grip, but he turned and hoisted her over his shoulder, carrying her further.

"Take me back," she yelled, hitting his back, kicking.

"We have to see. How far," he tried to tell her, bringing

her back down to face him. Her body was pressed tightly against his, his big hands palming either side of her face. "Jessamine. Hush. You'll wake everyone."

All her nerve endings, every place her body was pressed against his, was alight and burning with… something. "You know my name?"

"You know mine."

But she couldn't think of it. Couldn't remember. The only thought she could grab hold of was the need to go back. "I have to go back. I have to. Take me back." Tears filled her eyes and spilled down her cold cheeks.

With a sigh, the man picked her up again and carried her back to the manor, setting her down just outside the door.

She scrambled over the threshold, as if she were drowning and the only way to find a breath was to be inside. Once she crossed over, a weight slammed into her, and she grabbed hold of the doorframe.

Memories rose like a massive wave, then crashed down, rushing through her, covering her as if she were submerged in water. She turned to look at Johesha on the other side of the doorway, his dark gaze shining in the moonlight, assessing.

"I forgot everything. Everything except getting back here."

He nodded.

"How were you able to hunt?"

"It's the task, I think."

"Maybe focusing on the task for him kept you connected? And now?" He was still outside.

"Whatever the old woman did—a witch, I guess— broke the spell. I remember everything now, since meeting her. My head is clear."

She swallowed. "You're going to tell me everything you remember about meeting that woman, and I'm going to need a task."

His eyebrows arched.

At the sound of a door followed by footsteps, Jessamine whirled.

Johesha was suddenly there, his heat warming her back. She heard the click of the door as he closed it behind them. "Follow me," he whispered, grabbing hold of her hand and pulling her after him. "Stay down."

Jessamine ducked, the thick greenery a shield as they wound their way through the greenhouse to avoid whoever had come inside. Johesha stopped and waited, listening, watching then moving, pulling her along with him. She was afraid of her rapid breathing, sure her steps were too loud, but whoever was walking through the greenhouse didn't indicate they'd heard them.

Finally, they were at the door to the conservatory, still cracked open, and Johesha helped her through and then followed. But as she started for the morning room, he grabbed her hand with his and pressed a finger to his lips, pulling her toward a paneled wall.

"What are you doing?" she whispered.

Johesha flashed her a warning look, but it softened, as if he was asking her to trust him.

And she absolutely did. So she relented.

He tapped the wall, and it slid open to reveal a tight

spiral staircase that disappeared into the ceiling above. A secret passage! If she hadn't been terrified, she would have gasped in delight.

Johesha didn't give her time to gape in wonder, drawing her after him and pushing the panel closed so it clicked quietly back into place.

"How?' she whispered.

It was dark, so dark she couldn't see him. She could feel him, the way their bodies were pressed together. She tilted her head up, imagining where his face might be but unable to see anything. He was so large in the tight space, filling up every bit of it so that she felt enveloped by him. Her breaths came in shallow gasps, but it wasn't fear anymore but awareness of him, of his heat.

"I've lived here for over a year. I've had time on my hands."

To explore. To learn. To scout. To plan.

"This way," he mumbled, taking her hand once more and leading her up the steep, narrow spiral stairs. They were made of stone, like the old bits of the house. Places built into the home that told stories of its history. How she would love to know those stories. But now wasn't the time as she followed Johesha deeper into the dark, up and up each step, slow and deliberate. They'd wrapped around several spirals when the door below them slid open.

Johesha froze, his hand squeezing hers with a silent command, and she followed suit, holding her breath to keep from making noise.

It was someone who knew the passage was there, though perhaps that could be anyone who worked there.

Her instincts, however, told her it wasn't. Told her it was Crue. Maybe he'd placed spells around the property, wards to alert him.

There weren't any footsteps, just the oppressive silence of waiting and the burn in her lungs to take the breath she was holding.

Seconds ticked past, and after what felt like an eternity, the panel below them slid shut. Jessamine snuck a slow breath, and they waited a few more seconds, listening as only silence and the sound of their breathing answered. Then Johesha had them moving again, his hand firmly around hers. When they reached what looked like a dead-end, he pushed another lever, and another panel slid open, revealing a doorway into the gallery upstairs.

While it too was dark, windows lit the wide hallway which allowed her to see a shadowy version of Johesha as he shut the door. They started through the hall to the stairs to cut across to her room when a bounce of golden light started up the stairwell toward them.

"Shit," Johesha muttered and grabbed her hand, ducking down the back hall that led to the bedrooms. He pulled her into the closest bedroom. Empty.

"Do you think it's a servant?" she whispered.

He was moving around the room, looking at the walls, searching for something—a secret passage. "I don't know, but I know I don't want to find out."

"Why? They wouldn't say anything."

He was near the empty hearth of a large fireplace. "Want to take a risk that Crue would spell them into talking?" He stopped and turned to look at her, then waved his fingers in another silent command. "If he finds out I was with you tonight, I'm a dead man."

She followed his demand, offering her hand. "What? Why?"

"He warned me away from you." He stepped into the cold hearth.

She followed. "Does he know that we know one another?"

"I don't think so." He looked at her.

"Then why?" It was dark once more, the moon beyond casting only part of the fireplace in light. "Maybe he suspects." And though she couldn't make out his features, she could see the shine of his dark eyes. He didn't offer her a response, but his silence told her something, even if she wasn't sure what it was. "Do you think it's him?"

"I wouldn't doubt it. I think he's probably got this place so steeped in magic it's like a spiderweb. One move and he feels the vibration. We have to get you back to your room."

Just as she'd wondered. "Why, though?"

"Does he come across as a man who leaves much to chance?" He yanked on a lever, and the back panel of the hearth slid down, opening into the next bedroom. "I can guarantee he's going to check to see if you're there."

"But how?" Only now it was very obvious how. "Should we use the hall now?"

He shook his head. "The secret passages." He pulled into the room beyond. Another bedroom bathed in dark and moonlight. And Johesha didn't stop, as if racing. They ducked into the bathing room of the suite, and he went directly to a closet. He pulled her inside, and then they were stepping through a swinging frame of artwork into the next.

And so it went, room after room, until suddenly, they were stepping from a large mirror into her room. He pushed her toward the bed.

"Johesha," she whispered, holding on.

He hesitated, then, just a fraction of a moment, his hands tightening. Then the pressure was gone. "Go!" Then he was ducking back into the mirror and pulling it shut as she climbed into the bed.

She'd only just pulled the covers up over herself when a soft creak of a door on the other side of the room reverberated in the silence. Near the bathing vestibule. She couldn't remember a door there, only a wall, but she now realized there was a secret passage between her room and Crue's.

As the candlelight flickered, coming closer, she closed her eyes, willing herself to find what she hoped was the peace of sleep on her features. She stayed that way, trying to find calm as her heart slammed against the inside of her chest.

She didn't know how long she lay there, terrified of being caught, unsettled that Crue could infiltrate her room at will, and shocked at the secrets this manor held. But she knew one thing, there wasn't a single safe place here.

Johesha

Fuck!

Johesha stalled on the other side of the secret doorway outside Jessamine's room, conflicted. He was leaving her certain it had been Crue skulking about the manor after them, probably now inside her room as Johesha stood there debating a return. Except he needed a bit more time to figure out how to get Jessamine out, to see if Brendsen returned with orders from Lachlan. He had to placate the wizard just a little longer. He trusted Jessamine to know how to save herself. Besides, the wizard wanted her alive.

So he pushed away from the wall and hurried through the room to the next secret passage, worried that now Crue would come for him, come to check if he'd gone against the express order to stay away from Jessamine. He twisted and turned through the passages, one after the other, and moved down the hallway of the basement toward his room.

Light flared when he walked in.

"Huntsman." Crue stood just inside his room, the lantern in his hands casting strange shadows on the man's face.

"Sir?" Johesha asked and feigned confusion. He wasn't untrained in the art of subterfuge and knew that his training was what was going to keep him alive.

"Strange you're out and about tonight."

"Is it?" Johesha asked. "Had to piss."

The wizard snorted and sneered. "So crass." The man emanated an oily slickness that permeated the room. "And a lie."

Johesha didn't reply or respond, knowing that the other man was making guesses, unless of course magic was involved. He stood where he was, giving nothing, waiting.

Crue stopped an arm's length from Johesha and tilted his head to look him in the eye. Johesha met his gaze with confidence, then retreated, not to indicate guilt but rather submission. In his many years with the guard, from hand-to-hand combat, investigation, and training and leading others, Johesha felt himself a reader of men, and this man craved control and power.

So let him believe he had it.

The silence stretched awkwardly.

Johesha had no intention of breaking it. He was comfortable in silence and knew that the first to speak would be the first to give ground. Whether the wizard knew this or not was just a guess, though Johesha didn't think the other man was a student of this kind of tactical observation. Instead, his magic, his power, his manipulation guided him through interactions. Why would he ever need to study something like men and their responses with that kind of approach?

"I heard something earlier," the wizard said.

"What did you hear?"

"Sounds like someone was in the house."

"An intruder?" Johesha met the wizard's gaze, then to feign his concern.

The wizard tilted his head and studied him as if waiting for a crack in Johesha's armor. Johesha hoped Crue wouldn't find one, because there was a glaring one: Jessamine. The wizard couldn't ever know that.

"I wasn't able to check"

A lie.

"Did you need me to look for you?" Johesha asked. "Is that why you're here?" He looked at the wizard, a subtle reminder that he was larger, stronger, braver than the lord of the manor without saying it. "Where did you hear it?"

"The greenhouse."

Johesha made a show of moving through his room as he gathered a weapon, attaching a sheath to his hip before sliding in his dagger, then grabbing his bow. "Show me, sir."

After being driven through the manor checking room after room for non-existent intruders, the wizard called an end to the search.

"It must have been my ears playing tricks on me," Crue said, near the entrance to the basement inside his study.

Johesha could see through the man's ploy, self-deprecation to boost Johesha's ego. Another man might preen at the false praise, but Johesha remained calm and steady. "Are you expecting intruders, sir?"

"I did send a message to my daughter's mother. Let her know that she is with me and safe."

The obvious question—why—hung between them, but Johesha didn't voice it.

"She hates me. Hates that Jessamine has chosen me." Crue paused, turning toward the fireplace to break up the glowing embers. "It's late, huntsman, and I'm tired."

Johesha gave Crue a nod, then left him in the study to take the long way back to the basement. There had to be a passage in the wizard's study. That was how Crue had made it to the basement before him. He'd be sure to point it out to Jessamine later.

Once lying on his cot in the weapons room, Johesha stared up at the beams overhead thinking about all he'd learned. The spell impacted Jessamine the same as all of them. Crue was watching and most likely had set wards to alert him when they were triggered. Worse yet, Crue was wary of him. While Johesha understood, it made his job more difficult.

He'd give Brendsen and the prince another seven days to contact him with a plan. But then it was time to act. By then, maybe he'd have an idea of what to do that didn't involve putting Jessamine back to sleep to carry her away.

The next morning as he wandered past the wizard's workshop, he saw Jessamine there, somewhat to his surprise. Her head was bent over a book, her dress sleeves rolled, and an apron tied around her waist. With her elbows on the workbench, one of her hands fiddled with wispy strands of dark hair woven into a braid down her back, exposing the tender skin of her neck. The level of concentration she offered the open book, head bent, a finger pressed to its pages, gave Johesha the impression that he could walk inside, and she still wouldn't know he was there.

A quick image of seeing her like this, not here, but in a home they might share surprised him, and he shook the image away. He'd had the same impression upon his return, her standing in the kitchen in that yellow dress, her face unable to contain her happiness at seeing him. The tableau was an impossible one, considering his vow.

But as soon as he thought it, her dark eyes snapped up and caught his.

She straightened smiled. "Good morning," she whispered.

He was a moth tugged toward her light and stepped into the workshop.

The monster tittered from inside its prison.

"You are well?" he asked.

"Fine," she said, moving around the workbench toward him, her hands pressed against her apron and her eyes flitting to the door. "He has a way into my room."

Johesha had suspected and hated it. "Where is he?" He rolled his hands into tight fists to keep from reaching for her.

She stopped an arm's length away. "The greenhouse." Her dark gaze glanced over his shoulder once more, as if she didn't trust Crue wasn't there. "Getting something for this concoction." The flick of her head indicated the boiling liquid, but she didn't look away from him.

He licked his lips, thinking about wanting to kiss her, his body heating under his clothes. He could kiss her now, except…if Crue discovered them. He swallowed.

"Are you going hunting?"

He shook his head. "How long has he been gone?"

She swallowed, her eyes dropping to his lips. She took another step toward him. "He just left."

He matched her, so close now that if he just reached out, he'd be able to feel the fabric of her dark red dress hugging her frame.

"Johesha," she whispered and leaned toward him. "What are we going to do?"

Johesha leaned closer, wanting to tuck a stray strand of her hair behind her ear, but he didn't dare.

The creature clicked.

Johesha retreated, angry at himself for nearly caving. "We'll make a plan." He clenched his jaw tightly, offered a terse nod, and retreated further, refusing to endanger her for his own desires and impulses.

He stalked into the room where he worked the leather, tugging the apron from its hook as if it was the movement that annoyed him.

"Hesha?" Jessamine whispered.

He spun.

She stood just over the threshold of the room, her eyes drifting around, a frown pulling at her full lips, lips he'd once kissed and wished he could remember clearly.

"You're angry with me," she said more than asked.

"No." He shook his head, slipping the apron on. "I'm angry that—" He took a breath and moved toward her to grab a tool near her shoulder. She didn't move to give him leeway, so he reached and looked down at her lovely face as he did.

She took his hand with hers, her touch skimming his calloused skin, her palm meeting his, her fingers entwined with his. "We'll figure it out together."

"I need to get you home," he finally said.

She stood so close he could hear the soft rapid breaths breaking through her. "This is…" But she stopped.

He lifted his free hand to move a lock of her hair from her face, hesitating for a breath as his intellect reminded him this was a bad idea, that this was against his vow. And because he couldn't maintain his strength when it came to her, he capitulated to his desire and touched that lock of hair, moving it, reveling in the softness between his hardened fingers. When he slid it behind her ear, the silk of her skin made enticing promises. When her mouth parted at his touch, he drew in an uneven breath, his heart knocking wildly against his ribcage.

When her eyes closed, he leaned closer.

When his name left her lips on a quiet sigh, he drew in a deep breath. "Jessamine. I want to—"

"Jessamine!" Crue's voice called from somewhere down the hallway.

Johesha spun away and had the rough-hewn countertop between them by the time Crue appeared in the doorway. The man's eyes assessed both of them.

"What are you doing here?" he asked Jessamine.

"Asking for a bit of leather. For the potion." She turned her back on the wizard and looked at Johesha. Her cheeks were bright with color.

He found a scrap and held it out.

She took several steps toward the table between them. "Thank you so much." Her fingers brushed his when she took it, and that innocent caress dove straight to his groin. He was glad the table was between them. "I hope it works."

"Huntsman?"

Johesha looked away from Jessamine to Crue, struggling suddenly to find the balance that always kept him even. Dipping his head to look at the tabletop instead, he cataloged the fletching materials for the arrows and ground his teeth together, hating the man. It was a strange feeling, considering Johesha rarely allowed himself to feel at all. Feelings got in the way of logic and action. His split-second decisions were often a matter of life and death, so there wasn't time to weigh feeling. For over a year, he'd been at the whims of this man. Jessamine and every other person in this manor were at this man's mercy, and it wasn't mercy he displayed but manipulation and control.

Johesha wanted to kill him.

But now wasn't the time for action. Not yet.

A few more days.

"I need you to return to the market. Same vendor." Crue held out a slip of parchment.

"Oh!" Jessamine said. "Maybe I can go–"

"No," Crue interrupted. "You should return to your task. Let the huntsman go."

Jessamine glanced at Johesha, then disappeared as Johesha crossed to take the slip of paper.

"The rest of my order was ready days ago. If you'd be quick about it."

Without a word, Johesha strode down the hall, leaving Jessamine behind and hating the distance his steps created. His heart beat a complicated rhythm with which he wasn't familiar.

He set out for the market wishing he could make the journey to Sevens himself to find out what was the hold up. But there wasn't time, and he refused to put his access to Jessamine in jeopardy.

By the time he made it to the potter, he wasn't in any better mood. He held out the message. "From Crue." The potter looked up, alone this time, took the slip of paper, then disappeared into the curtained section of his space.

Johesha looked around, taking in the details of the market as if it were the first time, though he knew he'd been many times. But it was the first time since his meeting with the witch, the first time with a clear mind. He scanned for Brendsen, knowing he'd had enough time to reach the Fareviews but uncertain of the circumstances, the difficulties they might be facing. He'd hoped to see the guardsman's bright, convivial eyes, but he couldn't conjure him. He looked for the old woman too but didn't see her.

Before long, the potter returned with a leather pouch.

"Stash it under your clothes against your skin. It needs to be kept warm in this weather," the man said. "Wouldn't want it to be ruined before it gets where it's going."

Johesha nodded, tucking it into his shirt.

"Against your skin now."

Johesha walked away. When he'd reached a place beyond the potter's eyes, he pulled the satchel out and peeked, but whatever was inside was hidden from sight. Spelled. With a scoff, he tucked the pouch into the waistband of his pants, donned his winter gear once more, and set out for the mansion.

"You just missed Jessamine," Henro said as soon as Johesha entered the door. "I think she was waiting for you."

"Hello to you too."

The boy seemed to bounce on his toes as he avoided Johesha's movements through the room. "She's really pretty. Don't you think?"

Johesha smiled to himself as he pulled off the outer clothes. "Sure." He stopped moving to look at the boy, a memory of his own first crush when he'd been fourteen, then reached out and tousled the boy's blond hair. "Probably best if you wait to find a girl your own age. This one will just break your heart."

Henro blushed.

"I've got to get something to the Master," Johesha said and headed downstairs.

He'd anticipated the frustration of the wizard and whatever experiments he was up to. What he hadn't expected was the faint humming of a song. When he reached the doorway to the workshop, his eyes went to Jessamine, still there, looking much like she had earlier, as if he was getting a do over. Only this time she was singing, her voice a pleasant alto, full and rich. The muscle in her arms flexed and relaxed as she worked with the mortar and pestle in front of her, grinding something into a powder.

The monster was silent, but its claw-tipped fingers protruded from the opening of its door to curl around the bars of its cage, watching. At Johesha's awareness, the creature retreated, disappearing once more into the bowels of its prison.

And Crue was gone again.

Johesha stepped into the room, the leather pouch warm in his palm.

Jessamine looked up, her dark eyes connecting with his. "You're back."

Energy zipped from the base of his neck down his spine, radiating across his back into his shoulder blades, a sensation that took him by surprise. He cleared his throat and looked around.

"He should be back any minute."

Johesha walked deeper into the room, closer to Jessamine, and set the pouch on the workbench near her. "It's supposed to remain warm."

She wiped her hands on her apron and picked up the satchel. "What is it?"

"I don't ask those questions. I wouldn't get an answer."

She looked at him again, then around him.

Johesha followed her gaze to the empty doorway.

When his attention returned to her, he found she'd moved closer, close enough to touch.

"Are you okay?"

Though he was sure his outward appearance gave nothing away, his insides started and tripped at her question. No one asked him if he was okay. Never. That was his job. Always. The heat zipping around his insides intensified. "Fine," he answered, perhaps a bit too forcefully.

He watched her tuck the leather pouch into the open collar of her shirt and swallowed at the glimpse of warm skin, the swell of softness, but averted his eyes when his imagination offered the image of pressing his lips to that soft flesh, of tasting it with his tongue.

He cleared his throat and stepped back.

"Meet me tonight," she whispered. "In the third room. The one with flower painting above the bed."

He nodded, stepping back once more, then again to increase the distance, hoping his body would return to normal. That the awful, upended way he felt—a dangerous unpredictable rhythm that made him feel a bit wild— would ebb. Only as he returned to the project of repairing the arrows, that feeling didn't dissipate, and a lingering feeling of longing slipped in beside the anticipation knocking against his worry.

Jessamine

When it seemed the house was finally asleep, Jessamine tucked her pillows into the bed to make it appear she was there—just in case— then stole behind the mirror door into the secret passage. Using what memory she could of traversing these passages with Johesha, she made her way to the meeting place. When she entered the room, he was there, a single candle lit on a table in the sitting area.

She swallowed and found the will to move toward him. "You weren't waiting long?"

He shook his head, only taking a seat across from her

after she'd sat. "What are we doing?"

His clipped tone deconstructed her bravery for a moment, but then she wondered if perhaps he was as anxious as she was. Her own heart was in flight, fluttering with the fear of discovery and awareness of the man she was alone with. Was his trepidation for the same reason? She hadn't been able to get the moment in the under house from her mind, of his touch skimming her ear. She hadn't been able to get what he'd been about to say from her thoughts, finishing the sentence with various possibilities, all of them involving kissing.

"Planning, I suspect." She smiled. "I wanted to be able to talk to you without worrying about interruption."

"Yes. Right." He nodded and stood, putting distance between them. He was tense, the lines of his body coiled and tight, ready to snap at the faintest provocation.

She stayed where she was, watching him pace. "You're making me nervous."

He turned toward her. "I'm waiting for the prince. He knows where we are."

"How?"

"Soldiers. You remember Brendsen?" He sat once more as if talking about this made him at ease.

She did remember his guards, so she nodded and began to understand Johesha a bit more. He didn't like what was out of his control, clearly. Something about her made him feel out of control.

"We spoke. I'm just waiting for... something, a sign before leaving."

"I've been thinking about the task."

"And?"

"Ingredients. If our reason for leaving the manor is about me finding specific ingredients for a potion, maybe it will keep me focused and subdued."

"That could work."

She shivered, wishing she'd brought a blanket with her.

Johesha jumped up to pull a quilt from the bed, then draped it around her shoulders.

Before he could retreat, she grabbed his hand. "Thank you."

He didn't pull away. "You're welcome."

"For so much more than just this blanket."

He didn't reply.

She tilted her head to find his gaze. "What were you going to say… earlier?"

"Earlier?"

"Today? In the under house."

He cleared his throat. "It doesn't–"

"It has been on my mind all day," she interrupted and brushed her thumb across the back of his hand, noting the strength, the veins, and the smoothness of his skin in contrast to his palm.

"All day?"

She nodded. "I've been finishing it in my head."

He crouched down in front of her, his other hand on the arm of the chair. "How did you finish it?"

Heat rushed to her cheeks, and she looked down at her hand holding his. "I wasn't sure." It was a truth, but not *the* truth.

Silence settled around them, brimming with

possibilities, and Jessamine's heart filled her ears with noise. She braved a look at Johesha and saw that he was studying her, hesitating.

He opened his mouth as if to say something, then stopped and shook his head. "Nothing good will come of what I'd wanted to say." He stood. "We better get back before we're discovered."

Then he retreated, leaving Jessamine frustrated and antsy... for something.

The next morning, she was in the workshop again filled with an annoyance she couldn't contain.

"You're crowding me," she snapped at Crue.

The dim lighting and cramped quarters were grating on her nerves, and the man's constant hovering had barely given her a moment alone. The one moment alone had barely wrought a plan, and what she really wanted hadn't come to pass. Her patience was hanging by a tenuous thread.

"I need to see what you're doing," Crue retorted.

She stopped crushing the dried plant and turned to face him. "But I can't move, and the sound of your breathing is bothering me."

The darkling rumbled. A new sound she hadn't heard from the creature before, and she'd heard many since saving the footman. Crue now had her in the workroom, showing him her methods.

Jessamine glanced over her shoulder. The darkling's blood-red eyes watched through the small opening in the door. Had that been a laugh?

"You want me to stop breathing?" Crue frowned,

huffed, then mumbled something about not needing this headache or a daughter as he moved around to the other side of the worktable.

The surface was strewn with dried herbs and plants, though there was a method to her madness. Basim, rasput, grimmer bulbs, lakander blossoms, a glass vial of frasson. Crue had told her he could get whatever she wanted, and he hadn't lied. A glass bulb boiled and vented steam from its narrow neck, steeping a liquid base for an elixir she planned for Mr. Oto's gout. A blue flame sputtered mildly underneath the bottom bowl, and though the darkling had initially screeched with terror, when she hadn't used the flame to threaten the creature, its curiosity seemed to override its fear.

"It would help if you told me what kind of ailment you'd like me to prepare an elixir for," she said, sprinkling some of the crushed dried himit leaf into the boiling mixture. "Just asking me to make anything—this is what you get."

"What's that for?"

"Himit? It's an analgesic."

"For pain," Crue said, leaning toward her and watching as the liquid turned orange.

"But you know how to make potions." She looked around the room, though his ingredients were unconventional and frightening. She wasn't sure what one did with a bat wing. "You're... old."

He hummed an even note. "Yes. But I'm unfamiliar with the plants and herbs here."

She didn't understand but tried to put pieces of the

story together. "Because you're from Echo Landing?"

"Right." He wasn't affirming it or denying it, the sound of the word more like an agreement without offering anything new. "It's been many years since I was an apprentice to a potion maker. That's a different sort of magic. That's where I started. With potions. My strengths are found in conjuring and divination."

"I didn't know there were different kinds of magic."

"Many. And not every sorcerer has strengths in harnessing them all. This–" he picked up a red stalk of terris and spun it between his fingers, "–is a combination of alchemy and natural magic."

"Seems more like science to me," she said, thinking of her mother and all the lessons over the years about mixing herbs.

"Some would say the two are one in the same," Crue replied.

She hated that she found herself almost liking him this way, recognizing what was relatable in him as he hungered to learn something. He reminded her of a curious boy, and she could see the way they had this hunger for knowledge in common. The truth of who he'd shown himself to be wasn't far from her thoughts, and this Crue, she might believe her mother had loved. "Ailment?" She grabbed a pinch of salt to add to the mixture.

"Since I'm so old," he said, rolling his eyes slightly, "can you make something to make me young?"

"No. That *is* magic."

"You're right. Pure alchemy. But sorcerers through the ages have found ways to do it."

She looked at him. "Through herbs and plants?"

He shook his head. "No. That would be a first. Potions have staved off the process, but to truly stave off death, magician lore says it requires magic steeped in… a different kind of power altogether. But you're godblood, a healer. Perhaps…"

"I don't think that's true. My mother never stopped death."

"That's necromancy. The kind of magic, I mean," he clarified. "A magician who can control life and death would be very powerful indeed."

She pondered that and considered what her mother had taught her about healing, remembered the day they'd stood in a small cottage in the valley where a woman had died giving birth. Jessamine couldn't have been older than ten at the time, the father sitting at his dead wife's side holding their newborn boy who was squalling to be fed.

"Allow me," her mother had said, taking the newborn baby from the grieving father. She'd prepared a tincture she called first milk for new mother's and for occasions such as this.

"Can't you bring her back?" Jessamine had asked Scarlett. She remembered thinking her mother was capable of anything.

Scarlett had grabbed her shoulder, roughly, and jerked her into the other room. "Don't ever say something like that."

Tears had stung Jessamine's eyes, making the dark cabin swim in her vision. "I didn't mean—"

The baby had screamed, and Scarlett had pushed

Jessamine into a chair. "Hold him." Then she'd given the baby the draught. The little boy quieted, snuffling as he sucked on the liquid, satiated for the time being.

Later, as they'd ridden Wilhemina back home to Sevens, her mother had apologized. "I'm sorry I was harsh with you, Jessamine."

Sitting behind her, Jessamine had tightened her arms around her mother's middle, forgiving her even if she didn't understand. Scarlett had wrapped a hand around Jessamine's wrist, around the ribbon there.

"I know you couldn't know the power of your words," Scarlett had said, "but never forget that lesson, daughter. Your words, your thoughts—all of them contain power."

"Like magic?"

"Yes. And depending how you use that power, it can create light or darkness. What you asked me to do for that mother–"

Jessamine hadn't dared repeat it.

"–that is the way of darkness." Her mother's voice had tightened around the last word as if she were stifling a sob. Jessamine hadn't been able to see her, but she knew she'd gone somewhere difficult in her mind.

They'd never talked of it again.

She looked at Crue. "You practiced necromancy."

Crue's dark eyes snapped up to hers.

"You mentioned it at dinner the other night. For my mother's father."

He looked away, studying the liquid in the boiling flask. He grinned, but it wasn't filled with joy, rather chagrin. "I suppose my daughter would remember everything I say."

"Well, that is the advice of the ages: be careful what you tell your children."

He laughed. "That is what he hired me to do," Crue said, "but I didn't say I actually could, did I."

More revelations about this man's character.

"You're judging me."

"Did you expect me not to."

"Fair enough." He straightened. "I want to know an ingredient that strengthens tissue."

Jessamine could think of five off the top of her head, but rather than tell him, she paused, humming as if thinking about it. "I remember my mother teaching me about a mixture that could help someone who'd torn a muscle."

"What was in it?" The seriousness of his features told her he was hungry to know the answer.

She held back the information. "I'll have to try and remember. I wrote things down, you know, in a book I carried with me. It's not here. I could try and recreate it, but it might take some time to narrow down the ingredients."

"We have time," he said and started for the door. "Are you ready?" He hadn't really let her out of his sight since the dinner but to sleep, and there were mornings when she woke feeling as though she hadn't been alone.

"Have you heard anything yet?"

"About?"

"From my mother."

He frowned. "Not yet. Any day now."

She nodded and looked at the bubbling mixture. "May

I finish Mr. Oto's tincture?"

He glanced around the room and nodded. "Until dinner." Then he was gone, and Jessamine was finally alone in his workshop.

"You are awake."

Jessamine spun in place toward the voice. It was the darkling, hidden behind its cell door, but its voice was so… normal. She didn't answer and heard it sniff.

"You are her sister."

She knew it meant Tarley. "You're a monster."

"It is possible for every being to be a monster, yes?"

She furrowed her brow, confused by its lucidity, realizing she hadn't considered it a thinking being, even if it was horrible. Then she wondered what kind of monster she'd be if backed into a corner.

Jessamine

The following day, Jessamine stood in the basement once more fighting the urge to go into Johesha's space. She knew he was awake and could hear him moving around, but she didn't know where Crue was. She wanted to demand answers. She wanted to cry. She wanted to bury her face in his chest. She wanted to kiss him. She wanted to throw things at him. Despite all those wants, she couldn't identify the why. She just had all this pent-up emotion inside her without an outlet, and he was a hard man to decipher, his face never giving anything away, and though he agreed her idea was a good one, there was a nagging sensation in her body to push him to say more. She wanted to hear his voice. More of it, anyway. The man barely strung together multiple words, and in the few instances he had, the deep timbre of his voice had connected to her insides like a vital ingredient keeping her alive.

But she couldn't ponder the thought for long.

Crue entered the workshop, and with him the annoyance she felt in his presence. But he looked strange, less substantive. There were deep circles under his eyes, and a hollowness to his cheeks that hadn't been there before.

The monster screeched.

Suppressing the urge to cover her ears, Jessamine winced and returned to her mortar and pestle.

"I need more!" Crue yelled, rifling through his ingredients. "Huntsman!"

Gods, she wanted to crush his hand resting on the countertop.

Johesha appeared in the doorway, a cloth in his hands, his mask completely in place.

Stars, she wanted to kiss that mask off him.

Crue pulled the little pouch she'd given him from inside his shirt.

"What is it?" she asked.

Dressed in black trousers, Crue unbuttoned the top of his white shirt and watched her with that dark gaze. "A shifter's heart, still beating." He tucked the small bag back against his bare chest and held it next to his skin. "Still warm." He grinned, his eyes closing at whatever sensation he was experiencing. "I need more blood." He was manic.

Jessamine looked away, unnerved. "And what is that for?" She glanced at Johesha in the doorway, still waiting.

The darkling hissed. "I need blood."

Crue ignored the creature and crowded her space. "Tell me about this concoction."

She resisted the urge to step away from him. "It's just a simple mixture that helps reduce fever," she lied. It was a concoction she was hoping might impact her memory to get her past the spell. "Mother–"

"Yes. Yes. Taught you everything you know." Crue sounded bitter and moved away, turning to another space, then clapped his hands, startling her. "We need to determine the strength of your godblood."

"And what would that entail?" She glanced at the door. Johesha frowned.

She straightened, turning toward the man who claimed to be her father. She could see it now: the dark hair, the dark eyes, the bronze skin. Just like her. Her mother's fair features weren't hers, but she hadn't thought much about it growing up. It hadn't mattered. And she wasn't sure how to reconcile it now, but playing along with this stranger seemed the best way to get what she wanted. Freedom.

"Huntsman!" Crue yelled as though he'd forgotten Johesha was there. He turned toward the door.

Johesha's body filled the doorway, and her heart tumbled through her chest. His gaze connected with hers. Just a moment. It traveled her frame, assessing as quickly as a single breath before he was looking at Crue once more.

"I need you to hunt," Crue was saying. "I need more

fresh blood."

The darkling screeched. "Let me out," it hissed, the sound crawling up Jessamine's spine. She shuddered.

"Not you," Crue said. "And more antler, but a stag this time, a young buck. Look for the velvet-tipped antlers."

"Yes, sir," Johesha said with a deferential nod. He glanced at her one more time.

Crue turned back to her.

"I'd like to check your blood," he was saying.

Her eyes darted to Crue. "My blood?" Her focus was back on the danger in the room.

"Yes."

Johesha's frown deepened.

Crue readied a small knife, heating the tip. "It shouldn't hurt. Much." He reached for her, and she jerked away. "Just a small sample. Then I'll close it." He looked up. "Huntsman?"

Johesha didn't say anything.

"What are you still doing here?" Crue frowned.

Jessamine watched as Johesha went to war with himself, the desire to stay and keep watch or maintain the ruse. Though the man could probably be described as cold, the heat of his brown eyes meeting hers warmed her though. She could imagine he was contemplating slitting the wizard's throat, then gathering her against him and leaving, but that wasn't ideal to ending the spell on the manor, on her.

With a small nod of her head, she hoped to convey she was all right. Though his frown remained and those intense lines between his brow deepened, he eventually relented, disappearing from the doorway.

Jessamine readied herself for the coming cut. With a pinch, the sharp knife made it clean. She sucked in a breath.

Crue collected his sample in a vial.

The darkling moaned, she was certain because of her blood.

"Hush," Crue snapped. With his thumb he smeared some ointment over the small incision. "See. Not too much pain. You have been extremely accommodating, my dear." He grinned. "How about taking a stroll. I think you could use some fresh air, considering."

"A stroll?"

"Yes. You're looking a bit peaked. You could use some outdoor air, I think." He stood. "Come. I'll show you a secret of the house," he said and led her to a stairwell she'd never noticed. She'd never been this far down the hall, past Johesha's rooms.

She followed Crue to the top of the stairs into a dark landing, where she heard a lever depress, and something popped. A crack of light filled the small vestibule, and she realized she was behind a bookcase that opened into Crue's study.

"A secret passage?" She hoped her excitement sounded real. While she was happy to learn of another, Johesha had been the first to show her the house's secrets.

"I thought you would like it." He smoothed a lock of her hair behind her ear. She worked not to cringe away. "Meet me in the foyer in an hour's time."

She dipped her head and walked toward the doorway. "I will see you then."

He clapped his hands together, grinned, and retreated. "Dress warm. You have some new boots Mrs. Pennig placed in your room."

At the appointed time she descended the stairs into the foyer where Crue was waiting. When she appeared at the top of the steps, he nearly shouted, "There you are!" He watched her descend the final stair and cross the foyer toward him, that wild smile on his face and a strange look in his eyes. She had the impression he knew something she didn't and found it beyond unsettling.

"Here I am." She couldn't help her frown, so looked down at her feet to hide it.

When she reached him, he held out his arm. "It is supposed to snow later today. I thought we might take a longer walk into the village rather than just a turn about the house."

She gritted her teeth together, not wanting to take his arm but needing to maintain her freedom within the manor. So he threaded her arm with his. "Won't that take some time?"

"We should return before the snow is perilous. Besides, I have… abilities. I'd like to show them to you."

She refrained from rolling her eyes and instead bit down again to keep from saying anything.

The moment she stepped from the manor, her thoughts dissipated like grains of salt in warm water, and her will shifted, longing only for the warmth of the Master's attention. There was the whisper of a reason she hadn't wanted to be outside, but the sense of why disappeared.

Her first thought was to return to the Master, and when she turned her head, she saw he was with her. Her heart beat a joyous rhythm to find him there, and she smiled.

"Are you happy, my dear?" He led them down the cleared pathway toward the road.

"Excessively." She tucked herself closer to his side. "I'd been about to request to return to the house to find you, and yet here you are."

"Here I am. Ready?"

"What is your will, Master?"

They continued away from the manor. It hadn't snowed for nearly a week and a path had been cleared, wide enough for them to walk side by side. Her new boots crunched with each of her steps.

"Would you like to know what would make me happy?" he asked.

"I would relish the knowledge."

"I would prefer you call me, Father."

Jessamine grinned as happiness skipped along her skin with warmth. "I would be delighted."

Father watched her, the smile widening on his face. "Perfect. That is perfect."

They walked into town, Father talking about… things… though she couldn't recall what, and asked her… things. It was hard to remember with her focus on him and only him, but she held onto his wish for her to call him Father and did so. They went through the village, stopping at various shops where she met people she couldn't remember, their names, their faces, what they'd sold. Rather, she had a latent impression of them as if they were ghosts wandering her mind. Her whole mind focused on Father, being sure to use that designation whenever she was given the opportunity.

Father bought items, and when he was done, they started back toward the manor. It was cold, but she was warm in her garments and tucked against Father's side. She shivered.

"I'll warm us." He murmured a few words and waved his hand. A tiny pinpoint glow the color of peridot materialized between them, swelling to the size of a green pea then continuing to grow until it surrounded them like a transparent green bubble. It was so warm and cozy inside the sphere he'd created that she didn't feel any effect of the weather.

"What a wonderful sort of magic," she exclaimed. "I don't even feel the cold under my boots."

"It is but one of the spells I have learned over the years." They continued walking, arm in arm. Father broke the silence, "I would like to teach you. What I know."

"Really?" she asked, smiling at him.

"I'd thought perhaps it wouldn't work, that I would have to use you for a spell instead, but I'd like to make you my apprentice. You are my daughter, after all."

"That makes me so happy, Father!" she exclaimed, the bubble containing her excitement.

They walked on, Father talking of all the things he would teach her… things she couldn't recall but sounded so exciting to learn. Mostly she liked how he spoke to her, his attention undivided, so much so that when the manor became visible, she felt the rush of disappointment that this time and his attention would end.

As they walked across the field toward the manor, they came across a stranger.

"Huntsman!" Father called, waving.

The man turned; a deer draped over his shoulders.

He was a very handsome man, but she had eyes and heart only for Father and watched him closely. He was speaking with the stranger about the animal he carried.

"What do you think, Jessamine?"

"About what?" she asked. She hadn't been paying attention.

Father slipped a finger across her cheek, tucking some stray hair under her cap. She relished his attention and tilted her cheek. "You prefer to spend your time with me?"

"Oh, yes, Father." She closed her eyes, so grateful.

Father spoke with the stranger a bit longer, then pulled her away. "I have enjoyed our time, daughter," he said when they reached the door.

"I wish it could stay like this forever."

His eyes sparked with joy. "I can find a way to make that happen."

Then he led her across the threshold of the manor and every memory, every thought, every hurt and grief filled her like a flood. Her family. Johesha. Crue's cruelty. The darkling. She gasped under the barrage and reached out to grasp the wall as tears filled her eyes.

"Are you well, daughter?" Crue asked, his voice filled with mock playfulness.

Her back to him, she closed her eyes. "I'm fine," she lied. "Tired. I think maybe I overdid it today."

"Oh?"

She glanced at him over her shoulder and saw his eyebrow arched over an eye as if taunting her to lash out at him. She steeled herself against the urge. "Yes. It was taxing."

He hummed a note, then said, "Yes. You should probably rest before dinner."

She wanted to attack him, knowing what he'd done to Johesha, embarrassed she'd been unable to control any of it. Crue might not know that Johesha could remember, but she did.

"I am pleased. And I would like you to continue calling me Father, yes?" She didn't answer and was halfway up the stairs when Crue called out, "And Jessamine?"

She stopped but didn't turn.

"Remember who is in control, yes?"

She didn't respond and resumed walking.

"And don't be late to dinner," he called up after her.

She didn't stop until she was behind the closed door of her room, and only then did she burst into tears.

Johesha

When Jessamine returned to her room after dinner, Johesha was there, waiting. He'd been there hiding as Mary turned down the sheets, her lilting voice singing as she worked. He'd been there as Henro had arrived to light the fire, and listened to him chat with Mary as he did. Johesha had smiled at the boy's innocence, his heart warming at a story he told about finding a mouse in the woodhouse and making it a little nest, which was followed by Mary's warning that the mouse would be a problem come spring. After they left, Johesha walked around the room but missed finding anything that seemed to signify Jessamine, unsure why he was even looking.

His fingers skimmed the silkiness of the bedspread as he recalled her earlier that afternoon, her face tipped up toward Crue and shining with adoration. Johesha had known it was the spell and had played off his own devotion to the maniacal tyrant but seeing her like that reinforced his need to stay focused, to reorient to the goal of getting her home. He couldn't afford to be thinking about kissing her, about a future, about anything that split his focus. Now that they had ideas, he was there to plan the details. They had three days left to the deadline he'd given the prince.

When voices and footsteps sounded beyond the door, Johesha slipped behind the heavy curtain once more and waited for the click of the door.

He was standing in front of the window when she turned.

"Oh," she gasped quietly, her hand pressed to her chest.

"I'm sorry to startle you," he said, his heart beating a strange rhythm in his chest at the sight of her. Beautiful as always, she was wearing a wine-colored dress tonight, her shoulders bare. The silky fabric draped in a way that accentuated her lovely shape.

"Are you always so quiet and sneaky?" She smiled.

"Yes."

She made sure her door was locked, then crossed the room to a small green couch. Patting the spot next to her, she glanced over her shoulder. "Sit. Please. Your skulking makes me nervous."

"I don't skulk," he said, offended by the description.

Her smile deepened. "I've touched a nerve."

Annoyed by her observation, because he didn't have nerves, and if he did, they were as rigid as iron, he walked across the room and sat next to her. But the couch was small, and he was rather large, so there wasn't much space between them. Her body pressed against his side, and he was sure sitting had been a miscalculation on his part.

"I'm sorry about today."

"What about it?"

"Outside."

"Jessamine. That doesn't require an apology. I know it was the spell."

She made a humming noise as she smoothed her skirt. "I'm working on a memory potion."

He tried to ignore the heat from her body seeping into his. "And how would that work?"

"I'm thinking if I can just make a temporary potion to stave off the effects of the spell, it might give us enough time to get to wherever the witch is."

He cleared his throat. "And how will we know if this… potion works?"

"We'd have to test it."

He noted the turn of her head toward him in the periphery of his vision but refused to look, worried about how close that would bring their faces, because then he'd be tempted to look at her lips as he'd been doing every time he was near her despite every instinct in him that said to stop. That proximity might push him to test out their softness.

"Did he cut you?" he asked, staring at the fire instead. He hadn't been able to stop thinking about it. As he'd hunted, he'd thought about her. He'd pondered the thought of her blood as he'd spilled the young buck's. He'd pondered the anger he felt at the center of his chest along with the need to protect her. Seeing her at the wizard's mercy had been nearly too much. He didn't know how much more he could endure without snapping the sorcerer's neck.

Johesha stood now, needing to put distance between them. He could feel her eyes track him, boring holes into his back as he stopped in front of the fire.

"Yes."

He twisted to look at her.

She was studying her hand. "But it is healed." She held it up.

Johesha had an urge to hit something. No. Someone. The fucking wizard. "What the fuck for?"

She smiled, teasing him. "I didn't know men growled like that."

He narrowed his eyes.

She giggled. "Why does it matter? He did it. But I'm fine, as you see."

Inexplicably, Johesha closed the distance between them and took her hand in his to look for himself, forcing himself to be gentle. He looked at the skin at the base of her palm, at the neat, silvery line there, and ran his thumb over it.

She drew in a quick breath, her dark eyes jumping from

where his thumb caressed her skin to his face. "I'm okay."

"Fucking magic," he grunted and let go of her hand.

She swallowed, her throat working under her skin. Johesha wanted to look away, but couldn't, his eyes moving to her mouth.

"He wanted to check my godblood."

"Godblood?"

"Descended from gods," she said, drawing her hands back into her lap, "or some such thing."

He felt the surprise on his face, his eyebrows arched.

"My mother, according to our host, is both descended from kings and gods."

He drew away from her.

Her gaze dropped to his feet, watching him recede. "That's a problem?"

"Why should it be?" Johesha replied, attempting a respectful distance. A princess? A god? "The kingdom?"

"Echo Landing."

"I'm unfamiliar with it."

"Right." She nodded. "You're familiar with royalty. The prince's captain of the guard."

"Was."

"And why wouldn't you still be?" she asked, standing and crossing to a cabinet, removing whatever accessories Mary had added. Her hands were up behind her neck fiddling with the clasp of a necklace, the pinnacle of which rested between the luscious swell of her breasts.

"I left my post," he said.

"To follow me." She met his gaze in the mirror.

He nodded and swallowed, the intimacy of her actions

not lost on him.

"Help me?" she asked.

"Mary?"

"I told her not to attend me."

"And Crue?" he asked, knowing the wizard could sneak into the room as easily as he could.

"He hasn't returned since–"

"Since?"

"The night of the greenhouse."

That she knew of. Shoring up his defenses, Johesha crossed the expanse of the room, stopping just behind her.

"I can't unclasp it."

"My fingers are larger," he said, afraid to touch her.

"But I think your eyes will be helpful." He could hear the smile in her voice, along with the challenge.

Reaching out, he plucked the clasp from where it rested on the back of her neck, the pads of his fingers skimming her skin. Lightning sizzled up his arms seizing each of his joints with bright, white heat. She tilted her head to give him more room to work, and he suppressed the urge to press his nose against the skin there at her nape, his eyes moving across the flushed skin, the curl of dark hair, up to the mirror to look at her face.

Her eyes were closed. Her lips slightly parted.

Johesha swallowed. She was as moved by him as he was by her, he realized, and attempted to maintain his composure, his distance. This was a line he couldn't cross even if there was a riot inside him inciting it.

Once the clasp was undone, he allowed the necklace to droop, holding it out in front of her.

Jessamine held a hand under the metal and glittering jewels and curled her fingers around it when he released it into her palm. But then she surprised him, turning toward him before he had a chance to back away. "I think you want to kiss me."

He took a step back.

"I want to kiss you."

His heart sputtered, and he froze. "It's a bad idea."

"Why?"

"To keep you—"

She took a step forward. "I don't want to."

"It's safer," he said, backing up another step.

She followed. "For whom?"

"You. Me. Both of us." He took another step backward, his legs hitting the edge of the bed.

She nodded and continued crowding him. "You don't seem like the sort of man worried about a little risk. I watched you walk into a camp full of armed men all by yourself to rescue my sister."

"That was different." Pinned between her and the bed, he sat. "What are you doing?" he asked as she reached down and pulled up her skirts. He looked at her legs, and his body responded to the idea of following the outline of them to her center.

"How?"

"It—" But he clamped down on the words unwilling to admit that he wasn't interested in Tarley. Because that meant he was interested in Jessamine.

She ignored his nonanswer and instead said, "I have a curiosity that needs addressing." She climbed onto the bed and straddled his lap, her knees on either side of his thighs, hovering above him.

"Jessamine. This can't–" But he reached out despite his protest, wrapping a hand around the back of her thigh, the desire to touch her making him squeeze the soft flesh.

She smiled and sighed. "Tell me you aren't curious, and I'll stop."

He swallowed, sliding his hand up slightly and squeezing her leg once more, loving the feel of her skin against his.

"Don't make this more than it is," she said. "I just have wanted to know since laying eyes on you. You kissed me, and I can't remember it. I want to."

He swallowed harder.

"Is that okay?" She released her skirt, the extra fabric fluttering down between them.

His eyes darted to hers. Every cell in his brain said, "No. No. No!" while every fiber of his body screamed, "Yes."

She leaned forward, crushing the fabric between their bodies, the warmth of her body, of her breath enticing. She waited for his acquiescence.

Instead of answering with words, he grabbed the back of her neck and pulled her against him, his mouth crashing against hers.

Crue

After dinner, after Jessamine had retired to her rooms, Crue hurried to this workshop, his hand pressed against the little warm, pulsing pouch resting against his withered heart. He knew this wouldn't be enough—not without the real heart he needed—but this would serve the purpose. He also had her blood, after all.

Once in his workshop, he gathered the supplies, including the candles and the salt, and set everything on the center of the workbench. Keeping the still beating animal heart against his skin in its pouch, he set out

Jessamine's latest concoction she'd made for Mr. Oto's gout. He'd felt something as he'd watched her make it, an uncharacteristic feeling he couldn't identify, never having experienced it. Pleasant, if a little envious of her skill. She'd shared the different ingredients, creatively exploring different combinations he wouldn't have considered. Of course, she was godblood with a gift for healing; she might not have ascended to her power, but the gift was certainly strong and might prove beneficial for his own spell.

"Let me out," the darkling said.

Crue whirled on the wretched creature. "You want out?"

"Out!"

"For what? You know you can't leave."

"To hunt."

"Sure. I'll go right ahead and do that," he said, walking toward the door of the cell. Then he kicked it. "Tell me what I need to know to break the tether between us first."

The darkling screeched, a wail to beat all wails and rammed itself against the cell door. The lock rattled, but it didn't buckle or budge. The door wouldn't. It was spelled, and the darkling was weak with hunger.

Crue covered his ears but smiled cruelly at the creature.

Then he turned his back and continued working, spreading the bright pink salt in a square on the floor in front of the workbench as the darkling's cries faded. Next, he set a candle, one on each corner, representing the directions. Then he laid out the other ingredients: a spray of blue hellorne flowers between the line running north to east, Jessamine's elixir on the line running east to south, a cup of bitter milkweed running on the line between south to west, and a tip of fresh horn on the line between west to north. The final two ingredients—the sacrifice—he held onto until the spell called for them. Last and not least, he set the empty cauldron just inside the square of salt and filled it with the fresh blood from the huntsman's kill.

The darkling was silent, now.

This wasn't the first time he'd done this little ritual. Far from it. He'd summoned many times, the first to siphon off a piece of himself for more power. He knew power was all that mattered. He'd had so little of it growing up. Orphanages, cruel adoptive parents, a spinster aunt who might not have been cruel but certainly hadn't been loving. He'd thought that what he'd wanted was love, but really what he longed for was power. Power and the invincibility of immortality. Power over death.

Sitting before the north point of the square, Crue used a knife to cut his palm. He dripped his blood into the wax of each candle and recited the chant he'd intoned so many times he had to remind himself to invoke feeling and devotion. He repeated the chant a second time, and the candle smoke began to curl.

On the third recitation, a black shadow curled from the smoke and the blood of the cauldron, growing, building, until the partial view of a creature formed in the center of the square, as if standing but without legs, just smoke.

"Wizard," the monster said, blinking its yellow eyes and tilting its thick, wide head. Though the spell didn't allow for its corporeal form, the spirit form was frightening enough. Dark tusks jutted from its mouth along with rows of sharp teeth. The thick black tongue was grotesque. Its eyes were ugly and bulging as if when the creature coughed, they might pop out. Finally, its skin—or what Crue could see of it—bubbled with boils, some weeping thick, greenish liquid.

"Geragoth," Crue said, naming the demon from the Netherrealm.

"You call me from the deep. Have you offerings?"

"Poison, gluttony, bitterness, and pride," he stated, referencing each gift placed along the lines.

"What is your request?"

"I wish to strengthen the bond."

The demon's eyes narrowed. "Have you not siphoned enough power, sorcerer? You have borrowed a gift and failed to return it."

"I'm working on it." Crue tilted his head, his chin nearly touching his chest. "And yes. I have received it, but this body—"

"And what is your sacrifice? Will you offer your hands now? Your legs? What do I want with those? They barely make a meal."

"I am working on a godblood heart," he said, looking up, and pulled the vial of blood from inside his shirt. "Here is some godblood."

The monster licked its non-existent lips, leaving sludge along its tooth-filled maw. "Godblood?" It paused, eyeing the vial Crue held in his palm. "That will barely whet my appetite."

"But it will prove me true. I… the fade is pulling me."

"And it will always pull, sorcerer. You have stretched

your soul too thin."

"But godblood…"

The monster waited, considering.

"Prince of the deep, I have given you my true name and a thread of my soul–"

"You have threaded your soul to many! Do not speak as if I am somehow special and unique to you. My power is but one of many you might entreat if I say 'no'."

"Alea Maximora," Crue said.

"What of her? She is dead."

"The blood." He held up the vial. "Her progeny. I can get you a heart."

"The healer's heart?"

Crue's chest constricted as he thought about Jessamine, keeping him from saying 'yes.' He was realizing he wanted to keep his daughter for himself after using her to lure out Scarlett, but when he considered offering Scarlett or any one of the other children, he grinned. "I could give you two godblood hearts, Geragoth."

"Two healers?"

Crue hesitated. "Yes."

"Don't lie to me, sorcerer."

"No lies," he said and laid the vial and the still beating heart on the line of salt. "The heart of the animal beats true still." He glanced at the leather to be sure, the small pulsing of leather revealing that he'd spoken the truth. Were there two healers, yes, but did he plan on offering them both? No. "But I want the spell for immortality. No more tethers when I deliver."

The monster growled a sound of thoughtfulness. "Two

healer hearts and the return of my gift. You fail, and I take your tether, eat the bit of soul you have sold." Then the shadows flared, bursting out from the entity in the middle of the square.

Crue ducked, shielding his eyes as dirt and salt burst outward.

When he opened his eyes once more, the salt square, the gifts, the candles were gone, leaving only him behind and the surge of power flowing into him.

The feel of his lips against hers was better than she'd imagined. He had lips that somehow promised both sin and salvation and delivered both. With one hand wrapped at the nape of her neck and the other squeezing her bare thigh, he pulled her down onto his lap, fitting her body more tightly with his. His tongue teased the seam of her lips, coaxing her to let him in like the promise of possibility of other body parts.

When she did, the kiss burst into an inferno of sensation.

The warmth and sensuality of his tongue tangled with

hers. The needy sounds they both made. The rigidity of his body thrust up against the softness of hers, offering a delicious juxtaposition between them, of who they were at the core of their physical natures. And it was addicting. She ground her hips against him, wanting more friction, gasping around his kiss, at the deliciousness of it.

"Oh gods," she breathed and moaned into his mouth.

"Hush," Johesha groaned, and with very little effort, flipped them so she was suddenly under him, her back on the bed. "No one can hear."

Her curiosity more than satisfied, she spread her legs to accommodate the width of him between them, needing more.

But then, suddenly cool air expanded in the space between them, Johesha tearing himself away, leaving her alone with her need. One of his hands was pressed against his lips, the other against his erection, and her hungry eyes ate it all. He was amazing, his dark gaze feral with barely controlled need. She wondered what would become of it when he lost it. She wanted to know.

Coming up onto her elbows, she left her body spread before him, unwilling to hide the truth of all the feelings she was experiencing. "What's wrong?"

His eyes mapped her contours, her crevices. "We can't. I can't."

"Why?" she asked, unsure why he wouldn't want to relieve the ache. They were both consenting adults. They both had needs. It didn't need to be more than that, even if it was a lie she was telling herself.

But Johesha shook his head and turned away. "It isn't

smart. Dangerous."

Clearly, he'd enjoyed it, which bolstered her belief they could find some relief together, but his rejection stung. She sat up, pulling the billowing fabric of her skirt down to cover herself, then scooted to the edge of the bed before standing, needing to be on solid ground as she faced him. "Well, thank you for indulging in my curiosity," she said as if it had been nothing more than an experiment. It was a lie, of course, her heart bludgeoned against the inside of her chest. The words saved her pride.

He didn't say anything, a return to his usual silent reticence.

"When should we test the potion?"

"He isn't going to let you out of sight."

She turned away, unable to keep looking at his beauty, and finished removing the jewelry Mary had put on her: earrings, bracelets, fancy combs holding her hair in place. "He is. He's given me free reign of the house and thinks I'm making a potion for him. Showed me a secret passage to his study today." She loosened her hair, and the dark tresses cascaded over her shoulders and down her back as she glanced in the mirror once more.

Johesha's hands were fisted, his cock still hard in his trousers, his eyes devouring her. These were clues that he was battling with his attraction to her. It was satisfying to know it, and she wasn't above using everything at her disposal to upend the stoic man. So she pulled the ribbon at the front of her dress, loosening its hold on her breasts.

"What are you doing?"

"Undressing," she said and knew she was playing with

fire. Every muscle Johesha possessed was taut. She didn't hate the idea of getting burned. She was a twenty-eight-year-old woman who'd been locked in a spell, suppressed by another, and was finally awake, was finally the focal point of a man she was attracted to.

"Jessamine." Her name was a low growl, and her belly fluttered at the sound.

She turned to face him, pulling on the ribbon until the bodice of her dress was loose. "What?" She looked up.

His chest was heaving, his eyes even darker than their usually deep brown. "Do you know what you're doing?"

"What are you asking? If I know that I'm undressing? Or if I've ever had sex?"

His jaw pulsed under his skin as he put more distance between them, but he froze on the last question. "Have you?"

She ignored him. "I know who I am." She pushed the bodice from her shoulders, worked it over her hips. The dress collapsed in a heap of fabric at her feet. She stepped from it dressed only in her chemise. Everything inside her pulsed and ached. "It's time that everyone else understood who I am as well."

He swallowed, his Adam's apple bobbing heavily in his throat, and his gaze roamed over her body as heavy as a touch. "And who is that?"

She unbuttoned the top button of her chemise. "A woman."

He huffed a sound.

"Tired of hiding." She unbuttoned another button. "Who are you, Johesha?"

"Captain of the guard."

She looked around and unbuttoned another button. "What guard?"

His look shifted, his gaze narrowing as he took two steps to close the distance. But he didn't touch her. "I won't be manipulated."

"Who said anything about manipulating you?" She popped another button. "I don't think I'm being very covert or unclear with my intentions. I'm not trying to hide, am I. This is very overt."

His gaze dropped to her chest, then back up.

Jessamine removed her arms from the chemise. The top drooped over her hips, leaving her breasts exposed.

Johesha straightened, as if he were the one burned. "I have a job to do." He ground out the words through a clenched jaw.

"No one is stopping you," she said, pushing the chemise from her hips until it was a puddle of fabric at her feet, and she was naked before him. She was quaking and her stomach was a flutter of nerves. She'd never done something so bold.

He groaned again, grabbing hold of his erection. "It will complicate things."

She hummed a sound and nodded. "All right." With confidence she was faking, she walked past him and slid onto the bed grateful for the support of the mattress. Her limbs shook like branches in a storm. "I respect your decision."

He'd turned and faced her.

"We can test the potion the day after tomorrow," she

said and slid a hand down over her body, her fingers stopping at the top of her pelvis, she met Johesha's gaze. "That will give me one more day to tinker with the formula."

"Jessamine."

She lifted her brows and slid her fingers into the curls covering her sex, her fingers slipping through the wetness that had already prepared her. "You can stay and watch. You can join me." She gasped softly as her finger finally slipped across her clit. "Or you can go."

Johesha

J ohesha had killed men. He'd fought, he'd trained, he'd taught others how to disarm and kill. He wasn't averse to difficulties or challenges as a captain of Lachlan's guard but, standing there watching Jessamine with her hand between her legs, the other grasped onto the globe of her breast, and her mouth open on a mewling note, he wasn't sure he'd faced a challenge more difficult.

She was a goddess incarnate, and he fucking wanted her.

He knew he should walk away. He'd made a vow. He had a job to do, but that job suddenly seemed hazy. What was it, exactly?

"Fuck," he said on a breath and reached down to adjust his rock-hard cock in his trousers, pressing against it with a heavy hand as if it might alleviate the ache.

She used her fingers to split her cunt, opening it up so he could see her glistening center.

His mouth watered at the sight. *Fuck. Fuck. Fuck.*

His muscles tensed.

He should walk away.

Only he couldn't. And she was right, he didn't know this bold woman. He knew her as Tarley's older sister, a peripheral entity who he remembered in flashes of awareness. She'd been reduced to shadows. Much like he had his whole life as a guard, the waiting predator in the shadows.

But now, she was so central to everything that defined him, so bright and glaringly perfect, he couldn't get her out of his head.

Jessamine pulsed her hips into her touch. "Hesha," she whispered and looked at him, her dark eyes as black as night. "It's lonely without you."

Johesha groaned.

Every thread of logic tried to tie him up, but he cut through every one of them, undoing the ties of his pants and freeing his cock. He closed the distance to her and knelt on the bed between her spread thighs. He would touch her. He would fucking make her come undone. He couldn't go beyond that, wouldn't. But fuck, he needed relief.

"A finger inside," he ordered and watched as she

obeyed, gasping as she did, arching into it, her pert breasts, the dark areola and hard nipples needing his tongue. "Another one." He groaned as he spit on his hand and slicked it down his cock then back up, gathering the precum before doing it again, and again watching Jessamine fingerfuck herself.

"I need to taste you," he said. "Fingers."

She pulled her fingers from her cunt and held them up. With his free hand, he drew them into his mouth, licking and sucking all the essence of her.

"Godsdamned, Jessamine," he said, dropping forward and kissing her.

She grabbed his back, her nails biting into his skin through his shirt, and undulated her hips against him, seeking the pressure, the friction she wanted. "Please," she begged. "I need you."

"I need to taste this godsdamned cunt," he said and kissed his way down her body until he was between her thighs, holding them open. "Fuck I knew you'd be this beautiful. Tell me where you want my tongue."

His eyes jumped from between her legs to meet her gaze.

Her skin was bright and blushing.

"Don't lose that boldness now, Jess."

"I want you licking me."

"Godsdamned right," he growled and dove in. "Quiet now," he added just before his tongue slicked up her center.

She moaned the moment his tongue slid across her clit, her hands grasping at the bedding beneath her.

"You taste like fucking heaven," he said between licks and swirls of his tongue, loving the sound of her panting, moaning as he did. And she did taste perfect. The musk of her cunt was the perfect antidote to all the bottled-up need inside him. "Hands on me, love."

She listened, grabbing hold of his head, tugging on his hair, arching her greedy body against his greedy mouth. "I want to be closer."

He inserted his tongue, and she turned her mouth against her arm as she cried into it. He curled his tongue, lapping up the pleasure seeping inside to find the right spot. When she jerked beneath him, gasping out his name, he inserted his fingers and used his tongue on her clit in tandem, until she was a writhing mess of hushed noise, her cunt beginning the tell-tale flutter.

"Hesha," she moaned. "Hesha!"

"I got you. I'm here, love."

"I'm… I can't–"

"You can."

Her cunt tightened around his fingers, pulsing as she came, her cries music to his hardened heart. He eased off as her thighs tightened around him and kissed her pubic bone, creating a trail up her body, from the bones of her hips, across the valley of her stomach, spending time at the peaks of her breasts, kissing and suckling. If this night was all he was going to give himself, he was going to worship her. He created a trail over her collarbone, slid kisses up her neck, then followed the path of her jaw until he eventually reached her lips, and there he rested, his mouth pressed against hers, his cock rock hard between them.

She kissed him back, her hips undulating between them, as if seeking his shaft. "I need you, Johesha. Please."

He needed her too. Fuck he wanted her, but he was afraid. There wasn't much he was afraid of, but there was the threat that if he coupled with her completely, he might lose himself, lose everything that made him good at what he did. And if he wasn't good at being a guard anymore, what was he?

But he could make them both feel good. At least for tonight.

He knelt between her splayed thighs and held his palm up to her mouth. "Lick it," he ordered her.

She did, and his dick twitched at the sight. He pictured fucking that gorgeous mouth, pictured those lips wrapped around him, but that wasn't going to happen. It would ruin him.

He slid his spit-covered hand down his cock, then pushed his head through her wet core.

She moaned. "You feel so good. More."

"Oh fuck, Jess. You're so godsdamned hot. Hold your pretty cunt open for me."

She reached down and opened herself up to his gaze. He groaned and used his head against her clit.

She mewled, that sweet sound he knew would never leave his head.

"You like that, love. You like my cock splitting you open?"

"Yes. Hesha. Please. I want all of you."

"Not tonight, love," he said and sat up. "I'm going to milk myself all over you while you fuck your fingers. Got it?"

She nodded, her gaze devouring him as he took himself in hand, her slick coating his cock. Her fingers played with her clit as she watched him slide his hand down his shaft then back up, curling over his head, jerking back down to the base, then repeating the motion. Her gaze grew hazy as her breathy moans increased. He was so primed to unload, so hungry for her, it didn't take long.

As she gasped, "Hesha, I'm going to come again," he let go, releasing his own orgasm in bands across her breasts, her belly as she arched into her own orgasm. When he was spent, he sat back on his heels and looked at her, at the work of art she made coated in his spend.

He reached out and smeared his cum into her skin, coating her with it, wanting to mark her. "No bathing, Jess," he said, leaning down and grasping her cheeks, forcing her to meet his gaze. "I want you smelling like me. I want you to catch this scent tomorrow and remember what we did. How I made you feel. I want you to remember who played your body perfectly."

Jessamine nodded, then smiled. "You're bossy when you're having sex." She snorted a quiet laugh. "I like it." She watched him move away, climbing from the bed. "Stay," she said as she curled onto her side.

Johesha doused the lights and covered her up, bundling her under the covers. "You know I can't," he said, then, against his better judgement added, "even if I wanted to."

The last thing either of them needed was Crue stealing into this room and catching them in bed together.

He left through the secret passages, moving quietly down to the under house. Once in the hallway, a strange glow came from the workshop before it grew dark. He didn't dare investigate and ducked into the doorway just as Crue appeared in the hall.

Johesha held his breath as Crue walked past, humming.

Curious—even though he was pretty sure he should leave it alone, he snuck down the hallway into the workshop, but the light revealed nothing.

He returned to his own cot, wishing he were curled in bed beside Jessamine. As he lay there with his hand behind his head, he stared up at the open ceiling above, considering all the reasons he'd decided he couldn't be with her. The truth was, he had feelings for her. He wasn't sure if it was love, but perhaps it was something growing in that direction, like a plant growing toward the light. And if it was a possibility, wasn't that something he wanted?

He was thirty-six.

He'd been in Jast's guard for the majority of his life.

He was smart enough to know that he would have to pass the torch of his post as captain eventually.

It all came back to why he'd left his post.

Sure, he'd seen Jessamine in trouble. But he could have sent Jude to follow.

He hadn't. He'd chosen to leave his post as captain of the guard. That position was who he was, all he'd ever aspired to be, and still he'd followed this woman.

He'd told himself it was because it was his duty, but that was a lie. Jessamine had nothing to do with his duty to the royal family of Jast, to Lachlan. Jessamine was something he wanted for himself, and he couldn't remember ever in his life making a choice for himself other than the day he'd run away to join the guard.

The truth of it was the flimsy excuses he was making not to be with her weren't holding up anymore. He was going to stop making them, and if she was willing to have him, he was not only going to get her out of the mansion and away from Crue, but he was going to make her his.

Jessamine

"Jessamine," Brinna whispered, drawing her attention away from the man bathing in the pond. Jessamine wanted to remain hidden behind the shrubs to see his alluring shape. "Hush," she whispered back in a harsh tone, slapping at the insistent tug of her sister's hand pulling on her clothes. "I just need to get a look at his face." She was certain that if she saw his face, she'd know who she was going to marry.

Her mother had told them the story when they were girls of a young woman wandering the woods when she came across a sprite. Jessamine loved that story, could remember it like it was just yesterday, that twinkle in her mother's eyes as she told it.

Jessamine and her sisters would huddle around their mother's lap while Auri was tucked up on it, sucking her thumb, their mother's hand caressing her dark hair as she spoke. Mattias had not been born yet. The fire crackled in the hearth of the cottage and their father sat near it warming his toes from a day in the winter woods.

"Why did you stop," Brinna asked, like she always did.

"You want to hear the rest?" her mother asked.

They nodded, greedy for the tale.

"Once upon a time, a young woman running away from a tyrant lord got lost in the forest. She wasn't sure which way to go, except she couldn't–"

"–turn around and go backwards," Tarley finished.

"Right. So she walked onward, until a rascal raven called to her and she fell down a hole into another world. She walked some more in this new world filled with fantastical creatures like talking cows and met a sprite."

Jessamine and her sisters exchanged glances. She was getting to the good part.

"The sprite was very handsome and funny," Scarlett said.

"Like you, Papa," Auri pointed out.

They all looked over their shoulders at their father lounging in his chair, watching them with amusement glittering in his eyes and a smile on his mouth. He linked his fingers together over his belly. "You don't say? I'm honored you think so, Auri-girl."

"He is, isn't he?" Scarlett said. "Maybe he should give your mother a kiss for telling such a good story?"

They all made disgusted noises at the prospect.

"I want to hear the bath part!" Tarley said.

"Well, one morning, very early, just before the sun climbed into the sky, the young woman awoke, and she was alone. She called for her handsome sprite, but he was nowhere to be found. So she went off in search of him. What did she say? I forgot."

"My sun, my sun, where do you hide your face?" Brinna said.

"I'm afraid, I'm afraid, so I'll give thee chase," Jessamine added.

"Tell me, tell me. Leave me a trace," Tarley said.

Then, with their voices a chorus, they finished, "I promise, I promise to find the place." They all giggled.

"He's in the bath," Auri said, wrinkling her tiny nose.

"Sure enough," Scarlett said, "a bright light shone, and an old woman said, 'Daughter, why do you seek such a small soul?'"

"'Oh, but he's a giant,'" the young woman said, "'and I love him.'"

The girls giggled.

"'Then go to the pond and find your husband.'"

The girls snickered, hands covering their mouths.

"And sure enough. When she walked through the forest, she found the pond, and in it was her sprite, now a tall man. And they got married and lived happily ever after."

"Was he wearing knickers?" Auri asked.

"Certainly," their father replied, getting up and picking up Jessamine, Tarley, and Brinna all at once, making them squeal.

Now, Brinna was trying to get her to look away from the man in the pond, and Jessamine was certain she knew him—that rich, brown skin, the ebony hair, the wide back and tapered waist. "Stop. He's just going to turn this way. I need to see his face."

But just as he turned toward the noise they were making in the bushes, Brinna stood in front of Jessamine, blocking her view. "We know where you are."

And Jessamine's eyes snapped open.

Her heart thumped in her chest like Mrs. Gerrick moving pots and pans when annoyed. She looked around, forgetting for a moment, and the night before rushed in like a flash flood. She grinned, covering her face and kicking her feet happily under the sheets. She realized he hadn't stayed, but then, she hadn't really expected him to. Not with Crue.

But her smile faded as she pondered her forwardness. She'd felt powerful last night, emboldened, but what if he hadn't truly wanted to be with her. And he just… she swallowed as insecurity nipped at her.

She was still covered in him.

Her skin heated.

Mary!

She flipped the covers off, and hurried into the alcove, pouring icy water and hurriedly scrubbing at her skin.

Would she truly smell like him? She didn't know, but she couldn't traipse around Crue if she did. He'd find out, and who knew what the tyrant would do.

By the time Mary arrived, Jessamine was already dressed.

After a quick bit of toast with tea, she started for the basement, thinking about Johesha, trying not to fixate on the heat of the night before despite doing just that all morning. The uncertainty of what they'd experienced together plagued her. It had been so forbidden, wonderfully so, but they had left so much unsaid, even if Johesha had talked a lot last night.

She giggled.

She moved through the manor on the route she'd begun taking every morning. From the breakfast room, through the hallway to the main stairwell, down the curving ornate staircase to another hallway into the library off the study to access the secret door in the bookcase that led to the basement. As much as she wanted to explore the manor now she knew there were so many secret passageways and cubbies, she didn't dare. She didn't need Crue asking questions or suspecting anything.

With a pull of the latch, the hidden door in the library released, and she stepped into the small, dark vestibule behind the bookshelf, pulling the door closed. Darkness enveloped her, and she turned, knowing the sconce in the stairwell would offer her a bit of light.

But she couldn't see it. The darkness was pervasive and alive around her, as if it were breathing. Not easily scared, Jessamine reached out to feel her way to the doorway at the top of the stairs, knowing it was but three or four steps, and collided with an unforgiving mass.

"What are you doing to me?" Johesha's voice bit out in a harsh whisper.

She sucked in a breath. "Stars!" she whisper-yelled. "You are so sneaky." His hand covered hers over his heart. "And I'm not doing anything."

The rapid movement of his breath made the darkness come alive around them, and his hands suddenly gripped her hips, lifting her. "I can't stop thinking about you." He walked her backward. "I can't stop thinking about kissing you, about the taste of you on my tongue. I can't stop thinking about what you might be doing. I can't stop worrying that you're in danger. I can't get the image of you fingerfucking your cunt out of my head. I close my eyes and imagine you're squeezing my cock as you come."

With her back pressed against the backside of the bookshelf and her front against him, Jessamine gasped, her heart jumping in her chest at his bold words—the most he'd ever spoken at once.

"This isn't who I am. I don't fantasize. I don't feel unmoored. I don't lose my ability to concentrate." His nose slid along her neck, the warm heat of his breath, his body shimmering across her skin. "You washed."

She drew in a shaky breath, and her nipples pebbled under her shirt. She pressed her palm to his cheek. "I didn't want him to know."

He grabbed her wrist and pinned both of her hands over her head with one of his. "I'm going to take you apart and ruin you for ruining me. Do you understand?"

Unable to speak, her tongue thick with desire and shock, she nodded, whimpering and trying to find a way closer, only her skirt made it impossible.

The feral screech of the imprisoned darkling rent the air, followed by Crue's rampant mumblings.

With a groan, Johesha released her. "Go." He melted into the darkness, the sliver of light to the stairs showing her the way. Once at the top of the steps, she stopped to look back, at the bookshelf clicking shut, and she knew she was alone.

What had just happened?

Her trembling body nearly crumpled, not from fear but rather from need. She'd been in control the night before, until she hadn't been. Now, she realized Johesha had taken over, exactly where he liked to be. The realization made her want to find him and beg him to make good on that promise.

But she had a monster to appease and started down the stairs, gripping the wall to keep her upright. When she appeared in the doorway to the workshop, Crue was leaning against the workbench, his elbow pressed against the top and hands in his hair. She glanced at the prison door, at the beautifully elegant fingers wrapped around the peephole opening.

"What's wrong?" she asked.

"Where have you been?"

"I'm stuck in the manor. Where else would I be?"

"You're late."

"I'm on time," she said, and the darkling's fingers disappeared, enclosing the monster behind the door once more.

"Make me something new."

"What's the ailment?"

He looked up at her without removing his head from his hands. A cold fire burned inside the depth of their blackness, and she shivered. He didn't look quite right, even if he looked healthier. "Anger."

"A broken heart?" she asked.

With a feral cry, he swiped everything from the workbench, all of it crashing against the prison doors. The darkling screamed. With his back to her, Crue heaved with a foul energy that had her backing up, wondering if she should run. "She's fucking with me!"

"Father?" she asked, using the name that placated him.

Footsteps resounded in the hallway, cutting the fear that had permeated the room.

"Master," a small voice said.

Henro.

The boy started into the room; a bit of parchment gripped in his hand.

Jessamine held an arm out to keep him from entering, to keep him from getting too close to Crue, who didn't seem like himself, though she couldn't understand what had changed.

"What is it?" Crue said, his back still to them.

"A message sir," the boy replied and held up a folded piece of parchment with a purple seal.

Crue whirled, and Jessamine sucked in a breath. The man who claimed to be her father had looked like a strung-out version of himself the day before. It had been as if he'd removed his blood, his skin unusually pale and coated in a sheen of sweat. But today there were no circles under his glistening eyes. His form seemed taller, more muscular. And his lips curled in a smile that looked more like a snarl, his teeth sharper somehow.

"Give it to me," he snapped.

The boy made a move to start across the room, but Jessamine stopped him.

"Give it to me," she whispered, not wanting the boy near Crue, though she couldn't say why. "Then you go."

Henro nodded and pressed the parchment into her hand. Once she took hold, he turned and took off down the hall like a shot.

Jessamine carried the scroll across the room, and with the workbench still between them, laid it on the wooden table. "What's wrong, Father?" She worked not to choke on the word.

He scoffed, his eyes jumping to hers, clearly looking for the lie in her use of the word. "Hubris," he said and reached for the parchment. "Clean up the mess," he ordered.

With a swallow, she moved to the end of the bench and went to her knees, careful to avoid the glass. She heard the wax seal break and the unrolling of the parchment as she picked through for the big shards of glass.

She looked up at a huff of air. Above her, a set of dark eyes observed her through the opening in the door.

The darkling.

Though she couldn't make out the details of its face, she could see that it was changing shape, the shape of the eyes, the skin around those eyes, hair, lashes, and she was certain, though she couldn't see it to be sure, that it was now Johesha staring back at her.

Crue barked a single sharp laugh, drawing her attention.

"Damn her," he cursed, smacking a hand against the bench. "If that's how she wants it." He turned and looked at her huddling near the darkling's cage as she picked up the mess he'd made. "I'll just start sending you home to her."

He smiled an ugly, dark smile, his teeth somehow appearing rotted just then, and added, "one piece at a time." Then he stalked from the room, disappearing through the doorway.

Jessamine stood and swallowed, afraid he'd meant that and curious about what the letter had said. The movement of the parchment on the workbench caught her eye. She slid it toward her and read the words.

Johesha

When Henro ran into the kitchen, his face pale, breath heaving and pointing down at the basement, for the first time Johesha could remember, his heart jumped into his throat, undoing his thoughts. *Jessamine.* But then, as if his training reinforced what made him, he slid into the lowest common denominator of what he was. A predator. His emotions tempered. He cleaved to what was rational.

"What is it, kid?" He grabbed hold of Henro, then held the boy's small cheeks between his palms to force Henro's hazel eyes to his.

Henro babbled, something about men and messages. "Something's wrong." He panted the words between shallow breaths. "The Master."

Johesha didn't think. He moved, racing down the steps. Though emotion careened through him, his instincts took over. This is what he'd been trained to do. He slowed and stalked, pulling the dagger from the sheath at his hip. When he was outside the door, he listened, wondering what he was up against.

Only it was eerily silent. Even the monster in the cage.

He stepped into the doorway, and his eyes went to Jessamine. She was alone, holding onto a leaf of curled parchment, her face pale, but not harmed. His eyes cataloged the disarray. Plants up ended on the floor, their roots peeking from the strewn soil, broken glass, a toppled mortar and pestle. She looked like an angel in the middle of the dark chaos.

Her gaze rose from the letter, her dark eyes glistening with unshed tears. "It says they're coming," she said, and her throat closed around a broken sob. "But it isn't from my family."

Johesha shook his head. "But…" He crossed the room thinking about Brendsen and Kobb and the news they'd imparted to him. *We've been looking for you this whole last year.* The concern. Maybe this was what he'd been waiting for. "May I?"

She handed the letter across the table.

He looked at the seal: deep purple wax inset with a tree dusted with gold. "This is the Royal seal of Jast."

"It's signed Prince Lachlan."

Johesha's instincts kicked in. "Who did Crue send his message to?"

"My mother."

He opened the parchment and read the letter all the way though.

> *Safe and unharmed? Careful of your words, Lord Crue, if they ring with falsehood. A year has passed since we have laid eyes on Jessamine and therefore have just cause. Retaliation under the mighty banner of Jast will be the least of your worries should you be lying about Jessamine's safety. Leave your threats and bitterness aside, as it is inconsequential. Even with the treaty between Kaloma and Jast in effect, you have abducted my wife's relation, her sister, a fact I intend to rectify with extreme prejudice. There must be retribution for the harm you have caused this family, my family. There will be justice. I will send a group of convoy emissaries to collect my sister in two-days' time.*

> *Spies have discovered your location, and therefore it is unnecessary to send another missive. Answer if you will, but it will not deter the forward momentum of our mission: Jessamine's safe return. With the full might of Jast bolstering my royal party, only witnesses to Jessamine's proof of life by their eyes will substantiate your claims. Any duplicity on your part will be an act of war against Jast. Your safety is only guaranteed upon the safe return of Jessamine into the hands of my emissaries. Nefarious intent or actions will only reinforce the belief that your intentions are untoward. Exceptions are nonexistent but for her safe return. Evidence of her alive and without harm is expected, as a lock of hair isn't proof of life. Demands—your demands—will not be met. Moreover, should she come to harm in the exchange, this will be an act of war. Our rights as victims to your illegal*

deeds are to seek vengeance, but this conflict between you and Scarlett has gone on too long. Revenge, as a dish, is best not served but discarded. Expel the bitterness and hatred, and justice will be mete out with fairness. To ignore this offer would be foolish. In as much as there can be enmity between you, I urge you to consider this one and only offer of peace. My wife's happiness is paramount, and therefore your response will inform me as to how I should act. Enemy now, until you have proven otherwise.

Royal Prince of Jast, Lachlan Excelsior Orion Nicholas.

He read it a second time, his instincts twinging under his skin. He read it again, this time looking to see if the prince had embedded it with a code. This was a message to him as much as it was to Crue. Knowing that, the code was clear.

Johesha looked back at the parchment, then set it down on the table and leaned closer to her. "There's a code." He pointed to the first letters of each line. "See." He turned his face to see Jessamine's dark eyes tracking his finger, then she turned and looked at him. "Your mother is away."

She jerked back. "Away?" she hissed. "What does that mean?"

"I don't know, but–"

"He just threatened to dismember me. And send me to them in pieces."

"What?"

The darkling tittered behind the door of its cage.

Johesha glanced at the monster, turned back to Jessamine before turning once more to the monster, sure that he'd been looking at his own face behind the bars. He blinked, and the darkling wasn't there, having retreated into the darkness of its cell.

He glanced at the parchment on the table once more, committing the message to memory and opening his mouth to offer Jessamine something hopeful even if that wasn't his nature, but just then Crue walked back in and stalled at the sight of him, his dark eyes narrowing.

"Huntsman?"

"I came to help clean."

"I don't keep you to clean," Crue snapped and stalked back into the room, swiping up the parchment from the table. "I keep you to hunt for me, and I need more rabbit eyes."

Gritting his teeth, Johesha nodded.

"Well? Go."

He glanced at Jessamine, worried for her and unable to do anything about it. That alone enraged him, and all the feelings he worked so hard to keep bottled up threatened to overflow. But they wouldn't serve him and wouldn't serve her. He knew that. So he turned and left.

What he did know as he gathered his weapons: he and Jessamine weren't waiting any longer, two days or not. It was time to go.

Jessamine

"I don't believe that your mother isn't coming." Crue slicked a thumb at the corner of his grinning mouth as if wiping away the remnants of something he'd consumed. "Which means I must prepare."

"Prepare for what?" She hated the tremble of fear in her voice.

"Don't you worry about it." He looked better, now, back to the man she was used to seeing rather than the shade of who he'd been moments prior, but that didn't make her feel safe. It made her wonder what was happening to him.

"Are you going to cut me up?" she asked and grabbed a sliver of glass. The slip and burn of it as it sliced through the skin of her finger made her suck in a breath. She surged to her feet with a hiss.

The darkling tittered and rushed the door of its cage, banging hard against the door. "Blood."

"What?" Crue stalled and turned toward her.

She squeezed her finger, grabbing a cloth to staunch the bleeding.

Crue approached, taking her hand and pulling her toward him.

"You said you would send me to her in pieces." She tried to pull her hand away.

"I didn't mean it," he said, holding her tightly, his strength surprising. "Open your hand."

"It's bleeding."

"Let me look at it. I'll fix it."

"I'm the healer," she snapped.

"I'm the sorcerer." His hands began to glow, their warmth seeping through her skin. "I have access to power you can't imagine."

Jessamine glanced up from her hand to look at the wizard. His skin seemed to glow with a strange light, the power of which he spoke emanating inside out. His dark eyes were darker as if the magic were changing him. Pushing his thumb into her closed palm, he forced her hand open. Blood smeared across her skin, still welling from the cut before sluicing across and dripping down the back of her hand.

The darkling screeched, slamming up against the door of its cell once more.

The wizard hummed, whispered something, then swiped his thumb over the cut, smearing the blood even more. Heat from his hands burned, almost as if she were cutting herself once more. She drew in a breath and tried to snatch back her hand. Crue held her fast. The burning sensation waned, and when his thumb retreated, the cut was closed, the skin perfectly knitted together as if the wound had never been.

"See," he said. "I can heal." He took the cloth from her other hand and began to wipe the blood. "Your mother just… gets to me."

Unnerved, Jessamine took her hand back. "Thank you."

Crue sighed. "I have some things to attend to. Have to prepare, after all, for this happy proof-of-life reunion." He grinned again, and Jessamine suppressed a shudder. "I won't be joining you for dinner, my dear, but I will see you here in the morning, same as always."

She dipped her head in acknowledgement, afraid to say anything, and watched the door a few moments after he was gone, her heart knocking inside her chest that he would return unexpectedly. But the doorway remained empty, and the only sound was the movement of the darkling in its cage and the gurgle of steaming potions on the back counter of the workshop behind her.

She turned back to the mess littering the workshop and began to clean once more, listening to the strange noises made by the darkling. The creature drew closer to the door, its fingers—elegant and unmarred like those of a woman—wrapped around the bars. While she'd once seen the monster in action in a wooded meadow, this version of the creature was broken and pitiful. She couldn't help but feel sorry for it.

"I remember you," she said.

It didn't reply, its eyes tracking her movement.

"You went after my sister Tarley," she added. "You wanted to kill her."

"No," it hissed. "To satiate."

"What is that?" she asked, but the creature didn't reply, just watched her clean. "I don't understand why you're here, imprisoned. Is there magic in the bars?"

But it didn't reply and disappeared from view, slinking back into the shadows behind the door.

She stood, walking to the workbench and dumping some of the things she'd picked up on its surface.

"Did he hurt you?" Johesha asked.

Jessamine glanced over her shoulder. He stood in the doorway, and she knew he hadn't left, even though he'd been ordered to. He'd waited next door to make sure she was safe. "He left."

"Where?"

"He didn't say."

Jessamine couldn't look at him, too aware of him in the space, too aware of what they'd experienced together, too desirous to find her way back to that, too breathless, too worried, too much, too, too, too. She turned her back to him and busied herself with organizing the contents on the back counter. "We have to figure out if my potion works."

She reached for a bushel of tied herbs and rose up to her tiptoes to hang it from the hooks attached to a bar overhead.

Suddenly, Johesha's body heat crowded in behind her. His arm slipped around her as he took the bunch of hothouse grown lavender from her, his palm pressed against her belly. "Jessamine," he said, hanging the herb up on the hook above them.

She turned her head to look at him, moving upward from his chest to his face.

He glanced at her lips before his gaze rose to meet her eyes. He leaned closer, his lips and breath warm against her ear as he whispered, "We shouldn't talk in front of the creature."

Her gaze shifted to the cell door. She thought about the creature's ability to answer her questions and realized Johesha was right. When she looked back at him, she nodded her understanding.

He removed himself from her space. "Mrs. Gerrick wants to make jerky with the new buck. Is there any sage?"

"In the greenhouse."

He backed away. "Would you get me some?"

Then he left, and she knew she wouldn't be coming back.

Johesha

I t was time to go.

Johesha hurried back to the hovel that had been his over the last year and grabbed the weapons he was certain he'd need including the short sword and the bow with extra arrows. Next, he snatched the supplies he'd been stashing just for this moment. Finally, he hurried from the horrible workroom, hopeful this plan would work, that this would be the last time his eyes looked at this horrible, dank space. He moved quickly, taking the steps multiples at a time, knowing time wasn't on their side. Who knew where Crue was? With Jessamine compelled to return, they needed as much time as they could get for a head start.

When he strode into the greenhouse, Jessamine was there, dressed for winter in a dark, wool coat with a pack hooked on her shoulders. She whirled to look at him, taking in the bow, the rucksack, the dagger at his hip, the short sword strapped to his back.

"Are you sure?" she asked. "I feel as if I haven't done enough to discover his weakness, you know, should we need to know."

"Our window to learn is gone."

She took a deep breath, trepidation weighing the corner of her eyes. Then she lifted her hand, a short, dark bottle with a potbelly in her palm. "I don't know if it will work."

"That's it?"

She nodded.

"Is it safe? For you?"

She smiled. "Yes."

"But don't forget the task. What's the task?"

"I need winter Eldram berries for a potion he wants me to make."

"Winter Eldram berries? What are they for?"

"Does it matter?"

"If I know, then I can use any information to keep you focused."

She nodded. "They're poisonous, but if boiled and the pulp strained, what's left behind is an agent that attacks foreign bodies. I need them for a potion to fight infection."

Johesha nodded and grabbed her shoulders, turning her to face him, then placed his palms on her cheeks and tilted her head to force her to meet his gaze. "You aren't alone, Jess. I'm with you. I–" But he stopped as emotion climbed his throat, which he resented. He had a job to do, had always been good at his job, and why this was different he couldn't say. So he shook his head. "The plan is to make for the widow's cottage," he said instead. "We'll wait there for two days for the prince's emissaries and intercept them before they make it to the manor."

Her dark gaze searched his, then she nodded. "I trust you. I'm sor–"

"–stop. No. The spell isn't your fault."

She swallowed, her eyes dipping away from his as she glanced at the bottle, then lifted it to her lips and upended it, swallowing all the liquid inside. Her nose wrinkled and her eyes watered, but then she shook her head, her body shuddering. After a second, she sighed and nodded. "All right. Let's go."

His one regret as he stepped from the greenhouse was that he didn't have time to take the others, that he was leaving them behind. Henro. Gerrick. Mary. Oto. But they weren't his mission. He vowed he would find a way to return and rescue them from this prison.

They weren't five steps from the greenhouse when Jessamine said, "I need to go back."

"What for."

"I forgot something." She glanced at him, pulling on his hold. "My benevolent Master… I mean Father won't like this. Who are you?"

The potion hadn't worked.

"I'm the benevolent Master's huntsman. We're going

to get Eldram berries for your potion? Remember?"

She stopped struggling. "For a tincture. Yes. I need the berries." Her eyes searched his face. "And you're the huntsman?"

He nodded. "I'm here to help you hunt for the berries, to keep you safe, in case there are wolves."

Jessamine latched onto his arm and looked around. "Wolves."

"I promise to keep you safe."

Her dark eyes swung up to his. "How long will it take?"

"Most of the day."

She nodded, and they continued onward, putting more distance between them and the manor.

He was both grateful when snow began to fall even if it also worried him. Grateful because it would fill in their tracks. Worried, because they had some ground to cover before they made it to the cottage. But soon, the snow was coming down in flurries, and Johesha's worry turned to visibility.

"I need to go back," Jessamine hedged. "The berries can wait another day."

"It has to be today," Johesha said. "We promised the benevolent Master."

"He wouldn't want us to die in the snow." She was shivering now.

Johesha wasn't sure the Master would care if they died, but he picked her up. "Not much further," he said and trudged on.

Please, he prayed as Jessamine shivered in his arms. *Please.* Though who he was asking for help was unclear.

They were deep into the woods now, but the snow flurries were making it difficult to ascertain the landmarks. Everything looked the same, and he knew they should have been near the meadow by now. Except they were still surrounded by massive trees blocking some of the raging snowstorm.

"It's so cold," Jessamine said into his neck.

Please, he prayed again.

Suddenly, the snow parted like a curtain, revealing a path. He blinked and shook his head, wondering if his mind was playing tricks on him. But he started that way, deciding they couldn't be much further.

The wind picked up.

Snow flurries, obscuring his sight.

He swore.

Jessamine whimpered; her face pressed into his neck.

He hated to think he would have to turn around, but if he didn't find it, he knew there wasn't another shelter close by to keep them from the wizard's reach.

A few more steps, he told himself. One more. One more, he told himself.

He was just about to stop when the wind died, and the flurries tempered to reveal an opening between the trees. He stepped through and the meadow opened around them. Relieved, he continued forward, looking for the landmarks, hoping they weren't covered by snow, when suddenly he found them: the two stone faces marking the path, untouched by snow. *Thank you,* he prayed to whoever was guiding the way.

The wind whipped up again, raging around them as he

hurried toward the cottage.

"Here," he said, setting Jessamine down and holding her hand tightly. "Hurry."

"But the Master," she cried, tugging on him.

"The berries. He needs the berries!"

She glanced up the path. "The berries are here?"

"Shelter. The Master won't want us to die in this storm," Johesha yelled over the wind. He didn't wait for the spell to inform her otherwise and pulled her closer, taking her deeper into the woods, the storm quieting the further they walked into the darkness. The trees tightened, sheltering them from the snow. When the cottage appeared, dark and vacant—just like when he'd left it— Johesha didn't hesitate, hurrying the final distance with Jessamine tucked against him.

"I'll get us a fire going."

"I am so very cold. Father won't want me to die."

"Exactly." Johesha stomped up the front steps with Jessamine's hand in his. "I may have to find–"

But he stalled at the threshold when the door opened easily, no lock. He pushed it open, and instead of the dark, cold cottage he expected to find, a fire roared in the hearth.

Jessamine ducked under his arm. "Hello?" she called out. "We're sorry to intrude."

There was no answer.

"Hello?" she called out, then looked at him over her shoulder. "You're inviting all the cold air in. We'll look for the berries as soon as we warm up."

He nodded and walked in, looking around at the interior which looked nothing like it had when the old woman had fed him stew. The cottage still had a table and chairs, a kitchen, and a fire, but everything was… different. Rather than the roughhewn cabinetry covered with fabric, now they were finished. There was a black wood stove in the kitchen on which a pot bubbled and steamed as if someone had just left the room to fetch something. A table was set for two. There was a dark stone hearth alive with fire, a couch and chair facing it, and across the room, a bed large enough for two people rather than the old woman's small bed.

"Hello?" Jessamine called out again. "I'm Jessamine. We're sorry to barge in."

He walked around, checking, poking his head into doorways, behind curtains. "I don't think anyone is here."

"Were you planning on stabbing them, huntsman?" Jessamine asked, her eyes dipping to the dagger in his hand.

"If need be."

Jessamine snorted and pulled off her cap. "Do you think the owner will mind if we make ourselves at home?"

"Somehow, I doubt it." The widow's words came back to him. *Should you need me, just return here, between the stone faces.* Unless someone was perpetuating an incredible hoax, this didn't make sense. No one knew they were there—he hoped. But the widow's words.

Magic, Johesha realized but didn't say it out loud.

"This smells delicious. Do you think whoever lives here will mind our intrusion?" Jessamine asked, straightening up from looking at what was in the pot, pulling the scarf from around her neck.

"For some reason, I don't think so," he said, removing

his weapons, dropping them near the door. "I think they were expecting us."

"Expecting us?" Jessamine snorted as she unbuttoned the coat, removing the rest of her outerwear and laying it across the back of the couch. "Well, whatever this is, I am grateful."

Johesha watched her from where he stood by the door, the awareness of what it might have been like to have a wife, to come home to her, hitting him squarely in the chest. He sat on the wooden chair near the door, telling himself it was because he wanted to remove his boots, and ignored the strange weakness he felt trying to catch his breath.

Jessamine

Jessamine glanced at the huntsman sitting near the door. He was bent over, elbows pressed to his knees, looking down at his booted feet. And though she didn't know him, he had taken care of her, he had protected her. This wasn't the manor. But, she rationalized, this would do until they could return. That thought brought her comfort, even if the desire to return to the manor was an insistent and uncomfortable tug on her mind. The wind howled beyond the cabin, and she could see the snow sliding sideways between the curtains covering the window. Yes. This would do for now.

"Are you all right, huntsman?" she asked.

He looked up and his dark eyes slammed into her, nearly pushing her backwards with the intensity of his gaze. "I have a name."

She nodded, then turned away, not asking. She just needed to focus on getting back to the manor. His name was irrelevant. "Do you think it would be all right to eat? I'm hungry."

She glanced at him over her shoulder.

He was removing his boots, his shoulders shifting under his linen shirt. His forearms—visible because the sleeves were rolled to his elbows—flexed as he moved, and she whipped her head back around to the pot on the stove, unnerved by how attractive she found a near stranger! She lifted the lid and drew in a deep breath.

"It smells so good," she said. "Vegetables. Rosemary." She found a spoon and stirred. "Roast venison, I think." Her mouth watered, and she thought about the… there was a place she needed to go, but it slipped her mind for a moment. She turned to the table looking for the shallow white dishes set there, walked away from the pot, and picked them up. The manor! She needed to get back to the manor.

But food first.

"It does smell good," the huntsman said, just behind her.

She hadn't heard him move.

His presence sent pleasurable chills racing up her spine, and she suppressed a shiver. She turned with the first dish, holding it out to him. "For you."

"Thank you." He took the dish and retreated to the table.

Jessamine joined him with her own bowl and sat across from him. "Are you sure this is acceptable? It looks like someone was just getting ready to eat."

"Are you afraid of the food?" His eyes turned up along the edges, creasing with a smile, though his mouth didn't follow suit.

"More afraid of angering the occupant of this home." She glanced around. It was such a lovely place with patchwork curtains hanging over the windows, several tied rugs set in strategic places, a clean hearth with a blazing fire. Someone cared about it. "It doesn't make sense they aren't here."

"Perhaps they are." The huntsman took a bite.

She chewed her own bite, glancing around. "But where?"

"What if it's us?" His eyes met hers a moment as he reached for a roll.

She scoffed and finished the bite, swallowing and closing her eyes at how delicious it tasted. "Us? We're strangers, huntsman." She took another bite, finding his humor entertaining.

"I told you I have a name."

She studied him as she finished her morsel. "Do you know mine?"

He nodded. "Jessamine Fareview."

With surprise, she stopped chewing for a moment, then finished the bite. Warmth spread inside her, reaching all the places that had turned so cold. "How?"

"We're both from the manor," he said, dipping a bit of bread into the gravy. "We've spoken many times. It's because of the spell."

"The spell–" Jessamine stopped and looked down at her partially eaten food. The spell. Somehow, she knew what that meant. And she'd made an elixir intended to curb its effects. When she looked up, she knew exactly who sat across the table from her, knew why she was attracted to him, recalled what they'd already done, what he'd promised her just earlier that day. Her cheeks heated. "Johesha."

He smiled, then, one that illuminated his face, and it was breathtaking. "You remember?"

She nodded, realizing the last place she wanted to be was the manor. "Is my potion working?"

"Maybe. Or maybe it's this place. The magical meal you're eating."

Gods, he was so beautiful when he smiled, it hurt to look at him. "This place. It's magic." She looked around it. "This is the woman's cottage?"

He nodded, taking another bite.

"Where is she?"

He shrugged.

"Are we safe?" she asked, glancing at one of the windows. Though they were pulled closed she could see between the fabric's edges the darkness outside now, hear the howling of the wind.

"I don't think we could have been followed in this blizzard. Our tracks will have been filled in with the added snow. I think only magic–" He paused, frowning.

Both of them knew the wizard's abilities.

"We just have to make it two days."

She nodded. "It seems we have everything we need. And time." She felt the tension grow between them, as she chewed another bite, her mind on what he'd said earlier that day in the alcove of the secret passage. "Tell me about you, Johesha."

"What do you want to know?"

"Your story. Your family. How did you become a guard?"

"It will put you to sleep."

"It won't. I'm sincerely interested."

He swallowed his bite, then sighed. "I'm the son of a farmer and grew up learning how to work the land. I have two younger sisters, but I haven't seen them since I was fifteen. Rell and Reena."

"And how old are you?"

"Thirty-six."

She was sure her surprise was bright on her face. "Twenty-one years? You haven't seen them for that long? Your mom and dad?"

"When you become a royal guard, you take a vow to take the royal family as your own."

"Which is why—"

"I haven't seen my family. It's why I don't have one of my own."

"No wife?" Her heart twisted at the thought he might, suddenly jealous. That she hadn't even considered he might be married when she'd seduced him. What kind of person did that make her?

"No, Jessamine. No wife." He gazed at her with that

intensity she'd noted earlier, before looking down at his nearly empty plate with the ghost of a smile.

"You wanted to be a hero."

"And you?" he asked.

"You know my family. We've spoken about them—"

"True, but I want to know more about you."

"What would you like to know?"

"Everything."

"Let me think." She stood to break the tension threatening to drag her across the table into his lap and carried her plate to the small sink where there was a bucket of warm water. Magic. She barely had time to consider it when the heat of Johesha was behind her. There was no part of him touching her, just the insinuation that if he took a step closer, he would be, the hint of him.

"Why are you running away now?" he asked and reached around her to put his dish away. "Where is that brave boldness?" Then he did take a step forward, his body outlining hers, his hands on her hips.

"Are we rushing things?" Though even as she said it, she knew it wasn't true. She knew so much about him. His loyalty, his strength, his bravery and persistence. His devotion to the prince. His leadership, his kindness, his passion. This man was a dream. She imagined him in her dream, of his standing in a pond, turning to look at her.

"I'm learning you." His hands climbed up over her ribs, so big. Spanning most of her ribcage so that his fingertips pressed against the underside of her breast. "You are one of five siblings." Removing one hand from her rib cage, he grabbed hold of her braid and moved it over one of her shoulders, baring the back of her neck. "Three sisters and a brother." His breath was warm against her skin and shivers raced from the base of her spine up to meet that caress. "You're from Sevens and have worked alongside your mother as a healer. That you would take care of your parents, but that wasn't what you dreamed." He squeezed her ribs.

"What was my dream?" She tilted her head and sighed at the feel of his warmth caressed her neck.

His body pressed into hers, curving together perfectly and pinning her between his unforgiving form and the sink. "To travel as a healer. You're a caretaker. You're responsible. You love your family deeply." His hands slid back down over her hips, lower as his lips grazed the skin at the nape of her neck. "I know what you sound like when you come."

Her heart slammed hard against her ribs, and she sucked in a breath as one of his hands slid back up her thigh, under her skirt, the calluses of his palm rough and addictive.

"I know that I can't get you out of my head," he said, a hand reaching around to hold her belly, pressing her in against him and forcing her to lean forward, his hard length pressed against her backside. "The sound of your laughter is music and the sight of your smile, essential."

She grabbed hold of the edge of the sink.

"That I can't think of anything else but needing to be inside you." He rocked his hips against hers so she could feel his desire at the same time his hand slid between her legs, cupping her.

She gasped. "Johesha."

"I know everything that matters, Jessamine. And I know I want more of it. Is it rushing to accept what's between us as a gift?"

"Johesha?"

His nose ran the length of her neck, up toward her jaw, where he pressed a kiss against her pulse point. "What is it, Jess?"

"Thank you," she said, needing him to understand how much his presence meant.

Johesha stepped back so quickly, as if he'd been burned, leaving her back exposed and suddenly cold.

She turned to face him. "What is it?"

A cloud drifted across his features; one filled with the violence of an impending storm. "Don't thank me," he told her, shaking his head as if the words convicted him. Then he closed his eyes.

"You stayed. Even after the spell broke. I don't understand."

His eyes snapped open and mapped her face, but then he turned away, walking back to the table as if to busy himself, but the evidence that they'd eaten there was gone, the top cleared of their meal. "I told you I would always come back."

Jessamine followed. "Johesha? What's wrong?"

He put the table between them as if he didn't trust himself to be near her, that he'd avoid this conversation. Maybe he didn't trust her. "You don't have to thank me for doing my duty." But the words came out harsh and clipped as if he'd forced them out.

"Oh," she said. "You were ordered to follow and stay?" That made things different. "Well," she said weakly and swallowed, suddenly embarrassed. "I guess that still deserves a thank you." She crossed to the hearth and stood in front of the fire.

"No. That's not–" He stopped, expelling a harsh sigh.

"I don't want to pressure you. Not if all this is born from your sense of duty."

"I want to be honest with you."

She glanced over her shoulder, but he didn't look like a man struck with guilt. He looked like a man at war with himself. "That's all I want."

"The truth is, I don't know why you would want me. If I'm not a guard, I am not sure who I am. What I am." With a growl, she heard him cross the room. He grabbed her by her shoulders and turned her to face him. "I didn't follow because I was ordered. I didn't stay because it was my duty. That's a lie. I've been a guard for so long…" He stopped.

Jessamine searched his face and could see that storm at war with the clarity of a summer day on his features. This wasn't about her, she realized. This was about him and his own struggle.

"I love being a guard of Jast," he finally said, his dark eyes meeting hers, "but I followed you because I wanted to. It had nothing to do with being a guard. I left my post, abandoned it. How could anyone choose me when I broke a vow?"

She tilted her head. "You broke it for me?"

He shook his head and closed his eyes. "No. For me." Then he opened his eyes again, and with more conviction, admitted, "For me. I followed you for me. You kissed me the night of the prince's wedding…"

"I remember." Her heart was racing in her chest at his admission, unaware it had made as much an impression on him as it had her.

Running his hands down her arms, he wrapped her hands in his and pulled them up to his chest. "I wanted you for myself, Jess. And I'm not supposed to want…"

She tilted her head and studied him. "But why?"

"Because I made that vow."

She hummed in acknowledgement and looked down at his chest before looking back up and meeting his gaze. "Was it a lifetime vow?"

He shook his head. "As long as I am in my position."

"People change, Johesha. You've lived faithfully to your vow for twenty-one years. And perhaps choosing something for yourself just means you are ready for something different. Something new. Something all yours."

He drew in a steady breath, the sun breaking through on his features as if he was coming to his own realization. His eyes met hers, the depth of them shining with desire.

"Here I am." She stepped closer, disengaging her hand from his, and pressed her palm to his cheek. "Make me yours," she whispered.

Johesha didn't hesitate, crashing his mouth against hers and wrapping her in his arms. He kissed her with the ferocity of his nature. He was a predator, and she was his prey. He took and demanded, he gave and soothed. Jessamine gave it back, until he picked her up and walked her into the alcove where the bed waited, where he turned, set her down on the floor and sat, his hands on her hips.

He looked up at her. "Take it off. If I do it, I'll tear it." He curled his hands into fists and set them on his thighs as he watched.

She smiled, her fingers going to the first buttons of her bodice. "So bossy."

His gaze was a sponge soaking her in.

The adrenalin of anticipation slid through her, and she trembled. When the fabric split open, it revealed the ivory chemise underneath.

Johesha growled. "So many layers."

"Patience, Hesha. All good things come to those who wait." She pushed the dress over her shoulders, then over her hips, and he finally reached out and helped, tugging it to her ankles. She stepped from it.

"You aren't naked yet."

She giggled.

He picked up her foot, and she reached out to put a hand on his shoulder to keep her balance. With her foot in his lap, he undid the laces of her boot. When he was done, he kissed the inside of her knee and skimmed his hands up her thigh, his thumb caressing her seam over the fabric, making her gasp, then moving down the opposite leg for the other boot. "Up." He tapped her thigh and looked up. "Why aren't you taking that infernal layer off, woman?"

"It's that or my balance," she said.

He grunted, finished with the boot, and without any more patience, yanked her into his lap. He kissed her, melding his tongue with hers, his palms framing her face, then grabbed the back of her neck to hold her where he wanted her. "I've wanted this."

She mewled as his mouth traced a path across her skin. "Me too. I dreamed of you."

He pulled back. "You did?"

When she nodded, he groaned and kissed her again as if he were a starved man.

His real hands, his actual tongue, his firm lips were better than her fantasies. His palms ran up from the back of her thighs to her backside, squeezing, kneading, pulling, pushing, lighting a blaze between her legs. She groaned, rocking her hips, seeking more fulfillment. He pressed her harder against his erection, jerking his hips up with a grunt, and the friction it caused between her legs made her moan.

"Oh gods," she said into his mouth.

"Arms up," he ordered.

She lifted them, and he pulled the chemise over her head, tossing it away.

"Fuck, Jess." His eyes mapped the contours of her breasts. He lifted a hand, fisted it before touching her, then opened it once more and slid that calloused palm across her skin, lifting, molding and squeezing. "I can't stop seeing you... standing there like a fucking goddess. This is... mine."

She leaned into his touch. "Yes," she whispered, undulating against him.

He bent forward, his hands spanning her back to hold her in place and lathed one nipple with his tongue.

She wondered if she should be embarrassed by the noises she made, unable to help herself as he grabbed hold of his head. "That feels... good." The pulsing between her legs increased, and she rocked against Johesha's rigid cock, seeking the friction.

He hummed against her skin, "So fucking beautiful," then switched, offering his mouth to the opposite breast. "Use me, Jess."

Unable to still herself, not even if she wanted to, Jessamine stroked her clit against him in an addicting rhythm, his rock-hard erection offering her the friction she wanted. She mewled, moaned, gasped.

"Hesha. Hesha," she chanted as her body tensed, climbing to a place that emptied out all her thoughts but the sensations grabbing hold of her insides and tugging with pleasure. As her core began to constrict, she cried out, "Hesha. Please." He grabbed her hips, grinding up against her, leaning back and watching as she gasped as her body milked emptiness, as the pleasure overrode the disappointment of being empty.

Johesha flipped her onto her back and slid them both up the bed. "So godsdamned beautiful when you come. Perfect." He tugged at the ties of her bloomers and shoved them partway down her thighs. "This cunt is mine." He slid his fingers through her sex.

She opened her legs as wide as she could with the fabric still wrapped around her thighs and moaned at the blissful invasion of his finger. Then another. "Yes, Hesha! Yours."

His fingers retreated then entered her, in and out, the erotic sound of her sucking him inside making her moan, lifting her hips to meet his thrust. "You're such a greedy girl. And so fucking small. I need you ready for me, sweetheart." He pressed the heel of his hand against her clit, rubbing as his fingers fucked her. Then he added another finger and bit down on the skin of her shoulder, skimming it with his teeth.

"I want you," Jessamine said between pants. "Hesha. Please. Oh, stars. Yes."

"Come again for me, Jess. Open up for me."

Somehow, her legs were freed, Johesha doing something to relieve her of the bloomers, and she opened her legs wider, her feet against the bed, thrusting her pelvis against Johesha's hand.

"Yes," he growled. "Fucking take what you want, Jessamine. I fucking love it. You're so godsdamned perfect."

As if his words were what she needed, her body seized, clamping tightly around his fingers, and she cried out, the sound of his name cutting through the cottage, filling it with her ecstasy.

He groaned. "Fuck, Jess. I could come this way, and my cock hasn't even touched you yet."

As she came down from the orgasm, Johesha kissed down her body, making a trail to her core. She moaned. "I need you."

"Oh, I know, sweetheart," he said, his tongue, slipping softly against her clit.

She convulsed.

He chuckled, then drove his tongue into her, moaning as he did, his hands on her thighs, keeping them wide as he cleaned and slurped, making messy noises with relish.

Jessamine followed him, her body hungry for more of what he was giving her. She grabbed the back of his head, jerking against his mouth. "Please, Hesha," she whined, unable to help herself, unsure if she was begging him to stop or to continue, sensitive in a way that had her wanting to escape but also to stay.

He drew away and licked his lips as he got up onto his knees between her splayed legs. With a growl, he wiped his mouth with the back of one arm. That intensity devoured her as he worked to get his trousers open.

"I want you naked," she said. "I want to see you."

Johesha hesitated but then stood and shucked off his clothing a piece at a time revealing his form. Beautiful in its brutality. His broad shoulders, the curves of his biceps, the width and sculpted perfection of his chest and his abdomen that highlighted his narrow waist and hips. His muscles rippled as he moved, symmetry accessorized with scars. His shaft jutted up, and his massive thighs, his legs offered her a perfect specimen of a man. A soldier. A guard. A protector. A predator.

Jessamine moved up to her knees, reaching out to touch him. "Gods, Hesha. So beautiful." She slipped a hand over his arm, across his chest, and it jerked under her touch. She wrapped a hand around his massive erection. "You're… big. I don't know if…"

"It will fit," he growled, surging forward.

Jessamine was on her back again, covered by the massive man. "I haven't done this before," she admitted.

"Do you want to do this?" he asked, his mouth making art against her neck, her jaw. "That's the only important thing."

"Yes. With you," she breathed, sliding her hands up his naked back, feeling the scars against her palms. "Gods, yes."

He stopped kissing her and met her gaze. "Then we'll make it good. Together. You. And me." He kissed her between words.

She nodded, and he reached between them, sliding his fingers through her sex. He growled. "So fucking wet. For me." Then he grabbed his cock and slid it through her sultriness. His head caressed her clit, making her moan before notching it at her opening.

"Spread your legs, sweetheart, and take a breath."

She did.

"Release it slowly."

As she let out her breath, Johesha pushed in equally as slowly, gritting his teeth as he did. "Gods, Jess. Fuck, sweetheart, you feel so good."

She stretched and burned but didn't shy away from the discomfort. Instead, she sank into it, widening her legs. "More," she whispered against his skin.

He withdrew.

She cried out at the loss.

He sank in again, a little deeper.

"Oh," she gasped at the sensations alive inside her. "Hesha."

He withdrew again. "Hang on." Then he drove a little deeper, a little harder.

Jessamine cried out.

Johesha stilled. "Am I hurting you?"

She shook her head, trying to find words, but they were difficult to form in the mindless oblivion of passion careening through her. "No. No. You feel so good." She rocked her hips. "I want more. I want all of you."

Johesha groaned, withdrawing again before driving deeper. Again. Again. "Oh, fuck. Jess," he panted as he pushed all the way inside of her.

Jessamine cried out with both pain and pleasure, the pleasure overriding everything. "Yes, Hesha. Yes. Please."

The onslaught of his slow rhythm continued, diligent persistence to break her into a million pieces of want. She'd come on her fingers, his fingers, his mouth, but this was different as pleasure built inside of her. She couldn't control the sounds emanating from her, deep and guttural, needy and exclamatory. His sounds were different, but no less focused.

Until his controlled rhythm changed, until he pounded into her with exquisite savagery. Everything shook and rattled and rocked. Her cries gained strength, filling the room, and his grunts matched as he drove into her again and again.

"Oh. Fuck. Jessamine," he bit out. "You're breaking me, baby. I can't…" But his words were cut off as he lost the rhythm, his own need overtaking everything else. "I want to feel you–"

She wasn't sure what he meant, lost to her own pleasure, until he buried himself inside her, leaned back, and found her clit with his fingers.

"I need to feel you come," he panted, pulsing inside her with short, light strokes and thumbing her clit.

"Hesha," she mewled, needing the release, seeking it.

"Fuck. Fuck. Fuck," he chanted, surging forward, lifting one of her legs over his arm to spread her wider, locking her against him.

"Oh gods," she cried out as her body tensed, preparing for its release. "Oh. Hesha. Please," she begged.

"Yes." he grunted. "Yes." Slamming into her. "Fucking come, Jess."

And she did, crying out his name as everything inside her exploded in mass of wonder.

Johesha groaned. "Gods, Jess. You feel so fucking good. I'm–" Then he tensed, burying himself all the way, as far as he could go. "Fuck. I'm coming," he bit out.

She grabbed hold of his lower back, rose up, and held him tightly, needing him even closer, knowing they had achieved this paradise. Together.

Johesha

The wind was still howling outside when he woke, Jessamine's warm body tangled up with his. He glanced down at her nestled in against him, her cheek pressed against his chest, and a feeling he didn't recognize surged through him, nearly stealing his breath. He liked it, wanted more of it, and couldn't keep from running a hand over her head to make sure she was real.

Jessamine adjusted, tilting her head to look up at him, and smiled. His heart twisted with an unnamed longing he was afraid to name just then, and he realized fear had been controlling much of the way he responded to her. Fear, mostly, of his unworthiness, and now fear that he might let her down. Fear of losing someone that was so integral and important.

"You aren't sleeping," he said.

"Who could sleep like this?" She laughed quietly, resuming her watch. "Besides, I think I've slept enough for a lifetime." Her fingers traced the scars on his torso. "And I just wanted to be close to you."

He enjoyed the feel of her fingers traveling his skin.

"I've been listening to your heartbeat."

"What does it tell you?" he asked.

"How strong you are. How resilient."

Johesha drew her in tighter. "What are we doing?"

"Enjoying each other."

"Is that all this is?" he asked, suddenly afraid it was, and he knew he wanted, needed more.

She shook her head against his chest. "No."

He tightened his hold but didn't say anything. Neither did she, as if both of them understood there wasn't a future yet. They had to get Jessamine home, to break the spell and the wizard's hold.

"What if there wasn't a spell?" Jessamine asked, and she tilted again, glancing up.

"I would…" But he stopped, unsure. He hadn't thought about it before. His desires had only been to get past the spell, get back, face the consequences of abandoning his post. He hadn't thought this was a possibility.

"I'll go first," she said, as if sensing his struggle. "If there wasn't a spell, I would make you breakfast and make you tell me secrets about your childhood to get bites."

He chuckled.

"Your turn."

"I would take you out and teach you how to defend yourself."

She smiled with an airy laugh driven through her nose. "Said like a true royal guard. You can still do that with the spell."

"True enough."

"What if you were still in Jast?"

"Would you be with me?" he asked.

She turned, rolling over so that she was on him and could face him. "Yes."

"Then I would like to take you to meet my family."

She grinned, a blush staining her cheeks, and it made him want to kiss her again. Instead, he asked, "What if I asked you to come to Jast with me?"

Her eyes flashed to his, and she paused. He could see the thoughts drift across her features, and though in their scenario he wasn't asking, they both knew that was what he wanted to.

"Then," she said, "I would tell my family how much I love them, and they could come and visit me."

Stars, he wanted to kiss her again.

"What if I gave you another scar, on accident?" she asked.

He chuckled. "I would like to see you try."

"Oh?" She arched her eyebrows. "So confident."

"Yes. How would you do it?"

She shrugged, smiling. "Where is this one from?" she

asked, her finger following the outline of a scar near his ribs.

"Prince Lachlan wasn't the most… complacent prince in his youth. Spent a lot of time chasing him into misadventures. Got us into trouble more often than not. I think this one was from a band of outlaws that had been holding up an inn on one of those adventures. Broke a rib and nearly punctured a lung."

"Lachlan caused all these?"

He chuckled. "No. No. The idealistic ruffian just dragged me out looking for his next adventure, which usually meant finding unsavory characters doing unsavory things."

"It's amazing he's so pretty, still." She looked up at him with a mischievous gleam on her face. "I bet you had something to do with that."

Strangely jealous, he rolled her onto her back. "You think Lachlan is pretty, huh?" Next, he settled a leg in between her thighs, forcing them wider.

She laughed. Her fingertip traced a small scar through his left eyebrow. "Too pretty for me." She rose up and quickly kissed him. "I like my men with some edge." She kissed the scar near his eye, lingering. "And grit." She moved to a scar on his chin and licked it. "And strength." She leaned back and looked at him.

"Men?" he teased, sliding his hands down, and finding her wet, plunged his fingers inside her.

She gasped, grabbing hold of his shoulders, then sighed, "Man. Only one."

"That's better," he said with a smile against her neck,

his fingers creating a rhythm that had her breathing hard against his ear. The sound made him harder.

"Just you," she moaned as he paid attention to her clit.

"Perfect," he said and kissed her.

"Only you," she said against his mouth.

"Mine," he said, then spent more time proving it to her.

Later, after another quick round of sex, time spent talking and laughing, and a more languorous round of making love, Johesha fell asleep. He woke to the sun shining through the space in the curtains, Jessamine across the bed, her naked back to him. He rolled toward her, following the outline of her spine with his eyes, the curls of her dark hair against her skin, the blanket draped across the small of her back. As much as he wanted to wake her with kisses, he didn't.

Instead, he pondered the immediate future.

One more day.

He relished the thought of this purgatory. Of wishing it would last but knowing it couldn't. Even as he delighted in the idea, the reality of it weighed on him. They were too close to Crue, and by now, the wizard would know they were gone.

With a sigh, his body's needs pulled him from the warmth of the bed. After, he pulled on his trousers and undershirt before making his way in to light the fire, except the flames already danced inside the hearth. He'd anticipated black coals by now and had hoped for hot embers, but magic proved to touch the cottage once more. Thinking of food, he went into the kitchen to see what he could assemble for them, to search for any coffee. But even that had been magically tended, a pot percolating on the stove and food kept warm in the oven.

"Stars," he muttered. "I suppose I should say thank you."

The coffee pot bubbled a little faster. Or perhaps that was his imagination.

He prepared a tray for Jessamine and himself and carried it into the room where she slept. After setting it aside, he knelt next to the bed in front of her and gently slid the hair from in front of her face. "Jessamine," he whispered and kissed the corner of her mouth, lingering a moment to commit this moment to his memory. The feel of her soft skin under his calloused fingertips. Her silky hair curled wildly, rumpled from sleep. Her long, dark lashes that brushed a patch of tiny, barely perceptible freckles on her cheeks. Everything about her was perfect.

She moaned and stretched like a cat, then smiled. He was certain if she could purr, she would have. Her body was used thoroughly, and she was happy for it, if her smile was any indication. That look on her face made him feel a thousand feet tall. He hadn't known he could feel this satisfied, then again, he hadn't ever allowed himself to explore this possibility.

"What time is it?" she asked, her voice hoarse with sleep.

"Time to get up and eat," he said. "I brought you food."

Her eyes opened, blinking as she focused on him. "Am I dreaming?" she whispered, closed her eyes again, and moaned. "If I'm dreaming, please don't wake me up."

"Not dreaming." He smiled and dipped his head to kiss her again and found sliding into desire for her was easy. "Eat first."

"So bossy," she said and sat up, pulling the blankets up under her arms to cover her nudity.

He resisted the urge to pull the blanket from her body and instead set the tray of food on her lap. There were breakfast cakes and strips of bacon. Berries with whipped cream.

"You made this?"

"Would that surprise you?"

"Yes."

"I didn't. The cottage."

"Magic."

He nodded and sat next to her, taking a sip of coffee as he did. "I went out, and there it was all ready for you."

"For us." She smiled, shyly this time, as if she weren't sure she should lump them together.

Johesha found that he liked it, and it scared him. "Us," he agreed.

And so it went between them throughout the day. Laughter, diving deeper into the depths of one another's worlds, making love. The cottage took care of them, seeing to all their needs. From food to warmth to cleaning, they wanted for nothing. It was as if they existed in a bubble of magic where nothing could harm them.

Except both of them knew this magical respite couldn't last.

That night as they sat in front of the fire talking,

Jessamine chatted about remembering when her brother was born, about being there as a family, helping Scarlett through his birth. Johesha loved listening to her, and it made him glide into thoughts of his own family. Except, a thought consumed him that the next day the magic of this would end, throwing them back into the chaos of Crue's spell. That he might lose her, that he didn't have a family to go home to anymore, that maybe his guard family wouldn't want him anymore.

Fear clutched at his heart, and he grabbed her and kissed her.

She pulled back and searched his face, so perceptive. "What is it?"

But he couldn't get the words past his lips, wasn't sure what the words were, so instead decided to show her, to worship her. "May I?"

When she smiled and kissed him sweetly, he ignited the fire between them in front of the fire, kissing her with intention, drawing out her pleasure and prolonging it until she was a needy mess on the floor begging for release. Then he entered her from behind, marking her so she would always remember him in spite of the spell that would steal her away.

After their release, he lay with her in front of the fire, his heart warm with her even as the winter crept toward them, the darkness visible between the curtains reminding him that time was slipping away.

"Tomorrow?" Jessamine asked.

Johesha hadn't said anything right away. Instead, he'd run his fingers through her hair wishing this wasn't now.

"Tomorrow."

She turned to face him. "Do you think the spell will return? You know. And compel me to return to the manor?"

"I don't know."

She was quiet then, and Johesha allowed himself to watch her thoughts flit across her face like the light from the fire. "If it does," she said and swallowed. Then her eyes jumped up to meet his. "I need you to know something."

He slid his hand through her hair again, relishing the ability to touch her like this, the freedom to do it, hating that it would end. "What's that?"

"I love you."

He stilled, then blinked, his heart sucking in those words and allowing them to bolster the beat, recognizing them, knowing them, realizing that is what he'd been afraid to name.

"You don't have to say it back," she quickly said. "But I need you to know, in case I don't remember this. In case you're lost to me. I can't leave here without you knowing—"

But he didn't let her finish. Instead, he kissed her, in awe of her, in awe of her ability to let down her guard, in awe of her ability to love him. He rolled her onto her back and tried to show her what her words meant, how he felt them too, even if he was too afraid to say them.

Jessamine

The next morning, after eating and lingering and finding ways to prolong the inevitable, Jessamine faced Johesha at the door, bundled up and ready to leave the cottage. She'd told him she loved him, and though he hadn't said it back, she hadn't expected him to, hadn't said it for that purpose. She understood that the sentiment was hers, and she had no regrets. His response to her admission had been enough to reinforce her feelings and that he reciprocated them in a powerful way.

Now, her fear clung to her ribs like a spider in a web. She didn't want to leave the cottage, and it had nothing to do with the magic. The hope of the day should have been life-giving sunshine; she was to be reunited with her family. Except standing there with Johesha fussing over her outerwear, worrying that it wasn't warm enough, revealed a truth that even her admission hadn't.

She didn't want to be without him. Somehow, he'd become her family, and she didn't know what would happen when they found their way home.

"We'll head to the roadway," Johesha was saying. "Then we'll hide there to intercept them."

Jessamine grabbed hold of his face and pressed her lips to his. He stilled, surprised perhaps, but then kissed her back. Then she pulled away and pressed her forehead to his and took a breath, breathing him in before asking, "Are we still using the berries?"

He breathed with her, his hands gripping her hips, then nodded. "But we'll be headed back toward the manor, so if it comes to it, there's that." He lifted his lips to her forehead and kissed her, lingering as if to hold onto the moment as much as she was trying to.

"I'm afraid," she whispered.

He wrapped his arms around her. "You're not alone."

She leaned back to gaze at him and nodded.

Then, with her heart banging inside her chest like a horrible drum, she watched Johesha open the door and step out of the magical cottage, ignoring the weight of apprehension that everything was about to change. She hesitated at the threshold. Clinging to bravery she didn't feel but knew she needed, she followed Johesha, pulling the door shut behind her and closing her eyes, waiting for the spell to take hold. While there seemed to be a lingering desire to return, it wasn't an all-encompassing need.

Something had changed.

She glanced back at the cottage. "Thank you," she whispered.

"Everything all right?" Johesha asked, waiting for her a few steps away.

"I think so." She smiled and stepped after him with her snowshoes.

They'd only walked fifty paces from the cottage when the world around them grew colder, the snow turned to ice, and her shoes caught. She couldn't move. "Johesha," she cried out and looked, but he was also stuck.

"Johesha."

The voice froze everything inside of her. Crue. He clucked his tongue, but as Jessamine whirled her head around, she couldn't see him. She shivered, her breath crystalizing before her.

"How did you do it?" Crue called out from somewhere in the forest.

Johesha swore and struggled against the ice encasing his shoes. He didn't have any leverage to help him break free, so he went for the bow with a near preternatural speed she hadn't anticipated.

The clapping of hands resounded around them, the vibration bouncing through the trees, knocking snow from the limbs to the ground into deeper piles. The shadows between the trees deepened, but there was nothing else to mark where it originated.

Her gaze darted around, trying to locate the wizard.

"Did you think you would get away, huntsman?" Crue said and materialized from behind a group of trees near the path ahead of them. He was dressed in his dark clothes, looking like he always did, handsome and lethal all at once. A giant, dark shadow undulated directly behind the wizard as if it were his aura.

The darkling.

Jessamine's blood ran even colder. "Father. We were. Just coming back," she spoke the lie brokenly, the cold making her teeth chattering. "Eldram Berries. Potion."

Crue walked forward. "Awww, daughter. You don't expect me to believe that do you?"

"I just want to get back to the manor," she said through the chattering, deciding to pretend she was still under the spell's influence. "We got stuck in the storm."

Crue hummed, walking closer, the darkling floating behind him. "If that were the case, you would have returned yesterday. As soon as my back was turned, you betrayed me."

"Stop," Johesha said.

"Or what?" Crue asked, unfazed. "You'll shoot?"

Johesha let the arrow fly; it snapped from the weapon, whizzing so quickly that she was certain that Crue would be hit, but he waved a hand, and the arrow changed course, imbedding itself into a tree.

Jessamine's heart seized with fear, unsure what Crue would do. "Leave him alone," she begged.

Crue's eyes flashed at her. "I loathe your begging," he said, and she knew it. He'd said it before. "Too bad you don't have magic, daughter. It would be fun to see what you could do."

She would use it if she did. "Leave him alone or I will kill you."

"How?" Crue laughed, a sharp, short sound of incredulity, then pouted. "What will you do?"

Johesha yanked with his legs even as he pulled and nocked another arrow. The shoes cracked, giving way, but he wasn't free yet. Jessamine wasn't sure what would happen when he did get free, if Crue or the darkling might kill him or if it would be the other way around.

"I told you to leave her alone, huntsman. Remember?" Crue asked. "My message was clear. Gave you a chance to heed my warning, but obviously, you didn't listen."

With another tug, Johesha pulled his first leg free of the shoe, but as he planted his foot, it slipped, and he couldn't get leverage for his remaining leg. "You hurt her. I will kill you."

"You think I want to hurt her?" Crue offered him the tilt of his head and a deeper pout of his lips as he tapped them with a long, thin finger. The golden ring glinted in the light. "And no, you won't." His countenance brightened as he clapped his hands together. "I know! Let's play a game instead. What happens when the hunter becomes the hunted?" Crue chanted a chain of words, flicked his hands, and green light burst from his fingertips right into Johesha, who grunted, then yelled as the sound of his bones cracking filled the forest.

Jessamine screamed and continued screaming as tears flowed from her eyes and froze on her cheeks.

Johesha's form crumpled, then shifted. His clothes, his

skin tore until what was Johesha no longer existed and what stood in his place was a chestnut-hued stag, tall, proud, and angry. His antlers were broad and wide. The animal huffed steam from his nose and stomped at the frozen snow.

Crue laughed with delight, clapping his hands. "Look at that! Isn't that an amazing bit of work, daughter?"

"Johesha!" she screamed and bent forward in anguish.

Suddenly, Crue was at her side, dragging her up and holding her head to face the stag. "Look at him," he said cruelly. "This is your fault. This will be the last you ever see of him. Like this."

The stag reared up on his hind legs, kicking with his front.

"Run, beast!" Crue shouted at Johesha. "Darkling. Time to hunt. Bring me his heart!"

"No!" Jessamine screamed. "No!"

The stag darted away, and the darkling chittered, disappearing like a shadow between the trees after the deer.

Jessamine screamed.

"Hush, child," Crue said, pressing his finger against her temple, and everything turned black around her.

"Jessamine," a voice called to her from the darkness.

"Jessamine," it repeated. Even as the voice called, she didn't want to return to her mind and body. An empty maw of nothingness slid around her like slick oil, sucking up light, and joy, and goodness. The presence weighed her down, pinned her in the depths of her unconscious, but an inner voice warned her that she couldn't stay even if what lay ahead was worse.

"You aren't alone," a voice said, a conglomeration of her family, of Johesha, of someone else she couldn't name.

She blinked her eyes open.

Crue was there at her bedside—in the manor—sitting in a chair. With his long legs crossed, his handsome face devoid of any emotion other than boredom, he tilted his head. He was a spider, and she was caught in his web.

"You're awake. Excellent. It's been so tedious waiting for you. A day and a half, sleepy head! How are you feeling?"

She didn't answer as the recent events crashed through her memory. Tears filled her eyes, and she sucked in a breath remembering what had happened to Johesha. "I hate you."

"Join the club." He grinned. "It's a rather large one, I daresay. But even in spite of that, I have a gift for you. Even after you betrayed me. A token of my affection."

She watched him reach for an ornate silver box sitting on a table next to him. A small rectangle no larger than a loaf of bread, he fingered the silver latch and clicked his tongue. "I trusted you, daughter. Trusted that you were mine."

"I will never be yours."

He slammed his hand down on the table, and it rattled, tipping the vase with a single bloom. The water dripped onto the rug below. "Trusted you would never betray me with filth!" He took a deep breath, calming himself. "I trusted you would become my apprentice, but after this…" His voice faded. "I have doubts."

She refused to respond, even though that was what he seemed to want.

He lifted the box and studied it. "I could blame it on that horrible huntsman." He placed the container in his lap. "I wanted to tell myself that he forced you to leave me, that you were tricked, but I don't believe that's true."

He paused as if waiting for her to deny it.

She wouldn't.

"Then there's the matter of the spell." He ran his finger over the top of the box, lingering in the grooves of the plating. "I haven't figured out how you subverted it."

He stood, still holding the box, which he set on her lap. "I went to great trouble to get this gift for you, daughter. And there's a glorious tale behind what's in the box."

Jessamine shrank away, wary.

"You see, I had to send the monster on a hunt."

Her gaze jerked from the box to Crue, and she shook her head.

"Open the box."

She shook her head, tears pooling then streaming from her eyes.

"Open it," he said, the evenness of his voice terrifying. "You'll appreciate the trouble I went to get it for you. A little memento of your dalliance." He lurched forward and grabbed her cheeks, forcing her to look at him. "I sent my creature after the heart of the huntsman, turned into a stag." The sinister smile on Crue's face faded, and his eyes turned dark with rage and hatred. "Open. The. Box."

Jessamine mumbled "no" over and over again, squeezing her eyes shut.

"Open it!" he yelled.

She jumped, then shook her head.

"Open it," he snapped.

With trembling hands, she reached for the box, flipped the latch, and lifted the lid.

"Isn't it beautiful?"

Inside was the dark tissue of a gory heart, utterly still.

She screamed.

PART 3

"Now my charms are all o'erthrown,
And what strength I have's mine own, -
Which is most faint: now, 'tis true,
I must be here confined by you...
But release me from my bands
With the help of your good hands:
Gentle breath of yours my sails
Must fill, or else my project fails,
Which was to please: now I want
Spirits to enforce, art to enchant;
And my ending is despair,
Unless I be relieved by prayer,
Which pierces so, that it assaults
Mercy itself, and frees all faults.
As you from crimes would pardon'd be,
Let your indulgence set me free."
— William Shakespeare, *The Tempest*

Johesha

Johesha ran, the four legs spurring him through the forest with speed he'd never imagined. He could change direction with a thought, leap over obstacles that might thwart him as a man.

But the realization didn't matter. He was running for his life, a monster on his heels. He twisted, he turned, he crashed through the underbrush. He leapt rocks, a river. He squeezed between trees, raced through meadows, but never left the monster behind.

This was what it felt like to be prey.

His muscles began to ache.

His lungs.

His heart raced, taxed, feeling like it might burst from his chest.

The weight of his head—the antlers—caught and tugged.

He was going to die.

Suddenly, he emerged in a glen. He darted across the expanse, only to discover that hidden under the boughs of the trees was a cliff face. There was no way up. No way to skirt up the side. He was trapped.

He spun around to dart out, only the way was blocked.

There like a specter of shadow, the darkling undulated from the darkness of the trees. "I must take your heart," it said, its voice a horrific amalgamation of anger, hatred, and fear.

Inside the animal, Johesha crouched. He wouldn't die without a fight.

"At peace, huntsman," it said. "Mercy for mercy. My debt is paid." The darkling watched him a few more beats of his stag's frantic heart, then the creature turned and flew away into the woods.

Tentatively, the stag wandered back through the forest. He returned to the cottage where the evergreens offered shadows and darkness. He clung to the places where instincts told him he might be safer, unsure why he was choosing to remain where civilization could unmake him rather than drifting deeper into the woods where hiding was simpler. There was little more than the earth, the sounds of the forest, his hooves crunching in snow, and his senses guiding him. His instincts seemed to say, *"Here.*

This is where you need to be." A memory, perhaps that he couldn't recall any more lingered in the recesses of a human mind, attempting to hang on to a woman who seemed important to him.

He lifted his head, sniffed. His eyes, not as keen, searched for something, but the specifics of what were lost. The scent of evergreens, snow, and winter earth filled him with calm, central to his being, so he lowered his heavy head and chuffed at the snow, stepping forward as he foraged. He came to a lovely patch of grass to graze, the massive rack of horns stretching out in front of him as he relished the sweet, earthy flavor on his tongue. He didn't consider that it was the dead of winter, why might there be a patch of fresh grass at all.

The snap of a twig made him start, his head darting up with fear.

His heart pounded and his muscles tensed, readying for flight.

But it was an old woman standing several feet away, one that deep down, he was certain he knew. If he could just grab hold of the slippery memory.

He lifted his nose, taking in her scent, the sweet, pungent aroma of a spring day as dark earth splits open and new seeds cracking with life emerge. Her white hair was woven into a braid, her light skin wrinkled, but her nose and cheeks were flushed with cold. She wore a dark coat and shimmered with a violet light, absolutely still, as if she knew a slight movement would send him bolting back into hiding. All but for her eyes. Those moved, studying him, weighing him.

"Hello, hunter," she finally said. Her brow bunched and her gaze drifted down toward his hooves. "You still wear my gift." She nodded at the strip of leather tied around one of his forelegs. "Good."

His ears twitched at her words, the animal he'd become wary and uncertain, but the man trapped inside the animal cognizant.

She hummed a note, a thinking-note that told him she was deciding something. "I can't undo the spell." Her head tilted, studying him, and her voice was a hint above a whisper. "But, since you wear my thread, I might be able to modify it." She slowly crouched.

Johesha followed her movement, his muscles still tight with the power to bolt.

She opened her satchel. A patchwork of fabric and leather she'd had over one shoulder now set on the ground at her feet. "Always good to be prepared," she muttered as she reached in and carefully moved bits and bobbles hidden inside. There was clinking and thuds of heavy objects that certainly shouldn't have been inside a small bag.

Johesha's stag started but stayed.

"That should do it," she said, then glanced at him and added, "Don't go anywhere." With a snap of her wrists, she opened the mouth of the bag wider and stepped in. Johesha watched as she descended, as though she were descending a staircase. The bag swallowed her whole, then slumped back to the snowy earth.

And it was silent.

Johesha ate, one eye on the bag as he did. Time passed,

though it was more difficult to ascertain now, his animal brain in control, but eventually the bag jerked, and the old woman's fingers and hands arrived first, then her head, as if the patchwork tote now gave birth to her.

"There!" she said and looked for him, a smile growing on her face when she saw him. "Good! You listened." She stepped from the bag, freeing both feet from it and straightened. Facing him, she held out an object.

His nose twitched.

"I had to think about what a stag might eat," she explained.

In the palm of her hand was a shiny red apple shimmering in violet and golden light, a delicious perfume infiltrating and overtaking all his senses. He wasn't as afraid of her as his need for what she held compelled him. He took a tentative step forward, then another, then stretched, trying to reach the fruit she held. Another step closer and another, until his teeth clamped onto the fleshy apple.

"I'm going to touch you," she explained and tentatively reached out to grab hold of one of his antlers as he ate. Then she spoke: "Seek the tether between man and beast—"

Warmth moved through him.

"—sever the bond in two. One will use the light to feast. The other in the dark will rule."

He continued munching on the apple as the intensity of the heat inside him increased and spread.

"Seek and find the heart that's true to undo the tie that links their troth. An unending vow to bubble and brew, a steadfast oath to reunite them both. But beware that death to one is death, and neither will take another breath."

The heat wrapped around his innards, squeezed, then was gone.

Johesha jerked back, most of the apple finished.

"Here. The rest," she coaxed, undulating her palm to capture his attention. When he stretched out for the rest, she said, "You will be glad I give this to you." She laid something over his back, though he couldn't be sure what it was. "Go to Sevens," she continued. "Find the cottage in the woods. Save Jessamine."

With the apple gone, Johesha jerked away from the woman and darted back into the trees, but he stopped and looked over his shoulder. The woman raised her hand in farewell. "Don't forget, huntsman. A true heart is the key."

With a leap, Johesha left her behind and raced through the forest, headed north. He didn't consider stopping, a compulsion to keep moving his guide. He stopped to graze and drink water, his senses constantly on high alert, listening to the forest noises, evading predators. There were men in the forest, hunters. He skirted around them and ran away, cutting through the dense woods. As he sliced his way through the forest, he didn't ponder his existence. He just existed, his body and instincts guiding him. As the sun began its descent, he knew he needed to find a safe place to shelter and eventually found a thicket in which to hide. Exhausted, he slept.

And dreamed.

He was running through the woods as a man.

Confusion and fear rode his back, making his breathing ragged and his heartbeat erratic.

Something was wrong.

Something was after him.

He ran, turning this way and that, the snow and ice slippery. The woods were a maze, the path obscured by trees and bramble. He leapt over frozen streams, bursting through the bramble. The terror that followed on his heels was filled with sinister intent. He whirled around and there blocking his only escape, was the dark monster undulating in shadows.

"Mercy for mercy," it said.

Johesha's eyes snapped open, his heart racing in his chest.

The sun was down, inky shadows making the world around him dark. He stretched, his muscles burning strangely, as if they'd been torn apart and put back together. He blinked and realized that he was once more himself! He had his hands, his body. He tried to recall where he was, what had happened. He glanced at his surroundings, but the darkness made it impossible to ascertain much of anything. Tentatively, he reached out and felt branches, thorns, and realized he was in an enclosed nest made of bushes and bramble.

He sat up. Where was Jessamine? What had happened?

He closed his eyes, trying to remember.

He pictured Jessamine. Felt her skin under his palms. He saw her dressed, ready for a journey through the snow.

Then Crue. He had found them and cast a spell.

He'd been changed.

And he remembered running from the darkling, and when he'd been caught, the monster had spared him. "A mercy for mercy."

Johesha opened his eyes, and he held out his arms. How did he have his hands again, his legs, his feet?

The old woman.

He'd gone back to the cottage, as if it had been a fixed point in his internal compass. *Return here if you need me.* The appearance of the old woman had made it seem as if she'd been waiting for him. Though he couldn't remember the particulars, he could recall the sensations. That she'd spoken and touched him. He'd experienced warmth and comfort. She'd helped him.

He checked for her leather gift still on his wrist, and his gaze caught on a dark lump near his hip. His heart pitched wildly, unsure what lay near him. The darkness inside the bramble cave was filtered only by intermittent flecks of moonlight. Shoring up his courage, he reached out and touched the lump. It wasn't an animal but a bag, and he seemed to recall the old widow hanging it on him. Johesha pulled it toward him, but he couldn't see a thing, and instead of searching its contents, left the nest where the animal he'd been had taken him.

Once outside in the forest, the moonlight was a twinge brighter. Naked and shivering, Johesha opened the bag to see what she had given him. Clothes! Boots! A coat! He dressed. There were other things: a strip of leather, a small lantern, several bits of parchment labeled with names, a vial of liquid marked *'for Tomas,'* a dagger, and a bow.

Johesha lit the lantern and opened the parchment marked as his.

Dear Huntsman,

You won't remember the spell, but here is what you need to know: the wizard changed you into a stag. I have changed the spell so that when the sun goes down, you will be a man once more. But beware, the moment the sun rises, the animal will return. Be prepared for it. If you or the creature die, both of you will perish, so take care. To break it, you must find a true heart. Hurry to Sevens, to the Fareview cottage. I have enclosed tools to help retrieve the eldest girl. The end is near.

Johesha stuffed everything back into the bag, which was certainly too small to be carrying so much. It also wasn't heavy for so many things, but rather light. He didn't question it—not anymore. He'd seen too much, experienced too much to question the existence of magic.

Instead, he focused on what he could control and looked up into the night sky painted with a plethora of variations of blue sparkling with diamond stars. But he only needed to find one—Raffa's Heart—the brightest star that directed him north. It would help him navigate toward Sevens, toward the Fareviews, toward saving the woman he loved.

Crue

Crue marched into the workshop, darkness riding his shoulders. He tossed the box on the workbench, ignoring the crack of glass as the silver container smashed through the vials, not any happier for having taunted Jessamine. Her scream was still ringing through him like a discordant set of notes. A lament. But the vile deed had to be done. He was the one deciding things. He was the one in control.

His hands flat on the workshop table, he leaned over it, head hanging, and thought about King Zollah Cumbria—Scarlett's father—a man so wrecked with grief over the loss of his wife, he'd lost himself and was the ruination of a kingdom. Crue might have been a party to that ruination, but it had been for the greater good. Well, his greater good. There had been things to learn about the art of necromancy.

That had been a turning point in Crue's existence. A before Azleah and an after. Everything since Azleah—Scarlett, he thought with a sneer—had stolen his control from him. And that wasn't acceptable. This was him taking it back!

With a sigh he sat up once more and waved his hand over the mess. The shards of glass, the contents strewn across the countertop rose into the air. With a flick of his fingers, the glittering glass, the dried herbs and contents moved, swirling and shifting in front of him.

Crue hadn't meant to make such a mess of Cumbria's grief, of course, or of Scarlett's. He'd wanted to grant the man his wish to be with his wife once more, to find the means to control death. The experimentation hadn't gone as he'd hoped, leaving collateral damage. A necessary evil in the name of progress.

He separated the bits with his magic like a river splitting off into streams. Contents sorted, he collected the broken glass and with his power, melted it into pulsating globs, fusing the molecules together once more. Next, he reformed it into whole, cylindrical vials once more. Finally, like rows of ants marching from one place to another, he replaced the contents in the glass containers.

He could build things rather than only breaking them, but sometimes deconstruction was necessary to create the proper outcome. Separating Jessamine from the huntsman had been necessary to achieve the proper outcome for his goals.

He set the vials back into their holders, fixing the mess he'd made, and wondered if the mess with Jessamine could be fixed. Her grief worried him even if he didn't understand it. Certainly, she hadn't grown so fond of the huntsman in such a short time. He wasn't interested in fixing things with her, only coming to a mutual understanding. He had goals to achieve, bargains that needed to be kept. And he needed godblood hearts to do it. Granted, she had one. He'd hoped to groom her to be his apprentice, but if she refused, he had one heart to go. Scarlett's. That and the gifts she'd stolen. She would pay for her part in ruining his plans. Years! So many years.

Now, besides the situation with Jessamine, he had another mess to fix; he'd missed the messengers because of his daughter's flight. So much like her mother. That made him smile a bit, but then the small bit of warmth he felt along with the thought of his daughter faded. He needed to get to Scarlett.

"You hurt her," the darkling hissed from its cage.

The creature was satisfied for the time being having hunted and filled itself with the blood of the huntsman. Such a fitting end. A full circle comeuppance just like he planned for Scarlett. Poetic justice, if he did say so himself.

"What do you care?" he muttered as he retrieved a bit of parchment to pen a demand he would deliver to Scarlett posthaste.

"You do not love her?"

"What does love have to do with it?"

The darkling chittered in its cell but didn't respond.

"What do you even know about love?" Crue asked.

The darkling remained silent.

Crue was grateful not to have to talk to it any further and finished writing out his demands for the next meeting. He blew on the ink to dry it, then folded the parchment and melted the green wax, watching it drip like drops of blood and pool before sealing it with the figure of a crow. While he would usually lay it in the windowsill of the workshop, that was currently covered with snow, so he carried it up to the window of his study, opened it, and set the parchment on the window's ledge.

After, he refastened the window and returned to the workshop, constructed his summoning square, then stepped inside and provided his blood. With his eyes closed, he called to the spirit of the closest raven.

The next time he blinked his eyes open, he was the raven.

The blackbird took flight, drifting over the tips of the pine trees, ducking down and through them and over the landscape until the manor was in sight. The animal flew to the windowsill, took up the parchment in its talons, and set out for Scarlett's cottage.

The landscape rushed underneath him like the current of a summer-swollen river. The winter woods, the glimpse of frozen land and lakes. Winter rivers trickled with icy, winter shorelines, puffed with snow. He flew past other birds, drifted through low foggy clouds, until he soared over the thatched rooftops of the village, tendrils of smoke drifting up into the gray sky. The bird banked farther northwest, ducking down into the trees to sway between dark trunks, sharp branches, and through shadows of the Whitling Woods until the raven jerked upward at the encampment of soldiers. Woodsmoke drifted amongst the structures. Soldiers congregated around fire pits, some playing games, others eating and laughing together. Even more soldiers were at work on tasks while others kept watch.

Still, he flew until he arrived at the cottage.

The small structure was dark and dreary, as though no one lived there anymore. The first time he'd seen it, it had looked much the same, asleep with the occupants inside, frozen in time. Now it was frozen in time, waiting for the return of Jessamine. It gave him no small amount of satisfaction to recognize that the grief descended on this dwelling was because of him. Smoke drifted from the chimney, however, occupants still interred inside, as stuck in the winter as the landscape around them. He dropped the letter on the porch near the front door.

Then the raven's body hit the barrier, and it squawked, before it leapt onto a snow-laden flower box a few feet away to watch through a window.

One of Scarlett's daughters appeared, her hair the color of a shiny copper sunrise. "Did you hear that?"

Another voice murmured. The golden god appeared behind her.

Crue narrowed his raven's eyes and squawked. If anything could thwart him and his plans, the deities could. The only thing he had going for him on that count was their ambivalence and permissive distance from the affairs of mortals. And he was mortal. For now.

The front door opened, and though he couldn't see it, he kept his eyes on the window, hopping forward to get a better view.

"It's a message. From the wizard," the woman said, shutting the door.

She carried it to the god, and they opened it together.

Crue's raven eyes jumped about looking for Scarlett, but she didn't appear. Where was she? And Tomas? But he seemed absent as well.

This felt... wrong.

He closed his eyes and blinked out of the raven back into his own body within the workshop, his demands to meet having been delivered, even if it hadn't been very satisfying. He'd hoped to see Scarlett's tears. Even her rage would have brought him good tidings. But her absence left him feeling... bereft. Cheated.

He cleared away the summoning square and put away his tools, straightening his workshop so that it would be tidy and ready for the next time he had need of it. As he returned to the upper house, he whistled a formless tune, feeling content in the turn of events even though it could have gone so badly.

But then he frowned, pondering the absence of Scarlett and Tomas, his insides coated with righteous indignation. He was present for their daughter's heartache, ignoring for the moment he had been the cause of it. He couldn't fathom that Scarlett wouldn't be there awaiting word from him. An anxious premonitory concern slid through him. Where was she?

Jessamine

Jessamine stood at the window of the room with her arms wrapped around her middle, where she'd existed for the last several days. Outside, the depth of winter matched the depth of grief inside her. She was holding little more than sadness and desolation, a wilted bouquet which had taken root and grown since the darkling returned with…

A heart.

Johesha's heart.

Johesha was dead.

Her throat closed, and she clamped down on the sob

that filled her, a hand over her mouth. She squeezed her eyes shut and leaned her forehead against the cold windowpane as tears flowed down her cheeks. Her chest ached, her body, her soul ripped open and bleeding.

Hesha.

They were supposed to be on this journey together. She'd told him she loved him, and now she was utterly alone.

Imprisoned.

Since returning from their mad dash from the manor, she'd been confined to her room with only Mary for company. The maid brought chatter along with Jessamine's meals and information. She'd learned messengers had come and been sent away. That Crue was back in his workshop like nothing was different when everything was. But Mary couldn't bring what she wanted: Johesha and her freedom.

They didn't know.

A knock at the door startled her.

Jessamine turned away from the window and steeled her spine as she wiped the evidence of her grief from her face. When the door opened, Mary entered.

"Miss Jessamine. I brought you your lunch." Mary lifted the tray in her arms, the door swinging shut behind her.

"How do you get through?" she asked the maid, hurrying across the room to the door to study it. She'd tried to walk out the door the first day back but hadn't been able to pass over the threshold, as if there were a membrane stretched so taut over the opening it was transparent.

When she'd tried to push through, the membrane refused to budge so that she was pushed back into the room. Stuck. She'd tested it repeatedly to see if it might fail or change, but every attempt ended with the same outcome. She couldn't pass through the warded doorway.

"Through what, Miss?"

"There's a spell on the doorway. What did he do to allow you through it?"

Mary looked confused, glancing back at the door, and shook her head. "I truly don't know, miss," she whispered.

Jessamine believed that to be true but couldn't work out what made her different from Mary. How one could pass through, but she couldn't. She was an observer, however, trained by her mother from as young as she could remember to notice. Healers were observers of circumstance, of space, of time, of patterns. So Jessamine put those powers to use.

Mary carried the tray to the table near the hearth. She looked as she always did, dressed in her uniform of a long, dark dress—gray as usual with the characteristic white smock—and her hair was pinned up under a white cap. Jessamine didn't see anything different. No trinkets. No jewelry. Blood, perhaps? If she understood how magic worked, how he constructed his spells, perhaps she could deconstruct it, but as it was, she was stuck.

Mary bent to set down the tray, then stood, hesitated, and started toward the door. But before she went through, she turned and whispered, "What happened? Where is the huntsman?"

Jessamine's throat closed, and she sucked in a breath.

"Why?"

"The Master has hired a new man."

Tears filled Jessamine's eyes. "We tried to leave."

Mary swallowed thickly.

"We made it to… a cottage–" Jessamine stopped there and closed her mind to the memories of Johesha there. She couldn't think about the beauty of what they'd shared. Not just then. There was too much heartbreak taking up all the space inside her with its despair. "That's where the Master found us."

"Your father?"

"He's not my father," Jessamine said. "My father's name is Tomas Fareview."

Mary looked even more confused. "But–"

"The Master is a liar." Anger sparked inside her.

"You fell in love with him? Johesha?"

Jessamine nodded, and a tear slipped to blur her vision. "He used magic to kill him." Her throat closed around the last words, and a sob rippled up and out. "He killed him."

Mary gasped, her hands drifting to cover her mouth. "No."

Jessamine wrapped her arms around her middle and bent over with her sorrow, sobbing.

Suddenly Mary's arms were around Jessamine, holding her. "I'm sorry, my lady." Her soft, gentle words and compassionate touches offered Jessamine a respite from her isolation.

She huddled in Mary's embrace until her tears waned, then stepped free, wiping her cheeks. The spark inside her lit up the kindling of her anger. "I have to get away from here."

Mary squeezed her tighter. "I don't know how–"

Jessamine pulled away, sniffing. "Can you leave?"

Mary nodded, "But I do not remember."

Jessamine stood, putting distance between her and Mary as she got to her feet. Jessamine understood then, as she put all the other experiences together, that everyone in this house was trapped, not just her. She might be stuck in this room, but Mary and everyone else faced the spell each time they left. They were all prisoners here. "I need to find a way to break that spell."

"But how?" Mary asked.

Suddenly the door swung open, and Crue walked inside.

Mary started and curtsied.

Jessamine seethed. "It's rude to barge into a lady's room."

"Are you a lady?" he asked.

Her heart hardened and burned, the fire inside her strengthening and spreading, but even as her anger became an inferno, she recognized that she needed access to the basement. She needed to find his spells, and then she'd topple them one by one until all that was left was a mess of rubble and him trapped under it.

"Leave us," Crue told Mary, who bobbed another curtsy, then hurried around him out the door. He watched her go, then ran a hand over the front of his green brocade vest, buttoned over his slim form. He pulled a pocket watch from the slit in the vest, clicked it open, then snapped it shut. "You look well, daughter." He replaced the watch. "Better."

Her first inclination was to spit at him. To rage and tell him she was not his daughter, but she recognized the futility in it. This monster didn't have a heart. Therefore, she needed to think strategically. What she needed wasn't going to happen if she couldn't get him to allow her out of this room. But he'd also suspect something if she were suddenly complacent. So rather than say anything, she huffed indignantly and turned her back on him.

He chuckled. "I see you're angry with me." When she didn't respond, instead of insisting on her reply, he moved to the window to stare out at the winter white forest beyond the manor. "So this is the silent treatment. I always wondered what it would be like to be a parent, and I suppose this serves me right for my absence."

The creak of furniture drew her attention back to him. He'd sat in one of the chairs, his gaze on her.

"You had a man killed."

"One you liked."

"One I did… enjoy." It was so much more than that, she but wouldn't share her feelings with this monster. So she relegated Johesha to terms she thought Crue could understand, allowing her to distance herself from feelings this monster didn't have the privilege to know.

His eyes narrowed. "Enjoy," he huffed. "You betrayed my trust."

"I don't need your trust or your approval of my choices. I am my own person."

"You'd be wrong."

"You killed an innocent man."

"He would have killed me. Have you no heart?" It was his turn to be indignant, pushing a huff of air through his nose as his face twisted with annoyance.

"Why? Would you like it for your little box?"

"Your mother has made you weak."

She turned to face him. "Is that so?"

He snapped to his feet, but Jessamine held her ground as he started toward her. "All her beliefs about love and forgiveness—yes. They are a weakness. And she has ruined you."

She wanted to punch him in the throat, but it didn't serve her purpose. So she crossed back to a chair and sat, then ignored him by studying the items on her plate: buttered bread, a cup of creamy soup, some greens decorated with chopped eggs, cheese and fruit. Mrs. Gerrick had offered her beauty in addition to sustenance. There were so many of them trapped in this spider's web.

"Ruined?" She looked up and offered him a disdainful look.

"In more ways than one."

"That's disturbing." She feigned boredom in spite of her raging heart and slid the spoon into the soup to stir. "It sounds as if the man insisting he's my father is worried about my virginity." She suppressed a shudder then looked up at him with a sneer. "That isn't what you're insinuating, is it?"

"Of course not," he said, then shifted topics. "With good behavior, I will consider allowing you the run of the manor once more."

"And what constitutes good behavior, *Father*?"

"Following directions."

"Doing what I'm told, you mean."

"Well, yes. And you'll get your chance to prove your trustworthiness to me."

"Oh?"

"I've sent a reply to your mother's guard dog for a meeting with her and only her."

Jessamine's heart burst inside her chest, jolting then bolting as it raced. "Where? Here?"

"Information in due time." One of his oily, sly smiles grew on his face. "But you are to be most accommodating in the meantime."

"And if I am, you'll let me out of this room."

He offered a dip of his head to indicate that was his plan, though she didn't trust him.

"Fine," she huffed, determined to find a way to undermine him, to get even for what he'd done.

After Crue was gone—the spell still in place— after she'd eaten her dinner and spent time in front of the fire numbing her feelings, after she'd crawled into bed and spent more tears, she finally allowed herself to think about Johesha.

"What if I got lost in the woods?" she'd asked as they'd lain in front of the fire at the cottage, their *what if* game safer than making plans.

"I'd find you," he'd said, his thumb making lazy circles on her naked hip. "Nothing would stop me from finding you."

She'd rolled to look at him and grinned. "Not even your job as Prince Lachlan's captain?"

He hadn't been smiling, his gaze intense and focused. He'd leaned over her and whispered against her lips. "I'm here, yes?"

She recalled every moment from opening her eyes to his handsome face. From being carried into this room, to the greenhouse, to their flight through the secret passages, to their secret meetings–

Jessamine bolted upright in her bed.

The secret passages!

She flung the covers off, whipped a wrap around her shoulders, and stuffed her arms into the sleeves as she shoved her feet into slippers. Then, after arranging her pillows and adjusting her covers, she moved as quietly as she could to the mirror she'd once slipped through to meet with Johesha. She knew exactly where to pull the latch, and it clicked. The mirror popped open revealing the passageway beyond. Dampening her hope, she reached out to test the threshold. Her hand passed through. Nothing— no spell—impeded her.

Heart beating with hope, she grabbed a lantern and entered the passageway, pulling the frame shut behind her. She retraced the path she'd made to meet Johesha, taking it all the way to the end of the wing and the last room.

With the lantern out in front of her, she held it up and tested the doorway, easing it open, only to bump against that invisible wall Crue had set.

Jessamine swore, shutting the door and leaning against it to think.

Unsure of any other way from the room, she pushed off the door and walked back to the cold hearth to return to her own bedroom. Then froze. It didn't make sense there wouldn't be another passageway from that room. She pondered all the secret passages she knew, and every room in this wing had at least two including hers. Two means of escape.

Narrowing her eyes with resolve, she decided she should exhaust all possibilities and turned back toward the door, looking around the room. She started in the bathroom, checking the wardrobe, the frames, the cupboards, the walls. Nothing. When she walked back into the room she glanced around at the windows, the painting above the bed which was against the manor's outer wall, past the hearth where the first passageway was, then to the doorway framed by thick bookcases. She checked the bed, under it, the headboard, then sat with a huff on the end of the mattress staring at the doorway.

"Where are you?" she whispered.

But her eyes fell on the books, and she thought about the secret passage from the study into the basement.

The bookcase!

She stood and studied the framing for seams. When she was certain she'd located one, she searched for a lever, testing each of the books. Nothing. She looked for buttons or latches. Nothing. Out of options, she tugged on a slender candle holder. The bookcase made a chuffing sound as it opened. The door creaked as she tugged on it, and she froze, holding her breath as she waited for her discovery. But other than a strange humming of a breeze through the bookcase's corridor, there was no other noise.

After looking for the latch to reopen the door, and

though her heart was racing with fear, she walked with ease into the passage, no spell. At the top of a set of stairs that descended into the darkness, Jessamine shoved any trepidation she felt into the pit of her body and locked it up. She had only herself now. So, she pulled the door shut and with her lantern out in front of her, descended the stairwell into the dark. A wooden step creaked with her movement. She froze and waited.

When Crue didn't materialize, she continued, slowly and deliberately, down and down.

At another landing, another doorway waited followed by yet another set of stairs that continued down into the bowels of the house. After closing the door, she continued down the next set of stairs. When she reached the bottom, it seemed as if she'd come to a dead end, but with some prodding, she found a lever that clicked open a secret doorway. She stepped out into the dark, empty vestibule outside the kitchen. She secured the secret entrance and her way back and crept across the floor to what she knew was the entrance of the basement, the spell still nonexistent.

Crue had only spelled the main doorways of her wing.

Foolish. She smiled and continued her descent into the dark.

When she reached the hallway of the under house, she turned down her lantern and listened, but all she heard was the whisper of air and the eerie nothing of acoustic silence. No lights glowed from inside the workshop, so she opened her lantern a touch and moved quickly down the hall. When she reached the spell-work laboratory, she sighed, accomplishment pulsing through her.

A click and hiss made her jump.

"You are here?" the darkling asked, its voice always a disconcerting sound.

"Where else would I be?" she asked, looking around, but for what she wasn't sure. Then, rather than avoid the monster as she'd always done, her anger pushed her to walk directly to the outside of its cell. "Why are you still here?"

"I am trapped," it replied, though its voice had changed, becoming masculine, more familiar somehow.

"I hate you."

"A strong emotion," it said, "but not an unwelcome one."

She didn't reply, too angry. Johesha's name was too raw inside her chewed-up interior. So she turned away and began going through the items on the workbench, pulling bits of parchment, reading from them and matching things with the ingredients to see what Crue was using.

"My magic is tied to his," the darkling said.

"And if that tie was broken?" She continued through the items, shaking what looked to be a nearly empty vial of violet freeson petals, a poison in large enough doses. But in micro quantities? She wasn't certain.

"I will end the sorcerer." The darkling's answer was stark and honest, making her look at its cell door.

She knew she had every reason to hate the creature. Did hate it. With what it had done to Tarley and tried to do to Brinna. And now—

Her throat closed at the thought, and she caught the sob that threatened to break from her, pausing to lean against the workbench to compose herself.

She did hate it. But she also could see it was as much an instrument of Crue as it was to its own needs. And this might make them tentative allies. Or rather, she might be able to use its own rage against Crue.

"How is the spell between you broken?"

"I do not know," it answered.

Jessamine looked around and realized there had never been a truer statement. But she was resolved to find a way. Now that she knew she could return to the workshop unrestricted. "I'm going to find it." Tonight was the first night of the end to the man claiming to be her father, and she vowed he would learn just how weak she really was.

Johesha

The stench of a group of hunters hit his nose halfway through his journey on the second day to Sevens. As the stag, Johesha made so much more use of his four legs to chew up the distance in comparison to his two, but it also put his life in peril. So far, he'd been stalked by a mountain lion, nearly corralled by a pack of wolves, and now there was a band of hunters. They'd attempted to disguise themselves, coating themselves in wet earth, but underneath, the body odor of man was strong and stagnant. He chuffed a breath through his nose to clear it.

As a predator, he'd been on the offensive. Now, his mind was constantly on the defensive. He couldn't die as a stag, otherwise he would die as a man—the warning of the spell. He hadn't forgotten. That first night, Johesha remembered the widow's warning to prepare for the rising sun. So at the first hint of the light's descent, he stripped from the clothes and replaced them in the bag. When the sun collided with the dew of the grass, his body seized, shredded apart, and made way for the beast inside him. As a stag, he shook off the pain, rising onto his four legs and using his antlers to scoop up the bag, then churned up the earth toward the village of Sevens.

The only problem was keeping his priorities.

Johesha the man wanted to get to Sevens.

Johesha the stag wanted to eat.

Both of them were tired.

Getting the two to work in conjunction with one another proved a bit more difficult, but the stag seemed to instinctually remain headed in the right direction. It was a boon that the stag bedded down to sleep at the apex of the day and slept until nearly sunset. As the sun crossed the horizon, bringing on the night, Johesha's body ripped through the beast's, taking over. Rested, he cut the distance to Sevens.

He paused, sniffing the air, attempting to find a way around the hunters, except he couldn't find one. They'd spaced themselves out, setting a trap between them. So he backtracked, then shifted direction, but the further he paralleled their line, he couldn't find an end. The awareness that he would have to move through them made both his heart and body jerk with anxiety.

Johesha considered his options. He could dart through as a stag and risk being shot, or he could wait until after sunset and walk through as a man, chances being the hunters would have vacated their hunting grounds. But that option made him lose precious time. That was what he was spending. Every moment he wasted was a moment Jessamine had to live with whatever Crue was meting out. The sorcerer had threatened to cut her up, and who was to say he wasn't.

The thought terrified him.

But he knew he couldn't die, otherwise he'd never get to her.

He chose the second option, then, and settled into a burrow to await the setting sun.

He passed through without incident.

When he reached the village the next morning, just after he'd returned to the stag's form, he skirted the village, staying near the River Grimz, careful to avoid hunters, eating berries and grazing on foliage he could find but still wandering through the forest toward the cottage. Eventually, he sheltered in a thicket to bed down once more. When Johesha was finally back in control as a man, nightfall had descended on the Whitling Woods. He made his way through the woods to the muted, golden glow of the cottage, shining like a beacon in the night.

The Fareview's home looked the same as he remembered, though his memory of it was fleeting. The last time he'd been outside the cottage, the hedge had disappeared, and Crue had had Jessamine in his clutches.

The same day Johesha had left his post.

Now, light seeped through the leaded windows, drifting over flower boxes filled with snow. The thatched roof was coated in a thick blanket of winter white. Johesha shivered, grateful once more to the old woman and her help.

It was till early enough that those inside would be awake, so Johesha started for the cottage. Time was of the essence, since he knew the moment the sun rose, speaking would be an impossibility.

He crossed the road toward the house, having observed three royal guards keeping watch as they rotated around the property. It filled him with pride that he'd taught his men so well. As he neared the door, he expected interference.

"State your name and business."

Johesha stopped and raised his hands. The bow hung on his back, the satchel over his body. "I mean no harm."

"Captain?" The soldier, though his face was obscured by the deep shadows, stepped out from behind the barn. He wore black, his bracers and leather armor unassuming, but the tree on his breastplate indicated he was from Jast. At his collar, fastening the dark cloak, was the captain's pin.

"Jude." Johesha lowered his hands, relieved.

The soldier stepped into the light, his dark hair shorn and his facial hair trimmed and neat. "They told me they'd found you—" His eyes shone in the darkness as he crossed the distance and reached out to grasp Johesha's arm and smiled. "It is so good to see you, sir."

Several years younger than Johesha, Jude had been one

of the first groups of men he'd trained as captain to join his ranks. He could still see Jude then, a younger man with something to prove, a chip on his shoulder, the confident swagger. Though it wasn't unwarranted. The other man could smile good-naturedly in an opponent's face, get the other man laughing by drawing him in with what might be construed for weakness, then with lethal deftness slice his throat. Brutally perfect for his position.

"The prince here, then?"

Jude used his head to indicate that the prince was in the cottage. "Just inside."

"I need to see him."

Without a word, Jude led the way to the front door and knocked. A word inside bade them enter, and Jude pushed the door open, comfortable. Natural. But then, Johesha reminded himself, it had been over a year since he'd followed after Jessamine. Perhaps everyone else had been stuck in some way as well.

Johehsa followed Jude inside.

"What is it?" Lachlan asked, looking over his shoulder.

Johesha stepped inside behind Jude and faced the prince and his wife. They stood at the table along with the golden god, Lucian, and Jessamine's other sister Brinna. The table was covered with paraphernalia, as if it were a war room. Candles with wax dripping on papers were scattered across the surface.

"Captain Johesha," Lachlan said, but his eyebrows crashed together as he stepped in front of his wife, the swell of her belly indicating she was pregnant. "Is it really you or some dark magic that has conjured a version of you?

Tell me something only known between us."

Johesha sank to his knee and bowed his head, his heart buzzing at his prince's impending joy. "Your highness, when you were twelve, you decided that it was important to be able to ride a horse into battle with the ability to do tricks. You told me it might also gain you favor with Lady Catha, who you'd had a crush on at the time. I suggested that Lady Catha would return your affection because you were the crown prince, and that it would be better to be able to shoot a bow from the back of a moving horse. Undeterred, you decided you needed to use the horse as a shield. Your first attempt, you fell and broke your arm."

He looked up at his prince who was grinning. "It is you!" Lachlan crossed the space and pulled Johesha up and into his arms, hugging him tightly. "The last time I saw you... you didn't remember me." His smile faltered then returned to his face. "My ego and my heart were sorely crushed."

Johesha chuckled and hugged him back. "I'm sorry I left my post."

"Left your post?" Lachlan asked incredulously. "Thank the stars you did!" He released his hold, and with his hands still on Johesha's shoulders leaned back to meet his gaze, then pounded an open hand against him. "Because you did, we know where Jessamine is located."

"Is she with you?" Tarley asked, her eyes darting behind him.

"No one met the men," Lachlan said. "They went to the manor and were turned away."

Johesha looked from the prince to the other people in

the room wondering where everyone else was. Jessamine's parents? Her brother and sister? The dark god. "She isn't with me. I'm sorry. We were on our way here and were overtaken by the wizard."

"But you were able to get away." Tarley's eyes narrowed.

Johesha swallowed, guilt slamming into him. He lowered his eyes. "Yes."

Lachlan returned to his wife's side. "And you are able to remember now?"

Johesha nodded and looked around, trying to piece together the missing bits of the puzzle.

As if reading his mind, Lachlan said, "We're all that's here. The rest are on various assignments looking for the wizard's weaknesses. Seeking his true name to break the spell. Perhaps you heard it, having lived there for as long as you did?"

Johesha shook his head. "I didn't. He was only and always called *Master*."

Lachlan's lip curled up with disgust. "So Master, Crue, and the wizard."

"Where are they looking?"

"Auri and Nixus are at the library of Elcadia," Lucian, the golden god, replied. "Lexa, my sister, is searching the Netherrealm for any clues to the wizard's parentage."

"Mother and Father are with Mattias, who has taken them back in time," Brinna added, but her glance at Tarley gave Johesha pause.

"Back in time?" Johesha asked.

They all exchanged glances. "There's much to catch

you up on," Lachlan said. "But the most important bits of the story are that Scarlett is a descendent of a royal line and a goddess, which makes the Fareviews both royal and godblood."

"And the entire reason the wizard is after mother is for the powers she stole from him, which we now have," Brinna added.

"Like Mattias, who can travel through time." Tarley paused. "We haven't heard from them for months." She pressed a protective hand to the swell of her belly. "We don't even know if they are still alive."

"I refuse to believe that they aren't alive and well," Lachlan said, drawing her against him.

"Well, you are the optimist," Tarley said and turned back toward the table.

"Your mother is a force," he said. "She will return by stubbornness alone." He pressed a kiss to her temple. "Have faith, my love."

"But we're running out of time," Lucian said and slid the parchment on the tabletop toward Johesha. "The wizard wants to meet with Scarlett and only Scarlett."

"A new message?' Johesha stepped up to the table and read it. "And Scarlett isn't here, which is why you coded the message to me."

Lachlan nodded and smiled. "You got it." He looked around. "I told you. Didn't I? Nixus owes me a favor."

"There isn't a way to communicate with them?" Johesha asked.

"We're tried," Tarley said. "Auri tried using her mindspeak. Brinna's tried with dreams. Nothing."

Johesha felt confused, trying to keep up with all the new information, but remained silent, certain it would come together the more he listened.

"It's the time element," Lucian said. "If they were in a circle equal to this time, then communicating would be manageable. But they've gone into a different circle, back in time there. And for us to locate them without either complicating the timeline or messing with the future… it's just too dangerous…" Lucian stopped.

Johesha felt more confused.

"I've been dreaming with Jessamine," Brinna said.

"Dreaming?"

"My power," Brinna explained. "I can dreamshare. I tried it with Jessamine for a long time, but couldn't get through–"

"She was stuck in the sleeping spell for over a year."

Her sisters exchanged glances. "Over a year?" Tarley asked.

Johesha nodded. "The wizard couldn't break it."

"That's why I couldn't cross into her dreams. But she's awake now. The dreaming is different. She's interacting with me."

Johesha nodded. "I broke the spell."

"You kissed her," Lachlan grinned. "Now it's making sense."

"Hush," Tarley said and pinched him.

"I was given a love potion by an old woman in the woods." Lachlan's smile faded as Johesha's skin heated, explaining it. "That's how I was able to wake her. That's how I'm able to remember now." He held up his wrist, pointed to the leather band there. "She gave me this, which I think does something to counteract Crue's spell."

"Like our ribbons hid us," Brinna said.

"How is she?" Johesha asked Brinna. He wasn't ready to say what he and Jessamine were to one another here, but it didn't negate the fact he was worried for her. If Brinna had communicated with her, he wanted to know.

"She's sad. She dreams of death. Of you–" Her gray gaze pierced through him knowingly.

"You'll keep the meeting?" Johesha asked, hopeful that was the plan.

Lachlan nodded. "We thought perhaps we would stall him, get a sense of how he operates, maybe see if we can get Jessamine back. Jude." Lachlan motioned for the guardsman to step forward. "Now that the captain has returned–"

Jude moved to remove the pin.

"Wait," Johesha said. "I can't take it."

"Why not?" Lachlan frowned.

"There's more you need to know–" he started, then told them the whole story. About Jessamine sleeping for most of the year, about hunting and his inability to remember anything when he left the manor until he returned, and it would all flood back. He told them about meeting Brendsen, told them about the old woman in the woods and how her gifts changed things, about waking Jessamine. He told them about trying to run away and Jessamine not being able to remember beyond the manor's walls. While he held back the more personal nature of his and Jessamine's flight, he shared about Crue finding them, about the spell on him and the darkling's mercy. "So I can't in good conscience take the post, your highness."

"The wizard changed you into an animal?" Brinna asked. "But you're standing here."

"After the darkling left me, I returned to the cottage as a stag and the old woman was waiting. She rewrote Crue's spell with her own, somehow—because of this." He raised his hand and looked at the leather tie again. "She made it possible for me to return to being a man when the sun goes down. But upon the sun's return, I transform back into the stag." He paused, waiting to see if anyone had questions, but each of them seemed to be processing what he'd told them. "And–" –he pulled the satchel from over his shoulder and set it on the table– "there's another in this bag."

He removed the contents and pulled the leather strip from the contents, holding it up. "This. I think this is for something to be protected from the wizard's magic."

"What is the rest of this?"

They sorted through the rest.

"And this." Johesha indicated the bow and arrows strapped to his body.

"This one has our father's name on it." Brinna held up a vial, light shining through the liquid illuminating it a bright blue flecked with bright violet shimmers.

"Tarley?" Lucian asked. "Can you touch it, and see?"

Johesha wasn't sure what that meant. When Tarley reached out and touched the leather strip, she grew still, her deep gray eyes turning cloudy.

"What's happening?" Johesha asked.

"She's a seer," Lachlan said. "Her power, like Mattias's is time, and Brinna's dreaming."

Tarley blinked, the color of her eyes returning to their normal shade, which was unnerving. "Johesha is right. I saw the old woman, her magic as she infused it."

"Why didn't she give it to me to give to Jessamine?" Johesha asked, annoyed.

"May I touch yours?" Tarley asked.

Johesha held up his arm.

Tarley's hand wrapped around his wrist over the leather, and her eyes turned cloudy for just a second. "This one is different. Besides her magic, which is violet on both, yours has a green filament too."

"Crue's." Johesha said, knowing he'd seen the wizard's color again and again.

"I wonder if that is what allowed you to get past the wizard's magic somehow?" Brinna asked.

"But not the stag," Johesha said darkly. If it had that power, he would have Jessamine with him.

"It's probably a power thing," Lucian said. "If it allowed you through one spell, that doesn't mean it could empower you through another."

Johesha sighed. "I'm sorry. I tried to get her home."

Tarley squeezed his wrist before letting him go. "You're here now, and we're one step closer to getting Jessamine back."

"Check this one." Brinna held out the vial.

Tarley touched each item, sharing what she could, and though not everything revealed its purpose, they were given a bit more information about the old woman's intent.

They were to the last object—the dagger—which Johesha hadn't considered meant more than a weapon, but it was among the items in the bag. It was nondescript as daggers went. The blade was about fifteen centimeters in length and slightly curved, made of a buffed silver metal. The handle was made of bone, rough and textured for grip.

Tarley picked it up, her eyes turning that unsettling shade as she saw whatever she saw. Only this time her body tensed, and she whimpered, her eyes tearing up.

"Tarley? Sweetheart?" Lachlan asked, moving closer.

Then she dropped the object onto the table with clatter, slumping against Lachlan and turned into him, gripping him tightly.

Lachlan wrapped his arms around her. "I've got you, love. I've got you." He lifted her up and carried her to the couch a few feet away while the rest of them waited.

It wasn't a few breaths later that Tarley looked at Lachlan. "We can't wait," she said.

"But Mother–" Brinna started.

Tarley's gaze jumped to her sister, and she swallowed as she shook her head. "The vision showed me what I think is the wizard's intention."

"What is it?" Johesha asked, fear sliding down through his bones.

"To cut out her heart."

Jessamine

The workshop was strange at night. Though the light remained the same, there was something darker in the tomb of the place. Jessamine found that she had to face a deeper seeded fear inside of her each time she stole down into the basement in the shadow of night. But it didn't keep her from her desire to find a way to break the spell, to break Crue.

By day, she had visited the workshop with Crue, feigning his obedient daughter. They worked on various potions, and he taught her magic, but he refused to answer her questions, instead replying to "How did you get your power?" or "How can I get my own?" with "All in good time. Be patient." He forced her to eat her meals with him and returned her to her room where the spell on the doorway remained in place—one she couldn't figure out, not that she'd know how to break it. Then, by way of Mary, she knew Crue returned to the workshop to work on his own.

So the last two nights, she returned after the manor had gone to sleep. The darkling waited, watching her with curiosity as she worked through every ingredient, noting which ones Crue used, keeping track of their levels from their day work. Even so, without knowing each ingredient's purpose, his purpose, deciphering their importance was like finding a needle in a haystack.

She needed his spell books.

She turned toward the darkling. Next to the cell were stacks and stacks of books. She hadn't ventured near the creature since the last time, but she couldn't avoid it, now. With a glance at where it sat watching, its gaze sent a chill up her spine. But rather than ignore its presence, she settled on her knees near the cell.

"How were you caught by Crue?"

"The sorcerer came to my home." Its voice—a man's—was pleasant. Though she couldn't see all the creature, she could see part of it through the barred opening, offering her a small portion of its dark visage.

She didn't look up, certain it had changed form, and instead pulled a loose pile of parchment toward her. "Where is that?"

She flipped through the pages, recognizing some of the

spells that Crue had led her through. There were spells on changing eyesight, spells on changing hair color, spells for growing limbs, and one for growing warts. None of these were things she needed, but she continued looking just the same.

"Far away in the land of always-ice."

"Why did he look for you?"

"We can see magic," it said. "This is what he wanted."

"What does magic look like?" she asked.

"It is different for every magic maker. The Master wears his green magic like a fortress around him, the threads woven in and through him like skin and bones. But you–"

"I don't have magic."

"You do."

She paused, the paper in her lap, and looked at the darkling more closely. "How?"

"Your magic is inside you."

Godblood, Crue had called her.

"Because of my mother? That's what Crue said."

"The Master's magic is… taken," he said.

"What do you mean?"

"He wasn't born with it. He was taught it and then given power which he wraps around himself like a coat. He must take it or trade for it. A darkling's power is like yours. Inside them." She watched it shift inside the cell, though she couldn't see what it was doing. "Created, not stolen or given. This is why a darkling can see it."

"Which means I can see magic?"

"Perhaps."

"And my magic isn't like a coat?"

"It is a seed."

She imagined all the many seeds she'd planted in the soil over her lifetime with her mother.

"It glows in your heart, its power radiating beyond like…" it paused, considering, "like starlight, pulsing and golden."

"This is how you found Tarley?"

The darkling stopped speaking as if it understood it was venturing into dangerous territory with her, but then it spoke. "The other one. With the god of darkness."

"Auri." The first to lose her ribbon.

"I was taken by the wizard to find you."

"Taken?"

"He arrived in my land offering a deal, and I believed it. So I gave him my agreement, and then my name, which he used to tether us with a spell."

"Did he give you his name?"

"No."

"Perhaps that is how the tether is broken?" Jessamine hypothesized. "There is a balance to nature."

The darkling made a strange noise, unlike anything she had heard before. It wasn't mournful or angry, hungry or aggrieved. The course sound was even and monotone, stretching from one moment to the next as if it were considering what she'd said. "I agreed to his deal because my mate and I longed for our own progeny."

Jessamine stopped looking altogether, her eyes snapping toward the cell. "You have a mate? You can make little darklings?" The idea terrified her.

The monster made a series of clicks that she wondered about. Was it a laugh? "Not younglings. We satiate. There are only three at a time. We wanted to find our third, but these are hard to find in the land of always-ice."

"Because you killed everyone?"

"Because it is too harsh for your kind, human." It paused as if considering things, then said, "My mate and I were hunting when we came upon the sorcerer. We agreed he wasn't to be our third, and was to be food, but he was tricky offering passage and satiation beyond always-ice. The possibility of more food, more options was too tempting."

"So you agreed."

"He knew there was the link between us, to find your magic." It paused. "And yes. I agreed to the tether to go beyond after being tricked." Silence hovered between them a few beats as if the darkling was remembering, but then it added, "What you said about balance sinks teeth in me."

She didn't really like the image, but asked, "Why?"

"Too many darklings, that is all that will remain."

She hummed. "I see what you're getting at." She continued looking at the spells. "Like a seed needs both moisture and heat to grow. Life, growth, birth, death—it's nature's balancing act. It stands to reason that magic functions similarly, though maybe you aren't natural."

It didn't reply.

Jessamine thought that if she were called abnormal she might also refrain from speaking, but she was more interested in learning than in worrying if she'd hurt its feelings. "Your name linked you to him, maybe his could break it."

"He used the spell but not his name. Do you know the sorcerer's name?"

"I know the name he's offered, which he's already said isn't his true name. Maybe it's in these books."

The darkling didn't reply but watched her work in that unnerving manner, and Jessamine continued searching until she knew sleep was necessary. She left the darkling and workshop behind, thinking about the creature's story and hating that she saw it as trapped as she was, even knowing what kind of monster it was.

That night she dreamed of Brinna. Jessamine was in a dream version of the workshop, locked in the glass case once more. She was pounding on the glass trying to get out, screaming to be set free.

"Jessamine," her sister said, her voice clear but her face invisible.

"Brinna? Where are you?"

"Here."

Jessamine twisted in the glass case, looking, but couldn't find her sister. With an intense rage, she pounded on the glass once more, but it wouldn't budge. Eventually she stopped, her hands over her face as she sobbed. Her fists hurt, her voice was hoarse, and hot tears stung her eyes.

"Jessamine," Brinna called. "Try again."

Taking a deep breath, she drew in the calm and heard her words to the darkling: *it's all about balance.* She opened her eyes and looked at the unforgiving glass, strong and sturdy, and then with her finger, pressed the tip softly against the pane above her.

It shattered.

Jessamine climbed from the enclosure. "Where are you?" she called.

"Here!" And instead of the darkling inside the cell, it was Brinna holding onto the bars of the opening. "Can you open it?"

"It's locked," Jessamine said.

"That's okay. Just listen," Brinna said. "We're coming for you."

Then she was gone, and the dream broke apart as Jessamine's eyes opened to the light, unsure what left her heart racing. She sighed and searched for strength, because all that stretched out before her was yet another day knowing Johesha wasn't in the world with her.

Johesha

"What if the wizard suspects Mother isn't with us?" Brinna asked. Jessamine's sister, a sweet, gentle woman with looks to match her kindness, glanced around at the rest of the occupants of the table. Johesha followed her gaze. Prince Lachlan, fingering the handle of a mug of ale, sat next to his wife Tarley. The contrast to Brinna as Tarley frowned at her empty plate was stark and obvious. Tarley had an austere beauty that was slightly off-putting, like her caustic personality. Lucian leaned back in his chair, his golden gaze on Brinna, a focus that rarely wavered. Jude, Lachlan's new captain of the guard, reached for a stray berry. The missing family members left gaps and the reminder that things were amiss.

The remnants of their shared dinner on the plates littered the surface of the wooden table in the heart of the cottage. Mugs, partially filled with tea, ale, or wine rested in front of occupants. In the hearth, a fire flickered, and lanterns buzzed with light. Though a pall of disquiet hung about the party, they'd found moments of levity and laughter as they broke bread and reminisced. Over the last three days, most of their time together had been tight with tension.

The first day they'd composed a reply to Crue's message and sent it with Brendsen.

The second day they'd begun to plan.

It was now the third day, and they were still trying to decide the best course of action to meet Crue without Scarlett there. Tarley and Brinna were clearly worried with unspoken fears for their missing family members. Though no one voiced the questions, they remained at the forefront of concern. What if they never returned? What if something worse occurred? Even if those horrors weren't voiced, dread swirled in the anxiety that appeared like flashes of lightning of a distant storm in the dark.

"He won't know," Lachlan suggested, "that she isn't around. We could just say that he can't talk to her."

"But he expects her to be there." Brinna frowned, and Lucian wrapped a comforting hand around the back of her neck.

Johesha's heart contracted at the sight of the shared

affection between them, and he frowned. He thought about that last morning with Jessamine, her confession of love, and hated the feeling of loss that slid through him, angry at himself for taking so long to understand the gift he had with Jessamine until it was too late. It wasn't only the spell that divided him but his feelings when Jessamine needed him whole.

"You're thinking of Tarley's vision? Your dream?" Lucian asked, and Brinna nodded.

"It's his anger I fear," Tarley said. "What would he do to Jessamine because of it?"

Both sisters had been at the mercy of their powers. Brinna had shared a dream she'd had about Jessamine breaking out of her glass prison, of trying to tell her they were coming, while Tarley's visions had continued to include Jessamine consumed, withered away until all that was left of her was a small, golden seed that Crue ate.

The image brought him the phantom of a memory that floated away when he looked too closely at it, and he wished he weren't as unfocused as he was. Most of his thoughts circled around Jessamine, his worry, fear, anger, penitence, vulnerability. None of which, he knew, would get her back. And who he once was, the efficient captain of the royal guard couldn't find that balance inside him.

"Do you think he'd take out his frustration on her?" Lachlan asked Johesha.

Johesha took a moment to ponder what he'd seen and experienced. "Yes, but I don't think it would be directly. He never laid a finger on her in anger when I was there."

"Then–"

"He'll take it out on the darkling," he said. "And maybe others in the manor to manipulate her."

"What?" Tarley asked, her voice a low, withered pitch.

"There are more there? Trapped?" Brinna asked.

Johesha nodded. "The spell affects everyone. It's how he's stayed hidden."

"And he still has the monster?" Lachlan asked, his face dark with anger, an uncharacteristic look for the usually happy prince but certainly understandable considering what the darkling had done to his wife. And now with a baby on the way, Johesha could fathom the compounding of that rage.

Johesha nodded again. "Crue keeps it under lock and key. Tortures it."

"It deserves it," Lachlan muttered.

Johesha sighed, understanding Lachlan's enmity. "The creature extended me mercy. It's the only reason I'm here right now. It let me go when Crue ordered it to kill me." Johesha took his first sip of his ale and set it back on the table. He glanced around, considering next steps, tired and strung out. Had it been one of his men—former men—he would have excused them, telling them they weren't clear headed. But he knew he wouldn't have listened to that advice. This was Jessamine. And there wasn't the luxury of not engaging in this. "Don't hide it from him. At the meeting."

"What?" Lucian asked.

"Scarlett's absence. Use it."

"How?" Brinna asked.

Johesha stared into the amber liquid still in his glass,

thinking about everything he'd learned about Crue, remembering his rage when he'd discovered he and Jessamine at the cottage. How volatile the wizard had been. "He doesn't have to know that she is missing, only that she refused to attend. Crue wants the upper hand, and right now he thinks he has it over Scarlett. He wants to be in control. To manipulate things. Surprises will unsettle him, maybe push him to make a mistake. He's obsessed, which gives him a weakness."

"He does have the upper hand," Tarley pushed away from the table. "He has Jessamine."

"Yes," Johesha watched Tarley pace. "But he's going to want Scarlett begging him. What would it do to his head if Scarlett doesn't even show up? For him to think that Scarlett doesn't see him worthy of her time."

Lachlan leaned forward, his elbow on the table and his hand over his mouth as he hummed, considering. "It could backfire against Jessamine."

"Yes," he agreed, "which means we have to set her free, before he can do anything to her."

"He needs Scarlett." Lucian set down his glass of wine. "That's why he's using Jessamine. He won't harm the leverage he has over Scarlett."

"Without Scarlett, though," Lachlan said, "Jessamine is no longer leverage."

"Which is why he can't know—"

"—you want to play a mind game?" Tarley interrupted, her eyes bouncing around from face to face.

"With Jessamine's life on the line?" Brinna was angry. The ferocity of her gaze was antithetical to her usual personality.

"Jessamine's life is on the line regardless." Lachlan poured himself more ale. "Johesha's right. We have to change the paradigm to unsettle him. Get him rattled."

"Your last message did that," Johesha added. "That's how we were initially able to get away."

"I would like to see what Auri will say." Tarley's eyes held to Johesha as if she were seeing him as a stranger. "Her wisdom will help with this."

"Should I summon Nix early?" Lucian asked.

Tarley shook her head. "They'll be here in the morning. We can fill them in then."

"We have one more surprise," Johesha offered. When they all looked at him, he said, "Me. Crue ordered me killed, and I doubt the darkling returned empty handed."

Later, they cleaned up and went their separate ways to rest before reconvening the following day. Brinna and Lucian disappeared in that unnerving way the gods could, vanishing like moving dust motes in rays of sunshine. Lachlan and Tarley retreated to a bedroom. Johesha went outside to the barn with the other soldiers. He didn't like to sleep when he was in his human form, but then, it was important to offer the stag a rested mind for his own human clarity when trapped, otherwise he drifted too far into the animal's thoughts.

He bedded down in one of the stalls of the barn and laid there thinking about Jessamine, about her confession and how little he deserved it. He hadn't been able to save her, when that was what he was good at. He'd saved the prince over and over, though there was a recent black mark on him there too. He hadn't been able to save the prince when he'd gone over the cliff into the river when they'd been set upon by assassins, had nearly lost him and would have if it hadn't been for Tarley. Add to that failure, he'd now left Jessamine behind in the clutches of a madman. His defeats convicted his worthiness, and though he wanted to argue against it, he couldn't look past the truth of them.

Sometime later, just before the night began to wane into dawn, the sound of quiet footsteps in the barn drew his attention, and that of Jude.

He heard the new captain exchange whispers, ending with, "Yes, your highness."

Johesha expected Lachlan, but it was Tarley who entered the stall where he lay a few seconds later. He rushed to sit up, to stand, but she held up a hand to keep him where he was, then leaned against the wall. She didn't immediately say anything, just studied him. When the silence grew uncomfortable, she said, her voice a thin, breakable sound in the silence of the barn, "I can't imagine the circumstances around how the darkling let you go. Not the darkling I knew."

Still sitting, his back against the wall with his legs stretched out in front of him, crossed at the ankle, he nodded, looking down at his hands in his lap. "The wizard has been starving it. I started sneaking it food."

"Why?"

He could understand her incredulity, given the circumstances. "I was afraid of it."

"Explain."

"That it might escape and hurt Jessamine." He glanced at Tarley then.

Even in the deep blue of the darkness, he could see Tarley shudder and look down at her feet. She crossed her arms in front of her. "And rather than feed on you, it just let you go?"

"I'm not sure how I can answer it any more plainly," he said, then added, "your highness. I'm here."

She inadvertently placed her hands on her protruding belly. "How do I know you aren't the darkling? That it hasn't stolen your face?"

He frowned and crossed his arms over his chest. "Yet, you were willing to put yourself and the future king," he nodded at her, "at risk to come in here with that being a possibility." He paused, and when she didn't budge said, "Fine. You trusted me when I walked into that assassin's tent without even knowing who I was," reminding her of when he'd been the one to rescue her from Lachlan's assassins.

She took a deep breath. "Thank the stars."

"Why should they be thanked? Seems like a shitty situation."

She smiled then. "The darkling wouldn't have answered my last question like that. But Johesha, captain of my husband's guard, would."

"Not the captain anymore."

Tarley pushed away from the wall. "But the job is still yours if you want it, Johesha. You only need to decide." She started to leave then stopped. "Thank you."

"For?"

"For going after my sister."

Then she was gone, and Johesha settled back into the straw, willing himself to sleep. He dreamed of Brinna, who did much the same as Tarley, just in her own strange way. "I'm not the darkling," he told her as they stood in front of a rushing river.

"I know, but I wanted to see your dreams nonetheless."

"I wish I could stop the current."

"Maybe it's just a matter of building a boat."

He turned to look at Brinna, but it wasn't Brinna anymore, but a face reminiscent of hers. She smiled, leaned closer, and said, "Don't forget the seed."

The next morning when the sun rose, his skin tore from his body as he shifted into the stag, and he waited, panting to resettle into these particular bones.

"Captain." Jude stood at the half door of the stall.

Unable to speak, Johesha watched the soldier slowly open the doorway and walk inside with tentative steps.

The stag hopped up and tensed, unaware of Jude's intentions, watching warily, more interested in self-preservation.

Jude held out his hands and stopped. "I won't hurt you. I just wanted to see." His eyes drifted over the form of the stag. "Do you know the spell? Have you been working on it? To break it?"

The thought stopped Johesha's breath. He hadn't. Why hadn't he? He snuffed in answer, shaking his head, the antlers heavy as he jerked his head around. Then, he reached out his nose toward Jude's outstretched hand.

"Do you remember it?"

He twisted his head toward the bag on the ground at his feet. There was a written version of it on a sheet of parchment inside—a gift from the old woman, he was sure.

"May I sec it?"

Johesha nodded, the stag's giant head bouncing up and down.

Jude smiled and moved slowly to the bag, looking through the interior for it. "This, sir," he said, holding up the bit of paper for him to see. "This is what I'll be working on."

Johesha took a step forward and allowed Jude to run a hand along his neck. Then he tossed his head, making the soldier jump out of the way of his antlers before running from the barn.

Jessamine

ight after night, Jessamine snuck from her room after the manor settled down to sleep. Each time she retraced the path through the manor's secret passages to the workshop. The workshop at night was dark and lonely, yet somehow comforting in the solitude, the sole lantern she carried illuminating the quiet chaos of the space. Besides the ingredients and the tools for concocting, there were stacks and stacks of books along with handwritten slips of paper and journals to search for clues.

For the last five nights, by the light of her lantern, she'd begun searching through the notes and books Crue kept.

Some were Crue's scrawl while others were in the handwriting of others. None of them were organized, so discovery of something useful was like chasing a lone dragonfly along the River Grimz from Sevens to Jast.

"Have you found an answer?" the darkling asked one night.

"No," she answered with an angry whisper. She sat tucked in between boxes near the darkling's cage, hidden from view should Crue make an unexpected visit to the workshop.

"Read to me?" it asked.

Her anger surged, but she ignored the desire to lash out even if she wanted to, reminding herself that it was Crue who had ordered Johesha's heart in his hands. That it was Crue who had her trapped in a spell and stolen her away. That it was Crue who put the darkling in a prison and compelled it to kill. That it was Crue tethered to the monster.

She couldn't see the creature in the light, but its presence loomed near her, watching. It had changed its face, its voice pleasant when it spoke, and she tucked her face back into the book. "I won't be able to hear if he comes down here if I'm reading out loud."

"I will listen. Besides, I feel him. He sleeps." The creature's voice altered—familiar, somehow—as if in the resonance of Johesha, as if the monster had changed its skin again.

She wanted to throw the book at its cage, scream at it for killing Johesha, curse it back to the hell it came from, certain it was playing some kind of game with her. "Can't he feel you too, then?" she asked, instead.

"He doesn't pay attention to my feelings."

A nagging awareness twinged under her skin at the back of her neck and slithered its way into her gut. *Pay attention,* it seemed to say, almost as if the presence of a different spirit crouched next to her other side, urging her to press forward. *Tread carefully,* it added.

So she quietly read about magic, about potions, and noted the annotations in Crue's scrawl. One night after the next, she read to the darkling. The most interesting, she thought, were the journals Crue had written, even if they were droll. There was something more personal in them that allowed her to read between the lines of a very self-absorbed, dramatic, and manipulative person. And somehow, a little lonely and sad too.

Three of those nights, Crue was awake, at work inside the workshop making a potion of some sort and ranting at the darkling. "You're no help." He snapped out the words with loathing. "Worthless now that we've found them!" Something clanked—metal against metal. "How am I supposed to break this without your help?"

"You're the wizard," the darkling had replied.

Jessamine jumped in her hiding place at the bright sound of metal against metal again.

That first time she realized Crue was still awake, she'd initially panicked about being discovered, until she realized that he spoke freely to the darkling. So she tucked herself into Johesha's workspace next door and listened, piecing together parts of a story about the tether, what he'd attempted to try and break it, learned missing bits and pieces of how he'd known her mother, and heard confessions of deeds best kept in the dark.

The second time it happened, she secreted herself into the deep shadows of Johesha's room once more and eavesdropped. When the sound dropped away, she chanced a peek into the room and observed Crue in some kind of trance. He didn't speak, didn't move, just stood absolutely still in his workshop, his hand resting on a dark crystal and his eyes all white, oblivious to what was happening around him.

The third time, she realized that he was making an elixir. Though for what, he didn't say, the potion seemed significant—that strange feeling, that presence urging her onward.

"This should last until we meet," he said.

Jessamine wondered why that was important, wondered what purpose the elixir served. She needed a sample, she decided, thinking she might be able to deconstruct it. But when he finished and left the workshop for the night, and she snuck in after him to look for remnants, Crue had cleaned up. The elixir was nowhere to be found.

"Do you know what he is making?" she asked the darkling as she searched the counter, reading labels of mixes and potions. She'd already been through these, had used them before—

"A serum to reverse his aging," the darkling replied in Johesha's voice.

Her breath caught at the sound of Johesha's voice as well as the admission. Initially, the monster's change grated on her, but the more the darkling modified itself that way, the easier it was to talk to it. Hearing Johesha's voice, even knowing he was gone, gave her comfort and bolstered her purpose to avenge him.

She stopped her search and looked at the darkling's cage. "Why would he need a potion to make him young?"

"He is old like me."

"How old are you?" she asked.

"I am centuries old."

"Centuries! That's how long you've been tethered?" she asked.

"He only recently captured me."

"He's that old?"

The darkling didn't respond as she tucked herself into her corner with another of Crue's books. She set it on her lap thinking about that, surprised by the realization, and talked through her thoughts. "Certainly, he can't be more than a century old. Even with a magical serum, it would be difficult to find a way to reverse aging all together." She pondered what she knew about the body, the degeneration of cells. "A potion would only be temporary."

He was dying, she realized. That was why he was forced to make the potion. "Can you feel him dying?"

"Yes."

"Will you die, if he dies, or will the spell between you break?"

"I do not know, but I believe the magic will hold."

"How long would you live? Without the magic?" she asked.

"Not connected? Much, much longer. We live long,

love longer, but we are kept to a few. Too many and your kind would succumb, disappear, and we would go hungry."

"Because you're blood-thirsty wretches?" She snorted and adjusted the lantern, then opened the book.

"And you smell so delicious," it replied in its own slithering voice.

"Was that a joke?" she asked, glancing at the cage.

It didn't comment, leaving Jessamine to wonder. "We do not usually cross bodies of water," it admitted, its voice changing once more. "Not without necessity."

"A weakness."

"Yes. Water traps, ice traps, and fire–" it hissed.

"And that's how Crue caught you? With water?"

"Yes. Threatened my mate with fire, captured me with water, then offered his bargain."

Jessamine looked at the black ink scrawled across the page, noted the swirls and scratches, but struggled to concentrate, thinking about the darkling in the meadow when it had gone after her sister. "Were you going to eat Tarley?" she asked.

It hummed as if remembering, a sensuous, needy sound, as if the desire for Tarley still remained at the forefront of its immediate needs. "No killing. I chose her as the sacred three. For satiation."

Jessamine turned in her seat to face the monster's cage. "You wanted to keep her?"

Fingers, hands appeared, wrapping around the bars. "I wanted to create her. To take her home to be with me and my mate. Three is a sacred number."

"But that wasn't right," Jessamine said. "She didn't

want that. How could you force her to do something she didn't want?"

"I wanted it."

"Like Crue wanted you?"

The darkling went quiet, the hands withdrawing from the bars, and Jessamine sat for a few more minutes before she stood.

"You will not read to me?"

"Not tonight. I'm going to bed," she answered, returning the books back to their place and hurried back into her room where she lay in her bed struggling to find the calm to sleep. Eventually, she succumbed to the darkness and dreamt confusing dreams of Brinna telling her Johesha was there, of a woman who looked like her mother, but different, telling her to find the power inside of her. To trust her instincts.

The next night, she stood in the workshop looking at what was around her, pondering her next steps, recognizing that the problem would also always be that she couldn't identify important spells to Crue because she didn't truly know him. He might reveal he wanted Scarlett to pay, or that he wanted Jessamine to be his apprentice, but the true heart of him was hidden.

She turned back to the darkling. "He makes a youth potion?" she asked for confirmation.

The darkling affirmed it.

Jessamine looked at the treasure trove around her, and the darkness she knew slithered through her bloomed with her anger and hatred, her heart hardening. "Fine," she whispered. "You want darkness and unforgiveness, that is what you will get."

She spent the next several hours brewing a concoction not meant to heal, not meant to alleviate pain or malady, but instead to harm. She held up the pink vial to the lantern, knowing there was no turning from this path.

"We never harm," her mother instilled in her from the time she'd begun as her apprentice at ten, but then her mother had doused them with a spell. Perhaps it hadn't been intended to harm, but it had. So, she was going to use this lesson with poison instead. Jessamine might be justifying the choice to administer poison to Crue, but she also knew that this path, the darkness of it, meant facing truths about herself and who she was. She wasn't above it like Tarley, or sweet like Brinna. She wasn't idealistic like Mattias, or pragmatic like Auri. She hated that this proved the man who'd be partially responsible for giving her life right. She was a combination of both her parents, and this dark choice made her dark.

Despite all that, she still slid the vial into her pocket and cleaned up so that Crue wouldn't know she'd been at work all night. Then she stole up through the secret corridors and got some deep and dreamless sleep before the sun rose.

Crue arrived as she ate breakfast, that grin she hated on his face. "Good morning," he said as he walked into the room.

"Is it?" she asked, setting down her cup of tea.

"Why yes. And I think you will find it even more so when I reveal a second reason for my usual visit." He sat, picked up the tea carafe, and poured it into the cup

Jessamine had dosed. Then, as he always did, he added two spoons of sugar and a measured drop of cream. "You look—" he paused "—tired."

She didn't reward him with her curiosity or offer him any response and instead took a sip of her own tea to hide her glee as he followed the same routine he followed every morning. While many poisons had a flavor, she'd made this one to mimic the sweet on his palate, and she also only added a microdose. A slow dispensing of death. Time would do the trick.

"Since you aren't asking, I'll tell you. I heard from your mother."

Still, she remained silent but gave him her attention.

"There is a meeting set in seven days."

Jessamine set down her cup in its saucer. "And?"

"And then this will all be over. I'll have what I want."

"And I can return home."

He hummed a note that was meant to sound like his assent, but Jessamine saw the trick and watched him take a healthy swallow of his tea, unaware that his equivocation hardened her resolve.

Johesha

Just as he had for the last five days since he'd returned to Sevens and the Fareview cottage, he waited in the woods at sunset for the change rather than changing in the barn where his soldiers would witness it. Jude had, and that had been uncomfortable enough. It had been ten days since he'd been cursed, ten days of feeling torn apart and put back together, ten days since he'd seen Jessamine, ten days to harbor the anger and worry for her and what she was going through.

In the ten days, despite having returned, he didn't feel hope. He just felt furious.

Add to that: resurfacing as a man was becoming more difficult, as if the divide between his human form and the animal form was deepening, the stitches keeping them together tearing open. The returning awareness took him longer to forge, so after the change, he lay in the snow longer than he should, reconnecting to the essence of who he was. That clear chord that always guided him was thin, that who and why of him lost in the haze.

"That is rather impressive," a familiar voice said from the shadows. "Albeit inconvenient, I would surmise."

Johesha sat up and reached for the sack containing his clothing to dress, knowing who'd just witnessed his change, his weakness. A fact that grated on him. "Playing at Peeping Tom?"

The man laughed as the crunch of snow under boots worked its way toward him. Johesha looked up at the face of Nixus Uraiahs, god of night and darkness, pulling the shadows with him as he walked, that characteristic smirk on his face that set Johesha's teeth on edge. He stood and dragged on his pants.

"Peeping Tom," he scoffed. "You make it sound dirty that I wanted to see this spell in action. And I don't think Tomas would appreciate the disparagement of his name." He smiled, a grin that never looked friendly, but held a feral quality, as if he were deciding between the sharp edge of joking or planning someone's demise.

"Maybe I didn't want you to."

Nixus snorted, then clicked his tongue. "Pride goeth before a fall, as they say." He crossed his arms and watched Johesha dress. "It's for Aurielle," he said. "She needs all the information. She and that new captain have been working on your spell." He sneered at the idea of Jude.

It was Johesha's turn to smile. "Don't like Jude, I take it?"

Nixus waved a hand as if the question was inconsequential but didn't answer, then huffed a noise. "Auri has to do what she will do. And I will do what I need to do, which is to end anyone who touches what's mine."

Johesha shook his head as he donned the shirt. "Well, that sounds… healthy." He shoved his feet into the boots and considered he didn't feel any different when it came to thoughts of Crue hurting Jessamine.

"I am what I am, mortal."

Johesha held out his arms as a stark challenge for Nix's perusal. "Learn anything, god?"

"Other than you're weak?"

Johesha gritted his teeth at the criticism but mostly at the way it made him feel defensive. At the truth of it. But he remained silent and sullenly shoved his arms into the jacket before picking up the bag.

"No, but perhaps Auri will."

Johesha stomped through the woods toward the cottage.

"Have I upset you?" Nixus asked, keeping pace with Johesha.

"You just called me weak."

"Is it not true?"

"I'm not certain anyone wants to be seen as weak."

Nixus hummed a note. "Right. Well, we're not always strong though, are we?"

Johesha stopped. "What's that supposed to mean?"

"I haven't always been strong," Nixus said matter-of-factly, surprising Johesha.

"You're a god." Johesha had interacted with Nixus on a few occasions, and each time, Johesha had witnessed this terribly awesome deity eviscerate men with his shadows—even if they deserved it. He'd listened to him snark and joke, sometimes at the expense of his men. But he'd also seen him love, deeply, both Aurielle and his brother Lucian. Johesha had witnessed him succumb to death because he'd been separated from his true love.

"So? Am I not living?" When Johesha didn't move or say anything, Nixus continued, "I was trapped in a spell, yes? It was the love of a woman that bolstered my weakness. It was the vulnerability of women who gave me strength, who made me strong."

Johesha swallowed thinking of Jessamine's confession. Her love.

"Weakness is nothing to be ashamed of, Captain. It is part of the condition of life and gives us the opportunity to become better. To become more." Nixus reached out and laid a hand on Johesha's shoulder.

Johesha jerked back and started back through the woods. "I'd prefer not having to be ripped apart by a spell."

Nixus laughed. "Point taken." Then he grabbed hold of Johesha, and the forest around them blurred, eventually turning to dust as the cottage reassembled around them, making Johesha fold over at the waist to calm his stomach. "This was faster than your tromping through the woods."

"I don't tromp." Johesha straightened.

"Stomp then."

Johesha grunted.

"There you are," Lachlan said, smiling and taking a swig from a cup in front of him. "I was beginning to worry you'd take your own sweet time, Nix. We have things to do."

"Time away from my love is never sweet."

Auri looked up at Nixus and smiled, blushing. "Anything?"

"Would you like the images?" he asked her.

She nodded and closed her eyes.

"I'm censoring them." He looked pointedly at Johesha's groin and frowned.

Then Auri's eyes opened and snapped to Johesha. "It hurts?" she asked as if she'd been the one witness to his shame.

His face heated, and he looked at Nix.

"Don't worry. I filtered out all your impressive bits." He grinned. "Wouldn't want any comparison. Mortal. God." He used his hands to demonstrate who was who. "Favor's all mine." Then he laughed, absolutely at ease with himself.

"Yes. It hurts," he said to Jessamine's youngest sister, who had arrived the day before with Nixus and whose power had to do something with her mind and wisdom. She could communicate with Nix without saying a word, which was unnerving as the two stood silently speaking with one another, and she was working on managing that ability with others. Now, it appeared as if part of that ability was to see what Nixus saw, which was unsettling.

She hummed, thinking, and looked back down at the paper he'd given to Jude. "Do you remember the spell Crue cast?" she asked Johesha.

"No. Does that mean—"

She looked up at him and shook her head, as if knowing his question before he even said it. "No. It looks like the woman from the woods has given you the ability to break it here."

He joined her and Jude the table.

"Sit," Lachlan said. "Eat."

Johesha wasn't sure if he could, but he filled a cup with coffee and sat next to Jude.

"See this here." Aurielle pointed to some of the lines and read them, "*Seek and find the heart that's true to undo the tie that links their troth. An unending vow to bubble and brew, a steadfast oath to reunite them both.*"

"True love?" Jude asked.

She hummed, rocking her head side to side, considering it. "Maybe."

"What gives you pause, my goddess," Nixus asked her from her other side.

She glanced at him then back at Johesha. "It doesn't say love. It says heart. And—"

"—words matter," Nixus finished and kissed her cheek.

She smiled at him. "Yes."

"I hadn't considered that," Jude admitted, and Johesha agreed but didn't comment, unsure how to puzzle that out.

"But then—" —Jude pointed at the paper— "why mention a vow and an oath? That seems sort of lovey dovey."

"We took a vow to be royal guardsmen," Johesha reminded him. A vow he'd broken, not because he'd lay with Jessamine, but rather because he was certain he'd given her his heart.

"Vows and oaths can take many forms," Auri agreed. "The key is reuniting the animal with the man." She looked at Johesha. "The vow and the oath, whatever it is, should do that."

Shouts beyond the cottage sent Jude and Johesha running out the door only to witness a giant red dragon shrink down into a woman dressed in red, a dark gray monster with her. Though Johesha had met the goddess before, he'd never met the other unsettling creature. Johesha's eyes mapped the Jast soldiers camped around the cottage and their ease when they recognized the pair, as if this was common, the shouts good-natured ribs rather than those voiced in fear.

Lexa's eyes dipped, taking him in as she approached. She smiled, fangs glinting in her mouth. "Jude." Her eyes flicked over the other soldier, then she turned to him. "And the original captain of the guard."

"Johesha," he said.

Lexa was beautiful, though it was strange to think that considering her other form as dragon was equally impressive. Small but mighty was how he had always thought of her, though she wasn't probably very small. She was a storm, her dark hair sleek to her shoulders, her golden gaze as unnerving as her sharp smile. Her razor tongue could eviscerate and mostly did, but Johesha had once witnessed the tenderness and grief she offered Nixus as he'd died in a meadow.

"Goddess." Johesha dipped his head with respect.

The demon's eyes narrowed, the dark pupil—which had been slitted like a cat's—expanding across the green iris of his eyes. He was tall, as tall as Johesha, and lean with compact muscle. His smooth skin was a deep gray, showing off his muscular form under his black clothing. A warrior's form. His ears were pointed, clearly visible because his black hair was shaven on one side, revealing swirls of inked skin, and the length of what remained of his hair was braided and trailed down his back.

"It has been some time since I saw you. Before the spell broke." Lexa reached out and pressed a sharp nail to Johesha's bicep.

His heart picked up with trepidation not wanting the goddess's attention and not liking the other monster's. He moved to allow them to pass into the cottage. "Which?" he asked.

"Fair enough. The sleeping spell. The hedge. Take your pick."

He nodded and glanced at the other creature, unsure if he was safe, but Jude smiled at both warmly.

"Ozland." Jude tapped his breastplate, a greeting reserved for those respected in Jast.

"This is my demon," Lexa told Johesha.

"I am not yours," Ozland sneered at her, swinging his animalistic gaze back to Johesha. A predator meeting a predator, or so Johesha surmised. "Reformed demon," he stated. "I have been training the Fareviews with their powers. You were with the eldest?"

He nodded in answer.

"What is her power?"

"I don't–" Johesha started, unsure.

"Are you done with your pissing contest, Ozzy?" Lexa asked.

"Ozland, you witch," he said and moved into the cottage.

She tried to restrain her smile but couldn't, looking at Johesha. "It's too much fun antagonizing him," she whispered.

"I see where Nixus gets it."

Her smile widened, and she threaded her arm with Johesha's. "Lead the way into the chaos."

Johesha obeyed, believing no one ever denied the dragon goddess, and delivered her into the heart of the cottage, Ozland killing him—or Lexa since Johesha couldn't be sure—with his gaze. The small room was packed: Lachlan and Tarley, the god twins, Lucian and Nixus, Brinna and Aurielle, Lexa and her companion Ozland, Jude and himself.

"We weren't expecting you," Nixus said, hugging his sister.

She didn't hug him back but allowed his affection. "Yes. Well, we had information to share from our journey into the Netherrealm."

"The wizard's name?" Auri asked, hopefully.

"Unfortunately, no. Where is your duplicitous mother? We were hoping she would have that information."

Silence greeted Lexa's statement.

"What is it," she asked. "I haven't spoken of the dead."

Brinna blew out a held breath. "They haven't returned."

"They aren't in the Netherrealm?" Auri asked.

"Not on the death lists," Lexa replied. "I review them every morning." She took the coffee Brinna offered.

"I knew time would be complicated," Ozland said, leaning against a wall and crossing his muscular arms.

"No brooding," Lexa snapped. "My brothers brood enough for the whole of the universe."

"I'm entitled to my feelings, goddess," Ozland snapped back, and everyone seemed to take a collective breath and hold it, as if Lexa might flame him where he stood.

Except she didn't, and Johesha noted Nixus and Lucian exchanged a look when she seemed to ignore the reformed demon's temper and instead said, "We do have discoveries, though perhaps this information is useless if we don't have his name."

"Do tell," Lucian said. "We know you want to."

"Do you have to be so condescending, brother? You haven't taken father's place yet."

"Lexa." Lucian's impatience was a light on his already shining face.

She grinned. "Ozzy!" She twirled toward the monster. "Since you were so fond of the Netherrelm, you should do the honors."

He growled at her.

She laughed. "What?" She pressed a manicured hand, her nails sharpened into points, against her chest. "You don't want to?" Her lips puffed out in a pout, then, as if led by the flight of a falling star, she smiled. "Fine. I'll do it." She turned to the rest of them. "Who knew *reformed* demons didn't like being amongst the unreformed and were so moody about it?"

"I know you enjoy antagonizing us all, sister," Nixus said. "But if you would kindly get to the point."

One eyebrow arched. "The point." She tapped her mouth with a sharp nail. "I'm generally into soft things as opposed to hard ones, but perhaps I could be persuaded."

"Lexa," Lucian snapped.

She laughed. "The wizard has tethered himself to demons."

"Demons? As in more than one?" Auri asked.

She turned to Auri, a queen holding the attention of her court. "More than one is divine. A bit messy. You should try it sometime."

Nixus growled. "Lexa."

She laughed. "Still so possessive, brother. Loosen the leash. Yes. More than one demon. That is where his power is siphoned. Ask Ozzy."

Johesha glanced at Ozland again. "He'd have to have traded something," Ozland said still leaning against the wall, "made a bargain or a trade with the demons to be granted access to the power. To seal that bargain he would have had to give his true name."

"The demons didn't share it with you."

"They couldn't be persuaded," Lexa said darkly.

"They can't," Ozland added. "When the name is given, the power of it is drawn into the other, like a drop of rain on dry soil. The name is the collateral. If the demon speaks the name, the owner dies, but so too does the demon. No demon wants an end like that."

"Isn't there a way to magically get around that?" Tarley asked.

"In what way?" Lexa tilted her head. "Death is death."

"Maybe we could trick a demon to say Crue's true name," Brinna said.

"You think that would be easy?" Lexa asked, her eyes narrowing.

Brinna's hands fell to her sides. "Well, no. I just thought—"

"—thinking. Is that your strong suit?" Lexa asked.

"Lexa, if you'd like me to end you, keep going," Lucian said, his countenance dimming with displeasure and protectiveness. "I can make that happen."

"Ah, ah, ah," she said in a singsong tone, waving her finger back and forth. "Not yet, you can't."

"I can help him," Nixus said.

Lexa looked wounded.

"Stop being a bitch, Lexa," Auri stated, absolutely unfazed by the fact she was talking to the Queen of the Underworld. "You're deflecting, and it isn't pretty."

"She bites," Lexa said to Nixus. "I like it." She gave Auri a lecherous stare.

"Lexa," Nixus warned.

"Why would I deflect, Aurielle?" Lexa's voice was thick with sweet condescension.

"Because you couldn't fix this, and despite your airs, you want to. Now. Get to the matter at hand." Auri crossed her arms over her chest, facing down Lexa.

Lexa grinned. "I do love you, Aurielle. I'll only let you

get away with it because of Nixus."

"Fine." Auri arched an eyebrow waiting.

Lexa was silent, obstinate.

"The gods can't intervene," Ozland said. "It's the law."

Lexa rolled her eyes. "I was going for the drama, Ozzy. Why do you have to ruin my fun?" She sighed. "Our interference is against the Netherrealm Compact, which could free said demons."

"The underworld has a government?" Lachlan asked.

"But you're the queen?" Tarley asked. "Shouldn't you be able to make the rules?"

"If I was a bad one," she said. "I'm called the queen, but in reality, I'm the deity of the Netherream. I rule it, yes, but I oversee things. There are seven wards overseen by wardens. Agreements must be in place."

"Hence the compact," Lachlan said, nodding. "Why the stipulation against interference."

"That's not just the Netherrelm," Lucian said. "Immortal interference in mortal affairs is frowned upon, except in some circumstances."

"Convenient," Johesha muttered.

"Like this," Auri said. "Demons are involved. And Nixus helped me when Tarley was taken."

"And faced recompense for it with Father," Lexa said, looking at Nixus who frowned. "If we intervene, it could let loose at least three demons and give them a pass to reset until I capture them again, but who's to say the sorcerer hasn't tethered his soul to more of them?"

"So we need his name, which I don't think we'll have in time," Lucian said, leaning back in his chair.

"Which means the plan has to work." Johesha watched the fire in the hearth.

"So–" —Lexa clapped her hands together—"–what is the plan?"

Jessamine

Ten days. Johesha had been gone for ten days, and each one made her heart harder and more volatile. She wanted to rip Crue's heart from his chest and was only stopped by the understanding he was stronger and more adept at magic than she. So instead, she was a healer feeding him poison, nice and slow. It had been three consecutive days, and to her satisfaction, she was beginning to see the effects of it.

They stood in the workshop going over yet another potion that did nothing of consequence. This one was about changing one's looks to create a disguise, and her impatience was threadbare. She wasn't sure how much longer she could feign her obedience.

"You need three rat toenails," he said.

"Three more?" she asked.

Crue looked at her. "What do you mean, three more?"

"I already added three," she said.

He looked down at the slowly steaming position intended to provide unnatural, rapid growth. The thick, gray liquid plopped with a bloop, then sunk back into its heinous depths. Jessamine wrinkled her nose at the smell, a horrible sour stench akin to dirty, wet clothing roasting in a pile in the summer heat for too long.

Crue shook his head. "We added them?"

Jessamine forced herself to appear concerned. "Maybe you should go rest, Father. You seem… tired."

His dark eyes met hers again. "Yes. Yes. If we added the nails, we only need to leave this to cool before infusing the cold items." He paused and rubbed his forehead, his hand spanned over the skin. "I do have a headache."

It was the second day of the headache.

"We can finish later," he said as he walked from the room, grabbing the doorway to steady himself, then disappearing around the corner.

Jessamine hurried to the doorway to watch him go, grateful she didn't need to make any more poison. Her plans, however, now that she had some time, was to work on her memory potion. They were leaving the mansion soon, and she needed to be able to keep her head clear. Now that they'd been working on so many different magical mixtures, she had an idea of using what she'd already created and aligning it with one of Crue's.

As she assembled the ingredients, the darkling clicked at her. Over the last three days, with as much time as she'd spent in the monster's company, what used to unnerve her now seemed common. "What is it?"

"What have you given him?" it asked.

She paused as she reached for dried crow's brain, then grabbed the small container. "Why would you think that?"

"I share the tether with him."

"And what is it you think you are feeling?" She added a pinch of the matter to the mortar and returned the jar to the ingredients lined up and labeled along the wall. As much as it could be said Crue was a maniacal tyrant, he was an organized one.

"I am tired, but I fail to sleep."

She pressed the pestle into the mortar. "That could be many things. You are starving. It could be a lack of nutrients."

"I forget."

She paused again and turned to face the darkling. "Forget what?"

"From one moment to the next, like leaping over a ravine and forgetting I leapt."

"Also a lack of nutrients."

"You don't fool me."

She whirled back to her elixir, her hands flat on the table's surface. Her heart was hammering in her chest with unease, realizing she hadn't considered the tether. Then she went to war with herself wondering why she should care for the creature that had tried to end her sister. It killed

Johesha.

"I don't blame you," it said. "If I could, I would do it to be free."

She dumped the new dry ingredients into the base liquid she'd already tried. "You killed Johesha," she said quietly.

The darkling grew very quiet, uncharacteristically so. Even when it wasn't speaking, it was making noises. Clinks and chuffs, moans and screeches, huffs and hums. It rattled around in the cage constantly. This silence made Jessamine look over her shoulder.

It just made a noise, considering, and moved away from the small window, disappearing from view.

"What, nothing to say?" she challenged, but it remained silent.

With her window of time unknown, she didn't ponder it. Instead, she finished modifying her latest version of the memory elixir, grabbed a sample, and raced up to the greenhouse. Once there, she drank the sample and waited, counting to ten.

"Five."

She stopped in front of the door that led outside, thinking about the last time she'd gone through this door, the last time she'd ingested an elixir, her hand in Johesha's.

"Six."

Tears seeped from her eyes as she grabbed the brass handle and took a deep breath, clearing away the grief that threatened to keep her stuck.

"Seven."

She turned the handle and opened the door, unsure if

Crue had set a ward. She'd find a way to explain it away. A cold wind bit her bare skin, and though it was uncomfortable, she considered the beauty of pain she could see versus the wound she couldn't. The wind pinkened her skin while sadness rent her heart. She shuddered.

"Eight."

She closed her eyes and imagined Johesha, pictured him moving above her, his body buried in hers, his eyes mapping her face as they made love. *"You're everything, Jess,"* he'd said. Her throat tightened at the memory.

"Nine."

She imagined the way he looked when he smiled, the sound when he laughed, such a rare sound. Meditated one more time on the moment she told him she loved him.

"Ten."

She stepped over the threshold and gasped a deep breath, the cold seizing her lungs so that she doubled over. She waited, cognizant of where she was, what she was doing. With an anxious heart and a tentative step, she went a little further. Then a bit further.

She made it ten steps, and still there was no immediate desire to return. "It worked?" she whispered. Twirling, she looked at the door to the greenhouse. "It worked!" She did a little dance, then headed back toward the manor, stepping through the door expecting the crash of memory.

But it didn't occur. It didn't need to.

She'd done it!

With a heart filled with hope, she hurried back to the workshop. She needed to make enough for everyone in the manor, and for herself when they traveled. At the doorway, she slowed and glanced at the darkling's cell, guilt tripping up against her earlier conviction.

She wasn't a murderer.

Even if she hated Crue, her new awareness of the darkling made what she'd planned to do feel dirty and wrong. Ending Crue had consequences, and now that she'd found a way to counteract the spell with success, killing him might be the worse option.

With newfound purpose, she planned to use the time she had without Crue to make as much as she could.

The next time they met for tea, she didn't poison him.

Johesha

Darkness in the Whitling Woods felt heavier somehow, laced with deeper shadows, though Johesha couldn't be sure it wasn't Nixus's doing. The gods might not be able to intervene to end Crue like the mortals wanted, but Johesha didn't put it past the immortals to find ways to influence the world around them in other ways. Like this oppressive darkness. Even Lucian's light found in the moon and stars was suppressed, the reflection of the snow subdued.

Everyone except for Lexa and Ozland, who'd returned to wherever they came from, were getting ready for the journey south. Lantern light dotted the meadow fronting the cottage. Jast soldiers—those remaining from the first group—moved to and fro like worker ants. Brendsen and the younger soldier Kobb returned after delivering the final message to Crue, which meant it was time to enact the plan without Scarlett.

The first part of that plan entailed using the cover of night to travel, the idea to obscure who was in the party. Lucian and Nix decided to ferry everyone to a location that Brendsen and Kobb identified, which would get them there faster and without the ability to be tracked. Johesha didn't complain, since the dark kept him a man.

The soldiers remaining behind to keep watch over the cottage were to provide details should Tarley's family return. The prince and Tarley were in the mix of all that movement. But those soldiers were smaller in number. Lachlan was determined to make a good show of what had been in his missive, so the more soldiers the better.

"It's so good to see you here, sir," Brendsen said from Johesha's side as he watched Tarley speaking with a group of soldiers. She was pointing at the barn as she did.

Johesha glanced at Brendsen, nodded, then looked down, moved by the man's devotion, knowing that his dedication was what had uncovered him. Brendsen's persistence was what had led to the rest of them finding him and Jessamine. "Thank you, Brendsen, for not giving up on me."

Brendsen's heavy hand landed on Johesha's shoulder. "Sir, I would never. You–" He paused as if emotion caught in his throat, and Johesha turned his head. "Sir, you are everything I strive to be. Never a truer man have I known." His gaze met Johesha's. "Bringing you home, bringing Jessamine home was never a question, sir."

"Thank you. And it's Johesha." He offered the other man a short smile.

A crack in the forest made everyone whirl.

"Nixus?" Aurielle called. She held up a lantern.

Only Nix didn't step through the dark forest. Instead, several shadows approached. With focused speed he was grateful he hadn't lost, Johesha pulled his bow, Brendsen and Jude their weapons, the remaining soldiers positioning themselves between the prince and the strangers. While the fear was real, Johesha's instincts returned, his heart racing but his breathing calm, his eyes focused.

"Auri?"

Auri gasped and darted across the expanse, bursting through the soldiers' line of defense. "Mattie?" she cried. "Oh stars!" Her lantern lit the beleaguered faces of the missing Fareviews: Mattias, Scarlett and Tomas, and a strange woman Johesha hadn't met.

"Mom? Dad?" Auri said.

Brinna gasped and broke through the line to run across the meadow.

The party looked terrible, clothes torn, hair in disarray, almost like they'd been in a fight before dropping into the woods. Mattias and Tomas were still giants of men. Johesha was a large man at well over six feet, but these men had him by another head at least. Scarlett wasn't a small woman, but she looked like she was when standing next to her husband.

The stranger hung back. Johesha watched Mattias look over his shoulder at her and hold out his hand. She took it and stepped into his side. She was pretty even if her beauty was hidden under the mess they all made. They were dressed strangely, in old fashioned clothes that must have been from the time they'd just left.

"We're here?" Mattias asked. "What time is it?"

"The right time," Auri said, grabbing hold of him and squeezing him tight. "We were so worried."

"Stand down," Jude said, then maneuvered closer to the prince and his pregnant wife like a perfect captain. Johesha followed Jude's lead, noting Tarley didn't run forward.

"You're here. You're okay." Brinna was crying her arms around her father's middle. He hugged her back.

"It's so nice to be back," he mumbled into her hair.

"What happened?" Auri asked.

"I lost the threads," Mattias explained. "It's a long story."

"Lost them?"

"Jessamine?" Scarlett asked, looking around.

"We found her," Auri said.

Scarlett stalled, her eyes snapping to Auri's, then glancing around. "Where is she?"

"Not here yet," Brinna said, putting an arm around her mother and starting toward the cottage. "Crue still has her, but she's alive. It's a long story, but Captain Johesha followed her and has been with her the whole time. Except Crue put a spell on everyone where they couldn't remember anything."

"A memory spell?" Scarlett's eyes jumped across the sea of faces and connected with Johesha's. Her eyes narrowed, obviously confused.

Tomas followed, head and shoulders above everyone else except for Mattias, who trailed behind them.

Tarley stepped forward. "Mother. Father."

Scarlett's forward progress froze.

Tarley, with Lachlan standing behind her, his hands on her shoulders, wore her pregnancy regally, her protruding belly belying no secret to her impending motherhood.

Scarlett's hand covered her mouth with a gasp. "A baby?" She burst into tears. "How long have we been gone?"

Tomas didn't wait for Scarlett to find herself, stepping past his wife to pull Tarley into a hug. "You didn't tell us. Did you know? Before?"

She nodded, tears sliding down her face. "I didn't know you'd be gone for so long."

"How long have we been gone?" Mattias asked.

"Six months," Brinna answered.

Scarlett kept her distance from Tarley, waiting for her daughter's invitation into the moment she was sharing with her father. When Tarley looked up, she turned to her mother and threw her arms around her.

Johesha looked away, suddenly missing a family that wasn't his anymore, hadn't been for over twenty years. It made him feel... morose. The emptiness was a stark reminder of what he'd built over the last twenty years. Isolation. But he recalled another conversation he and Jessamine had had in the cottage during those dreamy two days. "You've built a family, though you've been separated from yours," she'd said. "Your team. The prince."

He recognized the truth of her words looking at Brendsen, Jude, Prince Lachlan.

Could he build something new?

I love you. Jessamine's words and smile hit his heart.

He wanted something new with Jessamine.

"Did you find his name?" Aurielle was asking as she passed him with Mattias, heading for the cottage.

"We have a name, but whether it's Crue's true name isn't certain," Mattias said. The other woman stood near him. He noted no one else seemed surprised by her, which made him think the family knew her.

Nixus and Lucian rematerialized into the low light of the yard. "Who's next," the god asked, grinning. His grin shifted when he saw them all, and he turned toward them. "Well, this changes things."

They'd settled into the cottage with some clean clothes and warm food, everyone now there, except for Jessamine. Scarlett, Tomas, Mattias, and the woman named Ruhnna sat at the table, bowls of steaming food in front of them.

Brinna set a basket of bread down, then joined them.

"Stars, I missed home," Mattias said, scooping stew into his mouth.

"We were gone for six months?" Ruhnna asked, the confusion crossing her pretty features. "It didn't feel like six months." She looked at Mattias.

He wiped his mouth on a napkin, then hugged the young woman against him. It was clear there was a bond between them, though what that bond entailed wasn't clear. Mattias turned his head and pressed a comforting kiss to her temple.

"We went through the doorway," Mattias explained, "then I used Mother's thread to figure out where she ended."

"You can see individual life threads?" Auri asked from the kitchen where she was making fresh coffee. Nixus was with her, his shadows keeping hold of her.

"If I know what I'm looking for," Mattias answered, reaching for a piece of bread. "Mother was with me, so it was easier to find it."

"And then what happened?" Brinna asked, glancing at Lucian as he sat next to her.

"When we got to Mother's time, we used the map," Mattias said.

A swollen silence filled the space, until Tarley asked, "What was it like?"

They all looked to Scarlett, who swallowed her bite, then glanced at Tomas. "Strange."

Johesha didn't know the whole of the story, but bits and pieces had been revealed over his days spent with the family. He knew that whatever had happened to Scarlett, the magic that had eventually brought her to Sevens had occurred under duress, and somehow Crue was behind it.

"Then what happened?" Lachlan asked.

"We used Scarlett's map," Tomas said.

"Found the old woman Mother remembered as Crue's aunt. She told us that Crue was adopted. So that's where we went. But we had to split up to look for the right orphanage." Mattias took a sip of his steaming cup of tea.

"We think we found it," Tomas added, providing hope.

"But we can't confirm it truly is Crue. We're guessing." Scarlett folded her hands in her lap, her stew barely touched.

"Then?"

The four of them exchanged looks.

"It all went to shit," Ruhnna said.

"The threads got tangled," Mattias explained. "Unraveling them to get us all back here was difficult."

"And how did you get here?" Tarley asked.

"Pax." Mattias glanced at Luc, though Johesha wasn't sure why that would be. "I'm glad he went with us."

"I'm surprised my brother didn't complicate things." Lucian chuckled. "I'm glad to hear he helped."

"How do we confirm it's his name?" Brinna asked, getting them back on track.

"We use it," Auri stated. "If it's his true name–"

"–we'll certainly get a reaction," Scarlett said, "if it is his name."

"I think we still go in as we planned, Scarlett and Tomas hidden at the camp," Lachlan said. "What do you think, Johesha?"

Johesha, leaning against the hearth, considered a moment, then nodded. "I think having him unsettled helps more than him being on firm footing."

"It would seem then–" —Tomas used his bread to clean the bottom of his dish— "–it's time to get our daughter back and end this."

Crue

The manor was a flurry of activity, preparing for the trek to the meeting place. The maids were assembling trunks of clothing and household goods to use within the tents being prepared by the porters. The cook was planning and packing food and utensils. The groomsmen were prepping the horses, carriages, and wagons. While that was taking place, Crue stood in the workshop staring at the darkling's prison, contemplating if he should take the creature. Keeping it close, he finally decided, using it in his final triumph over Scarlett, seemed the best option.

His body was jittery with nerves.

His existence for the last thirty years had focused on the moment rushing toward him now. It felt surreal and fantastical.

"We're going soon," he told the monster, placing some tools and ingredients in a trunk to take in case he needed them.

"Where?" the darkling asked.

"I'm finally meeting Scarlett. I'll be getting the powers back."

"And you will set me free."

"Potentially. I think I'm closer to breaking the tether." It was a lie. He wasn't any closer, but he was thinking that perhaps it would be a matter of trading the godblood hearts to break it and then end the darkling with fire. He couldn't have the creature wreaking havoc in the world, unchecked.

Footsteps at the door made Crue whirl around.

Jessamine—who he'd finally released from her confinement the day prior—walked into the workshop. She looked as lovely as ever, if a touch thinner. She hadn't been eating well since the demise of the huntsman, but she would regain her health when her sadness passed. He remembered the sadness when Azleah had fled, when he'd found her trail in the woods and found she'd changed her name to Scarlett and taken up with the tiny nymph, Tomas. How hurt and angry he'd felt she'd chosen such a weak creature over him. Crue recognized that his anger hadn't passed but had festered into what he was now, what had fed his obsession. But he'd been betrayed. Jessamine hadn't faced trickery by the huntsman, so he was certain her emotions over the man would wane with time.

"Daughter?"

Her eyes jumped from the darkling to him. "I came to see if you needed any help?"

The darkling chittered at the sound of her voice, drawing Crue's gaze. He narrowed his eyes. "No imprinting on her."

"I have not," the darkling said in a new voice. It had changed faces.

Jessamine cleared her throat. "Is there anything you need to carry to the wagon?"

"Leave it for the servants," Crue said and noted the high color in her cheeks. "You are excited."

"To be with my family again?" Her eyes were filled with that fire and rage. "Yes."

Crue knew she despised him. Her hatred didn't bother him, however, not completely, because she'd become a rather adept student. "We have a lot more work to do, though, daughter. You could stay—" The fact that he said it was strange, and he swallowed down the rest of the thought: that she might choose to stay. No one had ever stayed for him. Not in the entirety of his life. Her choice would bolster him, but she didn't have a choice. She would remain with him because he had no intention of returning Jessamine to her mother. Scarlett, plus any one of her other siblings, would be dead, and Jessamine would be his forever. The spell would make sure of her return regardless.

This brought him comfort.

She didn't reply and instead took the bottles of various

herbs he was holding out to her and put them in the open trunk.

"The darkling seems taken to you," he said.

Jessamine paused, her hands still in the trunk, the clinking of the glass inside subsiding. "What do you mean?"

Crue looked back at the cage, at the deep brown fingers, human, wrapped around the bars. "I think it likes you."

"I don't need to be liked by it," she said, continuing her organization of his supplies.

He liked having her with him. Over the last several days, teaching her had given him something he hadn't expected. A strange warmth in the withered muscle of his struggling heart. "It won't satiate if that's what you're concerned about."

She sniffed and took another bottle.

"On this trip, I'd like you to oversee its transport, look after its care."

Her eyes flashed to the creature, then back to him, her mouth opening as if she might protest. Then she shut her mouth, and her jaw clenched before she nodded. "Fine."

"Did you hear, darkling?" Crue asked loudly.

"I did." Its voice was decidedly human.

Crue turned to look at it, wondering what face it had taken, the tone and timbre decidedly familiar. "Are you using the huntsman's face?"

The hands wrapped around the bars shifted into the bony extremities wrapped in shadow, and the creature withdrew from the small window into the cage.

"What will I need to do?" Jessamine asked.

"Just keep it chained." He picked up a spelled chain glowing with the green of his magic, and it clanked on the countertop. "With this."

The darkling screeched.

"What happens if it isn't?"

"It will hunt, and controlling what it eats is impossible. It might eat your family. One can't predict these things."

He perversely liked that Jessamine shuddered at the thought. Maybe he should let the darkling hunt them, but then again, he needed godblood hearts and he couldn't risk losing one. The demons would collect, and that would mean harvesting Jessamine's heart. He'd already decided against that if it could be helped.

"Fine," she said. "I will take care of the darkling."

He smiled and finalized his packing. For the first time in a long time—since being with Azleah— he accepted the warmth of a pleasant feeling at work inside him, wondering if it was love. Or something like it.

Johesha

With the sun rising higher in the sky, Johesha moved through the forest in his stag form, using his animal instincts for stealth and silence, and his human instincts to bring him to Jessamine. She was the core focus of his purpose as the stag, and the motivation as a man to seek the layout of the enemy's retinue. He'd left everyone else back at camp just as the sun had risen, as the rest still slept before setting out for the confrontation with Crue. His purpose now was reconnaissance.

"Be careful of wards," Scarlett told him shortly before

dawn. They'd stood at the edge of the fire in the shadows. Jessamine's mother had been wrapped in warm clothes, her arms tucked up around her. "Crue won't leave himself open."

"For man or beast?" he'd asked.

"Good point." She glanced down at the leather strip tied around his wrist. "Perhaps it won't matter, either way."

"Because this can help me with his magic?"

She nodded and was silent for a moment. She swallowed. "Jessamine? Was she–"

"Healthy. Strong. Determined," he said. "She's a fighter."

Scarlett nodded, her eyes filling with tears she worked to keep contained. "I know that is meant to bring me comfort, but it also frightens me. I want her alive."

"She's smart."

She laughed through the tears. "She is. Has always been clever." She sniffed, her thoughts drifting somewhere Johesha couldn't imagine as she wiped the tears from her cheeks. "When she was little, we would walk through the woods collecting herbs. I would test her on them as we did." Scarlett paused, and Johesha waited, hungry for more stories of Jessamine, wanting to feel close to her, a part of her life. Scarlett smiled as she met his eyes. "She renamed the herbs to help her remember them. It was so cute."

Then her gaze drifted, her smile fading. She looked down at the cold ground before tilting her face up to meet his gaze once again. The vulnerability on her features, a tender openness that he didn't equate with Scarlett painted each line and plane of her face and made his heart pinch inside his chest. "Thank you, captain. For following her."

"Johesha. It was my honor." But it was more than that now. It was falling in love and made him wonder if perhaps it always had been, or the seeds of it, dormant in soil that only needed time to sprout and grow.

It wasn't much longer that he left her behind because the sunrise had threatened.

Now—the sun high in the sky—he moved through the trees using the shadows as he foraged for food and watched for signs of Crue, unsure what he might find. Besides the memory spell on whoever had come with the wizard, Johesha's role was to find them, deliver the gifts to Jessamine, ascertain the magic, then return. It took most of the morning, the beast looking for food with Johesha searching, but eventually he found the camp. Based on the flurry and activity of setting up, they'd only just arrived.

"Henro?" Mrs. Gerrick yelled, her voice sharp in the snowy forest, but muted by its density. "Help me start the fire."

The boy bounded from one of the dark green tents he'd been helping to erect toward his mother's voice. "Does the benevolent Master need a fire for his fancy pool?"

The memory spell was obviously still working, then. He'd anticipated as much and wondered what that might mean trying to get to Jessamine, wondering how to get beyond it.

Johesha caught sight of Crue, using his hands like that of a musical conductor and moving his lips as the tent appeared to erect itself. Johesha couldn't hear the man but watched as he conjured power to have inanimate objects do his bidding. When the tent was standing, the wizard walked around it, chanting. When he was finished, he started around the circumference of the camp. Johesha made sure to stay out of sight, watching as Crue put up magical wards. The barrier, coated with radiant green light, rose from the ground up, winding around the camp. As it curled over like a dome, the light flashed when it converged, then was gone.

Johesha moved on eager to see Jessamine, counting a total of four tents sheltered under the boughs of the trees, nicely camouflaged in the forest but for the snow around them. The evergreens offered some cover. The snow had been cleared for each tent, though whether it was human hands or magical ones wasn't certain. With the fires puffing smoke, Crue clearly wasn't worried about being discovered, which, Johesha decided, meant that the sorcerer was comfortable behind whatever magic he'd conjured.

Johesha circumnavigated the camp, grazing, foraging, and observing.

His head snapped up, his body tense as Jessamine emerged from a tent. The days between—fifteen—had been a lifetime. His antlers crashed against tree branches, causing a ruckus. Jessamine's head spun around toward the noise he'd made. His breath caught as memory and dreams and fantasy found handholds inside his lungs, making them feel depleted and needy. He understood, however, this wasn't just desire. His belief that he was falling in love with Jessamine was true but too thin to describe the depth of what he felt. He wasn't falling, he was already submerged in the deep drowning of it. He loved her with every fiber that made him. The awareness trapped him, unsure how that could ever work now, Crue's magic having changed him into… what he was now.

"Jessamine!" Crue's voice called.

"Yes, Father?" She turned back toward the wizard's voice.

"The darkling…"

"Yes, Father." She started across the camp, leaving Johesha behind.

He trailed her and watched from the shadows as she unhooked the cage door of a wooden container. She disappeared inside with a chain, and after a few moments, reemerged with the chain stretched between her and what was in the box.

"Come out," she coaxed and rather than pull the chain like Crue might have done, held out a hand.

The dark being's giant skeletal hand appeared and grasped hers, then it slunk out of the box, which was much too small. Standing at its full height, the shadow monster towered over Jessamine's head. Then suddenly it shifted, shrinking into a smaller being, a human one with brown skin, dark, curly hair, dressed… in leathers. It was him. Johesha.

His heart raced with terror.

"I don't like this face." Crue wrapped the creature's neck in a manacle.

The darkling didn't change back, just eyed the wizard, adopting Johesha's mannerisms.

Jessamine didn't shy away from it and didn't appear frightened as she led it from the box toward a tree at the other side of camp. It lifted its face—Johesha's face—and sniffed the air. With an animalistic groan, it shifted back into its massive, wreathing mass of darkness and growled, searching the forest. "Mercy," it intoned in that characteristic hiss.

It knew Johesha was there, and his heart raced, unsure if the mercy between them still stood.

Jessamine spoke to it, her mannerism kind whereas Crue was impatient and demanding, jerking the chain she'd handed the wizard. He fastened the creature to a tree. "There. Can't say I don't let you out."

"Give me freedom," it growled, though whether that sentiment was for Johesha or for Crue, he wasn't sure.

Johesha shuddered from a shadow where he observed. Jessamine, situated behind Crue, watched the exchange and inconspicuously lifted something to her lips. Johesha leaned forward, certain that he'd just witnessed something important. By the time Crue turned around, Jessamine looked as placid as before, smiling at the wizard with that characteristically empty look.

The afternoon waned into evening, and still Johesha watched. He had no intention of coming this way and not testing the wards, not trying to see if he could get to Jessamine. He had an assignment. So he waited and watched other animals cross the wards without problem, without the wizard coming to check them.

Just before sunset, he crossed into the camp and hid, testing his theory. No wizard, no magical repercussions.

Animals could cross whatever magic Crue had set. Even knowing that, Johesha knew he would have to cross back through as a man and hoped to be long gone before it mattered.

Using the brushes and bramble to hide, he worked his way around the camp from tent to tent to the one he knew belonged to Jessamine and waited for the change. As the sun ducked under the horizon, Johesha's human form tore from the body of the beast. He lay a moment in the freezing loam to catch his breath and wait for cessation of the burn that drove like spikes through his bones, muscles, and skin. When he could move, he quickly dressed, not wanting to waste time. Once he was done, he skulked from his hiding place to Jessamine's tent, which he was certain was empty but for her.

With a quick look around the front side which faced the center of the camp, he watched to see who might witness his arrival. Servants sat around a fire in front of the wagon, laughing, oblivious. The opening of Crue's tent glowed with light. The darkling was past that, somewhere in the dark, though Johesha couldn't see it. With a deep, settling breath, he ducked into Jessamine's tent.

Jessamine

The bath had cooled, now lukewarm. She'd fallen asleep, exhausted from having to pretend with Crue. Tired from the persistent ache that lingered in the center of her chest, missing Johesha. Weary of her mind spinning on how to get away from Crue now that they were beyond the manor. The memory elixir she'd made was working not only for her but for the three key people she'd given it to: Mary, Mrs. Gerrick, and Mr. Oto. The plan was to give the elixir to the rest of the household who'd come on this journey the day after she left with Crue for the meeting with her family. But what would happen to them after that? The circumstances were obscured and unpredictable.

She wouldn't have minded more hot water, but she'd sent Mary away and didn't have any warming on the stove of her shelter, which she might admire if it hadn't been made by Crue. Though it looked like a tent on the outside, on the inside it resembled a cottage filled with luxury. There was a wooden floor covered with plush carpet. A stove sat to one side heating the space, all of it insulated by thick, sturdy wooden walls that looked nothing like the walls of the tent. A bed was piled with thick blankets and pillows.

She sat inside of a copper tub near the stove with a thick robe waiting for her when she got out. She'd spent too much time thinking about how to get away from Crue, too much time wishing that what she'd heard earlier out in the forest, the shadowy outline of an animal, had been Johesha but knowing her imagination was playing tricks on her.

Johesha was gone no matter how many times her heart and mind wished it differently.

She couldn't cry, though. Not now, even if she wanted to. There was a plan to be figured out to get all the people stuck in the spell away from Crue, and it was on her to make it. While she didn't second- guess her decision to stop poisoning him, if she could have figured out how to do it without hurting the darkling, she would have. His magic was just so powerful. It seemed her only option was to get close enough to stab him in the back.

Or course, it wasn't that she liked the darkling, but

rather that voice inside her, the instincts skittering through her like the bubbles of a pot beginning to boil. That instinct insisted she keep the darkling safe from whatever machinations Crue intended. She didn't know them, of course, but offering the creature compassion seemed the right course. It was the one thing Crue never used and the one thing she could cling to in spades. The one thing that made her, well, her.

She stood.

The rush of air being drawn in like the harsh whisper of the window snapping through the trees was the first clue she wasn't alone.

She started to whirl, but strong arms encircled her and snapped her back against a sturdy body. Before she could scream, a hand clamped over her mouth.

"Shhh," a voice warned. "Don't scream."

He sounded like…

"Johesha?" she said behind the hand.

"It's me," he said into her ear.

"How?" As much as she wanted it to be true, how could it be. Was she still asleep? Tears pierced her eyes as she grabbed hold of the arm banded across her chest and pulled it away from her mouth. "You're dead."

"I'm not. I'm here, love."

He turned her to face him.

Her mouth dropped open as she gasped, her eyes cataloging all his features, looking for the trick. His face was perfect. That gorgeous rigidity that drew masculine lines of his jaw and nose, shaped his eyes fringed with those thick, dark lashes. He'd shaved his beard, but his hair was still long, perfect curls dripping to frame his beautiful brown face. His eyes were shiny, black orbs. Her gaze dipped to his damp shirt.

"Why are you doing this to me?" she asked, frowning.

"Doing what?" He held her by her upper arms.

She broke his hold, stepping from the bathtub and snatching her robe. Putting it on, she tied the belt with a jerky, irritated movements. "I asked you to stop putting on his face. Are you purposefully trying to hurt me?" She turned to face the disguised darkling, the tub between them. "How did you get in here anyway? Crue chained you."

"Who do you think I am?" he asked, tilting his head.

"Don't play coy with me. That's cruel."

"But it's me, Jess."

She paused, hope flickering inside her, but she squished it like a roving insect. "Oh. So the heart I saw? That was your idea of a joke?"

Awareness seemed to dawn on him. "The darkling is still chained up to the tree where Crue left it. It's me."

She swallowed.

He stepped closer. "I promise you. On my honor, Jess. Crue changed me into a stag fifteen days ago. The darkling hunted me, but then let me go, saying that it was paying its debt for my kindness."

"But," she stammered, still wary. "How?" He was standing here as a man, not an animal.

"The woman from the cottage. She changed Crue's spell somehow, so that I could walk at night as myself, the stag during the day." He held up a hand and pointed to the leather strap around his wrist. "Would the darkling know to mimic this?"

"It was you, outside today?" Her breath caught as a sob burst through the last word, and she covered her mouth with her hands.

He nodded. "I promise you. It's me."

Tears flooded her eyes, slipping down her cheeks. She'd accused the darkling of killing Johesha, she'd taken its silence for confirmation. "Oh gods," she whispered. "Is it really you?"

"Ask me where I've been."

"Have you seen my family?"

He nodded. "All of them." The man with Johesha's face took a step closer, skirting the bathtub. "I haven't stopped thinking about you telling me you love me and regretting every coarse and unworthy part of myself that I hadn't said it back."

With another sob, knowing it was him, certain of it, she rushed into his arms, her body awash with relief, remnants of grief, and a tumult of new emotions she didn't have the wherewithal to ponder.

Johesha's hands framed her cheeks, lifting her face to meet his gaze. "You consume me, Jessamine. Heart, body, and soul. I am yours."

"You're here," she said through tears, holding his strong wrists, then releasing them to touch his face.

"Of course I'm here. I am yours. There is nowhere else in this world for me but by your side." His hands slid down to her backside, and he lifted her, so she was even with his face. "I love you. Stars, I love you. I'm sorry I didn't say it–"

But Jessamine didn't let him finish, pressing her lips to his instead. His familiar scent—evergreen and leather, something the darkling couldn't replicate—wrapped her in a comforting embrace as she kissed him. His lips were as she'd remembered, divinely perfect, and reminded her of their stolen hours in the cottage, bolstering her with the awareness that she wasn't alone anymore.

When he pulled away to look at her, she finally gave him a teary smile. He set her back on her feet and wiped her tears with his thumbs.

"How are you able to remember me?" he asked. "I thought the spell–"

She shook her head, silencing him, then pulled him over to the end of the bed to sit. "I figured out the potion. When we returned to the manor, Crue started teaching me spells. I don't think he wanted me to learn anything worthwhile, the spells were silly, mostly. His intent was to manipulate me into thinking he was trusting me. But those silly spells got me thinking about how they were formulated, what the ingredients did. So I used some of them to reformulate the memory elixir. It worked."

He grinned, beautiful and vibrant and raw. "My brilliant girl."

"I made enough for everyone. I'm not the only one who has it. Mrs. Gerrick, Mr. Oto, and Mary do as well. They are giving it to the rest tomorrow after Crue and I are gone. Hopefully they can get away."

"And after that?"

"I hadn't gotten that far."

He chuckled and pulled her into his arms. "Your family is here. They are worried about you."

She gripped his damp shirt in her fists, climbing into his lap, her legs framing his. That made her happy, but not as buoyant as knowing he was here. "Is there a plan?"

He nodded and pulled a strip of leather from his pocket. It looked so much like his. "This was given to me by the old woman. I think it's touched by her magic, like mine."

"What's it for?" she asked as he fastened it around her wrist.

"We aren't sure, but if it's like mine, it seems like the best way to protect you from any of Crue's possible new spells. Hopefully to keep your mind clear." He looked around, then stood, pulling her to her feet, suddenly frantic. "We should just get you out of here. Get dressed and gather what you want. We'll run."

As much as she wanted to run with him, she hesitated. "But the others."

"They have the elixir."

"But it doesn't solve the problem."

Crue.

He hung his head, sighed, and nodded. "There's a plan."

"And does it involve me here or missing?"

He looked up and swallowed, his gaze searching her face. "Here."

She smiled. "Then I stay."

Johesha

Johesha didn't like it, the idea of leaving her there, but he understood. Rather than attempt to persuade her from a sense of duty he knew all too well, he acquiesced. What else could he do? She was ultimately trapped in a spell, the same as him. Different circumstances, but prisons, nonetheless. Besides, the plan did require her here. As much as he wanted to protect her now, he had to trust everyone else. This was out of his control, and as uncomfortable as it felt, he knew it was the right course.

"All right," he finally said.

"Stay tonight?" she asked and kissed the corner of his mouth. "With me?" She pressed her lips softly against his, and he kissed her back, relishing the ability to have her there in his arms, to feel her, to touch her.

That damned organ in his chest constricted, desire and need speaking more than his sense of honor, but he couldn't fall into the same pattern of withholding his heart. He moved her off his lap, and when she was standing, he went down to his knees before her.

"Johesha?"

"Let me speak. Please," he said, grasping her hips as he looked up at her face. "I need to say this before anything else."

She swallowed. "I'm listening." She reached out to touch him, but he grabbed her hand to keep from losing the concentration her touch stole from him.

"I am a lowly palace guard who forsook his vow to follow you. I left my post, dishonorably, in spite of my intentions. I come from farming parents and have a family I haven't seen in over twenty years. I am–" He paused, unsure how to say what he wanted to say, but forged ahead anyway, following the path as it was revealed to him. "Self-centered. I'm not... whole." He finally met her gaze. "And I love you. A woman who is a healer. A woman of noble and immortal birth. A woman who is superior to me in every way. A woman I don't deserve."

"Hesha," she whispered, shaking her head.

"I'm not finished." He shook his head. "Even still, that love—your love—has changed me." He looked up at her then, meeting her gaze. "I see the world through eyes brightened by you. When you aren't there, I can think only of having you near me again, for the world is dim without you."

"You are a good man."

"I might be a good man, Jessamine, but you have offered a path for me to be a better one."

"Hesha," she said, getting to her knees with him. "You forget, I am a woman raised as the daughter of peasants. I am a healer, but I have walked the world asleep, until you. You believed in me, so I found a way to be seen, to know myself." Her dark eyes shone with tears. "You have helped me find my courage, my voice." She smiled through her tears and pressed his hand against the center of her chest where he could feel the thumping of her heart. "I love you."

"Be my wife, Jessamine." He knew he shouldn't ask, not now, when he couldn't stay a man, and she was stuck with the wizard. But if something happened tomorrow, if one of them was lost, he needed her to know the depth of his love. "I want to wake up with you every day. I want to have dreams and make plans together. I want to build a life with you." He paused, realizing the truth and totality of the oath he was making. He wanted this more than he'd ever wanted anything, more than being a palace guard, could imagine the joy of a life shared with her.

Tears were streaming down her cheeks, but she was smiling through them. "Yes, Johesha. Yes." Then she was kissing him. "I vow to be yours, forever," she said between kisses.

Heat surged through him starting at the center of his chest, and unfurling outward. With a crackle, like wood splintering when chopped, something burst from inside him. A rush of wind swirled, lifting his hair, skittering over his skin, and then it was silent.

"What was that?" Jessamine asked.

"I think it was the spell." He looked around, chills racing along his skin, and his gaze met hers. "I think it's broken."

She kissed him again, her joy transferring into him. "Oh stars! Are we sure?"

"We'll know at sunrise." He grabbed her face once more between his hands and made her look at him. "I pledge my life to you, Jessamine."

She drew in a deep breath. "Please, Johesha. Too much talking." Then her lips melded with his.

He groaned and chuckled, feeling light, and followed her down onto the carpet. On his knees between her open thighs, he leaned back onto his heels and tugged at the belt tied at her waist. Then he spread the fabric, his palm sliding across her skin so he could see her body once again.

She shivered.

"Are you cold?"

She shook her head, another tear falling from the corner of her eyes. "I'm brimming with joy I can't contain. You are alive. You are here, and I feel as if I've come home."

With a growl, Johesha dropped forward and kissed her, then pressed a hand against her heart. "Home is where you are, my love." He kissed her with all that feeling, with everything he understood in his own heart, hoping she could feel that devotion down in the marrow of her bones.

"I love you so much," she said as he trailed kisses down her neck. Her gasp when he sucked her breasts filled his lungs with air. When she grabbed his head as he slid down between her legs and kissed her there, it added fire to his blood. He licked her seam, and she mewled with desire. "This is fucking home, Jessamine. Here." He licked her from her opening to her clit. "This cunt is mine," he said between licks and flicks of his tongue. She tasted like... his, and he groaned against her sex. "Fuck, Jess. I want you to come."

She moaned, panting and grasping at him, catching him with her nails. "Yes. Yes," she sobbed. "Oh gods. I missed you. I was so broken without you. Please, Johesha. I just need–"

"I know what my woman needs," he snapped, shoving a finger inside her and flicking her clit with his tongue. He pushed another finger inside her.

She cried out.

He covered her mouth with a hand, catching her sound, and fucked her with the other, his mouth and hands taking her apart bit by bit. When he felt the muscles of her cunt tighten around his fingers, and her cries grew more intense against his palm, Johesha inserted another finger and took her home with his tongue, leading her to complete annihilation. Her hips bucked against his face, and he welcomed the way her nails dug into his head and neck as she lost her mind.

As she convulsed with the aftershocks of her orgasm, he wiped his mouth against her thigh, then sat up and stripped off his shirt. Next came his shoes, then his pants, until he was bent over her again, sliding into the warm sheath of protection she offered his body and his heart.

She gasped, grabbing hold of him. "I'm yours," she said over and over as he moved in and out of her.

Unable to calm his own need, Johesha lost his rhythm, erratically thrusting. Understanding what he'd lost, and now what he'd regained undid him. He stopped, gathering his wits, his thoughts, backing away from the impending orgasm but kissing her. "Fuck," he said as he moved inside her. "You remake me, wife."

She gasped and smiled. "I like the sound of that, husband."

He groaned, giving her short pulses, then rolling and pulling her on top of him. She was beautiful, her gorgeous breasts dark and peaked, so he reached up and fitted them into his hands as she sunk down onto his cock again and again, her volume climbing again.

She bent forward to hide her cries against his neck, tilting her hips in a gorgeous rhythm but losing her momentum. Johesha grabbed her hips and helped her ride, helping her keep a rhythm that suddenly had him biting down on his own words. "Fuck. Fuck, Jess."

He rolled her again and abandoned all semblance of rhythm, pounding into her. Her cunt tightened around his cock, fluttering at the same time she whimpered, "I'm coming. Hesha." Her back arched, and his beautiful woman became a goddess in his eyes, her beauty as she succumbed to her orgasm the only thing he saw even as she squeezed his cock.

He didn't stop, pumping into her with a punishing power until he followed her into oblivion, panting against her neck and whispering "I love you" as he came.

Jessamine

They hadn't made it to the bed, still wrapped up in one another on the floor of the tent, covered by the robe she'd been wearing. She had rug burns on her shoulder blades and knees, but their presence made her grin.

"Finish what you were telling me." She loved how much he had opened up.

"They went back in time to your mother's time."

"I don't understand all that." She couldn't stop touching him, reassuring herself he was there.

"I know. I don't either. But your siblings have powers

and Mattias is able to move through time, somehow."

She leaned back to look a bit closer at Johesha and enjoyed that the corner of his eyes crinkled as he smiled. "Powers." She thought back to all Crue's ramblings. "Is this why Crue is after my mother?"

"Tarley said the powers were given to your mother by Crue."

"Tarley? And Brinna? Auri?"

"All here."

"I've missed them. I didn't think I would, you know. Sometimes being around my family felt so stifling that all I wanted was to get away from them. But being away from them all I have wanted is to return."

"Perhaps it's the circumstances," he said, "rather than the need to be apart."

She heard his own understanding in the depth of what he said.

They talked through the days they'd been separated, filling one another in on what they'd missed. She relished the feel of Johesha's fingers skimming her spine, his strength pressed against her, his arm around her, his deep voice vibrating in her own chest. He was here! Her throat tightened with the joy of him there, alive, with her. Giddiness and lightness at his confession, his vow planted happiness she was struggling to contain.

They spoke of what she'd learned about the darkling. Of what he'd learned from her sisters and their powers. They talked with *what if's* once more, Jessamine certain that this time those wishes were filled with more hope than before.

"What if in one year you want a ceremony, wife?" He kissed her shoulder.

"Then we have one." She smiled at him.

He sighed, looking up at the ceiling overhead. "I should go." He turned toward her, pressing his lips against her cheek, and it was clear he didn't want to as he pulled her closer.

She turned her head so her mouth met his, then angled her body, wrapping a leg over his thighs. "Stay," she said against his lips.

"What if the spell–"

"What ifs are only for good things," she said, looking down at him from her vantage point, her hands on his chest. "Sneak out just before sunrise."

With a relenting groan, he rolled toward her, reaching between them to grab his cock and notch it at her exposed opening. Then he sheathed himself inside her, and she gasped with the immense pleasure of him there, the rightness of it.

He made love to her with deliberate slowness, a savoring, whispering words of love and devotion. She moved with him, relishing the closeness, the fullness, the sensations he inspired inside her beyond the physical.

"I love you," she gasped, too full of him, too full of all the emotion as tears slipped silently down her cheeks.

"I worship you," he answered, kissing those tears as he moved inside her.

When the rhythm turned frantic, his kisses, his body provided the shelter she needed as desperation crested inside her, and she cried against his neck. He followed her into oblivion a few moments after, using her as a shelter, a fixed point on his compass, swearing against her skin as he succumbed.

After they'd come down together, giggling as they washed up with cold water and climbed into bed, Jessamine allowed the dream of this possible reality to settle inside her. "I don't want to sleep," she admitted. "I want to stay like this with you."

He kissed her. "This isn't an end," he said, a promise. "Not a what if. This is the beginning."

When she woke the next morning, Johesha was gone. She reached for him, but the sheets were cold, and she wondered if she'd dreamed the night before. Only the leather tie on her wrist remained and tucked under the pillow where he'd lain was a dagger proving it had been real.

"Good morning, my lady," Mary said, entering the tent.

Jessamine stashed the dagger, sat up, then realized she was still naked and covered herself with a sheet.

Mary didn't seem to notice, floating around the tent with purpose as she pulled clothing from trunks. "I thought the rose wool for today."

Jessamine tied her robe closed not caring what color she wore, and turned her nose against the shoulder, Johesha's scent lingering there. Then she nodded. "Does everyone have it?" she asked, her voice low.

Mary's bright gaze looked over her shoulder at the tent flap, then nodded, coming closer. "Everyone, but we might have a problem." She held up the underclothes.

Jessamine removed the robe she'd just donned.

"Why?"

"Now that they're awake and aware, some of them are threatening to run."

"They were supposed to wait until after we left."

"I know, but Mr. Oto–" Mary sighed.

"Can they be talked into waiting until we leave for the meeting?" She adjusted the ivory shift as Mary turned to grab the next layer.

"Mrs. Gerrick and Mr. Oto are working to keep everyone contained. I think their message has been that if they run, who knows if the Master won't harm them with his dark magic."

Jessamine nodded, turning for Mary to lace the stays at her back. "That isn't a lie."

Mary finished fastening the stays and turned for the first petticoat, a soft green. "And then?" Mary helped pull it over Jessamine's head, then pulled the drawstrings to fasten it into place before turning for the second petticoat, light pink speckled with darker roses.

She wanted to tell Mary the truth, but she couldn't. The woman needed hope, as did they all. "Well, I know the Prince of Jast is sending a contingent, and I'm hopeful that we'll be able to seek refuge."

Mary nodded and turned to grab the final layer of her dress, a thick wool gown the color of a perfect rose with long sleeves and a high collar that fastened with a row of buttons to her waist where the fabric flared out to her hips leaving the pretty petticoat exposed underneath.

"Let's do your hair," Mary said.

"I don't think it's necessary."

"No offense, but you look like you've been rolling around in bed with a lover." Mary's mouth quirked a smile. "That won't do to meet a prince's army."

Jessamine's skin heated at the truth of Mary's words, and she refrained from saying the prince was her sister's husband. "All right." She relented. "But something simple."

A few minutes later, dressed and warmer in an emerald, green cloak, Mary left, and Jessamine grabbed the dagger. She tried to find a place to conceal it and settled on the pocket of her cloak, hoping that no one would be able to see it weighting the garment.

Henro ran toward her as she stepped from the tent and handed her an oatcake. "The Master is looking for you," the boy said breathlessly.

She noticed he hadn't used benevolent preceding the word and reached out to put a hand on his shoulder, smiling. "Where is he?"

"With the monster."

She hummed a sound and started across the camp, thinking about correcting the boy now that she knew the darkling had spared Johesha. A mess of feelings about the creature were a chaotic storm inside her, swirling together: confusion, elation, doubt, gratitude, revulsion, hatred. Rather than say anything she took a deep breath to blow the mess away, the air and confusion escaping into the winter cold in a steady white puff.

The screech of the darkling rent the air and made her want to clap her hands over her ears.

Henro did, flinching.

"You go back to your mother," Jessamine told him, nodding the direction at him.

The boy hesitated a moment.

"I'll be all right," she added with a smile as the darkling voiced another horrible shriek.

Henro darted back toward the cook's wagon.

When she came around the opposite side of Crue's tent, she found the wizard yanking on the creature's chain, a blue fire glowing in his hand.

"Where have you been?" he snapped as he caught sight of her. "You are supposed to be doing this." The wizard threatened the creature with the fire, the darkling both struggling and cowering at the same time.

Jessamine wrapped a hand around Crue's, folding his fingers to snuff the fire. "Maybe if you used compassion, Father," she said, then took the chain and stepped between them. She hoped her countenance still disguised that she was under his memory spell.

The darkling quieted, its body shrinking as its fear ebbed. Its unsettling red eyes flicked from the wizard to her.

"As I was saying," Crue said, stepping up next to Jessamine. "You will go with us today, creature."

"And you will set me free."

"Yes."

She could hear the lie and glanced at Crue but kept her features serene. "Today is the day?"

Several beats of silence passed before Crue said, "I'd like to remove your chains, creature. For you to come with me willingly."

The darkling raised its unnatural hands, the gloom of it seeming to drip like suspended oil. Crue unlocked the manacles.

A little while later, the three of them moved through the forest as if in a funeral procession, the line somber and quiet. Crue led, followed by Jessamine and the threatening presence of the darkling behind her, sending chills up her spine. She didn't trust it, but she also found more grace knowing it had saved Johesha's life.

When Crue was far enough ahead she thought he wouldn't be able to hear, she spoke to the darkling.

"You spared him," she whispered.

"He showed me mercy. I offered it in return." Its voice was strangely subdued and quiet even in its monster form, as though perhaps it had modified its vocal cords.

"Thank you," she made herself say, for she was grateful.

The darkling didn't reply, and by then Crue had stopped ahead and turned to wait for them. "Hurry," he shouted. "Scarlett is waiting."

If she didn't know better, she'd have thought he was excited to see her mother rather than to bring her pain. Perhaps they were one and the same to Crue.

The farther they moved from camp, the easier she breathed knowing the rest of his household was making their escape, looting what they could to make a run for it. Jessamine had taught Mrs. Gerrick the elixir, but she was certain that the spell needed to be broken for the elixir to become unnecessary.

As the sun reached its apex, Crue stopped and turned

to the darkling. "Hunt. Animals only."

Jessamine blinked and the darkling was gone. "Are you not afraid it will disappear, Father."

"It can't," he said and led her toward a place where he lit a fire with his magic, then sat on a rock to wait. "It is always compelled to return, as I am to it, until we break the tether."

Jessamine made a show of sitting on a little boulder, cleaning off the space before she sat, adjusting her cloak around her. "That must be inconvenient, Father." She hoped he might release his guard to tell her more, confident in the spell being in place.

"Now, but in its infancy, it did exactly what I'd hoped."

She didn't ask another question, remembering the spell curbed her curiosity and filled her with only the desire to please him, to be complacent.

"Are you looking forward to seeing your mother?" he asked.

A trick.

"Who?" she asked. "I long only to look upon you, Father."

He nodded and watched the fire.

After the darkling returned and they ate, they resumed their hike to the meeting place. It seemed they were walking in circles, but then perhaps this too had been some test she didn't understand, contrived by Crue for one of his ulterior purposes.

Eventually, as the sun dipped behind the trees and cast long shadows, they stepped into a snowy clearing, and there a contingent of Jast forces ten men wide, ten deep, stood in a line framed by the wall of evergreens behind them.

Crue chuckled, walking forward.

Jessamine followed with the darkling moving alongside her.

She searched the line for her family, but didn't see any of them. No Johesha. Her spirit thinned with disappointment at their absence, even knowing this had been the plan.

"Who is your emissary?" Crue called out, his voice carrying across the snowy expanse.

"I am," a voice called from the ranks, and a soldier stepped forward. He was stocky and taller than she was, though not as tall as Johesha or her father and brother. His bright blond hair was shaved along the sides and the top braided, so it disappeared behind his back. He wore the leathers of Jast, its tree stamped into his chest, the rest of his attire black. His emerald cloak was thrown back, so it trailed behind him. A gleaming sword rested at his hip.

She remembered him!

"The messenger?" Crue asked incredulously.

"Ranger Brendsen Hargrave at your service." The soldier offered a short bow that seemed more sarcastic than formal.

Crue made an irritated noise. "Where is Scarlett?"

"She isn't here," Brendsen said.

There was a beat of silence as Crue processed this, the anger coming off him in waves. Crue's hand shot out and grabbed Jessamine around the back of her neck, and she gasped as he jerked her closer. "Then I don't need to wait to carve out our daughter's heart."

The sky around them darkened, as if the sun was going down more quickly than was natural.

Several Jast soldier's raised bows with notched arrows. "Light."

Their arrows burst into coordinated flames, then loosed with a yelled "fire." The darkling screeched, but the arrows didn't soar toward them, but rather a pile of wood set off to the side she'd failed to notice. The arrows arced across the sky and thudded—thump, thump, thump— into the wood in succession before the pile burst into flames.

Crue laughed.

Johesha

L eaving Jessamine's bed was the most difficult thing he'd had to do in his life, but being unsure about the spell and not wanting to shift within the walls of the tent propelled him. He dressed as quietly as he could, slid the dagger under the pillow where he'd rested next to her, and kissed her forehead before slipping from the tent. Returning to the bramble where he'd shifted only hours before, he stripped out of his clothes and shivered in the snow waiting for the magic to surge through his body once more.

The sun rose.

And there he remained, buck-ass naked and shivering in the snow.

Still a man.

He smiled, wanting to whoop and holler with joy, but didn't. Couldn't. Not if he wanted to sneak away without Crue knowing he'd been there. The spell, somehow, was broken, and he heaved a sigh of relief. He didn't know how. Didn't really care, content to focus for the first time on happiness overruling everything else.

They could do this. They could win, he decided as he dressed once more. Without delay, he crossed through the ward, certain his form as a man vibrated the web Crue had set, hoping the wizard blamed it on one of his own servants, and without hesitation, ran. He had a ton of ground to cover before the meeting, hopeful he'd get there in time traversing the ground on two legs instead of four.

He'd made it and surprised everyone that he was still a man.

"Is it broken?" Brinna asked with a smile.

He nodded. "It would seem so."

"And Jessamine is all right?"

He just smiled.

Auri watched him in that unnerving way of hers and tilted her head, then grinned.

Tarley's eyes cleared. "An oath."

"And a vow," Auri said. "The true heart was never in question."

Brinna seemed to know what they were saying even if he didn't, moving to stand in front of him, and wrapping her arms around him. "Welcome to the family, Johesha."

He spent the rest of the day preparing for Jessamine's arrival, and now the sun was dipping toward the horizon. The plan was underway. Johesha stood behind the ranks in the shadow of the trees with Jessamine's family, waiting for his sign to maneuver. The original plan had been for him in his stag form to work his way around to the rear of Crue. Even with the stag gone, Johesha could still follow his part of the plan, but now as a man. In either form, the wizard wouldn't suspect Johesha was alive. Hopefully, Crue would be more attuned to the spectacle in front of him. That way, if the name they secured wasn't the right one, Johesha would be able to deal the death blow.

Events were happening as if time had slowed. Brendsen was speaking to Crue in the distance. Tarley leaned her forehead against Lachlan's chest. Aurielle, with Mattias, watched Nix, who stood near her parents. Brinna was holding Luc's hand, her eyes squeezed shut.

"I told her, but she isn't sure she'll make it in time," Nix was telling Scarlett. Johehsa was certain he was referring to Lexa. "And if that isn't his true name, we have to rely on the backup plan." The dark god's eyes jumped to Johesha, and Nix nodded.

Scarlett turned to Tomas. "I don't like it, but you must decide." She handed him something.

"For Jessamine," he said.

Suddenly, someone screamed.

Jessamine.

"Then I don't need to wait to carve out our daughter's heart!" Crue yelled.

Johesha lurched, but a shadow burst out from Nix,

grabbing hold of him. "Don't. We need you. Stick with the plan."

He closed his eyes, imagining Jessamine and hating that he wasn't there to protect her. But he recalled his training, remembered his own mentor's words when he was a boy.

"Timing is everything, cadets." Master Himsley, a man of middling height, but whose presence felt giant to Johesha's sixteen-year-old mind had walked their ranks.

Breathing hard from combat training, Johesha felt the accusation of losing.

Himsley had observed, and Johesha hated that his commander had seen him lose to another cadet. The other cadet might have been two years older but being out maneuvered by the lug who'd gotten the best of him grated on his pride.

His commanding officer had stopped in front of Johesha. "Talent and ability don't guarantee winning a battle," he'd said as if speaking directly to him. "Timing is the difference between life and death. Understand?"

With a deep breath, Johesha calmed himself. This was about timing, so he nodded to Nix, who then removed the hold of his shadow before whispering, "Luc?"

Lucian nodded, and the sky darkened as Nix's power took over.

It was Johesha's signal to go.

The bows released their fire in the sky, lighting up the faces as Johesha skirted the edge of the clearing. The arrows hit the woodpile with a series of thuds before the timber caught fire. He clung to the shadows being chased by the light of the fire and relied on all the tools and tricks he'd learned over the years to guide him with secrecy.

"Secrecy," Master Himsley once told him just after he'd been selected for the Prince's guard, "is a bit like being a magician. It's sleight of hand." The commanding officer used a stack of cards and a coin to demonstrate a magic trick. "It's an opponent looking one way while you perform the trick where they cannot see it."

He needed to get behind Crue in the next few minutes while the wizard was focused on what was happening in front of him, so he pushed his pace without compromising his stealth.

Crue began laughing, his voice strange in the distance. "That is what you have for me? Do you not know who I am?"

Johesha curled around Crue's left, taking more care now with his stride. He paused, glancing over his shoulder to see all of Jessamine's siblings step from between the soldiers. Mattias at one end and Tarley at the other, Brinna and Auri between them.

"What is this?" Crue asked.

Johesha started forward again, taking care as he ducked between trees and bushes, staying out of sight. Once around Crue, he took a deep breath and picked up his pace.

"We're here to retrieve our sister," Aurielle called.

Johesha was close enough to hear the wizard snort but then ducked behind a bush as he moved into position behind the wizard and Jessamine.

"I believe I asked for your mother," Crue said.

"I believe we told you she wouldn't be here." Tarley, as imperious as usual.

"But all of you are. Curious." There was a pause. "Bring me Scarlett, or I kill her."

Johesha stepped out from behind his hiding spot, moving toward Crue's back.

Suddenly, he stopped. There in the shadows, free and unchanged, the darkling fluttered.

With the dagger clutched in her hand inside her pocket, Jessamine relaxed into Crue's hold, his arm wrapped around her shoulders and neck, his other gripping her arm—the arm she needed for the dagger—using her as a shield.

She was stuck and couldn't take the risk with the dagger. Not yet. Even if she could have tried to use it, there was no angle to kill him, and maiming him wasn't an option. She needed him dead. Her family needed him dead.

"Father? Why are you angry?" she asked, trying to hold onto her act and hoping her trembling voice wouldn't give her away.

Movement from the corner of her eye forced her gaze across the meadow. Her siblings materialized from between the ranks of Jast soldiers. Her heart alighted at seeing them. Though it had only seemed months, she knew it had been over a year, and she could see that now.

Mattias looked like a man two years older. He was tall and sturdy as usual but had become leaner and more angular. His face had the curvature of a carving, the angles more severe and his frown, menacing, which seemed a strange thing to see on her sweet baby brother. His dark hair was longer, curly around his face. He reached out to hold Auri's hand.

Jessamine's youngest sister also looked more mature, steady and wiser somehow. Her eyes were focused on what was happening between her and Crue. *It's all under control,* Jessamine seemed to hear Auri's voice inside her mind, *trust us.* Jessamine shook her head, thinking she must be imagining it, but recalled Johesha's revelation the night before about their powers. Tears filled her eyes, hoping the voice wasn't imagined.

"What is this?" Crue asked, his tone mocking. "I believe I asked for your mother."

Auri took Brinna's hand, whose generally serene nature had fled as determination and focus rode her brow. Seeing Brinna, her confidante, made the tears spill, blurring her sight. She thought about all the dreams she'd had with Brinna and wondered if she'd actually been with her sister. The thought brought her comfort.

"I believe we told you she wouldn't be here," Tarley

said, taking Brinna's other's hand. She looked as regal as she always did, her head steady, her mouth a line of determination, her spine straight. Jessamine's gaze drank in her siblings, snagging on Tarley's belly, a slight bump protruding from her parted cloak. She was carrying a child. Jessamine's throat tightened as she caught a mournful but relieved sob.

How she'd missed them. How much she'd missed.

"But all of you are. Curious." Crue's hold tightened on her shoulder. "I've upheld my end of the bargain–"

"–and we have upheld ours. We are here, are we not?" Auri called out.

"No!" he shouted, his tone now unhinged. "I said Scarlett, not her disgusting progeny she shares with the fucking forest sprite." His enraged reply sprayed spittle against Jessamine's cheek.

"Give us our sister back," Brinna said. "And you won't have to worry about being harmed."

Crue barked a laugh, and his grip tightened. "You think I'm worried?" He scoffed. "It's Scarlett or there's no deal."

"You've harmed her enough," Mattias snapped and appeared as if he might charge across the landscape between them.

"Harmed her? Harmed her! I helped her. I saved her from that disgusting creature she called 'father.' And how did she repay me? She stole from me."

Jessamine could feel the tension radiating off Crue's body.

"She stole our daughter from me!" He shook Jessamine slightly. "So I've taken her back. And when I get the rest of what she stole, then and only then will I leave her alone."

"You expect us to believe you?" Tarley asked.

Crue paused. "I see you're pregnant. Perhaps you'd like to trade your child for your sister."

The ranks of soldiers adjusted behind her sisters and brother as if ready to close ranks around their future queen carrying their future heir.

Jessamine wondered if now was the time to move. To stomp on his foot, drive an elbow into his gut like Johesha had taught her on one of the quiet nights in the magical cabin.

"I'm going to teach you how to defend yourself," he'd explained.

He'd taught her movements that would help her should she need it.

She moved through possibilities in her mind to determine the best way to get the dagger free, but then Crue shifted, tightening his embrace.

"It's always about the timing," Johesha had explained.

"I saved you from the darkling's imprint," Crue was telling Tarley.

"You think I should be grateful after you set the monster after me?"

Crue shrugged. "I could release it again."

He turned his head to look at the darkling, which had been fluttering next to them, only the monster was gone. Jessamine wasn't certain if she was glad or afraid, her eyes darting around the tree-outlined meadow to find it. Darkness had fallen, broken only by the undulating flames of the bonfire. She knew the creature would blend with everything, hiding by shifting its face. It could be anyone now.

Crue stilled, a split second long enough to tell her he was panicked at the realization. But this was Crue, and he pivoted, turning back to Tarley. "The darkling does like to hunt. Isn't that so, my daughter?"

Jessamine replied as placidly as she could even though it was at odds with her instincts. "Yes. But you never let it."

"See," Crue said. "My mercy controls it. And it is very, very hungry."

Though it had hunted only a few hours earlier, providing them with meat to cook for lunch, its belly was certainly full. Jessamine's was.

"Why do you wish to see Mother again?" Auri asked. "What does she have that you are seeking?"

Jessamine felt Crue shift behind her and imagined him tilting his head in that predatory way, as if sensing this was a loaded question. "I temporarily gifted her with four magical powers that were given to me for safekeeping. I want them back."

"Four?" Tarley asked.

Jessamine watched her siblings look around at one another. One sibling, each with one power. Johesha's story was alive on each of their faces.

A second later, Crue drew in a breath, as if every moment over the last thirty years suddenly made sense.

"She doesn't have them," he mumbled, his hold loosening. "She doesn't have them," he repeated.

Jessamine realized this had suddenly become more

complicated. Capturing Scarlett was one thing, but needing all four of her siblings plus their mother was something else entirely.

"Fine," he yelled, backing up and drawing Jessamine with him. "If Scarlett refuses to show herself, I refuse to acquiesce."

Suddenly, the air before Jessamine's eyes rippled like a pebble thrown into a pond. The space shimmered as if it had drawn the stars into those ripples, and with a breath revealed her mother, along with Nixus. The god disappeared, but Scarlett remained.

Jessamine hadn't seen her mother in over a year. She was thinner but her auburn hair was braided like it always was. Out of her face to make it easier to work. She wore dark clothing which made her skin glow alabaster in the light of the bonfire.

She tilted her head, her eyes narrowed, and a terrible, avenging smile graced her lips. "Hello, Altair Rook."

Crue gasped, stumbling back. "How?" His body tensed behind Jessamine's, and a green glowed at the edge of her vision, as if he were casting a spell, only it sputtered.

The darkling screamed.

"No!" Crue yelled, frantic, and shoved Jessamine away. "How? How?"

Jessamine flipped to face the drama before her, scrambling back on her hands and feet, the cold earth stabbing her palms. A glimmer of green light rolled from Crue's core outward, and he flickered from his corporeal body into that of three black crows only to return to his normal form. But where before he'd been a virile man in his prime, now his skin was lined, his hair turning silver.

"You bitch," he hollered, his hand struck out, catching Scarlett by her throat as his skin began to wrinkle and sag.

"Mother!"

Crue's eyes darted to Jessamine, awareness dawning, clearly realizing the web he'd spun was unravelling. He dragged Scarlett closer and shook her, spittle collecting on his lips. Her mother sputtered, clawing at his hand, her face turning red as the wizard squeezed. "What have you done?" The lines on his face deepened, his body shrank, his spine curving, his white thinning. "I will end you, then end your spawn to get my powers back."

Jessamine watched her mother smirk, his grip weakening. "You can try, Altair Rook," she gasped. "I found it, didn't I." Scarlett laughed, despite his hold.

Crue—Altair—screamed, squeezing and cutting off Scarlett's cackle.

"Release my wife," Tomas's voice came from nowhere.

Altair shrieked, releasing Scarlett's neck and shaking out his hands, his hair, but he moved like a puppet on a set of marionette strings, his body aging so quickly. He shook something off, as if he were covered by a meddlesome insect biting at his exposed skin. Then he flung something small and indecipherable away, streaking the air with magical violet light.

He conjured a spell, his mouth moving and the words bursting out of him in a horrible, undecipherable language. His body changed once more, returning to youth and vigor, only stronger somehow, as if imbued with the vitality of a man closer in age to Mattias. His face changed, becoming younger, exceedingly handsome.

He smiled cruelly at Scarlett. "Miss me?" he asked as he took a step toward her.

Jessamine scrambled to her mother, got to her feet between them, and brandished the dagger at the wizard. "You want her, you'll have to go through me."

He laughed. "I'm impressed, daughter. You found a way to counteract the spell. How did you do it?"

Jessamine didn't answer, even though her pride wanted to. Instead, she just glared and waited, her grip too tight, wishing she'd asked Johesha to teach her how to use the dagger. They may have practiced self-defense, but she was wholly unfamiliar with knives as weapons.

Crue lunged with a feral cry.

Johesha

Unwilling to wait for death, Johesha crouched forward, ready to spring into action should he need to, keeping his eyes on the undulating form of the darkling before him. He could hear the timbre of dialogue drifting from the meadow, though what was said was unclear. His attention was split, knowing they were counting on him to be ready.

Fuck. This was bad.

The darkling hissed. "I smelled you. On her."

"Thanks to your mercy." Johesha hoped that admitting

it would engender something in the creature that had saved him once.

"The sorcerer's spell?"

"Broken."

"How?"

The darkling's form changed. Johesha watched as it shrank down, the shadows reforming, becoming more substantive as if compressed as it changed into the perfect replica of himself.

Jessamine's confusion now made sense.

"I don't know. The witch of the woods, I suspect." Johesha took tentative steps, walking around the darkling who did the same, measuring, learning.

"Perhaps she would consider breaking my tether to the sorcerer." The monster was the perfect predator. Johesha would know as a predator himself; he also knew he was the creature's prey, having seen what it could do when hunting Tarley's former kidnapper through the woods. The eviscerated bodies, exsanguinated, their pulp left behind, unrecognizable.

As the darkling circled him, Johesha had the thought that the only way to kill it might be in this form as a man. That they might be equally matched this way.

"She wasn't able to break the spell, just change it, which helped me find the means to free myself of it. Maybe she could help you."

The darkling continued to circle. "If the sorcerer is unable, I fail to have faith in a witch."

"Fair enough," Johesha answered. "Are you planning to dispose of me now?" He figured it was better to know than try to guess.

"She is kind."

"The witch?"

"Jessamine."

"Yes," Johesha answered, wrapping his hand around the hilt of the dagger on his hip.

The darkling's eyes tracked Johesha's movement. "I find her to be... something I desire for myself."

Johesha gritted his teeth together, turning with the darkling as it circled him, hating that the darkling's face, its voice, matched his own. How easy it would be for this creature to take his place. "Like you tried to do with her sister?"

It hummed a note. "Tarley was a missed opportunity. The sorcerer broke the imprint. Jessamine, however, would be a delicious addition to my triad."

Johesha clenched his fists, knowing he would fight to the death before he would let that occur. "And your other partner? What would they think?"

The darkling stopped moving, and its eyes took on a faraway look, its form flickering as if struggling to maintain its hold. "They are so far away, I cannot feel them anymore, and it makes my insides feel empty."

"That is what it would feel like if you took Jessamine from me," Johesha admitted.

"Yours," it said.

"Mine."

The darkling shifted, drifting out of Johesha's form back into its own, growing so that it towered once more over Johesha. He tensed, afraid now, his heart thumping an erratic rhythm inside his chest, afraid that now he'd found Jessamine, this is how it would end. He knew he wouldn't be able to best this predator even with all his skill.

He readied himself to fight anyway, waiting for the creature to attack.

"Jessamine has made me see the truth," the creature said.

Johesha was afraid to let down his guard. "What truth is that?"

The darkling shifted once more, changing into the face of Crue. "That it is wrong to take."

Suddenly the monster screeched, its original form snapping back into place. Its back arched, a tendril of green light shooting out of it for just a moment, a rope tugged with tension, then going lax and dropping to the ground and writhing like an injured snake. The other end of the tendril led into the meadow.

"What is it?" Johesha asked.

"The tether," the darkling hissed in that horrible voice. "Frayed." The creature turned where it was and tried to flee in the opposite direction, but the rope grew taut once more and jerked the darkling backward. Despite its best efforts, it was unable to break whatever bound it to the wizard. It stopped struggling and the tether grew pliant. "The wizard's trap."

Johesha understood the darkling's sentiments. It too had been taken and trapped. "How can I free you?" He knew it was a gamble, freeing the darkling, but hoped that it might keep him, keep Jessamine alive.

"I do not know," it said.

"But just now?"

It looked toward the meadow but didn't answer.

"If I could free you, where would you go?"

"You cannot free me, huntsman."

Crue shouted, his tone angry even if his words weren't clear.

"I have to go help Jessamine, and I'll try. To free you. I owe you a mercy." He paused before heading into the meadow. "What will you do?"

The darkling's form undulated in the shadows. "What I must."

Johesha nodded, but when the wizard screeched and the darkling matched it, he knew he couldn't wait. He stole into the meadow to find Jessamine was sprawled on the ground, looking up at the wizard before her. Jessamine got to her feet, her face awash with anger and determination, and pulled the dagger he'd given her from her cloak pocket to rush Crue.

"You want her, you have to go through me," Jessamine screamed.

"I believe that has been the plan all along," Crue said.

Johesha's heartbeat magnified in his ears, his body burning as he rushed forward and grabbed Crue by the throat. "Touch her and you die."

Crue's eyes widened. "How?" Then his gaze flicked about. "Huntsman? But..." He shook his head, then relaxed slightly. "Darkling. Release me."

Johesha added pressure to the wizard's neck so that the man scrabbled for breath, his nails raking Johesha's hands. "It's Johesha. You should know the name of the man who will end you."

"How," the wizard gasped.

The darkling screeched, fighting, and doubt flickered inside Johesha as he thought of his own spell: *death to one is death, and neither will take another breath*. The darkling had shown him mercy not once but twice, it had changed. He had changed. For the first time in his life, Johesha hesitated.

With a blast of power, the wizard shoved him back, and Crue coughed. His magic flickered, his body broke apart into the three pieces that sprouted black feathers, but then his form snapped back together, and he crashed down to his knees. He seemed to wilt, withering like a dead flower.

Then his body surged once more, and he stood, looking over his shoulder with a dark look.

Johesha got to his feet.

"You think you can beat me?" Crue said.

"We know it, Altair Rook," Scarlett said, holding out her hand with Tomas—back to his normal size—at her side.

"I am a great sorcerer," Crue said, "tethered to greater demons of the Netherrealm."

"Yes. Um, about that," Nixus said as he appeared near Tomas. "My sister is on her way to take care of that now that we know your true name, Altair."

The sorcerer's eyes zeroed in on Scarlett. "You have stolen everything from me."

"You gave it to me freely," she answered. "Every power you bestowed of your own free will. What you have lost, are losing, is your own doing."

Johesha could feel the cornered man's rage seeping from him, a toxic response and quickening of last resort survival, just as Tarley screamed, "The dagger!"

But before Johesha could do anything, Crue reached out a hand, and his magic snatched the dagger from Jessamine.

She screamed, reaching as it whipped away from her, the hilt hitting Crue's hand.

With an awful yell, Altair rushed forward, dagger raised.

Johesha, thinking only of Jessamine and keeping her safe, darted from where he stood, and just as the blade drew a swift arc toward Jessamine, Johesha slid into place.

The dagger pierced his chest, golden light bursting from the blade as it slid home, but he didn't feel it, tackling Altair away from Jessamine. When he settled after the fall, his muscles felt heavy, every breath a battle.

"Got off me," Altair snapped, pushing Johesha off.

Jessamine was screaming, somewhere very far away.

"It's okay," Johesha whispered, his eyes unfocused, as shadows closed in.

His gaze grappled for something familiar, and he gasped for air, unable to take a deep breath. He watched a shadow slip from the tree line. The creature—the darkling—stood, watchful. And though the sound was fading, his sight darkening, he noticed how calm the monster was.

Johesha blinked.

He'd lived a good life, hadn't he?

"Jessamine?" he whispered.

There was a scream, but it was so far away, and he was so tired. So Johesha Malinor closed his eyes.

T he screaming surprised her, and the fact that it was coming from her, even more so. Johesha looked so still, and the wizard stood, covered in blood.

Altair smiled, a horrible smile. "I am invincible," he crowed, his voice a horrible reverberation across the meadow, the power sending chills across her skin.

Jessamine wept and started toward Johesha, but someone held her back. "Johesha. Johesha!"

"Now," Altair clapped his hands. "Let's get started. I need two of your hearts, and frankly it doesn't matter which two."

"That won't be happening," Luc said.

"Oh?" Altair raised an eyebrow. "But how will you stop me since the laws of your governance dictate you can't interfere?"

Nix chuckled darkly. "You think we aren't interfering?" He laughed again.

"We're just biding our time," Luc answered.

Altair looked unnerved, his usual arrogance and bluster flicking away.

"You forget," Nix said, "our sister is the queen of the underworld."

"And," Luc added, "we now know your true name."

A suddenly a burst of green light shot from Altair then dissipated into the darkness like fireflies, there then gone. The next moment, Altair's body hunched.

"One soul tether down. How many more to go?" Nix asked. "How much time do you think it will take our sister to get to each one, Luc?"

"Hmmm. If she already knows where they are? Should happen rather quickly."

"I'll bargain with you–"

"–too late for that, sorcerer," Luc said. "You threatened to kill my love."

"Darkling!" Altair cried out. "Come to me!"

A dark shadow appeared from the forest and hovered there, unmoving. "I will not," it hissed.

Altair spun toward the voice. "You must. I am your Master!"

The darkling floated toward the fire. "You promised. You lied. You broke. You stole."

"Darkling," Jessamine cried.

The monster stopped just short of the fire and looked toward her with its hideous face. "Thank you, Jessamine, for showing me the truth."

She knew it hated fire, and yet it still stood so close that steam was wafting from Altair's shoulders and head. "What are you doing?"

"Saving instead of stealing," it said, then it floated into the fire, screeching as fire licked at its form.

Altair burst into flames, screaming and scratching at his burning skin. A burst of energy bathed in green light exploded out of him. The ring travelled out, growing in circumference and spreading like a wave, hitting her with its power, passing through and disappearing as it moved on. And she knew the spell on her was broken, the spell on everyone was broken.

She broke away from whoever was holding her and rushed to Johesha's side, screaming his name, rolling him onto his back, seeing the dagger protruding from his chest. She shook him. "Please. Please. Don't go," she said. But he didn't open his eyes, and she knew. She knew. She knew. The wail that careened from inside her was an animal in pain.

"Hush, child," a gentle voice said, and a warm hand brushed her shoulder.

"Baba?" Scarlett asked.

Jessamine sat up, her hand still on Johesha but as she looked into the face of an old woman, her wizened face wrinkled with age. She smiled, only there was another smile on her face. An amalgamation of another woman was imbued in her features, this one, young but less corporeal. Ghostly but somehow familiar. Two women, one old and one young, one dark and one light, one there and one somewhere else.

Both women smiled, then looked down at Johesha and pulled the dagger from his chest. It disintegrated into golden grains of sand that floated away on the winter air.

"What?" Jessamine said, rocking forward to protect her love.

"I gave him a seed to hold," the younger of the women said.

"I gave him a spell," the older added, then looked up at Jessamine. "Did you give him your vow?"

Unsure and unclear what all of this meant, she nodded, recalling the night before. "I did," she whispered. "What is happening?"

A small golden light, no larger than a seed, rose from Johesha's chest, hovering like a pinpoint of light above his damaged chest as if waiting.

"You are godblood, child," the younger, less substantive woman said. "My godblood."

"Mother?" Scarlett asked from behind Jessamine.

The woman's ghostly eyes along with the old woman's rose to Scarlett, then back to Jessamine. "I didn't get to ascend," she said. "My power wasn't passed but through the blood. But I can gift it. Johesha has been holding onto it for me."

"You knew?" Jessamine asked. "This would happen?"

"Beyond the veil, there are truths that don't align with this side. The definition of time and space fall away and make way for infinity. I have seen and lived a thousand lives since leaving you." She looked at Scarlett again. "Watching but distant. I have met all of you in varied existences, Johesha included. Crossing is difficult, but Baba made it possible to be here for you." The old woman holding the young reached out and laid a hand over Jessamine's cheek. "When you needed me."

There was silence in the meadow but for the crackling fire, the awful scent of burned flesh, the pervasive heaviness of shock and loss.

"Take the seed, Jessamine," the young woman said. "Take it in and use the power, but you must hurry. Once he's slipped into the beyond, your abilities won't save him."

Jessamine reached out and pinched the golden seed.

"Eat it," the older of the two said.

So she did, swallowing the small morsel that effervesced into a larger existence once it was inside of her, bursting with power. The energy intensified, flowing through her like a raging river, as if she were nothing more than the canyon helping the river determine where to flow. Life was inside her. She was life.

Without being told, she laid her hands on Johesha.

"You are a healer," the women intoned. "Heal him."

With everything she'd learned, and with the power now flowing through her, she imagined his broken heart and stitched it back together with the love inside her. She caressed the muscle with her will and watched as it obeyed. She repaired what was broken, stitched what needed to be stitched. Then she leaned down and pressed her lips to Johesha's, breathing life into him.

"Wake up, Hesha," she whispered against his lips. "You pledged your life to me."

And Johesha Malinor opened his eyes.

450

Johesha

The farm was nestled in a picturesque valley of Jast. A golden green sea of wheat fields stretched to the forest of trees surrounding its perimeter. A ribbon of blue creek flowed past to the west, disappearing into the thatch of aspens. The sky was blue, patched up with white cumulus clouds as if holding the sky together. The farm looked as beautiful as he remembered it, a small but comfortable two-story white house surrounded by summer flowers. There were sprays of violet, red, pink, green, yellow, white and blue—his mother's pride and joy— framing a wraparound porch. He recalled running around in the yard playing hide and seek with his sisters in the heart of summer, of splashing in the creek. Remembered the time Reena, the youngest, was running through the grass and stepped on a bee. How he'd carried her inside for the poultice he'd known his mother would make. Then recalled the anger on his father's face as they'd watched him ride away.

"It's beautiful," Jessamine said on the horse beside him, drawing him back to the present.

He looked over at her, his wife, and his heart expanded in his chest, threatening to devour the rest of him. Her horse, a sweet mare by the name of Cinna, shifted her weight under Jess. His wife's hand shaded her eyes as she surveyed the farm where he'd spent the first fifteen years of his life, a beautiful smile on her face. Unable to contain the love bursting inside of him, he reached out, grabbed hold of her, and lifted her from her horse into his lap. Meha, his beautiful stallion, shifted to accommodate them both.

She squawked. "What are you doing?"

"I need you closer."

She laughed, a sound he would never tire of. "We were quite close just a little while ago."

He growled, shoving his face into her neck to both smell and kiss her. "Let's do that again." He slid his hand beneath her skirt up the outside of her leg and squeezed her thigh as he kissed her skin.

Jessamine squeezed her legs together. "Not here! Not where your mother could see!"

He chuckled and kissed her lips, thinking selfishly that

if he used his tongue, she would relent. But his wife was right, as she usually was, he'd learned. His mind was split between his desire for her and the impending reunion with a family he hadn't seen in twenty-one years. He pulled back and used his thumb to brush over his wife's ample bottom lip, then tugged on it a little, which ignited the beast inside of him.

It had been several weeks ago he'd woken up in a meadow, Jessamine glowing with an otherworldly power as she hovered over him, ordering him away from a dreamless sleep. He'd died—or had been close to it—by the wizard's hand. And somehow, she'd been able to heal him with her godlight.

With her tears, her kisses. "Don't ever leave me, Hesha Malinor," she'd said. "You promised."

"Not willingly," he'd told her then, and he meant it just as much now as they sat atop the bluff looking down at his childhood home.

She jerked her head away with a smile. "You're insatiable."

"For you."

"You should put me back on my horse, then we can ride down like a civilized couple."

"Who ever said I wanted to be a civilized husband to my wife?" But he urged Meha forward as Jessamine laughed, and the mare followed as they took the trail down into the valley.

When they emerged from the thicket of woods out into the fields, two figures appeared on the porch. The closer he and Jessamine rode, the clearer they became until he knew it was his parents standing there watching them approach, thinking them strangers.

Suddenly, as if they knew who he was, they descended the steps.

His mother began to run. "Joey! Joey!"

Tears pricked his eyes. No one had called him that but his mother, and it reduced him to his boyhood.

"Let me down," Jessamine told him and slid from his lap down to the earth.

He dismounted after her.

Jessamine took the reins. "Go."

He kissed her cheek, then took off down the lane through the field toward his mother. She was crying and waving. "My boy! My son!" Her voice rang out through the tall grass that grew around them.

When they met amid the chirping crickets, the soft breeze rustling the tall grass in rippling waves, amongst the buzzing of bees, his mother threw her arms around his neck, sobbing, and Johesha gathered her in his arms, swinging her around.

"You're here. You're here," she cried against him.

She was smaller than he remembered, but then he was so much bigger than the day he'd ridden over the hill, leaving them behind.

Leaning back, she looked at him, her brown face streaked with tears. Her curly hair was silver now, laced with black strands, which she'd braided. Her whiskey brown eyes twinkled with joy. "You're home." She pressed his cheeks between her palms.

"I am."

Movement caught Johesha's gaze. His father ambled up, his expression stoic and stern just as Johesha remembered. He wondered if he was still angry.

"Father."

He was tall, looming as large as Johesha remembered, but time had stolen from him too. His face was lined, his beard gray along with short, gray hair around the rim of his head. He wore spectacles over his brown eyes. He didn't respond to Johesha, just continued forward and wrapped Johesha into his embrace. "Welcome home, son," he said, and squeezed him a little tighter.

Johesha held onto his father, then pulled his mother into the reunion, unable to staunch the tears that filled his eyes. They cried together, clinging as if weathering a storm. There were things unsaid, still lingering from before with a lifetime to catch up on between them.

The crunch of gravel and the clop of horses' hooves made them peel apart.

Johesha turned to look at his wife, leading both of the horses toward them, and his heart was so glad. Glad to see her, glad to know she was his and he was hers, glad to be bringing her home. She was so breathtaking, so smart, so talented, and grew more important to him every day.

He smiled, wiping his tears, proud to present her, and turned back to both of his parents. "This is my wife, Jessamine."

His mother's eyes jumped from Jessamine to him, and a smile bloomed on her face.

"Jess, this is my father, Jomiah, and my mother, Rozzi."

"I've been anxious to meet you," she said.

"Well, don't leave her with the horses, Joey. You take care of those." Rozzi pushed past him to gather Jessamine, herding his wife toward the house. She looked at him as she passed, smiling.

"These are lovely animals," Jomiah said, taking Cinna's reins.

"They're from the royal stables."

His father hummed a noise. "Let's get them stripped and brushed."

Silence descended between them like it always did, but Johesha didn't want it that way if he could help it. "It's good to see you, Pa. The place looks perfect." It was risky bringing up the place considering he'd left it behind, which had been a source of conflict.

Jomiah looked across Cinna's back at him. "Thank you." He paused, then added, "I've had help the last few years."

Guilt moved down his gullet as he swallowed.

"Rell married a fine young man—Trig—who has always wanted to be a farmer."

Johesha couldn't look at his father, feeling accused.

"Johesha. Look at me."

He turned to face Jomiah.

"I'm sorry for the pressure I put on you. It wasn't fair. Knowing I'd let you leave thinking I was mad at you for not staying has eaten at me. I was angry, yes, but time, your mother, your sisters helped me see that you had to make your own way in this world."

Johesha swallowed again, pushing the guilt down to

make way for something else. "I'm sorry for taking so long to come home."

"You had your job." Jomiah opened the barn door and Johesha followed with Meha.

They tied the horses to the rails and began to remove the tack.

"Did your prince allow you some time off? Because you were married?"

Johesha dragged a brush over Meha's back. "He didn't have to. I retired from my post."

"Retired?" Jomiah didn't look up from his own brushing of Cinna.

"It was time. I broke my oath to the crown by falling in love with Jess."

His father's eyes jumped up to meet Johesha's, an indignant look on his face. "You were forced out."

Johesha smiled. "No. Prince Lachlan begged me to stay."

"And you didn't?"

"The oath is in place to keep the royal family safe. They become your world, as they should, and I knew I'd moved on."

"And he still wanted you to stay."

"He's…" Johesha paused, trying to explain the kind of bond he had with Lachlan. "He's a brother, now." Johesha grinned. "He's married to my wife's sister."

Jomiah's brows rose over his eyes. "I'd heard he'd married. Your wife's sister, you say?" His father made a whistling sound through his teeth.

Johesha smiled and finished grooming Meha before

leading the horse out into the paddock where he could graze. His father followed with Cinna.

"It's nice to have you home," his father said, and Johesha felt the truth of it inside him.

Later that night around the dinner table, Johesha sat with Jessamine to his right. His mother was at the head of the table with his father to her right, his two sisters, Rell and Reena and their husbands with his nieces and nephews in between. Dinner was filled with reminiscing, laughter, and stories as they filled him in on what he had missed, and he answered questions to curb their curiosity.

"What's he like?" his niece Timar asked. She was a gangly thirteen-year-old, the oldest of the children. It was hard to believe that he'd left only two years older than she.

"Who?"

"The prince!"

"A troublemaking whelp." He smiled. "I was always having to get him out of trouble."

"So now that you won't need to get him out of trouble, what will you do?" his father asked.

He glanced at Jessamine, and she just smiled, serenely. "Well, that depends on what my wife wants."

His family wasn't surprised by his answer. Everyone knew it was his mother who ruled the Malinor roost, even if his father's storm and bluster indicated otherwise. He happily submitted to his wife's wisdom on most occasions especially as it related to the family, and she left him to his devices for other matters.

"And what do you want, Jessamine?" Rozzi asked, setting down her glass of beer after taking a sip.

"Well, I'm not sure. My sister is at Jast's court now–"

"–oh is that all. The future queen is all she is."

Jessamine smiled. "Right. That's a strange thing to think. They have offered us both a position at court. Me as a healer. I think Lachlan wants me around when my sister gives birth."

"Both of you have a position?" Jomiah asked.

Johesha nodded, pressing a napkin to his lips as he finished the bite. "Lachlan asked me to be part of his royal council." Though that wasn't the exact title, the true nature of the offer was a bit more clandestine.

Though the rest of the family looked as if they were in suspended animation, Rell was the first to speak. "So you're like, part of the royal household?"

"If we accept, yes."

His sisters grinned at one another, and Reena turned to look at him. "The question remains, though, can we come to a ball?"

After cleaning up, enjoying more laughter and games, and telling stories to the children, Johesha's sisters and their families left, retreating to their own homes not very far from their parents. Johesha and Jessamine retreated into their room, his parents having retired to bed hours ago.

"They are wonderful," Jessamine said as she unbuttoned her shirtwaist.

Johesha smiled and reached out to help her, pushing her hands away, needing to touch her. "I'm glad you think so. I'm in agreement."

"Are you glad we travelled all this way?"

"Very."

"Do you wish you'd come alone?"

Johesha paused. "Why would you think that?"

"To mend things."

"Things are mended, I think." He finished unbuttoning and pulled the shirt from her skirt.

"Do you want to stay?" she asked quietly as he spread the garment wide, pushing it over her shoulders and leaving her only in her chemise.

He leaned forward and pressed his lips to her collarbone. "Is that what you want?" he asked and pressed another kiss to her neck.

"That's not what I asked."

He drew back and took her face between his palms. "I want what you want. I will go where you go. I will be home where you are. Because you, wife, are my heart and my home. So here or there or anywhere doesn't matter to me as long as I am with you."

She smiled and pulled the shirt hem from his trousers, then helped him pull it over his head. The garment dropped to the ground with a whisper. "That's quite a statement, husband." She pressed her lips against his chest.

He hummed, enjoying the sensation of her lips, the tip of her tongue as she traveled lower, taking him in her mouth. "You are quite a woman, wife."

After she'd worshipped him, he went to his knees to worship her.

Happily Ever After

"Hear my soul speak:
The very instant that I saw you did
My heart fly to your service, there resides
to make me slave to it..."
— William Shakespeare, The Tempest

everal months had passed since the events in the meadow, enough that their family had grown— Tarley and Lachlan's child had been born, a prince of Jast they'd named Rowan. Jessamine stood among her siblings on a dais in an amphitheater of sorts. They were dressed in white, around them a sea of faces, though the only ones that mattered were Johesha's, Scarlett holding Rowan, and Tomas. Lachlan sat next to Johesha and Ruhnna, Mattias's companion.

They'd all come to Elcadia for the ascension ceremony to claim their godblood among the gods, but more importantly for a vows ceremony between Brinna and Luc and Auri and Nix. While Jessamine was the only one to whom the god mantle had been passed by their grandmother, their ascension made it possible for other god gifts to pass to her sisters and brother and eventually to their children.

None of them needed it, but it felt like a kind of poetic justice for their mother, who'd been denied the opportunity.

While Crue's magic had been destroyed when the darkling severed their tether with fire and death—including the spell upon her, the manor, anything he'd cast, and the magic he'd gifted their mother—the passage of that magic to each of her siblings hadn't broken. Ozland and Lexa believed it was because those gifts hadn't been his magic, but magic he'd been gifted through the demon tethers, now destroyed, and the reason their magic didn't appear as god gifts.

"Are you nervous?" Brinna asked her, squeezing Jessamine's hand a little tighter.

She turned to look at her sister. "With all these strangers staring at us, yes."

Brinna smiled and nodded. "It's strange, isn't it? To think that this was our legacy all along."

Jessamine hummed a note. "Would you give up our childhood for this?"

"Absolutely not." Brinna squeezed her hand.

"Me either," Auri said from Brinna's other side.

Jessamine agreed but asked, "Why not?"

The hum of the crowd drowned out the silence

between them, until Tarley interrupted. "Our childhood made us who we are."

"Rich in love and abundance in what matters," Mattias agreed.

There was a burst of music from somewhere, and the room settled, people finding their seats and the hum of conversation faded until all that remained was silence. Jessamine glanced at Johesha again. He looked more nervous than she felt, his brow bunched low over his eyes, his mouth tight with tension. He looked ready to burst from his seat and snatch her off the dais. She smiled and whispered, "I love you."

His tension eased, and he mouthed it back. Not a single opportunity to share the sentiment was passed up by either of them.

"Welcome one and all," a voice belonging to Luc and Nix's father, Ur, intoned. "In light we rise. In darkness we sleep. In between we live."

The crowd of gods murmured a response. She caught sight of Luc and Nix. Of Lexa.

"Before us stand five unascended godblood passed through the name of Maximora on whom we wish to bestow godlight withheld from them and should they wish it, to receive power from the cistern in return."

Jessamine appreciated understanding what Ur was talking about, Nix and Luc having tutored them about what to expect. The cistern, as Jessamine and her siblings had learned, was the holding place for all godpowers. Once a god passed on and was stripped of their power or relinquished it, the force went into the cistern where it could be claimed.

"Is it full?" Mattias had asked.

"The cistern?" Luc asked. "No."

"So we might not even have access to a power? Not that I want one," Tarley said.

"You'll be added to a queue," Nix explained, "then when it's your turn, you'll have the opportunity to accept a power when called."

Jessamine wouldn't, since she already had her godlight power. She glanced at her siblings, wondering if they might ever have that opportunity and what it might mean but knowing they were already powerful with their gifts.

Ur moved them through the ceremony.

"One day this will be Luc," Brinna whispered to her.

Right, because he would take his father's power as the god of the cosmos. If Luc and Brinna had children, their first would take Luc's power, or it would go into the cistern.

Ur stopped in front of Jessamine, a cup in one hand and a plate in the other. Inside the cup, golden light swirled, and on the plate were small golden seeds—the godlight— much like the one her grandmother had given her. She knew she was to pretend with the seed, since she already had one, but was invited to sip from the cup. She did.

Ur moved down the row of her siblings, offering each of them a godlight seed from which their godlight would sprout, and a sip from the cup of power to encourage the seed to grow.

When the ceremony was done, they were congratulated by strangers and ushered to a party at Nix and Luc's parents' home in Elcadia.

Less than a week later, on the morning of the vows ceremony, Jessamine awoke in Johesha's arms, tightening around her as she tried to slip from his hold.

"No," he said, "not yet."

"You're so bossy," she said, turning toward him.

"I'll show you just how much," he promised, rolling her onto her back and Johesha indeed bossed her through several orgasms.

"That was—" Jessamine panted, pushing her hair from her forehead, unable quite yet to piece together the words to match her thoughts.

Johesha chuckled. "We should probably clean up."

She hummed. "We do have a double vow ceremony to get to."

He moved then, coming up onto his elbow. "Do you wish we had had a ceremony?"

She turned her head to look up at the ceiling, the open beams of smooth wood bright in the airy room of Sol, Brinna and Lucian's godseat, because looking at Johesha proved too hard when she had to maintain her concentration. She just wanted to kiss him.

She made a show of thinking about it for several seconds, then turned to look at him once more, smiling. "We did. Our ceremony was perfect." She meant it, the moment in the tent between the two of them warming her heart.

"In a tent, both under a spell, afraid to be discovered?"

"You said the sweetest things." She smiled and kissed him. "I truly wouldn't want it any other way." Then she withdrew to the bathroom where Johesha joined her and decided to boss her around again in the shower.

After they'd joined her family, Mattias whisked everyone to the venue. It wasn't as if they couldn't all use this new god power that allowed them to use the magic between space and time to move between places, but Mattias was as enamored by it as he was with Ruhnna. So they let him.

It was late spring in Elcadia, and the rose garden at Luc and Nix's family home in the country was blooming with rich fluffy blossoms. There was a maze, which Jessamine thought might be fun to get lost in with Johesha and his bossy nature later. There were arched walkways encased in green, a fountain with a fat cherub holding a bouquet that was spouting water. She hadn't been to many weddings, though the gods didn't call them that, but rather a pairing, and since this involved the godyoke, in Elcadian it was called *i une dio gere, i une au lora*, to make two into one. While she'd never been to a vows ceremony other than Tarley's before, most gods had never been to a joining.

They walked through the garden under an archway to where one of Nixus and Lucian's sisters, Ora, tall and thin and wraithlike, waited. "Welcome," she said, tilting her pretty blonde head. She had the perpetual look of youth, her cheeks blushed a pretty pink. "I would guess you're looking for your sisters."

They had met the night of the ascension celebration, though Nix and Luc's family was massive with so many half-siblings. Keeping them straight was going to be a trial in and of itself. Some of them had flirted with her. Johesha had growled into her ear that if she thought as a god she could even look at another man, he'd teach her where her eyes and body belonged. It made her smile knowing that he had a lot of growl and very little bite. Besides, she'd never look away from him. It was always good, however, to keep him on his toes, so she'd just smiled demurely. He'd made good on the promise to show her who she belonged to a little while later tucked in a closet.

She shivered now thinking about it. "Yes." The young goddess escorted them through the garden until they were moving through the lovely hallways of the house. When they arrived at a set of doors, Ora opened them to reveal Auri and Brinna, both radiant in their ceremonial attire, Scarlett moving around them, to make sure everything was just right.

"You both look beautiful," Tomas said, then looked around. "All my girls do."

Jessamine leaned forward and kissed his cheek when she noticed the tears in his eyes.

Scarlett came to his side. "Come. Let's get seated."

After giving Brinna and Auri hugs, Mattias followed them, until all that remained were Jessamine and her sisters.

"Do you know what to expect?" Tarley asked.

Auri shook her head. "Nix didn't know. A joining ceremony is rare. He just said an oracle will lead it."

"And Luc said something about stars, but there wasn't anything specific," Brinna added, smoothing down the fabric of her dress. It was the color of the sea on a bright warm day. Auri's dress was deep green, and brilliant like an emerald gem. They both looked breathtaking.

Tarley and Jessamine as their attendants both wore

matching blue dresses sparkling with silver threads embroidered in the shape of stars and sparkling when they moved.

"Are you nervous?" Jessamine asked.

"Excited." Auri smiled. "We've been through a lot. I can't wait for forever to begin with him." She blushed.

A knock sounded at the door and Ora—or perhaps it was Ifrit, one of her triplets—poked her blonde head inside the door. "They're ready."

Jessamine looked at her sisters. "You ready?"

Brinna smiled. "I am." She held out her hand to Jessamine and Tarley.

Auri joined from their other side until the four were connected. "I want you to make sure I tell you all how much I love you all. I am so blessed to call you my sisters." She squeezed Jessamine's hand.

The foursome collapsed into a clump as they hugged one another.

A few minutes later, they stood under an archway that led to a garden terrace blooming with an array of blossoms. Everyone who had been invited talked quietly in small groups across the space.

An oracle Brinna called Brother Rom entered the garden. His blue tunic was threaded with silver accents much like Jessamine's dress, his collar stiff with silver embroidery, and the keys around his belt clinking as he moved to the center of the group. He had a severe countenance, his face long and sharp. He looked around, then called out, "We call forth the stars."

That was Jessamine and Tarley's cue to appear and

walk the circumference of the garden. The crowd quieted as Jessamine helped those in attendance find their spot in the circle facing the center. Once everyone in attendance were situated, Johesha giving her waist a squeeze as he took his place, Jessamine walked to her spot on a parallel line with Brother Rom on one side as Tarley did the same on the other.

Luc materialized in front of Brother Rom, dressed in an ivory suit that fit him like a dream. The fabric had a sheen as if it shone like the sun when he moved. He looked like the embodiment of the god of day and light. His golden hair was as carelessly perfect as always, his face a broody mix of seriousness and careful hope.

Next, Nixus appeared, dressed in a black suit that seemed to effervesce with points of light like gems in the velvet, night sky. It was his turn to embody his role as the god of night and darkness. His shadows curled around his feet, tucked calmly as though they understood the momentousness of the occasion. His dark hair was a mess of curls, the edges and planes of his chin and jaw covered with that perfect day-old growth that never seemed to change. He grinned at his brother.

Ur and Aiah stepped forward behind Tarley.

Jessamine could feel Scarlett and Tomas move behind her.

Brother Rom looked at both and said, "There is order in life. Light and dark. Day and night. Life and Death. And then there is magic, love at home amidst that power. Above it all is fate. Today, under the witness of the cosmos" — Brother Rom waved a hand over his head in a graceful arc— "and amongst loved ones—" —he indicated the ring of guests— "we will close the yoke by completing the godyoke."

The circle parted in one space to reveal Brinna and another to reveal Auri, and both of her sisters walked forward.

Jessamine glanced at her new brothers, both of whom had tears in their eyes at the sight of their star mates. The emotion on their faces brough emotion to hers as she watched her sisters stop.

"The yoke," Brother Rom called.

Jessamine stepped forward pulling the golden ribbon from the pocket of her dress as she stopped in front of Brinna and Luc, now facing one another, as Tarley did the same in front of Auri and Nix. Both couples held hands between them, their bodies encapsulated in the golden light of the godyoke.

Jessamine laid the golden ribbon over their hands, then wrapped it around three times as Brother Rom said, "Once to signify love, twice to remember truth, and the third to seal it with faith."

Jessamine returned to her place, glancing at Johesha as she did and smiling when he winked at her.

"What the stars have destined to join only death will part," Brother Rom said. "It is done."

Jessamine watched Nix burst forward with brightness, his shadows careening out of him then encasing him and Auri in a cocoon of darkness. Luc and Brinna kissed sweetly, both smiling, both crying. Then all four turned to the witness, their faces glowing with joy.

Johesha's warm presence alerted her he was behind her before she felt him. His arm circled her waist, pulling her closer. "Are you happy, wife?"

She leaned against him and closed her eyes, allowing the moment to rush over her as if it were made of magic. Tilting her head so it rested against her husband's collarbone, she smiled. "Exceedingly."

Scarlett

Mattias, the wielder of time with the threads a tapestry only he could see, stood on the moor with Scarlett and the rest of her family. In the distance, a city lurked, though unlike any city Scarlett had ever seen before. She'd been to Fulstrom, but where that was a short, squatty city built behind a stone wall, this one was built unafraid, with metal and glass so that it shone in the light as if roaring back to the sun that it had no fear. Any remnant of what Echo Landing had been when she was a girl was lost to the ravages of time. She felt Ruhnna, holding her hand on her left, shiver with her own memories of her homeland, her time.

But they weren't here for Ruhnna. They were going farther back.

With her other hand in Tomas's, Scarlett glanced at her son, in awe of him, and looked around at the rest of her grown children, her heartbeat alive with pride. That they had become despite her.

"Be sure to keep hold of one another's hands," Mattais said, his hand threaded through Ruhnna's. He looked at her, love glowing through his eyes. "We don't want anyone lost."

Then there was the sound of a door opening, and the moor at the edge of the city collapsed into dust around them before it reformed into the moor of her childhood. Deep green rolling hills, black, sharp rocky crags, accentuated with thick patches of lavender and the white lox heather fluttering in the breeze around them, the sky a deep gray of melancholy.

The door shut, and when Scarlett looked around, her family was there: Tomas, Jessamine, Johesha, Tarley, Lachlan with little Rowan between them, Brinna and Lucian, Auri and Nixus, Mattias and Ruhnna.

They stood among the fallen, the burial mounds still there, though where they'd come from the funeral sites were gone, disintegrated to time so that names and stories were forgotten. It was a sad awareness that one day too, her story would be lost to that river's current. She looked for her mother's mound. When she looked up to get her bearings, everyone else's eyes lifted to something behind her.

Scarlett turned.

It was the castle. Dark stone walls were slick with moss and turrets rose high to mark the keep, the walkways and arrow slits. No Hale Sentries walked along the walls keeping watch. It seemed a ruin, as if asleep, though it still remained. But it was the single tower that caught her gaze, jutting up like the blunt tip of a sword. Her prison.

She whirled back toward the mounds and located her mother's. "This is the one," she said, ignoring the way her heart pushed violently against her chest. Coming back to Echo Landing was dangerous, but rather than touch down at her timeline, Mattias had taken them to a place in the *after*. After her father was gone; his funeral mound was near her mother's. After the kingdom had faded, the castle succumbing to disrepair and neglect.

Scarlett felt strange, standing there, knowing her mother was existing beyond the veil, that she'd seen her with her own eyes. It should have been a relief, but she struggled to catch her breath in the shadow of the trauma that still haunted her.

When Tomas's strong arms wrapped around her from behind, she took a deep breath, then another.

"I've got you," he whispered in her ear, and she rested in that truth. He always had. "You're not alone."

She wasn't. She and Tomas had made a family who stood with them now, healthy, hale, and growing. She glanced at Rowan, her first grandchild then to Jessamine and the slight rounding of her belly, her oldest daughter carrying Scarlett and Tomas's second grandchild.

Though they were spread across the cosmos, there

wasn't a timeline, a place they couldn't reach to get home to Sevens. Auri and Nix, Brinna and Luc resided in Elcadia. Jessamine and Johesha had returned to Jast with Tarley and Lachlan. Only Mattias and Ruhnna remained in Sevens, but she and Tomas knew it was temporary, Mattias and Ruhnna having returned to Echo over and over. This trip was also a goodbye. Her son had decided to return to Echo Landing to take her father's throne. *His death, the loss of his heir is the turning point in Echo's history," Mattias had said. "If I can fix it—"*

"What about Ruhnna? It couldn't ruin her line," Scarlett had asked.

"There isn't anything to ruin," she said. "It was already ruined."

"Are you ready, Mother?" Auri asked, drawing her back to the present.

She nodded. "Surround the mound," she told them. "And link hands."

Her family followed her directions, drifting around the funeral mound into a linked oval. She looked to Tomas, who gave her a short smile, though not because he was bothered, but because she knew he was measuring her emotions just as he always had. She squeezed his hand to let him know she was all right, and he nodded in answer.

The last time she'd been here, she'd been running from Altair Rook, though then he'd been Crue, her lover. She'd been pregnant with Jessamine, afraid and unsure. She'd used the same power Mattias had used to carry them there, only to flee.

She wanted to swallow down the memories for the newer, better ones, but she understood as she looked around at her family, that each of them existed because of what she'd been through. Her flight had taken her to Tomas. Her love with Tomas had beget Tarley, Brinna, Auri, and Mattias, and now Rowan. Every twist and knot in the tapestry had created this beautiful family. That awareness was nearly overwhelming.

She took another deep breath.

"I was thirteen when my mother died," she said. "I remember we dressed her and prepared her with lavender. I laid flowers over her eyes, then held my father's hand as he led the funeral procession here for her pyre. Flowers to celebrate the beauty of life, fire to wish the spirit reward in the next, and earth to offer strength to the ones left behind."

Scarlett paused.

"Nana sad?" Rowan's toddler voice whispered.

"It's okay Row," Tarley whispered back, picking him up to hold him. At two, being held wasn't his favorite, but he seemed to sense the somber moment and cuddled against his mother.

"She was a great mother," Scarlett added, looking at Rowan and giving him a comforting smile.

"Kisses?" he asked, his mop of brown hair flopping into his eyes.

"Good ones," Scarlett replied as Lachlan leaned forward and kissed his son on his cheek, Tarley doing the same from the other side.

"When the bones are interred," she began again, "everyone in attendance offers a tribute—a meaningful token and words. I gave her a lock of my hair and begged her to take me with her," Scarlett admitted. "I was thirteen."

They all laughed quietly.

"Today, I thought we could do that again, to honor her."

Auri stepped forward, offering a red ribbon she'd tied around her wrist. Though this ribbon wasn't spelled, Scarlett found her throat tighten as Auri laid the symbol of protection amongst the lox heather. "You watched over us, even when we didn't know you were there. For that, I thank you."

Tarley stepped forward, laying her red ribbon on the mound. "*Dwell near the earth, sweet mother,*" she recited the famous Kaloma poem, "*for the water and wind will take your strength and bring you near my heart for all eternity.*"

Brinna stepped up to the mound next, laying down her ribbon. She stood quietly, closed her eyes, and bowed her head. "In my dreams, I see you," she finally said, "and there you are happy. Thank you for meeting me there."

Mattias was next, presenting his ribbon. Rather than say anything he crouched down, leaned forward and pressed his forehead to the mound. He muttered something private before standing and stepping back, then gathering Ruhnna's hand in his once more.

Jessamine laid her ribbon with tears streaming down her face. "Because of you, I have my husband at my side, and a child on the way." Her hand covered her small belly. Unable to stop her sobs, Johesha folded her into his embrace.

Scarlett stepped up to her mother's death mound and

knelt. Tomas knelt with her, and though he didn't need to be there, he'd told her he'd wanted to honor the woman who had beget his love. Scarlett lay a lock of her hair, dark auburn and threaded with silver when it had once been bright red, tied with a slip of red ribbon. She placed both hands on the mound, one of Tomas's on hers, and said, "Thank you. Thank you for keeping watch. Thank you for your love. Thank you for making me stay."

When she was ready, she stood and looked around at her family. "I love you."

"Ready?" Tomas asked.

She nodded. "Let's go home."

The End

Playlist

I'll Get You Home - by the Coast

Arise, Love - Gray North & Anita Tatlow

Waiting In the Dark - Cathartic Fall

I Know You'll Follow - Snorri Hallgrimsson

Love Me - NANO

When the Lines are Curved - How Great Were the Robins

In the Shadows - Amy Stroup

Way Back Home - Ed Prosek, Portair, Driftwood Chair

This time I'll Save Myself - Tim Schaufers & Akacia

Evermore - Hollow Coves

Hold You Closer - Sod Ven

All My Love - Cathartic Fall

Acknowledgements

I'm sitting here at the computer screen. The cursor is blinking accusingly at me: *you have a lot of people to thank.* It's true. I do. But where do I begin? I've written my very first complete series even though it came about by accident! I did it! Feels sort of surreal. A little sad because I'm leaving these characters who have been such an important part of my life these last few years. So, to honor those characters along with those I need to acknowledge, I'm categorizing them.

To my Auris—the wise—thank you for helping me through with your wisdom and encouragement. To my editor, Kate, for your wisdom to get this story in the best shape we could. Any mistakes contained there within are mine to own.

To my Tarleys—the prophet—thank you for helping me see the forest through the trees. Thank you, Beth, your amazing insight helped me stay true to the vision, especially when I veered off in a random direction. Your ability to see the story clearly when I didn't kept me honest to the story. Thank you to my cover designer, Sara, who somehow just sees how it needs to go and makes it happen.

To my Brinnas—the dreamer—thank you to the readers and believers in this series. There was a moment as I wrote *In the Shadow of a Dream* when I wanted to give up, but you kept me going. "The red ribbons! I need to know what that's about," you said over and over in your messages, reviews, DMs. So, I knew I couldn't let the story go. Your support kept my own dream alive and made this story happen. Thank you.

To my Jessamines—the healer—thank you to those who listened to me when I dipped into darkness and helped me stand when I needed strength. To my Carpe Diem Crew who were there every step of the way, celebrating every win, crying with me in the deep, dark gulches. I'm so grateful for each of you. My girls I've been friends with since young-kid times: Shawna, Tami, and Sarah, who were there with girl's weekends, wine, laughter, and jumping in to share with anyone who will listen.

To my Mattiases—the timewalker—thank you to my husband, my family, my friends who understand that writing a book, creating a book, publishing a book takes a lot of time. Thank you for honoring mine and keeping it sacred so that I could do the work. I'm so grateful.

To my Baba—the magician—thank you to my Lord and Savior Jesus Christ. Through you all blessings flow, and I am so infinitely blessed. To you, I give all glory and honor.

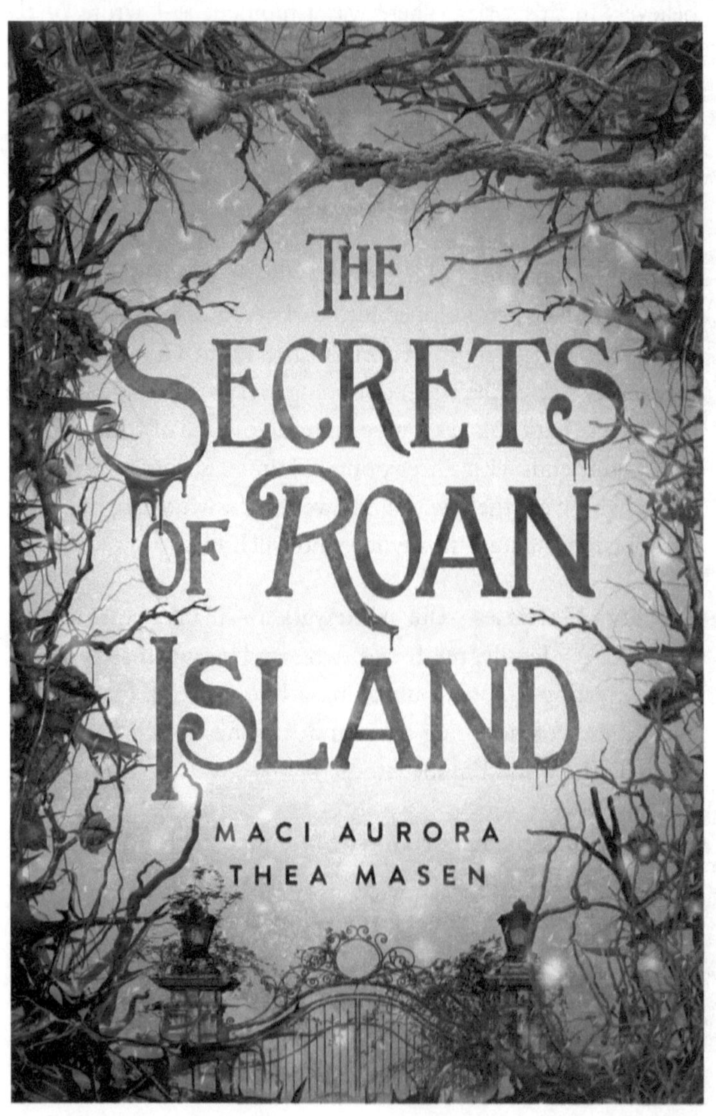

The
Secrets
of Roan
Island
MACI AURORA
THEA MASEN

1

Ruby

Visiting a stranger's home in the middle of nowhere, especially alone, isn't a good idea. Not that I'm particularly known for good ideas. Outlandish ones. Unhinged ones. Miscalculated ones. Among my colleagues at Essik College, my exploits are legendary. Especially among the men, who love nothing more than to laugh at me behind my back. Do I want to shut them all up? Sure, but there's more at stake than just my academic reputation. I'm desperate, and desperation makes people do inadvisable things. Which is why I'm alone with a boatman on the dock of Roan Island.

The narrow wooden dock is worn by age and sagging at the edges, like the smile of an unrepentant parishioner at confession. It creaks as I lift my skirts and step out of the steam-huffing metal boat onto the decrepit wood that appears as if it might disintegrate into the sloshing water below. It looks like this dock hasn't been used in decades, which doesn't line up well with the Roan family's reputation of vast wealth.

I glance back at Lake Nettor. The water we just crossed stretches to the horizon, crimson waves whipping up as the wind slices its way across the massive expanse. They say that the scarlet coloring is a result of some ancient deity who tore the island from the shore in a fit of anger and blood. True or not, the red expanse prevents me from seeing the colony on the other side, making my circumstances even more dire. Once the boatman leaves, I'll be utterly alone here with a family I don't know on an island that looks as if it hasn't seen civilization in years.

"Are you sure this is the right place?" I ask.

"That's it." The boatman nods with a grim frown at the roof of the house that rises above the treetops. "Not the place for a pretty thing like you."

For a moment, I consider turning back, but quickly discard the idea. If I want to keep my job, I need to talk to Hammish Roan, so I roll back my shoulders and raise my chin, trying to exude confidence I don't feel. I'm a fake-it-till-you-make-it kind of woman and very good at faking it. "I'll be quite alright, thank you."

The older man shakes his head and huffs an incredulous noise. "Suit yourself."

While he means nothing to me, his doubt grates against my insides like the incessant grind of the boat's engine as he cranks it to life with added huffs and pops of the metalwork and mechanisms putting it into motion. David used to assume that look too, as if I were nothing more than a child with whims and intellect to match. But I don't want to think of David. Not now. Not ever.

"You'll be back at the end of the month, as we agreed?" I ask, shaken by the eeriness and isolation of the island as I dig into my reticule for the agreed upon sum.

He takes the money, then glances at the woods as he pushes against the dock with his oar. "If you're still here."

A chill creeps up my spine as I watch the gears shift and turn on the boat, clicking like a metronome as it disappears into the fog. The only way back now is to swim.

Turning towards the house, I step from the dock to the rocky shoal of the island. Between the tall trees and the overgrown underbrush, the path from the dock is nearly imperceptible but for the broken cobblestone. With one hand, I squeeze my shawl tighter at my neck, and with the other the handle of my bag. Damp fog surges from the woods, curling around my boots and skirt, making me wish I'd put on my heavier stockings and an extra petticoat. The cold bites, and it'll only get colder over the next month.

With a shiver, I set down my satchel and pull out the parchment notice that brought me here. The dark burgundy seal of the Roan family is stark against the ivory paper staring back at me.

Dear Professor Rose,

I received your inquiry to meet and would like to grant you access to the interview you requested for your research.

Please join my family and me on Roan Island for the Winter Solstice holiday as my family's esteemed guest. Your housing, food, and clothing will be provided.

We look forward to the possibility of getting to know you over the holiday month, and to discussing your inquiry. I am hopeful we can come to a fortuitous solution.

Sincerely,

Hammish Roan

Even now, in this decrepit place, excitement courses through my blood as I reread the letter. The filthy rich family of philanthropists, whose name graces dozens of buildings and societies in New Essik Colony, received my letter and agreed to meet with me. *The* Hammish Roan signed it himself, inviting me to the estate for a whole month!

The Roan family is notoriously private, boarding on reclusive. Inviting me, a lowly college professor, to their estate is unprecedented. It's the best opportunity that's ever come my way, and the only chance I'll have to secure my position at the university. Their library at the estate is legendary, and access to it will give my next paper the validity it needs. A grant from the Roan family will do even more. If I can secure a grant for my department, the university will have to keep me on as a professor. The alternative is… well, I don't want to consider it.

Doubt creeps along my spine like the fog twisting around the naked trees as I glance up from the parchment, folding it once more. This place is nothing like I imagined. I'm surprised a family as wealthy as the Roans would let their land fall to such neglect. Perhaps they've had trouble finding a groundskeeper.

I tuck the invitation into my skirt pocket, wondering if

I'll need to present it at the door.

The wind whines over the water as I leave the lake behind and duck onto the path. The black trees press in on every side, like a corset that's tied too tight. They block the light, but not the heavy fog. It's difficult to see more than a few steps forward, which is why I don't notice the gate until I'm right in front of it.

Thick, climbing vines partially obscure the Roan family crest at the gate's center. A deep breath of relief fills my lungs upon seeing it. The gate looks ancient, as it should. The Roan legacy goes back a long way and their claim on the island is equally as old. The metal is rusted, a deep burnt red, and closed tight. Beyond it, the pointed tops of the trees compete with the steep roof. I can't see the full estate from the gateway, just slivers of stone and glimmers of windows. But from what I can see, the grounds are no better kept here than the dock.

"What have you gotten yourself into this time, Ruby Rose?" I mutter. I'm not easily deterred, though, and I need this, so I reach up and push on the gate. It doesn't budge.

Finding a boatman willing to ferry me out to the island for nearly all my mint was terrifying enough, but now a locked gate when I am supposedly expected? I swallow my scream and shake the rusted bars, pushing them harder this time. "Hello? Is anyone there?"

Besides the creaking of iron, the only answer is silence. An eerie silence. The kind that comes when a predator is near. Cold fear slides up my spine. I glance around, then pull my satchel more tightly against my side. I don't want to stand out here in the woods longer than I have to, which means I need to get past this gate. It's nothing more than another obstacle to what I really need: access to the Roan private library and their funding. Access to a future that has been unraveling over the past year.

There's a saying I came across once in my graduate work and wrote down in my journal: *Silent women lead silent lives.* It became the motto of the CWS, Conspirators Women's Society, of which I'm a founding member. I don't know who said it, but the sentiment has proven a necessity.

I need it now.

With a deep breath, I grab the hem of my long dress. "Dammit, Ruby. Why did you have to worry about how you look?"

Pants would have been so much easier than the socially acceptable dress I chose to make a good impression. With another fortifying breath, I tuck the fabric of my skirt firmly into my belt, sling my satchel across my chest, and start to climb.

The Secrets of Roan Island
is available on Kindle.

THE ACCIDENTAL SEREPH
MACI AURORA

ONE

Atlas

I straighten at the sound at the door of the garage. Being sure to avoid the car hood above me, I grab the blue mechanic's rag to wipe my hands and turn to watch two of my four brothers walk into the shop, their steps echoing against the concrete floor. I wait to hear how the hunt went, watching as they unbuckle and remove their leather harnesses, the weapons clanking as the metal of their knives, daggers, and other assorted weapons clash. Rome is silent but Samson hums. They're both clean, not a drop of gore anywhere.

Rome, the oldest of my brothers, hangs his harness in the cabinet, glances at me. "All good?" His intense, dark eyes bore holes into everything, including mine. His dark brows shift slightly, and that's about as much emotion as he'll offer. Fucking dipshit. But it's nearly impossible to deny Rome a thing due to that damn intensity. Fucker doesn't back down.

"Not really."

"Why not? Something happen?" I hear the concern in his voice, which sounds more like he's pissed. He might be emotionally bankrupt, but he isn't without emotions. They display in two ways: anger and angrier.

"All clear here. Chill out," I say and turn back to the car, releasing the hood so it slams back into place. "It's just being stuck here instead of hunting." My grumbling makes it seem like I'm pouting. Perhaps I am. I hate being left behind.

"Didn't miss much," Samson says as he flops onto an old red couch marred with grease stains, his gear strewn over the cushions next to him instead of put away. He leans his head back on the couch and rolls it to look at me. "A lot of nothing actually. Didn't need four of us. Didn't need two of us."

"And you're getting over an injury," Rome snaps again, over my bitterness. "You're too good a fighter. And if what the Grays have said is right, we need you healthy."

Samson makes a noise from his nose that sounds like he's annoyed. My middle brother is itching for a fight, like always.

"How did it go?" I lean against the car that occupied my hands while they are gone. I'd rather have had a bow at the ready. My four brothers might drive me crazy, but I love them. Being left behind isn't only about me, but because I worry when they're out on a job without me.

"Sammy's right. Nothing. Not a demon in sight."

Rome crosses his arms over his chest and scowls, making a huffy noise of disbelief. "The question is where they're hiding. With the summer solstice coming, they're around and will show up, surely." He walks across the shop to a counter where I know he'll find something to keep himself busy. He's always busy. "Luka and Tate back?" he asks.

"Not yet," I reply. "Tate wasn't happy you didn't take him with you."

"Is Tate ever happy with any assignment?" Samson asks with a snicker.

"You're always giving Tate the shit jobs—"

"Being the youngest sucks," Samson quips.

"Checking Grams' property isn't a shit job," Rome snaps, glancing over his shoulder.

Incredulous, I tilt my head and cross my arms over my chest, "Grams could kill a demon with that razor-sharp tongue alone."

Samson laughs. "Isn't that the truth."

Rome looks annoyed—as usual. "But she'd need help if multiples show up." He pulls his phone from his pocket and glances at it. "Bus coming into the Hollow."

Samson and I groan. Buses mean tourists. Obnoxious tourists drag in the demon riff-raff hiding among them, and they aren't usually the organized kind, but rather the fledgling demons or the deserters attached to the *taedae,* unsighted humans.

"Not it," Samson says.

"How's that injury?" Rome asks me.

"Not an injury," I repeat. "How many times do I have to say it?"

Rome looks me over, eyes narrowed, as if he can see beyond my skin and bones. "Fine," he relents. "You go into town. Wait for the bus to roll in, see if any demons have hitched a ride." He points at me. "But don't engage, not without backup."

I'm already walking over to the cabinet, pulling on my harness, sliding a sharpened dagger into a sheath, along with another into my boot. "Me? Engage?" I glance at my bow but leave it, knowing I probably won't need it. Those off the bus are rarely difficult to dispatch. I glance at Rome with a smile. "Never."

Samson laughs.

I shrug into my black leather jacket and grab my helmet before I'm out the door, headed for the heart of town. After driving past Lowry's Gas and Sundries, where the bus stops, and seeing the hulking, metal can is already empty, I ride down Main. I park my bike, cross to the other side, and duck into The Hole in the Wall, a small bar sandwiched between a diner called The Getaway, and a witchy souvenir shop that sells Carran Hollow guidebooks. One of these three establishments is often the first stop for tourists, and thereby their parasitic demons, when they reach town.

My eyes adjust to the dark. There's an older guy playing guitar near the door. The shiny wooden bar is on the left and runs the length of the room. There are a few people lined up along the counter, atop barstools. Booths—mostly empty—line the right wall and in between is a stretch of space big enough to walk between the two. I've been here before. I have been in every single shop in

Carran Hollow, every single home—though the owners haven't known I was there. The Hollow is my town.

The locals glance at me then look away, giving me a wide berth. They might know me. They might know I'm a Black. If they don't, they feel it—that sensation skittering across their skin telling them danger is near. That's all that's needed.

The bartender, Gus, an older guy with a huge mustache, tops off a beer before handing it to a patron. "What can I get you, Black?"

"A shot of whiskey."

He turns to the wall of bottles behind him, selecting one and a shot glass as the bell rings, indicating someone has walked in. I glance at the newcomer since it's never a good idea to be caught unawares. Walking across the room is a woman—twenties—with a duffle slung over her shoulder. She's dressed mostly in black: black jeans with tears at the knees, and a white shirt hidden under a black V-neck sweater, also sporting holes from wear and tear. Her silver hair is shoulder-length and wavy. She's pretty— gorgeous, actually. She's got one of those heart- shaped faces with giant eyes, a pert nose, and full lips, the bottom just a touch fuller than the top. It's too dark to see the color of her eyes, but I've got a pretty good suspicion they're green, because this girl's got an aura gleaming bright green, as bright as if I were standing in front of a flashing neon sign.

My body tenses as she passes, and power hits me—the raw magnetism of it slams into mine, grips my balls before sliding up to my pelvis then racing white-hot up my spine until it hits the back of my head. I blink and grab hold of the counter to keep on my feet.

What the fuck was that?

I was born a Sentinel, have fought with all manner of creatures, fucked a few more, and I've never experienced that reaction in all my twenty-seven years.

But I have an idea.

My calix has finally arrived.

The Accidental Sereph
is available on Kindle

ABOUT THE AUTHOR

Maci Aurora has been writing stories since she was a child. At eleven, she fell in love with reading Sunfire Historical Romances about girls who made a difference in their lives while falling in love. When she discovered Lavyrle Spencer and Judith McNaught, their novels cemented her own journey to tell stories about love. Since then, she's been forever lost between the pages of a book as both a reader and a writer. She's published several other books as CL Walters. For the most up-to-date news about Maci's upcoming releases, fun extras, and behind-the-scenes bits, sign up for her newsletter on her website www.maciaurora.com.